I
Had
the
Craziest
Dream

I HAD THE CRAZIEST DREAM

HELEN FORREST
WITH BILL LIBBY

Coward, McCann & Geoghegan, Inc.
New York

The authors wish to thank the following for the right to reproduce in full the lyrics to their songs:

Bregman, Vocco & Conn, Inc., for "I Had the Craziest Dream," lyrics by Mack Gordon, music by Harry Warren, © 1942 by Century Music Corporation, copyright renewed 1969. Rights throughout the world controlled by Bregman, Vocco & Conn, Inc. All rights reserved. Used by permission.

Cahn Music Corp. for "I've Heard That Song Before," words and music by Jule Styne and Sammy Cahn.

Mr. Gordon Jenkins for "I Had to Sing with a Band," unpublished specialty material written for Miss Forrest by Gordon Jenkins.

Warner Brothers Music for "But Not for Me," lyrics by Ira Gershwin, music by George Gershwin, © 1930 by New World Music Corporation; and for "It Had to Be You," lyrics by Gus Kahn, music by Isham Jones, © 1924 by Warner Bros., Inc., copyright renewed. All rights reserved.

The Welk Music Group, Santa Monica, CA 90401, for "All the Things You Are," lyrics by Oscar Hammerstein II, music by Jerome Kern, copyright 1939 T. B. Harms Company, copyright renewed. International copyright secured. All rights reserved. Used by permission.

Library of Congress Cataloging in Publication Data

Forrest, Helen.
    I had the craziest dream.

    1. Forrest, Helen.   2. Singers—United States—
Biography. I. Libby, Bill. II. Title.
ML420.F74A3   784.5'0092'4 [B]   81-7756
ISBN 0-698-11096-X   AACR2

*I dedicate this book to my son, Michael,
whom I love dearly.*

*And to my closest and dearest friend and personal manager, Joe Graydon, who has guided my career and whom I
also love very dearly.*   —Helen Forrest

*And I dedicate it to the late Richard Fraser and Alice
Longood, the best of friends.*   —Bill Libby

Acknowledgments

Most of all the authors want to thank Helen's manager, Joe
Graydon, for his contributions from start to finish. And Al
Lerner for his reminiscences.

The authors also wish to thank Dominic Scutti and other
members of the Helen Forrest Fan Club for all their contributions. (The Helen Forrest Fan Club, 1040 DeHaro Street,
San Francisco, California 94107.)

In memoriam, Earl Seaman.

They wish to thank Robert A. Sixsmith for his discography
and air-check listings of Helen, and for photos lent us.

Also Guy Richardson (91 Verdin Place, Reno, Nevada
89502) for a fine photo.

And Hugh Turner (1352 N. El Centro, Hollywood, California 90028) for photos from his extensive collection.

And Duncan P. Schiedt (RR 1, Box 217A, Pittsboro, Indiana 46167) for photos from his extensive collection.

They wish to thank Joanna Barker of ASCAP, Los Angeles,
for helping us locate the right music publishers.

And Allyson Adler and Laurie Libby for getting the pages
separated and in the right order.

And last but not least, they wish to thank Jackie Sommers,
our faithful transcriber of tapes.

Introduction

IT IS FORTY YEARS since Helen Forrest first sang "I've Heard That Song Before," "I Had the Craziest Dream," "I Don't Want to Walk Without You," and other hits with Harry James and his orchestra. When I hear those records from the Big Band Era it is hard for me to believe they are that old, and that I still am moved by music that old.

I think the truth is that they are timeless. There are those who think the music of that time, which extended from the 1930s through the 1940s, was the most musical, the most melodic of any that has attained popularity in any time. In any event, whatever shape pop music today takes, the pop music of yesterday is not forgotten.

There is hardly a major city in this country that does not devote radio time to the music of the Big Band Era. After a period of perhaps twenty years in which this music was not always available, concerts and dances featuring it draw capacity crowds. Those performing it are featured on musical shows and specials on television. The records, whether the originals or remakes, are selling.

The audience consists not only of the faithful past the age of forty, but many young people who listen to it, give it a chance, and find themselves attuned to it. The Big Band Era was a fascinating, tumultuous time, and its stars were as big then as the Beatles or Rolling Stones were in their time.

The Big Band Era began in the 1930s with the move away from vaudeville music, the advent of radio, and the success of the orchestras of Paul Whiteman, Jean Goldkette, Ben Pollack, and a few others. Many of the bandleaders who developed the music with discipline and drive and took it to its peak in the late 1930s and early 1940s came out of these orchestras.

Helen Forrest sang with three of the five or six most popular big bands of all time—the orchestras of Artie Shaw, Benny Goodman, and Harry James. The others were those of Glenn Miller, Tommy Dorsey, and, perhaps, Jimmy Dorsey. These were called swing bands, but Benny swung harder and less sweetly than the others. He played the jazz of the time, along with the Dixieland of Bob Crosby and Louis Armstrong. Their bands also were called dance bands, but people listened as much as they danced. The so-called "colored" bands of the day, such as those of Duke Ellington, Count Basie, Fletcher Henderson, Lionel Hampton, and others, were not as popular only because they played in an age of segregation. They did not play the Circle and other theaters I attended in Indianapolis, but I got the "colored" porter in my father's men's store to take me to the dances they played in the Negro neighborhoods so I could hear them. At times I was the only white in attendance. Sometimes a friend went with me and we were the only whites. But we never had any trouble, sharing with the others there a passion for the music that was played.

Those great black bands influenced enormously the white bands of Benny, Woody Herman, Charlie Barnet, Stan Kenton, Artie Shaw, and others. Some of the white bands eventually broke through the color barrier and used great black musicians. Artie was the first. Benny followed. The black bands of the swing era eventually achieved the recognition with the general public they deserved and Duke's band and the Count's band endured better than the white bands.

All the bands played dances, usually on one-night stands as they bussed across the country. But when the best of the bands played, the fans stood crowded around the bandstand, sometimes a hundred deep, not to dance but to listen. Bands like those of Les Brown, Charlie Spivak, Claude Thornhill, Glen Gray, and others swung, but they were primarily dance bands. Bands like those of Guy Lombardo, Lawrence Welk, Sammy Kaye, Kay Kyser, Russ Morgan, Freddie Martin, Frankie Carle, Hal Kemp, and others really weren't swing bands at all, but sweet bands that played dance music.

The big bands played ballrooms and college field houses and high school gymnasiums in every town of any size at all across the country. They played the big-town ballrooms like the Avalon on Catalina Island, the Palladium in Hollywood, the Aragon and Trianon in Chicago, Roseland in New York, and the Glen Island Casino in New York's suburb of New

Rochelle. They played the major nightclubs like the Latin Quarter in New York, Frank Dailey's Meadowbrook in New Jersey, the Blackhawk in Chicago, the Cocoanut Grove in Los Angeles.

They settled down for long stands in the swank supper clubs of the big hotels like the Lincoln, New Yorker, Edison, Taft, and Pennsylvania in New York; the Palmer House, Sherman, Stevens, and Drake in Chicago; the Roosevelt in New Orleans, the Chase in St. Louis, the Biltmore and the Ambassador in Los Angeles, the Mark Hopkins and St. Francis in San Francisco. Sometimes they stayed months at a time. Remote broadcasts of their music were an enormously popular part of late-night radio in those days: "Tonight we bring you the sounds of Harry James and his Music Makers direct from the Astor Roof in glamorous midtown Manhattan in the heart of New York City. . . ." Glenn Miller, Harry James, and others had their own early-evening radio shows which were among the most popular on the air.

Paul Whiteman, Ben Bernie, Rudy Vallee, Fred Waring, Lawrence Welk, and others had popular prime-time radio shows. Waring and Welk went on to prominent television shows. Welk remains a fixture. Novelty bands developed popular radio shows—Kay Kyser and his College of Musical Knowledge, Horace Heidt and The Pot of Gold. Ozzie Nelson and his singer Harriet Hilliard built a successful radio show around their family and became enormously successful on television.

Some who led the bands on the popular comedy shows on radio became radio stars in their own right—Phil Harris with Jack Benny, Skinnay Ennis with Bob Hope, just as Doc Severinsen has become a television star with Johnny Carson. Les Brown has been with Bob Hope for many years, working his television shows and worldwide tours with him.

Movies have been made of the lives of the Dorsey brothers, Benny Goodman, Glenn Miller, Red Nichols, Gene Krupa, and others. Steve Allen played Goodman, Jimmy Stewart played Miller, Danny Kaye played Nichols, Sal Mineo played Krupa. The bands of Miller and James and others were featured in films and received prominent billing because they sold tickets.

Many who sang with the big bands became movie stars—Bing Crosby, who sang with Paul Whiteman, and Frank Sinatra, who sang with James and Dorsey, as well as Alice Faye who sang with Rudy Vallee, Dorothy Lamour with Herbie Kay, Dale Evans with Anson Weeks, Jane Russell with Kay Kyser, Betty Hutton with Vincent Lopez, Janet Blair with Hal Kemp, Priscilla Lane and her sisters with Fred Waring, Marilyn Maxwell with Ted Weems. Television stars came from the big bands—singers Merv Griffin from Freddie Martin and Mike Douglas from Kay Kyser, musicians Gene Barry from Teddy Powell and Fred MacMurray from the California Collegians.

But the stars of the big bands were bigger than the movie stars in many cases. Popular music never has been as popular as it was in that era. Today the young go for the popular music of the day. Yesterday, young and old alike were tuned into pop music. And those of us who grew up in that era remember the big bands and their singers most fondly from their in-person appearances in movie theaters and from their records.

The big bands played four, five, six shows a day at the Paramount, Capitol, Strand, and other theaters on Broadway and at theaters in every city of any size at all across the country. They alternated with feature films, but it was the bands people came to see. Long lines of fans sometimes stretched around the block from early in the morning to late at night. Most of the crowd inside waited for the stage show to end before leaving. Once inside, they might sit through the movie twice in order to see the stage show twice.

I can still remember the thrill I felt when the curtain parted and the bandstand, often rising mechanically from the depths, came into view. I can still hear the theme songs—

Benny Goodman's "Let's Dance," Artie Shaw's "Nightmare," Harry James's "Ciribiribin," Glenn Miller's "Moonlight Serenade," Tommy Dorsey's "I'm Getting Sentimental over You," Jimmy Dorsey's "Preludes," and Woody Herman's "Blue Flame."

Lionel Hampton's band played for my graduation dance at Shortridge High School in Indianapolis in 1945. Woody Herman's band was playing at the Circle Theater downtown. The last show ended at midnight, when the dance started. Some of Herman's best musicians came over to sit in with Hampton's men. Flip Phillips, Chubby Jackson, and Davey Tough played with Arnett Cobb, Cat Anderson, and Hampton. Phillips and Cobb had what we called at that time a "cutting" session on sax, soloing to outdo one another. Hamp wrapped it up by pounding the piano, vibes, tom-tom, and drums in a half-hour rendition of "Flying Home" that left everyone in a sweating frenzy. A few weeks later, Herman's Herd was heard on the radio playing "Flying Home."

The most frenzied of us knew well the great sidemen with the great bands—Bunny Berigan, Ziggy Elman, Roy Eldridge, Lou McGarity, Ben Webster, Vido Musso, Georgie Auld, Johnny Hodges, Toots Mondello, Jess Stacy, Teddy Powell, Charlie Christian, Bobby Haggart, Gene Krupa, Buddy Rich, so many more. We could listen to new records and pick them out from their solos. They were marvelous musicians. I do not think they are matched by those in the rock groups of today.

The best of the big bands came up with outstanding instrumental hits—Benny Goodman's "Sing, Sing, Sing"; Artie Shaw's "Begin the Beguine"; Harry James's "You Made Me Love You"; Tommy Dorsey's "Song of India" and "Boogie Woogie"; Glenn Miller's "Moonlight Serenade," "In the Mood," and "String of Pearls"; Woody Herman's "Woodchopper's Ball" and "Apple Honey"; Count Basie's "One O'Clock Jump" and "April in Paris"; Duke Ellington's "Take the A Train" and "Mood Indigo." We bought those old 78 rpm records—one song to a side—by the millions and played them on the jukeboxes of the day. We heard them a thousand times, yet still thrill to them when we hear them again. They are more than monuments to a past time, they hold up today, they endure.

In time, however, the records these bands made with their singers became the most popular, and they are among the most memorable today. Through many of those years it was wartime, when lovers were apart, a time when songs of sentiment were sung, such as "Sentimental Journey" by Doris Day with Les Brown, and "I Don't Want to Walk Without You," "I Had the Craziest Dream," and "I've Heard That Song Before" by Helen Forrest with Harry James; also, of course, "All or Nothing at All" by Frank Sinatra with Harry James, "This Love of Mine" and "I'll Never Smile Again" by Sinatra with Tommy Dorsey, "Marie" by Jack Leonard with Tommy Dorsey, and "Green Eyes" and "Tangerine" by Bob Eberly and Helen O'Connell with Jimmy Dorsey, among many more. Hearing them again takes you back to the best of times, the worst of times.

Singers were a big part of the big bands from the time Bing Crosby sang with Paul Whiteman and Russ Columbo with Gus Arnheim. Many of them moved from one band to another from time to time, but basically, Billie Holiday came out of Artie Shaw's band, Ella Fitzgerald out of Chick Webb's, Mildred Bailey out of Red Norvo's, Lena Horne out of Noble Sissle's, Kay Starr out of Charlie Barnet's, Rosemary Clooney out of Tony Pastor's, Connie Haines out of Tommy Dorsey's, Peggy Lee out of Benny Goodman's, Anita O'Day out of Gene Krupa's, Eydie Gormé out of Tex Beneke's, Frank Sinatra out of Tommy Dorsey's, Dick Haymes out of Harry James's, Perry Como out of Ted Weems's, Joe Williams out of Count Basie's.

Some did not go on to great success beyond the big bands, though many have had long and varied careers. These, who were among the most popular of the era, included Helen

O'Connell and Bob Eberly with Jimmy Dorsey and his band, Ray Eberle and Marion Hutton with Glenn Miller, Jo Stafford and Jack Leonard with Tommy Dorsey, Kitty Kallen with Harry James, Bea Wain with Larry Clinton, Ginny Sims with Kay Kyser, June Christy with Stan Kenton, Wee Bonnie Baker with Orrin Tucker, Eddy Howard with Dick Jurgens, Kenny Sargent with Glen Gray. And, of course, Helen Forrest with Harry James.

Also, there were enormously popular groups—the Pied Pipers with Tommy Dorsey, the Modernaires with Glenn Miller, the King Sisters with Alvino Rey. Singing groups were popular in those days—the Mills Brothers, the Ink Spots, and so forth. But the most popular singers—with the exception of a Dinah Shore or a Bing Crosby—were those with the bands. The musicians' strike, which took the bands out of the studios for fifteen months starting in 1942, forced many singers out of the bands to make a large number of records with canned or chorus support. This started the trend in popular music from the bands to the singers. Many remember the Big Band Era as fondly for its singers as for its bands.

Helen Forrest generally is regarded by the experts as the best of the big band "girl singers," although Helen O'Connell may have been more famous and is better remembered. Helen Forrest was the first to have songs shaped for her rather than for the band, the first to have records shaped for her rather than for the musicians. Before her, the bands usually opened and closed the songs with the singer singing a chorus in between. After her, the singer opened and closed and the band played a chorus in between. An instrumental remained an instrumental, but a vocal for the first time became a vocal. Helen sang with Artie Shaw and Benny Goodman in the old way, but when she went with Harry James she was able to go her own way. Others followed in her footsteps.

She grew as a singer, rising rapidly in newspaper and magazine polls conducted annually to determine the most popular swing band and sweet band and small band and the most popular singers. In those days, the results of the *Down Beat*, *Metronome*, *Esquire*, and other polls were almost as important as the Academy Awards. A few years into the 1940s she was winning regularly. In the 1943 *Down Beat* magazine poll, for example, while Frank Sinatra, Bing Crosby, and Bob Eberly were the top three among male vocalists, Helen Forrest, Helen O'Connell, and Anita O'Day were the top three among female vocalists, followed by Peggy Lee, Jo Stafford, Dinah Shore, Billie Holiday, Marion Hutton, Mildred Bailey, Lena Horne, and Ella Fitzgerald.

Helen had five records with Harry James that sold a million or more and she has sold ten million records in her career. In her heyday critics called her the best in the business. She was a star, not only on the bandstand but in the gossip columns. Her romances, real or unreal, were reported regularly. Her real romance was with Harry James and it was riotous. She was engaged to marry him until he left her to marry Betty Grable, the pinup queen of the day. Helen took a walk around a window ledge. Instead of jumping, she walked out and went her own way.

She lived that strange, narcotic, nocturnal life the members of those celebrated bands lived during their short, sweet heyday. And she has revealing stories to tell of it. She sat on the bandstand with Billie Holiday when that late tragic lady was breaking the color barrier with Artie Shaw's white band. Helen was singing with Shaw when that intellectual, temperamental man walked off the bandstand in the middle of a set at the Pennsylvania walked out on a million dollars' worth of bookings, walked out of the business at a time his band was the best in the business, and went to Mexico.

She sang with the brilliant Benny Goodman and found out why he was referred to as "The Prince of Poison," rather than, as he was publicly known, "The King of Swing." She was, as were others like her, the one woman on the bus with thirty men. The bands had a girl singer and a boy singer and she sat demurely in front of the bandstand, smiling sweetly, making a show of moving to the music, and waiting for her turn to walk up to the microphone and sing. But the girl singers were not always sweet and demure and a lot went on away from the bandstand. Like the time Helen unknowingly carried marijuana across the border for a super sax man who wound up doing the music for a recent big band movie.

Just as Benny Goodman made it big for the big bands with an appearance at the Paramount in the late 1930s that had the audience dancing in the aisles and attracted nationwide attention, so did Frank Sinatra make it big for the singers with an appearance at the Paramount in the early 1940s that had the girls screaming and swooning and moved him toward a superstardom that has endured all these years. Helen went on her own at this time and teamed with Dick Haymes on a radio show that was tops at the time. Haymes actually was stronger than Sinatra for a time.

Helen had an association with three of the greatest "womanizers" of their time—Haymes, Shaw, and James. James married three gorgeous showgirls, notably Grable. Shaw married eight beauties, notably movie stars Ava Gardner and Lana Turner. Haymes married six, notably the star Rita Hayworth. Helen, herself, made three marriages—and divorces—during a tempestuous personal life. She was born in Atlantic City and reared in Brooklyn, and her home was a whorehouse for a while. She fled a bad childhood to seek the good life of show business. This is, after all, her story, and her personal story is as strong as the story of her show business life.

By now she has had close to forty years on her own, much of it on the road, some of it in nostalgia shows, some of it in saloons. She has had the knack of being in the right place at the wrong time. She was working with Frank Sinatra, Jr., at Tahoe, for example, when he was kidnapped and held for ransom. She has survived serious illnesses and is working today, in her sixties; this book is as much about the music business today as it is about the business yesterday, and should appeal as much to the young as to the old. The real roots of this business and what they developed into can be found in this book.

She is stuck forever, I suppose, with being a "girl singer," but she no longer is a girl. If she was not one of the great beauties of her heyday, she was, especially after a much-publicized nose-bob, an attractive lady who had, as one of her bandsmen put it, "a figure that wouldn't stop." Well, it didn't stop and she is what we might call a full-figured female. She is a tiny woman with a big laugh. One of the things a writer cannot put on paper properly is the sound of a person's laughter. Helen has one of those special laughs. It is a sort of war whoop of delight that bursts from her whenever something strikes her funny, quite often something she has said about herself which strikes too close to the truth to be entirely comfortable. It is my conviction, working with her to put her autobiography down on paper in her words, that she is a woman of great strength and good humor who is not afraid to tell the truth about herself and her life no matter how much it may hurt at times, and is perfectly prepared to laugh at herself at those times. If you can imagine this whoop of delight in your head and substitute it wherever I have put "ha!" you will have it.

Today she lives in Calabasas in southern California, but her home remains largely on the road. For about ten years into the late 1970s, she lived in Phoenix, where her one child, a son, now lives. Since her last marriage ended, she has lived alone and traveled alone, although her closest friend, her manager, Joe Graydon, sometimes travels with her, especially if she is going with one of those big-band nostalgia tours he puts together. She has had some problems with her hearing and her general health, but she battles back and is a lusty, lively lady who works almost every weekend of the year, as well as a good many weeknights, is paid very well for it, and earns her pay.

When I first met Helen, she told me she was singing better

than ever. I smiled and nodded as if in acceptance of this, but I did not believe her. I'd been a fan of hers in the old days and I remembered her singing very well, and there was no way I could believe that forty years later she possibly could be singing as well, much less better. I'd heard too many of the old singers. I figured it was just something an old singer would say. And then I heard her. Her voice is clearer and warmer than it ever was, and she always had a clear, warm voice. Her range is much greater than it was. She has lived a lot over the years and her feeling for a lyric and her phrasing provide a depth of meaning to a song beyond anything that was possible for her in her youth. I think she is singing as well as anyone who is singing today, maybe better than anyone. It is even more difficult to capture the sound of a singer on paper than the quality of her laughter and I wish that you could hear her as you read this.

She does not sing the songs of today. Her faithful fans will not let her. She sings the songs of yesterday. But many of these songs are as timeless as she is. She draws large crowds wherever she sings, and her reviews are better than ever, full of surprise that she is so good. But she seldom has the opportunity to sing to the millions who could see her on television and no longer gets a chance to sing to the millions who might listen to her on new records. She no longer is a star, but she shines as brightly as ever. Her best days may be past, but she is full of life. She should not be forgotten.

She is a great lady and has a great story to tell. Here, in her own words, is that story. If you cannot at this moment hear her sing, you can at least hear her speak.

Bill Libby
Westminster, Ca., 1981.

I Had the Craziest Dream

In a dream the strangest and the oddest things appear
And what insane and silly things we do.
Here is one I see before me vividly and clear.
As I recall it, you were in it too.

I had the craziest dream
Last night, yes I did;
I never dreamt it could be,
Yet there you were in love with me.
I found your lips
Close to mine
So I kissed you,
And you didn't mind at all.
When I'm awake
Such a break never happens,
How long can a gal
Go on dreaming?
If there's a chance that you care
Then, please say you do (Baby),
Say it and make
My craziest dream come true.

1.

I HAVE SIXTY YEARS to tell you about. I have a lot of stories to tell. It's hard to believe, but the best times were packed into a five-year period from the late 1930s through the early 1940s when I sang with the big bands of Artie Shaw, Benny Goodman, and Harry James. The most dramatic moments of my life were crammed into a couple of years from the fall of 1941 to the end of 1943. They seem to symbolize my life, so maybe I should start with a little of the story of those years.

That was the peak of the Big Band Era when the music of the dance bands was the most popular music in the country and I was the most popular female band singer in the country and Harry had the most popular band in the country. It didn't last long, but it sure was something while it lasted. Everyone should have something like it at least once in their lives. I'm grateful I did.

Whether we were going by bus cross-country from one one-nighter to another in dance halls or auditoriums or gymnasiums or playing a theater or ballroom for a week or settled into a hotel for a month, doing movies or radio shows, or cutting records on the side, we were always on the move at a dizzying pace. Wherever we played, we played to capacity crowds of adoring fans. To many, we were as big as movie stars.

I had hit records. Number one, number one, number one. I also had Harry . . . for a little while. Number one in my love life. I've had three marriages and I never married Harry, but he was the love of my life. Let's face it, I still carry a torch for the so-and-so.

Harry was a so-and-so. Still is. And I still love him. You know how it is—you can't help loving the man you love. Harry always did just what he wanted to do. Still does. It's his right. And it's my right to bitch about it.

Harry had one of the most popular of the big bands in those years. Benny Goodman was still big. Tommy Dorsey, Jimmy Dorsey, and Glenn Miller were big. But they didn't have the personal appeal Harry had. He played the sweetest trumpet in the world and when he put that horn to his lips, he melted the hearts of the hardest of ladies. He certainly melted mine.

He could have had almost any woman he wanted. And did. Beautiful, ugly, tall, short, thin, fat, Harry had all he could handle, and he handled all he could. They rolled in and out of his room at an alarming rate, some of them so homely you couldn't believe he'd bother. The boys in the band used to say Harry would go to bed with anything in a skirt even if he had to put a bag over her face.

Harry would laugh. It flattered the hell out of him to be told he was a sex symbol. He loved it. He loved the ladies. And he didn't care what they looked like. Not that he didn't get his share of beauties, because he did. But he also took on the homelies others in his position wouldn't have bothered with. Harry was very democratic. As long as the lady had the right equipment, Harry wanted to try it.

I've said that Harry must have had two of those things men use because he couldn't have done all he did with just one. It

23

does seem that way to me, too, though I know he had only one. It's a wonder it didn't wear out, but he used it very well. In fact, I hear it hasn't worn out yet. Would I like to find out for myself? Maybe not. I know you can't turn back the hands on the clock. What once was can never be again.

He wasn't the handsomest man in the world. Tall and skinny. But he was attractive and charming. He could sweet-talk his way out of any situation. He was one of those people who could get away with murder. Like Huck Finn. Or Peck's Bad Boy. No matter what mischief he got into, you couldn't get him out of your heart. There's a lot of little boy in him. You laugh about him and love him, no matter what.

Of course, I wasn't a raving beauty. People kept telling me I wasn't too bad, but I was never too sure. Even after I had my nose bobbed. I never really liked my looks. I was flattered to be a woman that Harry wanted. A lot of guys wanted me. Only girl in the band on the bus on the road. A big singer. Maybe not too bad-looking. But I didn't care about them. I cared about Harry. As the song goes, I was just wild about Harry. He was the one I wanted.

I was virtually a virgin when I got together with Harry. Oh, I was married, but still practically untouched. I'd married a drummer from Baltimore when I was with Artie Shaw's band. I met him while I was working in Washington. He stayed at home playing drums in Baltimore, while I went on the road. We never really had a marriage. We didn't see each other very often, much less sleep together much. There just wasn't a lot to our relationship. I hadn't had any real relationships with men before Harry.

Harry was still married to his first wife, but their relationship had long since ended. I wonder why. Could it be that he couldn't be faithful? Harry was the most faithless son of a gun who ever lived. Yes, his later marriage to Betty Grable lasted a long time. But I wasn't surprised to hear it wasn't much of a marriage. Marriage didn't stop Harry from running. He was the world's champion long-distance lady-chaser.

Harry was a great musician. His trumpet excited everyone and he found a formula for a sort of sweet swing that worked wonderfully well. To some extent, he made me a singer. I'd had success with Artie Shaw and Benny Goodman, but I was still just the girl singer with the band like the others. I did the vocal refrains between instrumentals, and I didn't have a lot to do.

When I told Harry I wanted to do more, he told me to do it. When I told him I wanted to sing the whole song, he said sing it. He had arrangements built around my vocals and featured me on many of his records. He made me a star. I learned a lot about singing from the way he played trumpet and I loved working with him and his band. We made marvelous music together.

In bed, too. I don't remember the first time we went to bed together. Really. It just happened. Maybe two or three months after I joined the James band in September, 1941. I had been laughing off offers from bandsmen for years. I'd tell them I wanted to be their friend, not their lover. We'd laugh about it. We were friends. I was young and the guys in the band became my friends and my fathers. They'd protect me from the fellows who came after me. But no one protected me from Harry. One night I looked at him and he looked at me and we went into his room and I got into his bed. I don't think that one word was said. Whenever it was, it was as natural as falling out of bed. Or into bed.

Not only was he the greatest trumpet player in the world, he was the greatest lover in the world. Not that I know. A lot of ladies are more qualified to comment on that than I am. But he was the best I ever had. By far. I learned more about making love from Harry than from any man I ever knew. I'm not talking about tricks. Different positions and things like that. That doesn't interest me. I'm speaking about love, pure love, passionate lovemaking. Harry was my teacher and he was a great teacher. Very gentle, kind, caring about your pleasure as much as his. Harry loves ladies. He not only likes

25

to make love to them, he loves them and cares about them.

I never lived with him. We never shared a room on the road or anything like that. But for about a year and a half we were together in his room or my room every night. We were still married to others and you didn't move in with someone as easily in those days as you do today. The boys in the band knew about it, of course, but they liked Harry and they liked me and they didn't make a big deal about it. It may sound like it was cheap, but it wasn't. I loved Harry and he loved me. We were going to be married when we were free. He asked me to marry him and gave me an engagement ring. I wore the ring, but didn't make a big deal about our engagement. We were paired romantically in the press. Our picture together was a regular feature of the gossip pages. But I didn't tell anyone we were engaged. The guys in the band knew of course.

Harry wanted to keep it quiet until we both were free to marry. I went along with that. I asked my husband for a divorce and he wouldn't give it to me. Maybe he had more hope for our marriage than I did. I was frustrated by that. Harry told me he was trying to talk his wife into a divorce, too. Maybe he was and maybe he wasn't. He did get one somewhere along the line because he was free to run off and marry Betty, but he never said anything about it to me. This was before Betty, and we just went along the way we were going.

He gave me more than a year, I'll give him that. I won't say he was true to me for that whole time, but I will say he was very discreet about his women for about a year. I knew him well enough to suspect him but I couldn't catch him in the act. As time wore on, he became less and less discreet. Once he was sure of me he wanted others. At that point he wasn't tired of me, he still wanted me, but he wanted other women too. And they were lined up for him. I'd see them going in his door, then he'd deny they'd been in there. I'd confront him with it and he'd deny it. I'd begin to boil and start to scream and throw things. He'd duck and sweet-talk me, and calm me down, and win me over.

I want to tell you this lady has a temper. I try to be reasonable, but anyone who's worked with me can tell you I can be one tough broad when I want to be. I wouldn't have taken what I took from Harry from any other man I've ever known, but I guess we all run into our Waterloo sooner or later and Harry was mine. I wanted him so much I would forgive him anything. I figured it wasn't his fault, it was just his way. Which was true. And he was otherwise good to me. He gave me more than anyone else ever gave me. He showed me he cared for me in a million ways.

Our relationship was a romantic comedy, like one of those 1930s movies. We were on a roller coaster and it was a wild ride. I'd accuse him of running around on me and he'd swear he hadn't and I'd start to steam up and lose my temper and scream "you no-good, sweet-talking, two-timing, so-and-so . . ." and literally throw things at him and he'd duck and laugh and say he knew I didn't mean it, he knew I loved him, and he loved me, and on and on. We put on a show after every show.

I remember best the time we had a long stand in Hollywood in the summer of 1942. He rented a two-story house and rented me an apartment down the hill. He wouldn't let me move in with him, but he always wanted me close to him, within reach. But some of the guys in the band were camping out at his place and bringing girls in and I knew he was getting his share.

One night he was supposed to come down to the apartment to be with me, but he called to say he had some business to do and would be late and would call before he came. I knew he didn't have any business to do. Harry didn't do business. Pee Wee Monte, who had been Benny Goodman's band boy, was Harry's manager by then. He did his business. When Harry didn't call, I figured some funny business was going on.

I called and got him. I said, "Harry, what's the holdup?"

And he said, "Oh, Helen. I just haven't finished up yet, honey." And I could hear giggling in the background. I said, "Harry, I can hear the giggling." And he said, "Oh, oh, that's just some girls the guys brought in. They're having a party, kind of." And I said, "If you're having a party, I want to be a part of it." And he said, "I'm not having a party, the guys are. I don't want you to come up here. I want to come down there. I want to be alone with you." I said, "Like hell you do. You want to have a goddam party with every goddam woman in the world." And he said, "I swear I don't have anyone with me. Sid will tell you. Here, Sid, tell Helen I don't have anyone with me."

And he put Sid Beller, the road manager, on. Sid was one of my buddies, but I knew he'd lie for Harry. Sid said, "Harry doesn't have anyone with him, Helen." I said, "C'mon, Sid, tell me the truth." He said, "I swear it. Some of the guys have some girls in, but Harry isn't part of the party. He's finishing up some business with Pee Wee. He says he'll be down to see you in a little while." I was so mad I hung up on him. And decided to head up that hill right then and there.

I don't think they expected me. I burst in, boiling. There were couples in all kinds of positions. There were some screams and everyone started to cover up. I yelled, "No one has to worry about me except Harry." And I started to yell for Harry. "Where are you, you two-timing trumpet player?"

I heard a door slam upstairs and knew where he was. The boys were giggling as I went up the stairs two at a time, which was some feat because women didn't wear slacks at that time and I had a long, tight, heavy skirt on. I burst through Harry's door, but the girl was gone. I was sure she'd been there. All Harry had on was a pair of pants and he was still zipping them up when I walked in. "Hi, Helen," he smiled. I said, "I'll hi-Helen you, you no good . . ." and picked up a hairbrush and hurled it at him. He ducked and laughed and ran from the room. The boys had been drinking and they were feeling good and laughing and hollering up to Harry, "Hey, Harry, you still there? Has Helen belted you yet?"

Harry went to the balcony overlooking the living room and leaned over it, bare from the waist up, and said, "I'm fine, Helen's fine. Just a little fit of temper. You know Helen." And with that I really let him know Helen. His skinny butt was a beautiful target. I followed him to the balcony, came up behind him, hiked up my skirt, and gave him as good a kick in the rear as anyone ever got. I heard his howl of surprise as I turned around, ran down the stairs, ran out of the house, ran down the hill, and returned to my apartment.

As I walked in, the phone was ringing. I let it ring. I was so mad I couldn't speak. It stopped and started to ring again. Finally, I picked it up and it was Sid. He was laughing so hard he could hardly talk. I could hear a lot of laughter behind him. I'd booted the boss and the boys loved it.

Sid said, "I don't know how the hell you did it, but you kicked him so hard he darn near tumbled over the balcony and fell down on us. He had to hang on. His scream was the highest note he's hit all year. It was beautiful. The boys loved it."

The more he talked, the madder I got. "Why did you call?" I asked. "Why didn't Harry call? I'm gonna kill the son of a bitch. I swear, one of these days I'm gonna kill him." And he said, "Hell, he isn't even mad. He laughed as hard as any of us. He said to give the girl credit for having guts. He said to tell you he loves you."

But he didn't call and he didn't come down to my place that night. And soon he wasn't coming to my room or asking me to his room a lot of nights. That first year and a half no one had to ask. He knew we would go off together, to get a drink or a bite to eat before going to one of our rooms. We waited for one another. But soon after he was starting to make excuses. He had to go here, he had to go there. He was arranging a date for the band. He had to be with Pee Wee on business.

I knew what was happening, but I was hanging on to him. We were still going together, we were still engaged to be married, I thought we would still be married sooner or later.

I'd humiliate myself by running after him and asking if he wanted to go out that night or was going to come over later. I don't think he wanted to humiliate me. I think he still wanted me. But he was to the point where he wanted the other women again, as well. It was a way of life to him and he liked his life. He wanted me and he wanted the other women. He wanted to have his cake and eat it too.

And I still loved him. So I bit my tongue. I tried to control my temper. Out front we were still the big bandleader and the popular singer, making wonderful music together, but behind the bandstand it was a very tough second year for me.

Then we went back to Hollywood to make a movie. Betty Grable was the star. The band and I were featured. Harry met Betty. He told me he didn't like her. He didn't seem to. I don't know why. But before I knew it, they liked each other a little too much. They started to turn up together. They were an item in all the gossip columns, pictured in the newspapers here and there.

I began to brood about it. How could I compete with the pinup queen of the world? I didn't know if it would last, but I knew I was losing him. It is very easy to look back and say I should have said the hell with him and held my head high, but when you are really in love with someone it is very hard to do that. And losing someone you love is very hard to handle. I couldn't deal with it.

One night I was talking to Sid Beller on the telephone about it because he was one of the few I could talk to, and he was trying to console me and tell me Harry wasn't worth it and I was telling him maybe he wasn't, but life wasn't worth living without him. The next thing I knew I was standing outside the window of my apartment, on a ledge about three stories high, and Sid and Sam Kaplan and some of the other boys were standing down below, looking up at me, yelling up at me to go back in, not to be foolish.

I don't remember a lot about it. I guess I've blocked a lot of it out. I guess I was hysterical. I remember I was crying uncontrollably and couldn't stop. I was crying so hard I couldn't see and could easily have fallen. I don't remember going out there, but I remember being out there. It was night and dark and kind of cold and I was standing there and crying and thinking that I should jump and just be done with it.

I don't know if I was so far gone that I would have jumped, but the next thing I knew someone grabbed me from behind and pulled me into the room. I don't remember much more about it. I remember the boys talking to me and putting me to bed. I guess some of them stayed through the night to be sure I wouldn't take another walk.

When I woke up I felt better. I guess I'd gotten it out of my system. I imagine seeing how far I might have gone showed me what a fool I'd been. I didn't love him quite as much after that. Because of what he'd done to me. Oh, I still loved him. He didn't do it deliberately. He didn't want to hurt me. He did what he had to do. But I could see he wasn't the man for me. Funny thing is, there never really has been a man for me. I tried to find one. Married a few. But the right one never turned up. Harry was the one for me, but even he wasn't the right one.

I don't know if Harry ever knew about that walk I took around a window ledge. The guys must have told him, but he never said anything to me about it. I guess maybe I wanted him to know, as if knowing would maybe scare him back to me, but I never told him. I don't think the guys ever told anyone else. It never made the newspapers. It's not a story I've heard about from those days. The guys never talked to me about it. They helped me through it and that was that. The boys in the band were very good to the girl singer. They made me a part of their music, their team, and their lives, and I love them for it.

I left the band and the band business not long after that and went out on my own. Harry got his divorce and married Betty and they were a very glamorous couple for a while. But a couple of months after that a funny thing happened. I was working a theater in Hollywood and Harry and the band were working the Palladium and I went over to see the boys one night. He gave me a big greeting and asked if I'd have a drink with him at the bar after the last show. I said I didn't think I would. He said, "Oh, come on, honey, for old time's sake." I couldn't believe it. I said, "No, Harry, not for old time's sake or any other sake." He grinned and I grinned right back. We both knew what he was talking about. I asked, "Where's Betty?" And he said, "She's home." I said, "Go on home, Harry. Go on home." And that was that. I don't know how often he went right home. Knowing him, it wasn't too often. Even with Betty in his bed.

Well, it was good while it lasted. The roller-coaster ride was fun while it lasted. It was wild going up and wild coming down. I have led the sort of life I wanted and I really have no regrets, not about the bad times and certainly not about the good times. There have been a lot more laughs than there have been tears and you learn to take it in stride as you go along. I got a great deal more out of life than I ever could have expected when I was growing up. Come to think of it, I've gotten a kick out of life. Especially that one kick that one night.

I still have my engagement ring, by the way. I had it made smaller so I could move it to my little finger. I still wear it.

2.

THE INCIDENT that I remember most vividly from my childhood was seeing the boogeyman—a large, dark monster of a man—looking in the window of our back door.

My mother had been yelling at me for being bad and when she did this she always threatened that the boogeyman was going to get me. I doubt that I had been very bad. I was only two or three years old at the time. But my mom was always yelling at me. I was scared of the boogeyman. I suppose it was just a man passing by and glancing in, but the monster seemed very real to me. All these years later I have not forgotten him. Perhaps he is symbolic of my childhood, which was not as good as it could have been.

My mother had three boys before me. When she was having me, she prayed for a girl. Shortly after she had me, she lost my father. He died during the flu epidemic at that time, suddenly, young. And she blamed me, believing that God had taken her husband from her to make up for having given her me.

Any happiness she felt when she had me turned into

33

unhappiness with me when she lost her husband. Maybe it was unreasonable, but that's the way it was.

I was born Helen Fogel on the twelfth of April 1917 in Atlantic City, New Jersey. In those days the little town south of New York was a summer resort town for vacationing easterners, the boardwalk by the sea.

I don't remember it very well because we left when I was still very young, but I later worked there many times—on the Steel Pier and the old Million Dollar Pier, where the entertainers worked. It never seemed much like home to me.

I don't remember my father at all. He married my mother when she was only fifteen or sixteen. They had a little grocery store, and after my father died my mother tried to run it herself and didn't do very well.

They were Louis and Rebecca Fogel. They were Jewish and kept a kosher house—no meat and dairy products served together, and so forth—but I don't think they had a kosher grocery. I don't think there was a Jewish neighborhood there and they were just trying to get by. I know we never had much there when my mother was trying to make a go of it with the store. And this was during the Depression.

My older brothers were named Harry, Ed, and Sam. Harry died four or five years ago. Ed is living with his wife in Florida. Sam is somewhere. They were never very nice to me and we were never very close and I haven't kept track of them. Ed and his wife came backstage to see me one time after a performance, and he was upset that I didn't even know him, but I had nothing to say to him.

Ed was a musician and had a band for years and I did get my start as a singer with his band so I have that to thank him for, but I think the only reason he let me sing with his band was he didn't have to pay me what he'd have had to pay another singer. I'm not sure I even wanted to be a singer or sing with his band at that time. I was only about fourteen years old, still in grammar school, and I only sang for him a couple of weekends at dance marathons during the summer.

Harry was my favorite and later on when he married I loved his wife, Peg, and ran to her with all my troubles and she taught me about the birds and the bees. But he hurt me too. I was living with them for a while. I was very young. I went to the refrigerator to get some milk and he saw me take the bottle out and grabbed it from me and screamed at me that I couldn't have it, that it was for the baby. It was like being slapped in the face and I remember it as if it were yesterday. I remember I started to cry, and now when I think about it I still feel like crying. I was so young; what did I want that was so much? Of course it was during the Depression and he was having a hard time of it and they did have a little baby that needed milk. He later explained to me he simply couldn't afford another bottle. But at the time it was as if he were telling me he didn't love me. It left a scar on me.

I remember when I was very young back in Atlantic City one of my brothers put a slice of orange in my mouth. When it dropped from my mouth, it fell into something, but he picked it up and put it back in my mouth. I wound up with a serious infection and had to go to the hospital to have it treated.

I was in the hospital there four or five times. Twice I went to the hospital with bites from jellyfish, poisonous fish that look like globs of white jelly and swim in the ocean close to shore. One time they had to cut the creature off my leg, which left a scar.

One time I had scarlet fever, which was serious enough to cause a hearing loss that has become progressively worse over the years and has threatened my career and bothered me a lot. I had an operation that helped for a while, but it has become worse again. I haven't always heard the music as well as I would want to, which is awful for a singer, but I have learned to live with it.

Most of my memories of my life in Atlantic City are not good ones. I guess my mother had a hard life, but she was not kind to me, and my older brothers didn't stand up for me. In fact, the only one I can remember standing up for me back then was a colored cop who used to come into my mother's store.

He was kind to me. He'd take me on his lap and try to make me stop crying. My mother made me cry a lot. He'd tell my mother not to blame me for my father dying. She must have complained constantly to everyone or he wouldn't have been so aware of the situation.

I remember she was always crying in those days, complaining about how her husband had been taken from her, blaming me. She always went to bed crying, I remember.

I call him a "colored cop" because that's the way we described a Negro policeman in those days. We called blacks "colored" and there couldn't have been many on the police force at that time. I'm glad he was there for me.

He used to tell my mother I would be famous someday and she would be proud of me, but I have no idea what he was thinking. I suppose he was just trying to make me seem important, to my mother and to myself.

He passed through my early life only briefly, but I remember him fondly as a sort of father figure, one of the few men from that time who was nice to me. This may have affected my feelings about men later on.

I made good friends among the men in my life, but I never got a lot of real love from men, not from the beginning. And my stepfather, who was a real monster, was the next one to come into my life and hurt me.

When I was still young, maybe ten or eleven, my mother and I moved in with my brother Sam in Brooklyn. My other brothers were old enough by then to be on their own, and they stayed in Atlantic City. Later, Sam moved out.

I finished grammar school in Brooklyn and went to two high schools there, first Girls' Commercial, then Tilden. We moved a few times, the last time to an apartment on Eastern Parkway. I don't know why we moved around, maybe because of the cops. We got into a bad business.

After we got to Brooklyn, my mother met and married a man named Feigenbaum. He was called "Fiegy." She had been alone a long time and I'm sure she was lonely. He wasn't a bad-looking man and I'm sure she thought he was the best-looking fellow in the world. He had a way with the ladies. A bad way. He was a bad guy.

He became my stepfather, but I never thought of him as my father. I don't know if he liked me, but I never liked him. When I began to mature, he began to make passes at me. He always had his hands on me. I'd tell my mother, but she'd say he just liked me.

I didn't know anything about sex. The first time I got my period and started to bleed, I ran to my sister-in-law Peg, thinking I was dying. I never would have asked my mother about anything.

Mother was strict. I remember when I started to date, I started to go with a boy who had a lame leg. I liked him and didn't think anything about his lame leg. He used to give me a candy bar when he walked me home from school. He was sweet. We didn't even neck.

I brought him home one time to introduce him to my mother. She wasn't even polite to him. After he left, she turned on me and screamed, "What're you running around with a cripple for?"

I was upset. I still am. But that's the way she was. I didn't bring any more boys home to meet her.

Her man was no prize. He was a house painter, but that was his "straight job." On the side, he was a pimp. Or, at least, became one. Times were tough, but he made out. In time he turned my home into a whorehouse. Mom went along with it. I guess that made her a madame.

We moved to a bigger apartment on Eastern Parkway. They used to tell me not to come home right after school.

37

They used to tell me they had business to do. They never told me what kind of business. My mother arranged for me to take piano lessons at Honey Silverman's house. Everyone called her Honey. She was a nice lady, a widow who gave piano lessons to support her family, and my mother had met her at the temple.

Sometimes when I got home there would be girls at the apartment. I know now that this would be when I got home too early. I didn't think about it a lot. I thought they had something to do with the business. They did, but I didn't know what the business was.

They were nice girls, neighborhood girls. Pretty girls, at least fairly pretty. I'd talk to them about this and that and they were nice to me. One of them told me she was doing some things for my mother and stepfather. I knew her family needed money.

Then I started to hear things around the neighborhood about men going up to my apartment to be with the girls. Your mother and father are too old to be friends with those young girls, they'd say. They're using those young girls to do business with men. I didn't want to believe it, but I was suspicious.

One day I really got home too early, but it didn't look like anyone was home. Then I heard a noise in my mother's bedroom. I thought she was home so I went in. I saw my stepfather in bed with a girl. They were so busy they didn't notice me.

I closed the door quietly, left the apartment, went downstairs, and sat on the steps. Thinking about it was one thing, but seeing it was another thing. Seeing it made me sick. I didn't want to go home again. I hated my mother for making that man my father. I didn't want to see him again.

I didn't tell my mother. What was the use? I used to tell her about my stepfather putting his hands on me and things like that. She'd deny it. She'd say I was making it up. Or that I was leading him on. I was growing up, getting a figure. She'd say I shouldn't show myself around, but I never did. I wouldn't walk around that man unless I was covered up, even in my own house.

He'd pat me on the rear end. I was getting a rear end. I didn't find anything funny in the way he was back then. He'd ask me why a daughter wouldn't give a father a kiss. I'd say because I wasn't his daughter and he wasn't my father and I hated him. He'd laugh. Mom didn't want to hear about it. I guess he was all she had. She didn't want to think about the truth.

She knew what he was. What they both were. She was to blame as much as he. I went home early and hung around the hallway out of sight a couple of times and I saw the guys and gals going in and out. I hadn't known that my home was a whorehouse during the day and I hated it. No one said much about it in the neighborhood, but I was embarrassed by it. I was fifteen or sixteen years old and didn't know what to do.

One day I got home late and it looked like no one was home. But I didn't check the bedroom this time. I went to my own bedroom. Then to the kitchen. I was standing at the sink, at the counter making myself something to eat, when my stepfather came up behind me and put his arms around me and put his hands on my breasts.

I tried to pull away and told him to get the hell away. He said, "Let's go to bed. All the other ladies who come into this house go to bed with me, why shouldn't you? What are you, too good for me?" I kept struggling, but he only held me tighter.

I was getting desperate, realizing I was about to be raped. The silverware drawer was open and somehow I twisted around and got one hand on a knife and started to stab him. He pulled away, but I slashed him on the arm and it started to bleed. He started to curse as he grabbed his arm. I ran free, screaming from the apartment, down the stairs, and away.

I went to Mrs. Silverman's house and told her the story.

She sympathized with me and told me to tell my mother. When I told her my mother wouldn't do anything about it, she asked me if I wanted to move in with her for a while. I was surprised and pleased. At least it gave me somewhere to go to get away from home. I guess Mrs. Silverman knew what my home was.

Later, I went home and told my mother I wanted to move in with Mrs. Silverman. I don't know what my stepfather had told my mother, but she must have seen he'd been cut and had asked him about it. We didn't talk about it, but I guess she knew. It was bound to be easier for her without me. So she said it was probably best and let me go.

I moved in with Mrs. Silverman. I called her Honey. Her own kids called her Honey. She had two daughters, natural redheads, beautiful girls, who were a little older than I was, and a son who was a very sweet boy. They were a fantastic family. They didn't have much, but they made room for me and accepted me as a member of the family.

Every day when I came home from school, I'd take piano lessons from Honey. When she found out I could sing, she started to ask me to sing all the time. She saw that I was a better singer than I was a piano player. She knew I was never going to become a piano player, but she thought I could become a singer. She told me so. She was the first one to make me think I could be anything, the first one to make me think about becoming a singer.

Her lessons became more singing lessons than piano lessons, but she wasn't a singing teacher and I never really took singing lessons. Singing came natural to me. Anyway, Honey Silverman did more for me than my mother ever did.

When I told my brother Ed I was singing he listened to me and brought me to Atlantic City one summer to sing with his band. I didn't know how to sing, I just sang. The people seemed to like me.

We played for danceathons. Danceathons started there, I think. Couples would dance until they dropped. They'd dance for days, round the clock, with very few rest periods. They'd eat while they danced. One would hold the other up so one could sleep while they danced. People would pay to watch. It was depressing. But it was Depression time and people were desperate for prizes offered.

You had to have music. And entertainment for the customers and dancers. So I sang. We had an emcee. His name was Red Skelton. He wasn't anyone in those days, just a young guy from Indiana trying to make it in show business. He made it, of course. I've talked to Red about it and he remembers it very well.

Frankie Laine, one of our greatest pop singers, used to dance in the danceathons. I think he was the world's champion or something. I guess you've got to come from somewhere. There was a movie made about it a few years ago, *They Shoot Horses, Don't They?* with Jane Fonda. It won an Academy Award for Gig Young, who played an emcee.

Anyway, that's how I got started, that's where I came from. I don't know what happened to Honey Silverman, but I hope she's happy wherever she is. If she's passed on, I'm sure she's in heaven. My mother died in 1955. I don't know if she's in heaven, but I don't wish her bad. Life didn't give her a whole lot and I can't blame her for being bitter. My stepfather also died a long time ago, in a veteran's hospital. Someone sent me a clipping. If there's a hell, I hope he's in it.

He broke up with my mother some time after I left. Before I went with the bands I was working in Washington, and I took her to live with me there. Later, after I'd been with the bands and was on my own and living in Los Angeles, I brought her out to live with me there. At the end of her life, she was so sick and feeble I couldn't take care of her and had to put her in a convalescent home. I asked my brothers to help with the bills, but they wouldn't. I paid the bills myself.

I don't know why I did all this, but, after all that had been between us, she was still my mother. I guess that's what a good Jewish girl is supposed to do, be good to her mother. And when she first moved in with me she was very proud of me. She never encouraged me to be a singer and I'm sure she never thought I'd make anything of myself, but when it happened she was a typical Jewish mother—my daughter this and my daughter that to everyone she met.

My stepfather seldom was mentioned. She'd mention him once in a while. If I said something bad about him, she defended him. I never mentioned our whorehouse, so she didn't have to defend herself. We got along all right, but I never became a big enough star for her. She used to say, "You sing better than Dinah Shore, why aren't you a big star like Dinah Shore?" I'd say, "I'm not as pretty as Dinah Shore." She'd say, "You're prettier than Dinah Shore." And I'd say, "I'm not prettier than Dinah Shore."

She'd say, "You should sleep with a producer. That's what a singer has to do to be a big star. Dinah Shore slept with a producer and she's a big star." Ha!

As far as I know, Dinah never slept with a producer. I tell the story because it's so typical of my mother to say something like this to me. It may not be typical of the typical Jewish mother, but it was typical of my mother.

You know, she may have been right now that I think about it. I became a star, I guess, for a while at least. I never slept with a producer, but maybe I should have. Maybe I'd have become a big star.

1932

The Depression, crippling this country's economy, was the main issue as Franklin Delano Roosevelt soundly defeated incumbent President Herbert Hoover. Unemployed men wan-

dered the streets, sold apples, lined up for handouts, and formed protest rallies. There were riots. Some eighteen million adult men were out of work.

A "bonus army" of twenty thousand camped out in Washington in quest of promised payments for World War I service. When Congress voted them down, most left, but the last two thousand had to be forcibly driven out by troops led by General Douglas McArthur. . . . The League of Nations was seeking unsuccessfully to impose arms limitations on the countries of the world.

Gangster Al Capone began serving a ten-year prison sentence for income tax evasion, but Prohibition, which inspired his reign of bootlegging, still existed. . . . Jimmy Walker resigned as mayor of New York City under charges of corruption. . . . Amelia Earhart became the first woman to fly solo across the Atlantic. . . . Charles Lindbergh, Jr., was kidnapped and found dead.

The New York Yankeees, led by Lou Gehrig and Babe Ruth, swept the World Series from the Chicago Cubs. . . . Jack Sharkey regained the heavyweight boxing title from Max Schmeling. . . . Figure-skater Sonja Henie and speed-skater Irving Jaffee were the stars of the Winter Olympics at Lake Placid, and Babe Didrickson stole the show at the Summer Olympics in Los Angeles.

Radio, which played an important part in the election for the first time, was in its infancy. Rudy Vallee and Ed Wynn had popular shows, while Jack Benny and Fred Allen began their shows. . . . Radio City Music Hall opened in New York. . . . Grand Hotel won the Academy Award. Wallace Beery (The Champ) and Frederic March (Dr. Jekyll and Mr. Hyde) tied for one acting Oscar, while Helen Hayes (The Sin of Madelon Claudet) won the other. . . . Paul Whiteman and Gus Arnheim had the big bands of the day. . . . Bing Crosby was the singing star. His big song was "Just One More Chance."

3.

I NEVER HAD any real training as a singer. I just sang. I listened to the way others were singing the music of the early 1930s and sang as best I could, developing a style as I went along.

I never learned to read music, and sometimes I'd get into a situation where they'd think I couldn't do the work without knowing how, but I proved I could to anyone who gave me a chance. I only have to hear a song once and I remember it. I may have to learn the words, but play me the music and I'll remember how it goes from then on. It was a knack that helped me from the beginning.

I was fourteen or fifteen when I sang briefly with my brother's band in Atlantic City and started to sing in high school musicals in Brooklyn. It didn't amount to much.

I got a job as a salesgirl at a discount drug store. I may have been the worst salesgirl in history. The customers had to point out the cosmetics and things they wanted because I could never find them.

I wanted a career more than I wanted an education. I got terrible grades in school and I didn't want to give up my job, so I quit school before I started my senior year. I was sixteen and I wanted to be a singer.

I started to visit the offices of the song publishers on Broadway to get the sheet music to learn new songs. Sometimes I'd try them out there. A song plugger sent me to audition with a band that needed a singer. That was one week at the 500 Club—not the famous one in Atlantic City, but one in New York on Fifth Avenue. The band had a fifteen-minute air shot on a local radio station. I sang one song. Moments before I went on, a sax man whispered he didn't like my name, it sounded too Jewish or something. He suggested I should take a stage name.

I said, "All right, what?"

He thought a few seconds and said, "Forrest. Helen Forrest."

"One 'r' or two?" I asked.

"Two," he said.

And that was that. In a few seconds, on an impulse, my name was changed forever from Helen Fogel to Helen Forrest. I never had it changed legally, but I've used it, even on legal papers, ever since. I used a lot of different names in the early years.

In 1934, when I was seventeen, I got my first full-time job singing at WNEW, the big radio station in New York in those years. A lot of great musicians started there—Benny Goodman, Teddy Wilson, Charlie Spivak, Erroll Garner, Mitch Miller, Frank Sinatra, Maxine Sullivan, Eileen Farrell, Dinah Shore . . .

I auditioned and landed a job singing commercials. There were a lot of singing commercials in those days and several of us ran from studio to studio doing commercials live or recording them. Dinah was one of the other girls running from studio to studio. They kept us busy from early in the morning until late at night. I also sang on Alan Courtney's early-morning musical show. I used different names, usually only first names—Helen, Helene, Marlene, Arlene. I was paid twenty-five dollars a week, but I learned to sing anything any time. It was great training for a singer.

After about a year I went to WCBS—the CBS network station in New York—for the same money, but a better job. They made me "Bonnie Blue, The Blue Lady of Song" on *The Blue Velvet Hour* with Mark Warnow and his Blue Velvet Band. Would you believe, we played Blue Velvet Music?

That was in 1935 and I was eighteen. The show was self-sustaining—no sponsors—but pretty popular. The identity of Bonnie Blue was kept secret. Mark wanted it that way. He was the star. Whoever sang with him used the name. I sneaked in and out of back doors of the studio so nobody would see me. If anybody had, he wouldn't have known who I was. But I was told I'd be fired if I told anybody who I was.

Mark Warnow, who went on to fame as the orchestra leader on the old *Hit Parade* show, had a great studio band—thirty pieces. Bunny Berigan, one of the greatest trumpet players who ever lived, was in the brass section. Don Lamond, who played for Woody Herman later, was the drummer.

I was becoming sort of famous as Bonnie Blue, singing strictly ballads, slow-tempo stuff, until one day Mark asked me to sing a jump tune, an up-tempo thing. It was "There's a Small Hotel," which can be sung as a ballad but which he wanted done as an up tune. I said, "I sing ballads. I don't sing jump tunes." I do now, but I didn't then.

He said, "I want you to sing this as a jump tune."

He was the boss, but I thought I was a star. I said, "I won't do it." I pointed out, "You can't fire me."

I guess I thought that as Bonnie Blue I was irreplaceable. Ha! Two of the things I have learned in this life are "never say never," and never say "you can't."

He fired me.

I was so furious I went to see the head of CBS. He told me, "If Mark Warnow fired you, you're fired."

I found out I wasn't as important as I thought I was. Anybody can be replaced. Benay Venuta replaced me and went on to do very well. I don't know that anyone even noticed there was a new Bonnie Blue. They also added a new male singer, Buddy Clark. I like to think that it took two singers to replace me.

Years later I went to sing on a recording session. Mark was the orchestra leader. When he saw me, he asked, "Why won't you sing 'There's a Small Hotel'? " We both broke up and he walked over to me and gave me a big hug. I was well known by then and all was forgiven.

But when he fired me I wasn't in a very forgiving mood. I cried for a while, then started to ask around for another job. Brother Ed was working in Washington by then and he called to say there was a temporary opening for a singer with the band at the Madrillon Club. Mom was separated from her husband by then and living there too.

I took a train and auditioned at the club. Even though I couldn't read music, I convinced them I could do the job. And I did. I was supposed to fill in for two weeks and wound up staying two years. I don't know what happened to the singer whose place I took, but it was a big break for me. That was late in 1936, when I was nineteen. I moved in with Mom and turned my paycheck over to her. She'd give me a couple of bucks back for carfare to and from the club. I was making twenty-five dollars a week again. I think I thought that was all singers could make in those days.

But it was a great job for a young singer. I learned to work before an audience. A young singer who worked mainly in studios had to get used to working to real, live people, who made noise and weren't always very respectful. It was a very popular supper club—music for dinner and afterwards for dancing. This was during Franklin Roosevelt's first administration and the Madrillon was a popular place with the politicans. Many were well known and whatever the band was playing or whatever I was singing we'd stop and launch into his favorite song when one of the better known walked in.

47

The band had only eight pieces, but it was a great band. Washington always has turned out a lot of great musicians and some of them played in that band. The great trumpet player Ziggy Elman, who also was from Atlantic City, asked Ozzie Nelson to listen to me. In any event, Ozzie came in with his singer, who was also his wife, Harriet Hilliard, to hear me one night. He offered me a job with his band for eighty-five dollars a week, which would have been more money than I ever dreamed of making. But I turned it down.

It's funny, but I always had a gut feeling about different jobs. I have made decisions on impulse and I didn't think this offer was right for me. Not that Ozzie didn't have a good band at that time. He was from Jersey City and he'd brought the band out of Rutgers College in New Jersey, played three straight summer seasons at the Glen Island Casino in Westchester County, and three straight winters at the Lexington Hotel in New York. He was building a national reputation too.

Later, he was the band on radio's *Joe Penner Show*, *Robert Ripley Show*, and *Red Skelton Show*. He made some movies, then started the *Ozzie and Harriet* comedy show on radio and later took it to television.

Harriet Hilliard had joined his band as his girl singer in 1932 and he married her in 1935. She wasn't a great singer, but she did a nice enough job with novelty tunes and up-tempo songs. He played the sax and sang a lot of duets with her. But he'd been looking for a ballad singer.

He said, "Why don't you come with us? Harriet will do the jump songs and you can do the ballads."

I asked, "All the ballads?"

He said, "Of course."

I asked, "Even the good ones?"

He said, "Yes."

I said, "Ozzie, I'm very flattered to be wanted, but Harriet is your wife as well as your singer and I'll bet you all the money in the world that when a good ballad came along, you'd give it to her. True?"

48

He laughed and admitted, "I guess so."

I said, "See! I just don't think it would be wise for a girl singer to join a band where the girl singer is the leader's wife. But I thank you for coming to hear me, and I am thrilled that you wanted me with you."

We parted as friends. I don't know what would have happened if I had joined the band, but Harriet left it the next year, 1936, when their first son, David, was born, so the way would have been cleared for me.

Four years later their second son, Rick, was born. And David and Rick became a big part of the *Ozzie and Harriet* show, which was a true family show.

Many years later I found myself standing next to them at Saks Fifth Avenue in New York. Ozzie turned to me and said, "You should have become my ballad singer. I might have made you famous." I laughed and they laughed and it was all right. It does seem like you never forget the little things in this business.

It would have been some sort of turning point for me, this fork in the road I didn't take. I couldn't have gone with a nicer man. I was sorry when I heard he died in 1975. His show is still in reruns. But I did go with a better band.

I might have gone with any number of bands. I was beginning to get a reputation as a good singer. There were close to a thousand bands touring nationally at that time and all of them had singers and many needed a singer at any given time. A number of bandleaders came in to hear me when they were in town.

At the urging of Ziggy Elman, Benny Goodman came in to hear me, but he didn't like what he heard and walked out in the middle of my first song. That was the first time I found out what a fine, courteous fellow BG was. I couldn't have been too bad; a few years later he hired me. Benny was a beauty.

Next, Ziggy sent Artie Shaw to hear me. Artie liked what he heard and said he wanted me with him. I didn't think I wanted to go out on the road I was going with the Madrillon band drummer, Al Spieldock. He was maybe the only unattached guy in the band and it sort of fell to him to see me home after the last show and we sort of fell in love. He was my first real boyfriend and I didn't want to leave him.

I say we "sort of fell in love" because there wasn't too much to it. He lived with his father and I lived with my mother and we weren't alone very often and didn't go to bed or anything like that. This was 1937, remember, and a nice boy and a nice girl didn't go in for that sort of thing, even a drummer and a singer. And he was a nice boy.

Maybe because of my background I wasn't too keen on men or experienced with them. I was still a virgin, and while I was singing songs of love I didn't know much about it. I was still young, just twenty years old, and I didn't feel like I was ready to take on the whole world. And Artie, who was a wise man, saw it.

Artie told me when I thought I was ready to send him a demonstration record so he could hear how I was singing and if he liked it and had a place for me, he'd give me the job. I wondered if I'd passed up my big chance.

Artie's was becoming a big band. He had some big records. In the summer of 1938 he recorded "Nightmare," a wild, bluesy thing that became his theme song and that the band played whenever the curtain parted and a set started. Shortly after that, he recorded "Begin the Beguine," which became the biggest record he ever had, one of the biggest any of the bands ever had.

At summer's end I decided it was time to take Artie up on his offer. I don't know why I made my decision at that time, but I always have made sudden decisions based on my feelings, intuitions, hunches—whatever you want to call them— and it seems to me these have been right for me. I decided it was time to leave Washington and the Madrillon, go out in the world, and go for the big time.

Al didn't want me to go, but I was twenty-one and I figured if I didn't go then, I never would. He wanted to marry me, but

I wasn't ready to settle down. I wasn't sold on Al anyway. I was a lot more sold on singing. A lot of people told me I could make it to the big time as a singer and I wanted to find out for myself.

I cut a demo and sent it to Artie and told him if he had an opening, I wanted to try for it. I remember I did "Embraceable You" on one side. I did "Solitude" on the other side, a Jimmy Lunceford arrangement of a Duke Ellington tune. Artie listened and sent for me.

I was scared half to death. My knees were shaking so I could hardly board the bus for St. Louis. But I got there. Artie explained to me that Billie Holiday was still with the band but was getting ready to go out on her own. He was willing to take me on even before Billie left. I said I was ready. That was in September 1938 and my real life was beginning.

1938

Franklin Delano Roosevelt was serving his second term as President of the United States. The Depression had ended, but a recession had set in and FDR got the Congress to authorize funds for new public works projects and more relief for the unemployed and the poor. Expelled from the American Federation of Labor, the United Mine Workers formed their own organization, the CIO, headed by John L. Lewis.

While America remained isolationist and its political leaders plotted courses they believed would keep them clear of foreign entanglements, Adolf Hitler's Nazi Germany occupied Austria and Czechoslovakia, and Europe trembled on the brink of World War II. The U.S. Congress authorized funds for beefing up American armed forces. Reports of anti-Semitic terrorism in Germany increased, and FDR said he "cannot believe such things could occur in a twentieth-century civilization."

In June, heavyweight champion Joe Louis avenged his only defeat with a first round knockout of the German Max Schmeling, "a triumph for blacks and freedom." Hank Greenberg hit fifty-eight home runs, but it was Joe DiMaggio and the New York Yankees who won their third straight World Series title, sweeping the Chicago Cubs in four straight games.

In October, Orson Welles' radio adaptation of "War of the Worlds," presented as if an invasion from outer space really was happening, frightened thousands and created tremendous controversy. Many fled from their homes.

Jack Benny and Fred Allen were radio favorites. A Frank Capra comedy, You Can't Take It with You, was the most popular movie and would beat out The Adventures of Robin Hood, Alexander's Ragtime Band, Pygmalion, and others for the Academy Award. Spencer Tracy would win an Oscar for Boys Town and Bette Davis one for Jezebel.

The Big Band Era was approaching its peak. Benny Goodman had the biggest band, and early in the year he introduced swing to staid old Carnegie Hall with a concert that attracted tremendous attention to the music. Later in the year, another clarinetist, Artie Shaw, posed a challenge to Benny's popularity with a swinging instrumental recording of "Begin the Beguine" that was the hit of the year.

4.

I BECAME A BIG BAND SINGER and part of the Big Band Era in September of 1938 when I joined Artie Shaw's band. I was twenty-one years old, just a scared kid with very little experience. Artie's recording of "Begin the Beguine" had just become one of the biggest hits of all time and his band would beat out Benny Goodman's as the swing band of the year in the *Down Beat* magazine poll.

Swing music was the popular music of the day, though it ranged from the hot sounds of Benny and Duke Ellington to the sweeter sounds of Tommy and Jimmy Dorsey down to the saccharine sounds of the Guy Lombardos and Russ Morgans. Glenn Miller's unique sound was just starting to catch on. Harry James had just left Benny to form his own band. The band was the thing, not the singers. Frank Sinatra was a year away from his first hits.

The big bands were tremendously popular and the big bandleaders were stars. They crisscrossed the country in buses, playing one-night stands in ballrooms and dance halls, one-week stands on theater stages, sometimes month-long stands in hotel nightclubs. Their music was carried live on late-night "remote" broadcasts and some of the better bands had their own radio shows and made movies. Some of them released a record a week, those old 78 rpm one-song-to-a-side discs.

The bandleader got all the money from the personal appearances, records, radio shows, and movies although the band members usually were paid extra. The best bands made maybe $1,000 for a one-nighter, $3,000 for a week's stay when expenses were less, but these fees doubled in the next few years. Most of the band members made $100 to $125 a week, though one who was a star in his own right might make $150 to $200. In a few years a few stars would make three or four times as much.

The singers were not stars. I was offered $65 a week when Artie first asked me to join his band and got $75 a week when I did join. I was one of the first band singers to be considered a star in her own right and I did get a couple of raises, but I was still making only $185 a week when I left Shaw. Helen O'Connell became a star with Jimmy Dorsey, but I doubt that she made much more. Bob Eberly was a star with Jimmy and I don't think he made $200 a week with him. Sinatra started with James at $75 a week and went to Tommy Dorsey for $200 a week.

It was a living for a lot of us, but the competition was terrific. The big bandleaders made big money but there were only a few at the top, a lot in the middle, and a lot more at the bottom. There must have been close to a thousand bands working here and there, reaching for success, all but a few failing. Those musicians who thought they had something special would leave a band to form their own band, but frequently fold within months or a year. There were thousands of singers and maybe twenty thousand musicians reaching for the brass ring and all but a few fell short. They hit the road and a lot fell by the roadside. There were a lot of broken hearts along that hard highway.

Artie Shaw was born in 1910, so he was only seven years older than I was, but he seemed much older and was sort of a father figure to me. He was the most intelligent man I ever met. He was interested in everything. Music was only one of his interests, which was one of his problems. He never was as dedicated to it as the others who reached the top. But he was an outstanding musician who had marvelous musical ideas.

The only child of a Jewish tailor, he was born on the lower East Side of New York and later moved to New Haven. He studied the saxophone, showed up whenever a band came to town, and at fifteen was playing with the best dance band in town. He traveled with different bands as far away as Florida and once was stranded in Kentucky and had to hock his horn to get home. He played with pros at a theater that played for the silent films of the time. He even played at a Chinese restaurant on the side.

Artie was just beginning to play the clarinet when he joined the Austin Wylie Orchestra in Cleveland. Artie all but took over the band and Austin later became his road manager. Artie then joined a band that was bound for New York. In Chicago he jammed after hours with whatever musicians were in town at the time, such as Louis Armstrong, Jimmy Noone, Benny, Bix Beiderbecke, Eddie Condon, and Gene Krupa.

When the band left New York, Shaw stayed behind. He got his union card and played alongside Goodman, Condon, the Dorseys, and others in theater house bands and background studio orchestras. For a while, he was on staff at CBS. Invited to take part in a swing concert at New York's Imperial Theater, along with Bunny Berigan, Tommy Dorsey, Bob Crosby, and others, he contributed a jazz piece for clarinet and string quartet that was the surprise hit of the show.

Artie then got backing for a band of his own in 1936, opened at the Lexington Hotel, and hit the road. But the band had more strings than brass, the public wasn't ready for it, and it died. When he talked about his early days, Artie said, "Everybody liked the band except the audience." Bitterly, he reformed a band with the standard instrumentation, heavy on brass, and swore it would be "the loudest band in the world." It may have been, but it wasn't the best, and it struggled.

Artie said he took some time off to listen to Benny's band and others that were making it and decided the simpler the sound the better. But he still wanted to play good music and decided he would swing the Broadway hits of George Gershwin, Richard Rodgers, Cole Porter, and others. He hired one of his former violinists, Jerry Gray, to set these in swing arrangements and out of this came the great version of Porter's "Begin the Beguine," which made Artie a star. Gray later contributed a lot of the charts that made Glenn Miller's band a big hit.

I don't know whatever happened to the clarinet, but Benny and Artie were the big stars of the business when I joined Artie, and there were a lot of arguments about who was best. Both were brilliant. Benny was technically better and played faster and swung harder, but Artie had a better sound, played warmer, and swung in a different way. Artie used to say, "I was playing, he was swinging." I think down deep he wanted to be considered better than Benny, but he never would admit it, and he used to say he didn't care whose music was supposed to be best, he just wanted his to be accepted.

Benny had better musicians with him, but Artie had some marvelous musicians too. When I joined Artie's band he had fourteen pieces—John Best, Chuck Peterson, and Claude Bowen on trumpets, George Arus, Russ Brown, and Harry Rodgers on trombone, Tony Pastor, George Koenig, Hank Freeman, and Ronnie Perry on sax, Les Burness on piano, Al Avola on guitar, Sid Weiss on bass, and Cliff Leeman on drums. Later, George Wettling, then Buddy Rich came in on drums, and Georgie Auld on tenor sax, but most of the guys were happy with Artie and stayed with him; there wasn't the moving around there was in a lot of bands, and the band stayed pretty much the same during the time I was with it.

It was an outstanding band and I learned a great deal just listening to it. I had to listen to it a lot because like the other singers of the band days I sat on the bandstand and smiled a lot and kept time to the music and had to look like I was listening. I really was. Many singers with lesser bands were not. I sang maybe a couple of songs a set, which lasted about an hour. I never sang an entire song. The band would start and finish and I'd sing a chorus in between. That was the custom in those days. The band was the thing and the arrangements were written for the band, not the singer, not even on the vocal numbers. The band didn't back me up. I had to fit my singing to the tempo the band played. The arrangements and tempo were made for dancing.

When I joined the band, Billie Holiday was still with it. She is considered the greatest jazz singer ever, but she had a unique style that was not suited to big band music. She was having a hard time establishing herself, had gone with Count Basie's band for a year, then went with Artie. He admired her and made her the first black vocalist to be featured with a white band. It took guts on both their parts, but that was still a bad time in black-white relations in this country and it wasn't working out.

She'd had a hard time in her life, reared in a whorehouse, raped at ten, arrested for prostitution at fourteen, starving in Harlem at sixteen when she started to sing in New York's small clubs. She was only a couple of years older than I was, but she seemed older. If my childhood was hard, hers was harder. All she'd been through showed through in her singing. "Lady Day" was a lady with a lot of dignity, but the white audiences saw only her color and didn't hear her singing.

The guys in the band loved her and her singing, but they couldn't do much for her. Artie and Tony Pastor and others

57

defended the right of a black to be with the band, but the time hadn't come for racial freedom in this country. Those were segregated times and there weren't always facilities for blacks where the white bands played, especially in the South. The hotels we stayed at wouldn't give her a room and she'd have to find a place in the black part of town. The diners we stopped at on the road wouldn't serve her and she'd have to wait on the bus to be brought a sandwich. Chuck Peterson, the trumpet player, took her into a bar for a drink one night in Detroit and when some of the men there complained they didn't want a "nigger" served alongside their wives, he ploughed into them and they beat him up.

I feel bad about her. Maybe we should have backed Billie better, but we couldn't play the black places and if we didn't play the white places we had no place to play. Some places canceled us out when they found out about Billie. Artie was just starting to make it and he might have gone broke and the band might have vanished if he'd continued to buck the times. He hoped that with her he'd break through the color barrier, but he couldn't. He kept saying he'd take care of any problems that came up, but he couldn't. Sometimes red-neck cops or sheriffs ordered her out even when the audiences wanted to see her. He was frustrated by his failure. At least he tried. He used to say, "I tried."

I envied her singing, if not her life. I found her a good gal. I was new in the business and I didn't want to get into the color wall that followed us around. It was so much easier for me just because I was white. She was tough, but her life with the band was tougher. She said, "Finding a place to sleep, finding a place to eat, even just finding a place to go to the bathroom is a mess."

She treated me well. The band's vocal arrangements were written for her, so I sat around. She'd say to Artie, "Why don't you let this child sing?" He'd say, "She hasn't got any arrangements yet." And she'd say, "Well, let her use mine. But don't let her sit there doing nothing all night." But we sang in different keys and her arrangements didn't fit me. She taught me some tricks of phrasing, but her style was different from mine. We weren't really in competition, even though we were both singing with the same band. The only boy singer we had was Tony Pastor, the sax player, but he did novelty tunes, not ballads. Billie and I did the ballads and we were very different.

We both recorded "Any Old Time" with Artie. I never asked Artie why, but I think that after she left the band he felt that he could keep the number in his books if I recorded it too and developed an identification with it. Actually, that was the only number she ever recorded with him. And she was never on his remote broadcasts. A lot of people including his managers, booking agents, and producers put a lot of pressure on him not to use her and he used her less and less as time went on. He had it in his mind that he wanted to do right by her, but his skull was caving in from the pressure.

Lots of times she wasn't even allowed to sit on the bandstand with me. She had to use the back entrance and wait backstage to go on. Artie used to say she had to sit on the stage or the band would walk off, but she'd beg him not to get into trouble because of her, and he'd give in. If I didn't want to sit on the stand without her, she'd tell me not to cause trouble for myself, and I'd give in. The funny thing is everyone says she finally gave up when the band got to New York for its big opening at the Lincoln Hotel and she wasn't allowed to sit on the stand, but the fact is there wasn't any room for any singers on the bandstand and we both waited at a table up front for our turn. Maybe the fuss was because we sat together. The fact is Billie had told us she was leaving long before. Artie knew it when he hired me, which was one reason he hired me. We weren't together with the band for more than a month or two.

I used to tell her I didn't want her to leave, that the thought of her leaving made me feel bad, and I hoped it wasn't because of me. She said, "Sweetheart, it's not your fault. The band's got the greatest singer in the world and it doesn't need me anymore. I don't want to be a band singer and the life I've been living is not for me. I got to go and I'm going." When she left, I felt terrible. She kissed me goodbye. I wish I could have done more for her. But I was white and she was black and the gap between us at that time was just too much for us.

She, of course, became a great star, but I don't think she ever made the money the white stars made. She had a small voice, but she made big use of it. More than a voice, she had style. The Diana Ross movie about Billie, *Lady Sings the Blues*, shows a musician in her white band turning her onto drugs, but I never saw a sign of anything harder than marijuana while I was with Artie's band and Billie looked clean to me. She later said she smoked her first pot at a party at the home of Joe Louis in Hollywood long after she left Artie, was turned on to pot and harder drugs by her husband, Jimmy Monroe, and she really got hooked in the 1940s when fans at the clubs along Fifty-second Street used to bring her white gardenias and white junk. She spent time in prison, wasted herself, overdosed on heroin, and died in her early forties in 1959.

After Billie left Artie, I was the only real singer with the band, although Tony Pastor continued to do novelty tunes. Tony had a pretty big record hit, "Indian Love Call," but the flip side unexpectedly became the biggest of hits, the instrumental "Begin the Beguine."

I cut my first side for Artie the month I joined his band, September 1938. It was "You're a Sweet Little Headache." I wish the first one could have been a better one. Terrible tune. I did the flip side, too, "I Have Eyes." I did a terrible job on it.

Washington is sort of southern, hard on Maryland and Virginia. Without realizing it, I had picked up a sort of southern accent. I sounded like I had just come from Alabama. "Ah only have eyes. . . ." When I hear it, I get sick. Fortunately, I realized I had picked up an accent and dropped it fast.

I recorded some good songs along the way with Artie— "Day after Day," "Deep Purple," "Bill," "I Didn't Know What Time It Was," "All the Things You Are," and others. I don't think I sold a quarter of a million copies of any of them, which is what you had to do to have a hit in those days, but I did sell a lot of copies of a torch type of tune, "I'm in Love with the Honorable Mr. So And So."

However, my most requested number by far in my personal appearances was "All the Things You Are." The song was written by Jerome Kern and Oscar Hammerstein II for a Broadway show that failed, and Kern thought it would die with the show. It followed a kind of complicated line melodically and wasn't easy to sing, but Kern credits our recording with bringing it to life and making it the standard it became. It was one of his favorites and is one of mine. I think it was one of the most beautiful songs I have sung and I am happy to have been associated with it all these years.

Over a period of about fourteen or fifteen months I recorded forty-one sides for Artie for RCA Victor's Bluebird label. I was able to check out the exact number because a friend and a member of my fan club, Robert Sixsmith, has compiled a discography of every commercial record I ever made and the acetates of songs I sang over radio. Many of these were later released on records. Dominic Scutti and the late Earl Seaman formed my fan club and members always are coming to me to autograph records I forget I made. Sometimes I'll swear I never recorded a tune and argue about it until the fan brings me a copy of it to prove I did. Over a period of more than forty years I recorded more than 250 sides and a gal's got to forget some of them. Ha! Some of them are best forgotten.

With Artie, about half the time I'd do both sides of an all-vocal 78, half the time just one side with an instrumental or a Tony Pastor novelty on the other side. Of course, most of Artie's releases were instrumentals on both sides, featuring his fantastic clarinet, Georgie Auld's hot tenor sax, Tony Pastor's cool tenor, Johnny Best's strong trumpet, Les Jenkins's strong trombone.

The most popular records—the ones people played on the jukeboxes of the day in soda stores and bars, restaurants and dance halls, bowling alleys and so forth, or bought to play on their Victrolas at home—were the ones they wanted to hear in our in-person appearances. The band had only to hit the first notes of one of the more popular instrumentals or vocals and the fans would go "aaahhh" and start to applaud.

In the magazine polls covering the year 1939, the bands of Artie, Tommy Dorsey, Glenn Miller, and Benny Goodman were at the top. Benny's Septet and Bob Crosby's Bobcats were the top small groups.

In the *Down Beat* poll, Harry James and Ziggy Elman were the top trumpet players, Tommy Dorsey and Jack Teagarden the top trombonists, Coleman Hawkins and Charlie Barnet the top tenor sax men, Johnny Hodges and Toots Mondello the top altoists.

Georgie Auld was sixth among the tenor men.

Benny and Artie were tops among clarinetists, Bob Zurke and Jess Stacy the leading pianists, Bobby Haggart and Artie Bernstein the top bassists, Charlie Christian and Carmen Mastro the leading guitarists, Gene Krupa and Ray Bauduc the top drummers. Buddy Rich was fifth among drummers. Benny, Harry, and Artie were one-two-three among soloists.

Benny's "And the Angels Sing" was the number one record of the year, followed by Glenn Miller's "Moonlight Serenade" and Woody Herman's "Woodchopper's Ball."

Artie's number one hit of the year before, "Begin the Beguine," still was in the top ten, as was his "I Surrender Dear."

Also in the top ten were Miller's "In the Mood" and "Little Brown Jug," Benny's "Jumpin' at the Woodside," Harry's

"Ciribiribin," which became his theme song, as well as Glen Gray's "Sunrise Serenade" with his Casa Loma Orchestra.

The leading male vocalists were, in order, Bing Crosby, Jack Leonard, Bob Eberly, Bon Bon, Ray Eberle, Tony Pastor, Jimmy Rushing, Jack Teagarden, and Louis Armstrong. Although Bob and Ray were brothers, they spelled their names differently.

Frank Sinatra was twelfth. He'd had one hit with Harry James's new band, "All or Nothing At All," and was just beginning his rise to the top.

The leading female vocalists, or "fem chirpers" as the magazine put it, were, in order, Ella Fitzgerald, Mildred Bailey, Billie Holiday, Bea Wain, Helen Forrest, Helen O'Connell, Irene Daye, Ginny Sims, and Louise Tobin.

I, too, was just beginning my rise to the top.

I'll be honest with you. I think I'm a pretty good singer. No false modesty for me. While I have liked a lot of singers over the years, I haven't envied many. I think I have been able to sing with the best of them. I think I am singing better than ever now. But I wasn't too good in the beginning. The public thought I was pretty good. The press praised me. Artie was happy with me. To this day, people bring me copies of records I made with Artie and tell me how much they still love them and how they think I've never sung better. I can't believe it because they were mostly pretty bad. My voice was thin and high, I had no depth and little range. I would sing only the chorus of a song and I hadn't developed my own style.

I started out copying Mildred Bailey and Ella Fitzgerald and picked up a bit of Billie. Mildred listened to Bessie Smith and Ethel Waters and the great black blues singers of the early days and was the first white woman to sing like a black blues singer. She married Red Norvo, the great jazz vibist, and developed a distinct style of phrasing with his band. Billie probably had the purest jazz phrasing of any singer. Neither had great range. Ella, of course, has a pure, rich sound and

63

a great range, but she was just beginning in those days and, in fact, had her first hit in 1938, a novelty tune, "A-tisket, A-tasket (I Lost My Yellow Basket)" with the band of the great jazz drummer Chick Webb.

I don't compare myself to them. They were in a different world. They were black singers, even Mildred in her way, born out of the blues and with a jazz upbringing and background. I was influenced by them at first, but I am a white singer, born out of the big bands and with a background of swing music and show tunes, and I had to find my own way with a song. I was starting to find it in those days. I'm probably too critical of myself, but my time with Artie was primarily a learning experience.

Musicians—and singers are musicians—can learn from listening to the sort of music Artie made in those days. His and Benny's were the best bands then and Artie was catching Benny in the polls in 1938 and passed him in 1939. Artie's music had a simplicity to it that was remarkable. He knew what he wanted from music and he got what he wanted out of that band. He didn't give a damn what they did away from the bandstand, but he drove them hard on the bandstand. He rehearsed the guys until he got what he wanted from them and it showed in the band's performance. The band was a hard-driving collection of excellent musicians, especially after Buddy Rich got behind it on drums, and it played its music with remarkable consistency night after night.

Artie later said it was the best band he ever had. He said, "It was a bitch of a band. It breathed together, thought together, played together. It was as close to black music as a white man can get. I never played better. I can go back to those records and tell. At that time I became an artist. Not to sound pretentious, but to say I was doing something better than I had to do it, I had my band playing better than it had to play. I was the happiest with that band I ever was. We played well night after night."

After a while, however, the nights get to you, the night-after-night gets to you. They got to Artie, they got to a lot of the guys. When you are as successful as Artie was, you can play every night, so you play every night, and a lot of days, too. You remember the lean years and you dread the lean years that may lie ahead so you get fat while you can. You grab all you can while the sun is shining so you can put it away for a rainy day. You bus from one one-nighter to the next and when you get to the big town and stay put for a while, you cut records in the studio in the early morning and you play hotels and do radio late at night. The days get away from you, the weeks, and the months, and there's nothing in them but the music and, after a while, it isn't enough, you want something else, too. There were a lot of laughs along the way, but also a lot of outbursts of temper here and there. You got tired. You were always away from home. You had no home. The road was your home.

All the Things You Are

You are the promised kiss
Of springtime
That makes the lonely
Winter seem long.
You are the breathless
Hush of evening
That trembles on
The brink of a lovely song.
You are the angel glow
That lights a star,
The dearest things I know
Are what you are.
Some day my happy arms
Will hold you,
And some day I'll know
That moment divine,
When all the things you are
Are mine.

5.

I HAD JUST LEFT the stage door at Loew's State on Broadway after my last show for the night with Artie's band when my fans almost strangled me. Ha! It was winter and cold and I was wearing a black Persian lamb coat I had just bought. I had the collar up, held up by one of those twirl ropes they used to tie around the collars in those days. Our fans were waiting for us as we came out. Mine came up to me asking for autographs, wanting to touch me, crowding around me.

I had tied the rope in front. There was a small ball at each end of the rope. Seeking a souvenir, one fan grabbed one end of the rope, another grabbed the other, and before I knew it the knot was being drawn tighter and tighter and I was starting to strangle to death. They didn't realize what they were doing and I couldn't talk to tell them.

It seems funny now, but it was scary then and I thought the end was near. Fortunately, a security guard saw what was happening, yelled, "My God, you're killing the lady," got them to release the rope, and walked me back into the theater, where I was helped into a chair and gasped for a while before I got my breath back.

We were stars. I don't know if I deserved to be one yet, but I was. Anyone in a popular band was a star of sorts. The top performers were stars. The singers, who were more easily identified than the musicians, were stars. And the bandleaders were the biggest stars of all. Many of our fans were respectful, but others went into a frenzy over us. The fans who hollered and danced in the aisles at Benny Goodman's important Paramount Theater appearance and those who screamed and swooned at Frank Sinatra's solo singing breakthrough there later were comparable to those who still later went crazy whenever Elvis Presley made a personal appearance or hounded the Beatles wherever they were.

Because we made so many more personal appearances than those performers the fans, frequently crowding around the bandstand, were often able to get closer to us than can fans of musical stars today. When Paul McCartney or the Bee Gees play a concert today, they are sneaked in and out of the arena and protected as much as possible from the crowd, but when we were in a theater or at a ballroom we were really within reach and we loved it, we loved the adulation, all of us except Artie.

Artie hated this sort of hysteria. He did not want to be touched, reached for, screamed at. He wanted to perform his music in the purest possible way and be appreciated for it in the purest possible way. He thought too many of the people were crazy and he used to say, "I don't know what the hell gets into them."

The only way he used his popularity was with the ladies, but even then he didn't go for the ones that pushed to the front of the bandstand or waited at the stage door. He was famous and successful and wealthy and he had a fine mind and he always was with the finest-looking, the classiest kind of lady. He spoke exceedingly well and he had a great wit and charm. He also attracted the highest type of female—society gals and movie stars.

Eventually, he was married eight or nine times. Two of his wives were among the most beautiful movie stars of all time, Lana Turner and Ava Gardner. A third was another attractive movie star, Evelyn Keyes. One was Jerome Kern's daughter, Betty. Another was Kathleen Winsor, the author of *Forever Amber*, the sensational and successful novel. Another was high society's Doris Dowling. He admitted to me that if he had a weakness it was for lovely ladies.

I couldn't compete in that kind of company. He never came after me and it never occurred to me to go after him. He liked me and I liked him. We were friends, as much as a bandleader and a band singer can be. We were together a lot and we talked a lot. I learned a lot about music and about life from him. His interests went beyond music into every aspect of life. As I have said, he was the most intelligent man I ever met and you had only to listen to him to learn from him. I took my troubles to him and we talked them over and he helped me with a lot of good advice. I wish I could have helped him with his love life. Ha!

The boys in the band didn't need any help. They didn't deal at Artie's level and they weren't as selective. The girls were there and the guys took them. The girls crowded around the bandstand with their shining faces looking up in awe at the musicians, and the boys made dates to meet them later. The girls waited for the guys at the stage door and the guys went off into the night with them. Most of the girls were young. My God, they were babies, a lot of them! But they loved the music and so they loved the musicians who made the music and they were soft touches for the guys, some of whom scored every night.

A lot of the men were married, but their wives didn't travel with them. The musicians were on the road most of the time and home maybe six or eight weeks a year. They were lonely a lot of the time. They worked late hours and wanted to let off steam later. There was too much temptation to resist. It was an accepted thing. It was the way it was.

On the other hand, the boys in the band protected me as if I were a kid. I wasn't, but I was a little like one, new to the business and all, and really inexperienced. Guys would come around the bandstand trying to make time with me, and Georgie or Tony or someone would come over and tell them to beat it, to let the lady alone. Some of the men who came around were good-looking and I didn't always want to be left alone, but the fellows in the band were like big brothers to me and they were determined to protect me even when I didn't want to be protected. It was nice, but it was annoying at times, too. Good-looking guys would wait for me at the stage door, but the boys in the band would hustle me away from them. They didn't think about the fact that I was alone much of the time.

There always was a lot of talk about the girl singers in the all-boy bands. A lot of it was true, too. There were singers who took on all the guys in their band at one time or another. They were all together in this thing and the girls didn't want to play favorites. Tonight, the brass section. Tomorrow night, the reeds. You know. And of course there were the girl singers who just got involved with one guy and really had a hot romance with him and maybe wound up marrying him. And the girl singers who put out for the leader. A lot of them had hot romances with their leaders and quite a few wound up marrying them.

But there also were the girls who stayed straight. I was one of those until I got to the Harry James band and it seems to me that if you set your standards high and stuck to them the guys would accept it. Oh, they were always fooling around. Georgie Auld, for one. He'd make a pass, half-kidding, ready to make more of it if I'd let him, I'm sure, and I'd say, "Hey, Georgie, I don't want it, I'm not looking for it, and I don't need it, so please lay off," and he'd laugh and that would be the end of it.

Once in a while on overnight trips we'd take trains. On one trip, we had a sleeping car with those enclosed bunks. I had gotten into my bunk and was almost asleep when I felt some-one in the bunk with me, feeling me. I let out a screech and leaped out of the bunk. The lights came on and all the guys were leaning out of their bunks laughing. Georgie leaned out of mine. He'd gone in as a gag and all the guys were waiting to see how far he got. I laughed too. It was funny. It was all in fun. I just wanted to keep it that way.

One night at a hotel I was standing at the bar with the boys when Georgie tried to talk me into having a drink. I didn't drink in those days and Georgie was always trying to change my mind. I kept saying, "No, I don't drink and I don't want to start to drink." And Georgie kept saying, "Just try one. You'll never know if you like it if you don't try one."

Finally, in one of those moments of weakness that comes over you every once in a while, I said, "All right, Georgie, if it'll make you happy, I'll try one, just one." He ordered me a Pernod. I didn't know what it was. What it was, was about 200 proof something. It smelled like licorice. I'll never forget that smell as long as I live. It tasted sweet. It felt warm going down. I don't know how much I drank, but suddenly I realized the room was spinning around.

I had enough sense left to figure I had better get to my room. I left and ran into an open elevator. Georgie was right behind me, but the door closed right in his face. When I got out at my floor, the door closed behind me. When I got to the door of my room, I heard the elevator door open. I got into my room and got the door closed behind me just as Georgie came running up.

He knocked on the door, asking, "Helen, are you all right? Is anything wrong?" I said, "I'm fine, just leave me alone." And at that moment I started to feel sick, ran to the bathroom, and started to throw up. Georgie was pounding on the door now, calling, "Helen, Helen, are you all right? I'll take care of you. Helen, let me in and I'll take care of you."

I was so sick I couldn't even answer him. Soon, I guess, some of the other boys came to the room because I could hear their voices saying, "Let us in, Helen. C'mon, Helen." I think they were scared because they knew Georgie had tried to get me drunk so he could make a pass at me. They were just trying to help.

I was just a young girl who'd gotten drunk and sick on her first drink, but I'll remember forever how sick I felt and I was angry as I could be. I finally told them all to get away from my room and it got quiet and I fell into bed with the room spinning as I passed out. The next morning I felt awful. I don't think I talked to Georgie for two weeks. But I could never stay mad at him. He was the kind of cut-up character you couldn't stay mad at.

I was still a virgin when I married Al Spieldock. Good old Al. My boyfriend from the Madrillon in Washington. From the day I left to join Artie in St. Louis, Al wrote or telephoned me once or twice a week. I guess he was in love with me. I don't think I was in love with him. But he was a very nice guy. He was a good drummer, but I don't think he had the drive to make it with a big band. We were bound to be apart, but he was bound and determined to marry me. He kept talking to my mother about me and she was all for my marrying him. I know what she was thinking. She was thinking that it would be bad for me to be the only girl traveling in a band of fifteen or sixteen men and if I was married I would be safe.

After I had been with the band less than a year, in the early summer of 1939, I gave in to the pressure and told Al I'd marry him. I found out when I had a few days off and we set a date to be married back in Baltimore, where he lived with his father and some cousins. He also had about a hundred relatives there. They all set about making arrangements. And my mother was very excited about it.

I Had the Craziest Dream

When I told Artie, he asked me up to his suite in the Lincoln Hotel, where we were staying at the time, and tried to talk me out of it. He said, "I know your family must be worried about your traveling with a bunch of men and I know you may feel trapped at times among so many men, but you also must know we respect you and love you and would never take advantage of you, so you don't have to get married to feel safe with us."

I said I knew that, but I loved Al and had planned to marry him for some time. I didn't tell the truth because I was unsure of myself and wanted to justify myself. Artie said, "Maybe, but if you're going to be a big star in this business—and you are becoming a big star—you're going to have to travel and you won't be able to take him with you. You've seen enough by now to know it's not good to be married in this business, it just doesn't work out too well. Do yourself a favor, give yourself some more time. Go on back, but come back with an engagement ring instead of a wedding ring."

I said I couldn't do that. His family had planned a wedding and it wouldn't be fair to back out at the last minute. It was going to be a Jewish wedding with a lot of people and I couldn't back out on Al and his family. Artie was Jewish and he knew about family feelings and he understood. He said, "I just hope you're not making a mistake."

I said, "I hope so, too." But I was.

I went back to Baltimore and married Al and spent my wedding night with him and flew back to New York without him the next day and rejoined the band. I was no longer a virgin, but I didn't feel any more real love for Al than I had before. To this day I don't know why I married him. We had nights here and there together, but his father or cousins were always around and we had little time alone. We talked on the telephone and wrote each other, but as time went on we talked and wrote less and less. We just never had a real marriage.

His hobby was photography. He was a better photographer

than he was a drummer. Eventually he turned to photography and gave up the drums. After we were divorced, I heard he remarried. Later, I heard he was one of the top child photographers in the Baltimore area. I guess he's still there, but I haven't seen him or spoken to him or heard from him or about him for many years. I don't want to put him down but our marriage was a mistake and at all a marriage.

My life was the band. About a month after I joined the band at the Chase Hotel in St. Louis, in October 1938, we went into the Blue Room of the Hotel Pennsylvania. It was our first major New York engagement on the heels of the hit record "Begin the Beguine" and we were a big hit. We got great reviews and drew great crowds. The band was making marvelous music and joined the Benny Goodman and Tommy Dorsey bands as one of the most popular in the country at that time. We began to get a lot of national exposure on radio and our records really started to sell. The talent agency behind Artie was flooded with offers and we were booked solid a year in advance all across the country.

We went to Hollywood to make some shorts and then a feature. Musical shorts were popular in those days. Along with cartoons and newsreels, they played with the double features that movie houses ran if they didn't have big band stage shows. We made one short in the summer of 1938 and two in the summer of 1939. In the first, I sang, "Let's Stop the Clock." In the second, *Class in Swing*, I sang, "I Have Eyes." In the third, *Symphony in Swing*, I sang "Deep Purple."

While we were making the first one, Artie met and had an affair with, ironically as it turned out, Betty Grable, who was making a movie called *Campus Confessions*. When we made the feature film *Dancing Co-Ed* in 1939, Artie met Lana Turner and started a romance which led to marriage. Artie always liked those campus co-eds. I did not sing a song in the movie.

We filmed during the day and played the Palomar Ballroom at night while working the Old Gold *Melody and Mad-*

ness radio show in between. We supplied the melody, along with an added singer, Dick Todd, to do the boy ballads. Robert Benchley provided the madness. A writer who made movie shorts and feature films, he was a very funny fellow with a sly sense of humor. But I seldom saw him. He did his stint separately. The show was on once a week for almost a year—from November 1938 through August 1939—and when we weren't in Hollywood we always had to get back there to do the show.

We also put in long stays at the Blue Room of the Hotel Lincoln and the Café Rouge of the Hotel Pennsylvania, as well as the Summer Terrace Roof of the Ritz Carlton Hotel in Boston, from which we did late-night broadcasts almost nightly. And when we were in New York we played Loew's State or the Strand or the Capitol Theater from nine in the morning to one in the morning, six or seven one-hour shows a day, and squeezed in a couple of one-hour stints at the Roseland Ballroom at night.

In between, we traveled on tours of one-nighters in which we played ballrooms and dance halls and field houses and gymnasiums in towns across the country and one weekers at hotels in Philadelphia and Atlanta and New Orleans and Houston and Chicago and St. Louis and Kansas City and Denver and San Francisco and so forth, and at theaters in Pittsburgh and Birmingham and Indianapolis and Minneapolis and Dallas and Detroit and Cleveland and Phoenix, etc., etc., etc. We were always on the move and we never really knew where we were. We were always exhausted and punch-drunk, but we just went on and on. Every time we were on the bandstand we got fresh life and made beautiful music. The people loved us for it. We got a lift from the fans and inspiration from their cheers.

6.

WE TRAVELED mostly by bus. On a few long trips we took trains. On a few short trips we drove cars. Except for the train trips, Artie didn't travel with us. He drove his own car. Most of the bandleaders did. Sometimes the band manager drove. Sometimes one of the musicians or singers went along with the bandleader for the ride. I went with Artie a few times. I liked going with him because he was interesting to talk to.

Once we were driving down a dark strange road, talking, when he suddenly slammed on the brakes. I was almost thrown into the dashboard, but he yelled as he braked and I put my hands up in front of me. They hit so hard they hurt. We sat there silently in the dark for a few seconds while I tried to figure out what had happened. Suddenly, a train came roaring by, right in front of us, no more than a few feet away.

I recall it clearly. It was so eerie. We had seen nothing, heard nothing. Artie admitted that later. He said he sensed something wrong and reacted to it. Maybe he thought we were about to drive off the end of a cliff. Maybe he heard something without realizing it. But we didn't see any railroad crossing signs. No warning light came on. No bar dropped across our path. There was not one light on that train when it went by. And I didn't hear it until it was in front of us, passing by, I sat there, frozen with fear. I still tingle when I think about it. That could have been the end for both of us.

We shook it off and went on. I don't remember where it happened. I don't think it matters. Half the time we didn't know where we were. Most of the time we were trying to find our way to some town, driving down some dark, deserted highway, or in the town trying to find our way to some ballroom or dance hall or school gym through dark, strange streets. Woody Herman was almost killed in a car crash. Hal Kemp was killed in a car crash in 1940, driving from the Cocoanut Grove in Los Angeles to the Mark Hopkins Hotel in San Francisco. Many musicians have been killed driving late at night in strange areas, perhaps driving too fast, perhaps fortified by a few drinks, perhaps stoned in some way.

Mostly I went on the band bus. We'd charter a bus and hire a driver for a tour. I was lucky in that I never had an accident on a bus, but many did. We were lost a lot of the time, but that was the driver's problem. We drove in rain and snow, in midsummer heat and midwinter cold. The buses weren't cooled or heated in those days the way they are today. We'd strip down (to a limit) or bundle up and make the best of things. The longer trips took eight, ten, twelve hours. The movies of that time always showed the fellows whipping out their instruments and making mad music on the bus. The instruments were locked in the luggage compartment. No one made music on the bus. A lot of the guys played cards. Some talked. Most slept.

I never could sleep on a bus, which was a terrible handicap because I always arrived tired. I'd read a little, look at the scenery, wonder when we were going to make a rest stop. I'd talk to Tony Pastor or Georgie Auld or the other boys. Tony had played with Artie in some early bands and joined Artie when he formed his own band. Tony was an older guy and a steadying influence on the younger guys, many of whom were eighteen, nineteen, twenty years old and new to the road and to the business. Tony played great tenor sax and brought a lot of personality to a novelty tune; off the bandstand he was a solid, dependable guy.

After Buddy Rich joined us, I talked to him because no one else would. And I liked him. If you've seen him guesting on the Johnny Carson show in recent years, you know Buddy to be a wisecracking smart aleck. We who knew him in the early years knew him as a wisecracking smart aleck. He hasn't changed a bit, except maybe to get worse. But I got along with him. Buddy was my age when he joined the band, but he seemed younger. He was a cocky kid who was afraid of being in the wrong. If someone told him how to do something, he'd tell them off. He threw his drumsticks at sidemen who messed up during a number on stage and threw his fists at some offstage.

Artie put up with Buddy because he was a great natural drummer, maybe the best that ever lived, one of the few white musicians that black musicians really have admired. He's been the best technically and maybe the best at giving a band a driving beat. But he had the worst temper of any person I ever met. He was a brat who used to say the only people he had trouble with were grown-ups. Buddy saw that I liked him and he'd listen to me. I'd say, "Buddy, you're being obnoxious again." And he'd grin and say, "Am I, Helen? I guess I'll have to stop. But only for you, Helen, only for you."

I met his parents and they were the nicest people, quite unlike their son. He'd talk to them about me, and one time when we were at a hotel in New York and I was sitting with them, Buddy's mother said, "Why don't you marry Buddy? You're the only one he listens to. You could straighten him out." And I laughed and said, "I love him, but not that much." After that, Buddy's mother or father always said, "You really should marry Buddy." And I'd laugh and say, "I'm too smart." And years later Buddy would ask, "Why wouldn't you ever marry me?" and I'd say, "You never asked." But there never was any romance between us, just a kind of cockeyed friendship.

He did get married and has remained fiercely loyal to his wife, Marie, and daughter, Cathy, who sometimes sings with his band. He is loyal to his friends. He has fought for the rights of black musicians. But the last thing in the world he wants to be known as is a nice guy. When he left Artie, he went with Tommy Dorsey. Frank Sinatra was singing with Tommy. All three were temperamental. Buddy had fights with Tommy and threw his drumsticks at Frankie. But Frank later shelled out fifty thousand dollars to back Buddy and a band and lost it. Fans would tell Buddy how great a number was and Buddy would ask them what the hell they knew about music.

Some years ago I ran into him in Pittsburgh, where his band was playing. His bass man had just quit and Buddy had hired another he'd heard of out of Las Vegas. He hadn't heard him play, but I had, and I told Buddy he was one of the best, outstanding. But there was bad weather and his plane was grounded on the way. All Buddy knew was that he was on the stand ready to play a set and his new bass man hadn't arrived yet. He took the mike and told the crowd, "Ladies and gentlemen, my new bass man hasn't arrived and I can't play without a bass man." And he walked off the stage, leaving the musicians sitting there. I grabbed him and told him I knew the band couldn't get a good sound without a bass man, but he was not treating the paying customers right. He said to "screw" the paying customers. I decided against it.

A half-hour or so later I spotted the bass man at the door, looking all dishevelled and worn out, lugging his big instrument. I went to the poor guy and he was relieved to see me. He asked what I was doing there, and before I could answer him he asked where Buddy was and how angry was he. He was a young man and he'd heard how bad Buddy was. He was late and he was scared to death. I said Buddy wasn't too bad, he wasn't too mad, I was a friend of Buddy's and I'd told Buddy how good he was. And he said, "You can't be a friend of Buddy's. I heard Buddy doesn't have any friends." He hadn't even met Buddy and already he disliked him.

I took him to Buddy and introduced them and Buddy just looked him up and down, asked him where the hell he'd been, didn't wait for an explanation, and said, "I hear you can play. Prove it." He took the kid to the bandstand. By that time the kid was so nervous he couldn't play. All you have to do is hit one bad note and Buddy believes you can't play. He'd been known to stop in the middle of a number and ask a player, "Who the hell ever told you you could play?" Well, the kid hit a bad note right off, and Buddy waved off the musicians and asked him, "Who the hell ever told you you could play?"

They finished the set and Buddy stormed off and yelled at me, "I thought you said the guy could play." And I yelled back, "You never gave him a chance to play." The poor bass player was practically in tears. He lasted only until Buddy found someone to replace him. He never had a chance. You had to be tough to endure in the business and guys like Buddy and Benny and Basie didn't make it easy on you. The Count used to walk behind the guys in his band during rehearsals and if one of them wasn't playing right Basie would bash him in the back of the head with rolled-up sheet music.

It was a tough life, but the boys in the band frequently acted up to relieve the monotony. Once we moved into a hotel in Hollywood. As I was unpacking my bags, good old Georgie Auld telephoned me and told me to look out my window. I looked out and saw a double row of palm trees extending as far as I could see. Then I saw some of the boys setting fire to one of the trees. It was midday and they were cold sober, but they were like college kids playing a prank with whoops of joy.

Setting the fire at the base of the tree, they ran for the hotel and their rooms. Soon the tree was flaming and smoking and the sirens were screaming. Fire engines pulled up and doused the blaze before the hotel caught fire, but the boys were laughing so hard some of them almost fell out of the windows. They were "the boys in the band" then, just a bunch of over-grown boys.

A lot of them drank a lot. There's a story about the great trumpet player Bunny Berigan. He was a heavy drinker, but everyone wanted him because he played so well. Tommy Dorsey once hired him for a big NBC radio show. He agreed to buy Bunny and his wife dinner before the show, telling his manager to pick up the tab at a nearby hotel. When Bunny showed up at the studio and stood up to solo on the air, he fell off the bandstand. When Tommy checked Bunny's meal check he found it consisted of a dozen Scotch-and-sodas and one ham sandwich.

The boys used to bring bottles in brown bags aboard the bus and drink the stuff straight, passing it around, especially on cold winter trips. Life on the bus and on the road was so difficult I can understand why so many used hard drugs to get by, but I never got into that and I never saw any of it in my day. Liquor and marijuana were what I saw. Marijuana was bad business in those days. As I understand it, the stuff was so straight and so strong it was practically a hard drug. And so many of the guys were turned on to it that the bus used to fill up with that sickening, sweet-smelling smoke so you could hardly breathe.

They used to keep the front window seat for me and even on the coldest days I'd have my window wide open so I could breathe. The smoke would get in my hair and I'd stick my head out of the window to try to get the smell out. My gown would hang in the back of the bus and by the time we finished a trip it would smell like a "joint." I'd grab it when we got in and try to air it out, but I went up on the bandstand smelling like a joint many a night, and I didn't even smoke. It was only when you stopped in a place for a few nights to play a hotel or theater that you could get your clothes cleaned. Otherwise, if there was an hour to spare, you'd run for the nearest laundromat. And the guys were always asking me to do their underwear for them. Ha!

One time we were getting on a bus on our way to Toronto when one of them asked me to hold a brown bag for him. It was tied up with a thick rubber band. Georgie had his hands full with his instrument case and I had one of those huge handbags. Without thinking, I said okay and stuffed it into my bag. We got to the Canadian border at Toronto and immigration authorities pulled out the luggage and went through it and boarded the bus and searched through it and even body-searched Georgie Auld, who was a Canadian from Toronto. They couldn't find anything, but they held us up for a long time until some of the boys suggested I make a fuss. I did. I said, "Guys, we have to get going. We've got a date to play in Toronto. We're running late. You haven't found anything. There's nothing to find. C'mon, give us a break." They finally did and let us pass on through. They never did search me.

We did the date and the boys went through another rough search at the border. We bused back to our hotel in the states. It was late, but they called me into the bar to have a drink with some of the other boys. I ordered a Coke and stood there talking to Georgie and the others. I realized they were all standing around sort of expectantly with a funny kind of look on their faces. You can tell when guys have something up their sleeves. I knew something funny was going on but I couldn't figure it out. Then one said, "Helen, I forgot, don't you have a brown bag of mine in your purse?" and I said, "Oh, yes, I do," and took it out and started to hand it to him. And they all started to laugh, and I finally got suspicious.

I don't know why it didn't dawn on me earlier, but I never thought about it from the moment I stuffed that bag into my purse until the moment I started to hand it back. Suddenly, I knew what it was—marijuana. I threw it in his face and started to tell him off. "You rotten so-and-so . . ." Everyone in the bar turned around. He started to back out of the bar and I started after him. He darted out through the revolving door and I followed him through with all the guys following us and laughing. He ran down Broadway and turned the corner with me trying to catch up to him and cursing, "You rotten bastard, how dare you do such a thing to me!" And every once in a while he'd turn around and run backwards a few steps, looking up at me, laughing, pleading for mercy. We went completely around the block, me chasing him and yelling at him: "You no good . . ." and him staying just ahead of me, laughing, pleading for mercy.

I was wild, just wild. It was five o'clock in the morning and I didn't give a damn that everyone in the world was stopping to watch us, looking out windows. I couldn't believe he had done that to me. They put people in jail for possession of marijuana in those days. They'd have put me in jail if they'd caught me. My reputation would have been ruined forever. Sure, he was playing a gag on me. The whole band was in on it. But it wasn't funny. I still would have paid a heavy price if they had caught me. I wanted to kill him.

We got back to the hotel and he hid while the other guys calmed me down. Then he came to me and said he was sorry. I said sorry didn't do it. I asked him if he realized what might have happened to me if I'd been caught. He said, "Helen, I just didn't think." I said, "That's the trouble with you, you never think." That was the one time I couldn't laugh off something as a bad gag. I laugh thinking about it now, but it really wasn't funny. If I had gone to jail, I'd still be living with that.

Artie hated it when the guys came to play drunk or stoned. He wouldn't stand for it. He got the reputation of being a tough boss because of that, but he didn't dissipate and he believed the guys that did couldn't play the music the way they should. That was one of the things that bothered him about the business. But the guys usually cooled it before a performance. Even though they really believed they played better when they were high on "hash."

I remember one night Georgie came to me and said, "Wait 'till you hear me play tonight. I feel so good. I'm really ready to blow." I could see he was stoned. He had a kind of glazed look on his face. He went out there and he played with so much passion on that tenor of his it was unbelievable. It was wild. But it was all emotion. Now, Georgie really was a great player. I believe if he hadn't been white he'd have rated right up there with Coleman Hawkins, Ben Webster, Lester Young—the great black tenor sax men of the day. I believe that there was a tendency to think that a white player couldn't play as well as a black player. But Georgie really could play. When he was at his best he played with a lot of feeling and a lot of imagination and he put a lot of love into it. He had his feet on the ground and you could see him thinking which notes would fit best as he improvised solos full of feeling, imagination, and love. But when he was high he was walking on air and his solos were all emotion. At his best he'd punctuate them with shrieks in the high register and growls in the low register, but when he was stoned he'd stay with the high notes until your ears hurt. Then he would get in that guttural groove and stay there until you were ready to scream. He just got out of balance.

He came off that night saying he'd played for me and asking how I'd liked it. I didn't want to hurt his feelings so I said it was great. But a couple of days later I was sitting on a bus with him and I told him the truth about what I really thought. I said, "I'm sorry, but I don't think you play as well stoned as you do straight." He said, "That's funny, because when I get high, I get such a feeling of strength I feel like I can do anything. All I can say is I sound good to me. I'm sorry I don't sound good to you." He was hurt. He didn't want to face the fact that I might be right. Maybe I was wrong. You know, a jazz musician might play every night, while his fans might

see him only one night a year. He has to improvise imagina-
tive solos every night because the fans who are there that
night expect it of him. That puts tremendous pressure on him
to be at his best night after night. I guess some guys go for
anything that might give them that something extra. I guess
they get so high they can't see what's real. They go into
another world and they hear something we don't hear. And I
suppose some do play better when they're relaxed by drugs.
In the long run, though, it destroys them. Fortunately, there
are not nearly as many on drugs as the public is led to believe.
I've been around and I haven't seen many. But every one is
one too many.

Georgie later led some small combos and had his own big
band for a while. He was never as successful as he should have
been. But he's still playing. He taught Robert DeNiro how to
handle the sax and played the sound-track solos for him in the
movie about the Big Band Era, *New York, New York*. And he
played marvelously. He's living in Palm Springs, last I heard,
and I'd love to see him sometime. He was a handful while we
were with Artie, but looking back on it, I think he made it
more fun than it otherwise might have been. I really liked
him, and I really miss him. It was a hard life for those guys. A
lot of them had a lot of talent and got very little out of it.
George was one of the great talents and he never got rich at
it. He never really was famous and he's not too well remembered, except by those of us who were there with him and by
a few loyal fans.

The bandleaders were the only ones who really made good
money, and only those who made it to the top did. Most went
broke and are long forgotten. They paid the guys and gals
small salaries with maybe a few extra bucks for a record date
or radio show. They paid for the bus, but we paid for our
rooms and meals. They'd drive ahead of the bus and stay at
the best hotels, while we scrambled around for rooms we
could afford. If a guy had a home and a wife and maybe some
kids he sent money home, seldom got home himself, and lived

an unreal life. He made maybe ten or fifteen or twenty grand a year and spent half of it sustaining himself on the road and maybe the other half sustaining a family at home.

The big bandleaders made a hundred to two hundred thousand dollars a year and maybe cleared half of that, depending on how much they were willing to work and how tight they were with money. There were maybe ten who made big money and maybe another thirty or forty who did well, but it was a brutal business for them too. The demands made on them and the pressures put on them were really heavy. Many couldn't stand even the good times. And when the good times came to an end, many more couldn't handle that. Tommy Dorsey choked to death in his sleep after taking some pills in 1956. Brother Jimmy died a year later. Artie was long gone from the business by then.

7.

ARTIE LOVED the music part, not the business part of the music business. His theme song, "Nightmare," and his big hit, "Begin the Beguine," were worked out while he was fooling around on his clarinet in hotel rooms with some of the fellows. He was always trying to work out something new and different. He gave his musicians and his arrangers a lot of freedom to do new and different things. He was convinced that within the context of swing music with a dance band he could combine jazz and the classics. His first band had strings. He regretted it had flopped. He was ahead of his time.

After the hit with "Begin the Beguine," Artie was booked so solidly he had little time to develop new ideas and he didn't like it. The booking agents, the record producers, and the fans wanted everything he played to sound like "Begin the Beguine," and Artie hated this. He used to say, "It's like Beethoven writing his Eighth Symphony and everyone saying 'That's enough.' He'd never have written his Ninth if he'd listened to others." Artie felt he wasn't free to experiment. Out of pride he kept rehearsing the band so it would sustain its excellence, but it bothered him that his audience didn't care. As long as the band played its favorites, the fans didn't care how well it played.

Artie used to say, "The music is everything. I don't care about the audience. I know when the music is good, the audience doesn't. I only want an audience there because they pay the tab so I can play the music." But early on, the manager of a dance hall told Artie, "I don't give a goddam about the music. I don't know a goddam thing about music. I'm paying you to play your goddam music so we can get some goddam customers in here and make some goddam dough. What do you think we're running here—a goddam concert hall or something?"

After "Begin the Beguine," Artie was a celebrity. Although he was cold to the fans on the bandstand, they were hot for him, climbing on the stage, trying to get to him. He couldn't step out of the stage door for a breath of air without being besieged by them. He couldn't get into or out of a ballroom or a theater without having security cops to get him through the crowds. He was good-looking and he played a passionate clarinet. He went with glamorous gals. He hated it that he couldn't go out with a lady without photographers snapping away and reports on his romances appearing in all the gossip columns. He was featured in *Life* and all the big magazines. He used to shake his head and say, "It's like living in a fishbowl."

He was making big money, but he didn't care about the money. He later said, "Money got in the way. Everybody got greedy. Including me. I'd do something I didn't want to do because of the money and I hated myself for it. I hated it when I became a commodity to be bought and sold. Fear set in. I was afraid of making a mistake. I was making myself sick."

Twice during his biggest year he collapsed on the bandstand. The second time came late in 1939. He had a strep

throat, took an overdose of a new miracle drug, and developed a blood disease that was serious and sometimes fatal. He
was sidelined six weeks and Tony Pastor took over the band
temporarily. We were really worried about Artie.

He rejoined the band at the Pennsylvania Hotel in New
York. He seemed all right and everything went fine for a
while. Then on the night of December 19, after some fans had
crowded around the bandstand asking for autographs, he suddenly walked off right in the middle of a set. He just walked
off and disappeared.

We were startled. We didn't know what to do. Then Tony
took over and we finished the set without Artie, playing the
tunes we could do without Artie. When we finished the set,
Tony got a message that Artie wanted to see us in his room
upstairs in the hotel.

We all went up and crowded in and there was Artie, bags
partly packed, clothes strewn around the room, propped up in
bed. He said, "I'm leaving the band." Tony asked, "Are you
sick?" And Artie said, "No, just sick of the business. And I'm
finished with it forever." We just stood and stared at him.
We couldn't believe it. Someone said, "You've got a million
dollars' worth of bookings." Artie said, "I don't give a damn
about that." Someone said, "They could sue." Artie said,
"Let 'em sue. If I don't have a band, what're they going to sue
me for?"

Tony asked, "What happens to the band?" Artie said,
"You can have it. You've been leading it anyway." Tony said,
"I don't want it without you." Artie said, "How about you,
Georgie, you want it?" Georgie said, "I don't want it. What
do I know about business?" Artie asked, "Any of you guys
want it? We can work out something about the arrangements
and things. You can have it all. You can pay it out. I don't
care. Anyone want it?" All the guys shook their heads. Artie
asked, "How about you, Helen? You want to try it?" I said,
"My God, no."

Artie said, "Well, then, that's it. The band is through. I'm through. I like the music, but I'll never play again. I hate the business. I hate selling myself. I hate the fans. They won't even let me play without interrupting me. They scream when I play, they don't listen. They don't care about the music. I'm sorry, but that's it, guys."

One by one they filed out, some of them stopping to shake hands with him. They were shocked. Most weren't making a lot of money. Suddenly they were out of work. Most would catch on with other bands, but it was a bad time. They couldn't believe this thing had happened so suddenly. They had developed a great band together, and suddenly it was finished.

I was the last to leave. I asked Artie, "Are you sure you want to do this?" He said, "If I don't do it, I'm going to have a nervous breakdown." I said, "Okay," gave him a kiss, and left. I was suddenly out of work, too. I'll never forget how lost I felt that night.

I heard later that when his agent rushed over he pleaded with Artie to stick it out "just two more years" and he'd never have to worry about money again as long as he lived. And Artie said, "If I stay two more years, I won't be able to worry anymore."

They say an executive of RCA Victor rushed over a spiritualist to try to talk Artie out of leaving. They thought he was crazy. But Artie packed up and disappeared into the night. The story is he took a taxi to the airport, caught a plane, and was in Mexico the next morning. And never played again. It's one of the most famous stories in show business, but it's not told accurately.

No one says how sick he was and how he'd been thinking of quitting for a while. And he drove off all by himself and didn't get to Mexico for several days. And it's not true by a long shot he never played again.

He had fallen for Judy Garland, twelve years younger than he was. He'd met her in 1938, the year she first became famous at the age of sixteen with her rendition of "Dear Mr.

Gable" in a movie. She went backstage at Loew's State to tell him how much she admired his music. Later, when she played the same theater, he went backstage to tell her how much he admired her singing. They started to see each other socially, but Artie was almost thirty, while Judy was seventeen, and Judy's mother would have none of it. Then their careers took them away from each other.

Artie telephoned Judy from a motel in Little Rock, Arkansas. Wondering what to do, he was tempted to go to a house he had in Hollywood. Judy supposedly told him the world was going nuts because he was among the missing and maybe he better cool it for a while. Artie went to Acapulco where he lay on the beach, swam, fished, and thought about his life. After Christmas, he drove on to L.A.

He and Judy dated for a while. Judy had her old pal, Jackie Cooper, pick her up several nights a week so she could get out of the house, but he'd drop her off at Artie's house. When Jackie backed out of this arrangement, Judy would say she was going to her sister's and have her sister cover for her.

Artie always said he divided his women into two categories—those he talked to and those he went to bed with. Apparently he put me in the first category. And Judy's sister believed he put Judy in it too. But Judy wanted more.

The Wizard of Oz was a big hit and Judy was a big star, but she was working hard and was unhappy, and she had started to take sleeping pills so she could get some rest. He encouraged her to take some time off. She encouraged him to go back to work.

"You can't sit around on your ass and do nothing," she supposedly said.

He was supposedly engaged to—irony of ironies—Betty Grable, but he was seeing other beauties, and early in 1940, he and Lana Turner, only nineteen at the time, ran off to Las Vegas and got married. Although Judy's mother never wanted him to go with Judy, the mother supposedly sought out Artie and told him his marriage to Lana was the reason

Judy had gone on pills. He denied it and remained friends with Judy to the day she died from pills many years later.

Artie did go back to the music business in 1940. He formed a new big band, this one with his beloved strings, and in March took it to a recording studio to fulfill a contract he had with Victor. He recorded a song he'd heard in Mexico, "Frenesi," and it turned out to be his second biggest hit of all time. Before he knew it, he was big again and back on the road.

When we entered World War II, Artie enlisted and was assigned to form a band that would tour service installations. He formed a great band and toured the South Pacific, often performing where the sounds of music were mixed with the sounds of nearby battle. After two and a half years of this, the band was brought back to the States, supposedly suffering from battle fatigue. Artie admitted, "We were beat."

Out of service, he formed one new band after another, often loaded with strings. Back to pioneering, he employed such brilliant black musicians as trumpeters Roy Eldridge, Red Allen, and Hot Lips Page, trombonist J.C. Higginbotham, alto sax man Benny Carter, and singer Lena Horne, as well as such wonderful white musicians as trombonist Ray Conniff, guitarist Barney Kessell, drummer Davey Tough, and singer Mel Torme.

He had some big hits with instrumentals of such great songs as "Stardust," "Dancing in the Dark," "Summertime," "The Man I Love," and "I Surrender Dear." In response to Benny Goodman's success with small groups, Artie put together the Gramercy Five with Billy Butterfield on trumpet, Johnny Guarnieri on harpsichord, Al Hendrickson on guitar, Jud DeNaut on bass, and Nick Fatool on drums, and had a series of swinging hits, including "Back Bay Shuffle."

But the last band he formed, in 1953, was bad. Artie didn't want to form another by then. Artie had bought a farm and he said he had to "feed the cows." He had an agent hire fourteen musicians for one hundred dollars a week apiece and took them on the road. He was so disgusted with the grind, he started to clown around on stage, in contrast to the old Artie. The fans loved it. After a dance at an American Legion Hall in Pennsylvania somewhere, the proprietor said Artie's was the best band to play the hall since Blue Barron. Artie quit on the spot. And, finally, for good. And to the best of my knowledge, though he sometimes fools around on the piano, he has not picked up his clarinet in more than twenty-five years.

We had dinner one night many years ago. Artie had called the business "a racket" and the jitterbugs "jerks," but I asked him how he could leave something at which he'd been so successful. He said, "I didn't want to be a half-assed human being just so I could be a whole-assed musician." He said he had begun to feel like "a sideshow freak." He said, "I didn't want to walk out on the music, I wanted to walk out on the whole human race." He said he was happy. I hoped he was. It was a wonderful evening and I just love the man and miss him.

He married and divorced a lot of beautiful ladies, wrote a book about his life, produced some movies, hosted some talk shows in which he talked freely about his life, lectured on the college circuit on such topics as "The Artist in a Materialistic Society" and "Consecutive Monogamy and Ideal Divorce." He lived in France and Spain and in recent years has lived almost like a recluse in California. I have no idea how he has managed financially. I have no idea how he has managed without music. I know there is more to him than his music. There is more to me than my music. But I don't think I could live without singing. And that night in 1939, when he walked off the bandstand, I was suddenly left without a band to sing with.

8.

BENNY GOODMAN was by far the most unpleasant person I ever met in music. Almost anyone who ever worked with him will agree. He is a legend because he has lasted so long and played so well. He practically invented swing music and he is still playing it, as well as classical music. While the clarinet is no longer a popular instrument, he is one of the greatest clarinetists who ever lived, he is playing as well as ever, and he is still listed among the best in the jazz magazine polls. He is in his seventies now and has endured for more than fifty years. He has been a remarkable musician and a remarkably disagreeable man.

When Artie's band broke up, I went back to Baltimore and to my husband, but I really didn't want to settle down and be married to Al. With Artie, I had risen to the top ranks of female vocalists in fifteen short months. Fifteen months! I can't believe it was no longer than that. I guess you can live a lifetime's worth in fifteen months. I guess the highlight of your life can come in one day, one hour, one minute.

The fifteen months I spent with Artie's band were among

the most memorable of my life. So were the twenty or so months I spent with Benny. They felt like twenty years. Looking back, they seem like a life sentence. But I heard Louise Tobin had left Benny to have a baby and he was auditioning to find a new singer, so I called him up and asked to audition. He said I was his singer. I didn't even have to audition. All I had to so was accept a cut in pay from the $175 a week I'd been making with Artie to $85 a week with Benny.

I took it. I wanted to work. I wanted to sing with Benny's band. From year to year one hot band or another might finish ahead of Benny's band in the polls, but everyone knew Benny's band was the best musically. I joined him in New York in December 1939, only a week or ten days after Artie disbanded.

Actually, some of Artie's guys were so desperate to work that they did stay together and Georgie agreed to act as leader. I could have rejoined them. But once the ties were cut I didn't want to go back. And Georgie wasn't cut out to be a leader. The band didn't last long. And before long Georgie had joined Benny too.

I don't know why Benny took me. A couple of years earlier he had walked out on me in Washington, saying I couldn't sing. Maybe I couldn't. Maybe I was singing better by the time he took me. But I don't know that he ever really listened to me. I think he took me because I was becoming a big singer and he had to have a singer and he didn't care about singers anyway, and he figured he could do worse.

He never said one kind thing to me about my singing, but then he never said one kind word to anyone about anything. He had some of the greatest musicians in the swing world with him at one time or another and he couldn't bring himself to compliment them no matter how well they played.

However, aside from the fact that he was a great musician, the one kind thing I can say about Benny is that he wanted great musicians to play with him. No, there's one other thing.

He wanted great musicians so much that he, more than Artie, broke the color barrier by adding great black musicians to his band.

Over the years Benny had such brilliant black musicians with him as Lionel Hampton, Teddy Wilson, Charlie Christian, Cootie Williams, Roy Eldridge, Sid Catlett, and others, and brought in Count Basie to record with him.

Although black and white musicians have played alongside one another in jazz for many years, it was new then, and there always has been a feeling among many black musicians that it is their music and whites do not play it as well. It is a tribute to Benny's musicianship that black musicians wanted to play with him. Benny is color-blind in that he does not distinguish between black and white musicians. He also is insensitive. It took courage to feature blacks in his band, but he did no more for them than he did for the white musicians.

As it had been for Billie Holiday with Artie, the road was very rough for the blacks in Benny's band. Somehow a singer is spotlighted more, so the reaction of the red-necks to Billie was worse, but the blacks with Benny could not stay at the same hotels with us, eat at the same restaurants, use the same facilities where we played a good part of the time. Benny could not be bothered with this. His attitude was you were his when you were on the bandstand and you were on your own when you were off. He provided the bus and that was that.

A few of the fellows stood up for the blacks as certain situations developed and the guys got along among themselves fine. Just having whites and blacks in the same band, however, did much to break down these barriers of bigotry and contributed to a gradual acceptance of integration.

The great white musicians wanted to play with Benny too, of course, and over the years such superb players as Harry James, Ziggy Elman, Bunny Berigan, Billy Butterfield, Lou McGarity, Toots Mondello, Vido Musso, Bud Freeman, Georgie Auld, Johnny Guarnieri, Joe Bushkin, Jess Stacy,

Red Norvo, Terry Gibbs, Artie Bernstein, Gene Krupa, and Davey Tough did go with Goodman. Many left, too.

Toots walked off right in the middle of a set one night, saying "I've had it." He picked up his sax and stormed away. When Stacy left, he said, "I never want to play with that man again. You never know where you are with him."

Benny never fired anyone. But he made many want to quit. He was a tough taskmaster. So were others—Artie, Harry, the Count, Tommy Dorsey, Glenn Miller. Tommy put up his fists and fought with some. Benny never fought with anyone. He fixed him with a look that left him frozen when he was displeased with him. He aimed his eyes at a spot on the forehead just above the eyebrows and bored a hole with it. It became famous within the fraternity as "the Ray"—"the Goodman Ray"—and it enraged some, embarrassed others, and irritated everyone. He never told anyone he didn't like what he was doing, he just stopped the music, turned the Ray on him for as long as a full minute, then started the music again. The Ray reduced many a strong man to a nervous wreck.

As great as these musicians were, Benny never called them by their names. He never called anyone by his name: He called everyone "Pops." He even called me "Pops." He just couldn't be bothered to remember anyone's name. Once, many years after I had left him, he called me on the telephone to ask me to work a date with him. He called me "Pops." I had never said anything to him about this, but finally this time I did. I said, "Benny, I worked for you for two years. You've known me for thirty years. You've never called me anything but 'Pops.' My name is Helen. H-E-L-E-N, Helen. You're calling for a favor. Please call me by my name, call me Helen." He said, "Oh, yeh, sure, Pops." I turned down the date.

He was notoriously absentminded. He forgot anything and everything. One time he got into a taxicab to go cross-town and just sat there, lost in thought. The cabdriver sat and waited to be told where to go. The stalemate lasted a long time. Finally, the cabdriver turned to Benny and said, "Hey, mister." Benny looked up, startled. And asked, "Oh, yeh, Pops, how much do I owe you?" The wheels hadn't turned.

Benny was always in his own world. He passed you without seeing you. You talked to him and he didn't hear you. Benny lost himself in his music. He practiced more than any musician I've known, and when he wasn't playing or practicing he was thinking about his music. He often didn't hear people when they talked to him and ignored those around him to the point of rudeness. Accused of this, he once admitted, "It's true. When I'm into my music it has my total concentration. I'm completely absorbed by what I'm doing. And everyone else should be, too."

No one wanted to travel with him. Fortunately, he drove to most of his dates, like most of the bandleaders. Maybe his manager drove him sometimes, but none of his musicians ever drove with him that I remember. I certainly didn't. I drove with Artie sometimes and, of course, with Harry sometimes, but never with Benny. Artie was great to talk to. Benny had nothing to say.

No one even wanted to eat with him. We'd rush to fill up a table when we'd stop at a diner or go into a restaurant so there would be no empty chairs when he came by. "Got an empty chair?" he'd ask. Someone would say, "No." And he'd wander off. He always read the newspaper while he ate. Usually the sports section. He did like sports. He wouldn't look when he ate. He slurped his food. The food fell all over him. He was a slob. And he never talked to people, even if they talked to him.

One time somebody got up and moved to another table just before Benny arrived. There was an empty chair and he grabbed it, much to our regret. He stuck the newspaper in front of his face and ignored the rest of us. When the waitress came, he didn't even look up when he ordered scrambled eggs and toast. He just kept reading, turning the pages, grunt-ing.

When the food came, he started to shovel it in, grunting, continuing to read. Suddenly, he spoke: "Somebody pass the catsup." Ziggy picked up a bottle of catsup, loosened the cap for him, and passed the bottle to him. Benny took it up and started to douse his eggs with it without looking. The cap fell off in the middle of the eggs as he shook catsup all over them. He heard it fall, looked down, and saw it in the middle of his eggs. He shrugged a little, turned back to his newspaper, and continued to eat all around the cap. We couldn't believe it. And I have never forgotten it.

Another reason no one wanted to eat with him, besides the fact that he never talked to anyone and ate so sloppily, was that he never picked up a check. He was making the big mon-ey, mind you, not us. But he'd sit at the table behind his newspaper, eat, and when he was finished, he'd fold up his newspaper, get up, and go. He never looked at the check, never paid it, never paid even his share, never even left a tip. When he was in a taxi with others, he'd be the first one out, leaving the others to pay. Whether it was the band mana-ger, the band boy, whoever he left behind, that person had to pay. When he took a taxi alone, the cabbie practically had to tackle him to get his fare. And never a dime more than the fare.

Getting an extra dollar out of Benny was next to impossi-ble. He made great players plead for raises and just grunted. I got a couple of raises out of him. When I left him I was mak-ing $125 a week, or $50 a week less than I'd been making with Artie two years earlier.

Traveling with Benny's band was not as much fun as it had been with Artie's band. Traveling never was fun, of course. Maybe I didn't mind it as much when I was starting out and it was new to me. It was kind of exciting to see all the cities. But before long you realized you didn't really see the cities. You saw the countryside as you drove in. You saw the four walls of a hotel room. If you stayed at one. And the ballroom or the theater or the auditorium or the field house or whatever. And you saw the countryside as you drove out.

It all became a blur—the town, the time of day, the day of the week, the date. Someone else told you when to go and where to go and you went. But the guys in Artie's band were more fun than those in Benny's. At least for me.

The black musicians didn't talk much to the white vocalist. No bad feelings or anything, they just didn't. That's just the way it was. I talked to Hamp some. But he was a little like Benny. A lot friendlier, but he also called everybody "Pops." And he grunted, too, and was hard to understand. He was sort of hyper, full of energy, which showed in his playing. He played the greatest vibes ever, drums, an incredible two-fin- gered piano. He worked over his instruments like a madman and really swung. And he was a nice guy. Teddy Wilson, a great pianist, was a great gentleman. Charlie Christian, an incredible guitarist, was a quiet man. He never was well and died a few years later of tuberculosis.

I was closest to Ziggy Elman. And Toots Mondello, until he left. Ziggy, whose real name was Harry Finkelman, was, like me, a Jew from Atlantic Cty, two or three years older than I was. He put a Yiddish flavor into his solos. His most famous was on "And the Angels Sing" with Benny. And "Well Get It" later with Tommy Dorsey. He was a fantastic trumpet player and was voted number one in the polls several times in the forties. And he was a sweet man. Toots was fan- tastic too on alto, and a thoughtful fellow. If I had problems, I took them to these two. You sure didn't take your problems to Benny.

A man could say "Good morning" or "Good night," couldn't he? But that was Benny. He didn't have the time of day for his best friend. He didn't have a best friend. He didn't have a friend. Maybe John Hammond, the critic and record man. Or Willard Alexander, an agency man. They believed

With Harry James and his Music Makers playing behind her, Helen
sings a ballad. (*Helen Forrest collection*)

Above, Helen sings with Harry James in the movies. *(Courtesy of Universal Pictures, Inc.)*

Left, Helen sings as Artie Shaw plays behind her during her early days in the big band business. *(Duncan Shiedt collection)*

Right, Georgie Auld swings away.
(Duncan Schiedt collection)

Below, on the bandstand with, among others, Benny Goodman, Toots Mondello on sax, Ziggy Elman on trumpet, Nick Fatool on drums, and Johnny Guarnieri at the piano, Helen waits to sing. *(Photo by Hugh Turner from Robert Sixsmith Collection)*

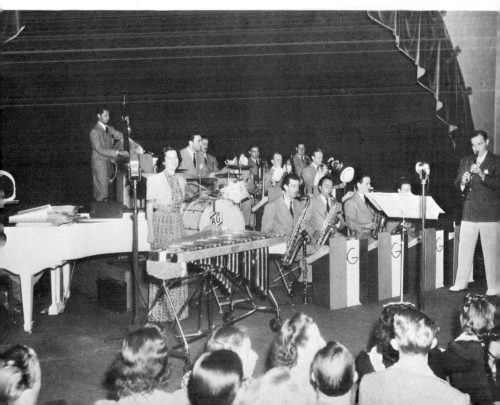

Left, bad-boy Buddy Rich, Helen's buddy with the Shaw band.

Below, Artie Shaw with wife Ava Gardner at the Hollywood Paladium in 1944. *(Photo by Gary Gray)*

Above, Harry James with wife Betty Grable at Hollywood Park Race Track in 1946.

Right, Dick Haymes with wife Rita Hayworth in 1955 when she returned to Columbia Studios and moviemaking while he was fighting deportation because he was born in Argentina and studio boss Harry Cohn wanted him away from her.

Helen in 1948, late in her blond period.

Right, Helen, gone blond, chats with Dick Haymes at the mike in a wartime appearance at a Navy base.

Below, the crowd gathers near the marquee of the Strand Theatre on Broadway where Harry James, Helen and the Golden Gate Quartet were performing in 1942. *(Photo by Arsene Studio)*

Above, actor Dick Foran gets in front of Harry and sings to Helen in a scene from the movie *Private Buckaroos.* *(Courtesy of Universal Pictures, Inc.)*

Right, orchestra leader Raymond Scott and Mark Warnow buss Helen, who was fired by Warnow from a WCBS radio show many years earlier.

in Benny and contributed to his career. We never thought anyone would marry Benny, but Hammond's sister Alice did. And they had two daughters.

Perhaps because he had so few friends, Benny relied a lot on family. He ran his band like a family business, like the corner deli. At one time or another, Benny had in his band one brother, Harry, on bass; another, Irving, on trumpet. Another brother, Eugene, took care of the music, while yet another, Freddy, was the road manager. And a sister, Ethel, ran the office.

The rest of us were really just outsiders, working for a living. And Benny was the boss.

9.

Here I go again,
I hear those trumpets blow again,
All aglow again,
Taking a chance on love. . . .

WHATEVER ELSE you might say about Benny Goodman, you have to say he was a fantastic musician, and still is. He and Artie may have been the best clarinetists ever. Artie played more romantically and with a better tone, but Benny was quicker, more versatile, and truer to swing music and to jazz. Benny improvised better than Artie and was more inspirational to others.

Although most of the numbers were built around Artie's clarinet, his band often played very well when he wasn't with it. As many great musicians as he had, and he had more than Artie, Benny's band never really came to life until he started to play.

Artie and Benny had a lot in common. Both were born into

poor Jewish families in ghettos—Artie in New York, Benny in Chicago. They came along at about the same time, both played the clarinet, and they played alongside each other in studio bands before they went on their own with their own bands. Neither went well at first, but each eventually caught on and went to the top.

Benny began by playing in a band on a steamboat that took tourists across Lake Michigan. He joined Ben Pollack's band at the Venice Ballroom in California in the middle 1920s. He also played with Isham Jones and Ted Lewis, and in studio bands. He made a name for himself as an instrumentalist when he recorded with Red Nichols and the Five Pennies.

Late in 1934 he formed his own band and broke in at Billy Rose's Music Hall in New York City. He then played the Roosevelt Hotel and on NBC radio's *Let's Dance* show. But he didn't attract a large audience or much attention and took off on a cross-country tour.

Broke, he was about to disband after his last stop, the Palomar Ballroom in Los Angeles. He had been playing the slow, sweet stuff of the day, but there he decided to try some fast, hot arrangements Fletcher Henderson had written for him.

They say he lit into "Sugar Foot Stomp" and the audience let out a yell and went wild. He recalled later, "That was one of the greatest sounds I ever heard in my life." Word of this swinging band spread fast. Radio picked him up. The big houses booked him. The swing era was on.

Benny's band went into the Congress Hotel in Chicago for two weeks and stayed seven months. He broke through the color barrier there by hiring Teddy Wilson to play piano with Gene Krupa on drums and Benny himself on clarinet in the debut of the Benny Goodman Trio.

Later he brought in Lionel Hampton on vibes and made it a quartet and then Charlie Christian on guitar and Artie Bernstein on bass to make it a sextet. Using different combinations, he recorded some of the swingingest small group performances ever.

The big bands really hit the big time with Benny's stay at the Paramount Theater, beginning in March 1937. Fans waited outside in line for hours to get in, and those inside jitterbugged in the aisles and gave roars of approval to every number. The theater seated thirty-six hundred people, but they seldom were seated. More than twenty thousand passed through the first day. The theater was packed the entire stay. By then, Benny had been crowned "The King of Swing."

He became real royalty when he played the World's Fair in San Francisco, the Hollywood Bowl in Los Angeles, and Carnegie Hall in New York. His was the first popular band to play that citadel of classical music and that January 1938 concert produced the enduring classic "Sing, Sing, Sing," featuring Krupa on drums.

In those days you weren't supposed to record a number longer than about three minutes, or one side of one of those 78-rpm records. But "Sing, Sing, Sing" took twice that long, was released on both sides of a record, and became one of the biggest instrumental hits of all time.

Benny later played classical clarinet at Carnegie Hall with symphonic groups in 1940 and 1941. And he took swing groups to the legitimate musical theater in Swingin' the Dream in the fall of 1939 and The Seven Lively Arts some years later.

To some extent, Benny's became the first concert band in the history of jazz and Benny really didn't like that. He actually played few concerts after Carnegie Hall. He used to say, "I grew up with dance music and think in terms of dance music." His theme became "Let's Dance" and when the audience crowded around the bandstand he'd sometimes say, "Aw, c'mon, kids, let's dance."

But first Fletcher Henderson and then Eddie Sauter gave him some great arrangements and when Benny's band played you wanted to listen. Some of his sidemen such as Krupa, Hampton, and James became as famous as anyone in the business and later led their own successful bands.

In fact, Benny backed Harry in his first band and almost lost his money, but Harry finally hit and wound up having to pay Benny a big profit to buy back his own band. Harry had already gone when I got on board with Benny so our meeting was to wait a little while longer.

The band I joined was sensational. Again, I learned from listening. Few special arrangements were written for me. I sang choruses. I made myself fit to the music. Benny used to drive me crazy by "noodling" behind me on clarinet when I sang.

Benny drove all the band members crazy by noodling behind them on clarinet while they played their solos. He was doing just that the night Toots gave up, got up, and walked out. It distracted the soloist and attracted attention away from him.

The first side I recorded with Benny's band is never to be forgotten, but not for the quality of the song. It was "I'm as Busy as a Bee, I'm Buzz-Buzz-Buzzin."

I recorded fifty-three sides with Benny in eighteen months from late December 1939 through mid-June 1941. These included "How High the Moon," "It Never Entered My Mind," "I Can't Love You Anymore," "The Man I Love," "Cabin in the Sky," "More Than You Know," "I'm Always Chasing Rainbows," "Perfidia," "Lazy River," "I Found a Million Dollar Baby," and "Smoke Gets in Your Eyes."

Most did very well and I had one big hit, "Taking a Chance on Love," which was one of the ten best sellers for ten or twelve weeks, hit number one for a while, and was my first million-seller. The hit of the year was "I'll Never Smile Again," sung by Frank Sinatra and the Pied Pipers with Tommy Dorsey. It shot Sinatra to stardom. "Taking a Chance on Love" moved me up, too, but I had left Benny before the record was released. It's a great song, and I still sing it.

Lionel Hampton also asked me to record with him and I cut two sides with him in the summer of 1940—"I'd Be Lost Without You" and "A Ghost of a Chance." The sidemen on these were interesting: There was the Nat "King" Cole Trio with Nat on piano, Oscar Moore on guitar, and Wes Prince on bass. Cole was a great jazz pianist and his trio was a great jazz group before he went on his own as a romantic singer.

And the drummer behind Hamp was Al Spieldock, mine own husband, who was traveling with me for a short time.

My career went up a couple of notches while I was with Benny, partly because of the one big hit, partly because I'd been in the spotlight three years or so, was becoming better known, and was moving up in the polls. I was developing my own style, my own way with a song, and was increasing my confidence as I went along. People were responding well to my work.

But life with Benny was difficult, even if it was always exciting musically. Early in my stay with him we played the Waldorf-Astoria in New York, easily the fanciest hotel in the country at the time. But early in 1940 he was so troubled with phlebitis—the same condition that sidelined Richard Nixon: blood clots in the veins of the legs—that he took some time off.

Wearing a brace on his leg, he played a benefit at Chicago's Hull House, where he had learned to play. Then he went into the Mayo Clinic for corrective surgery. He was out for three or four months.

But the band went on, led by Ziggy Elman. Ziggy never made it on his own as a leader, but then he never had a band behind him like this one. At least life was fun for us while Ziggy was out front.

There were the same marijuana–smoke-filled buses and rooms with Benny's boys, just as there had been with Artie's outfit. Some drinking. No hard drugs. Benny's boys were not as much fun as Artie's had been. But no romances here, either, though that was just ahead.

Benny came back with the Ray and the tension returned. He was strictly an instrumentalist and the need to have vocals were a pain to him. He had fewer than any other major band-leader. He forced Martha Tilton out. Helen Ward left.

Peggy Lee followed me. At that time she wasn't the singer she was to become. Benny kept glaring at her. When she asked him what was wrong, he muttered something about her phrases. She didn't know what she was doing wrong, but it was hard to understand Benny.

One night Harry James stopped by to hear the band and Peggy told him tearfully of the problem. Having worked with Benny, Harry understood. He told her to tell Benny before the next performance that she now knew what the problem was and would do what he wanted.

She did, but Harry also told her to sing exactly as she had been singing, and she did this, too. When she was done, Benny smiled at her, pleased. It was one of the few times he ever showed approval of anything.

He did not try to tell her how to sing again. He was satisfied after that. Peggy was mystified then and still is. But Benny was a mystifying fellow.

When I went with him, I thought Louise Tobin had been my immediate predecessor. She left to have a baby. Whose baby? Ironically, Harry James's, who was her husband at the time. When I got there, I found out Kay Foster had been there for a brief stay, but had been done in by the Ray. Benny simply wasn't satisfied with her. I guess I satisfied him, but he never said so.

After he returned, we played the Cocoanut Grove at the Ambassador Hotel in L.A., the Avalon Ballroom on Catalina Island, the Steel Pier at Atlantic City, and the Hotel Sherman in Chicago, among others. We did radio remotes from these places and we did *The Old Gold Show* and *The Fitch Bandwagon* out of New York. Along the way, I wanted to quit and threatened to do so several times.

Finally, when we reached the Sherman in Chicago the first of August 1941, after a night in which he had noodled behind my meaningless vocals, I told him, "This is it, find another singer, and find her fast."

He hired Peggy Lee, but I still had a month to go on my contract. He said, "Stick until your contract runs out." I sat alongside Peggy on the bandstand and didn't sing a note for four weeks. She'd get up and sing, but I never got up. When people would ask me why I wasn't singing, I'd say, "Ask Benny." They'd ask him and he'd say, "She's got laryngitis." I was healthy as a horse.

That was the longest month of my life. Finally, my contract ran out and I left. Benny went on very well without me, of course. And Peggy did well with him, having a number of big hits, notably, "Why Don't You Do Right?"

Years later, when I was working as a single, Benny and one of his daughters came to hear me in a hotel dining room. I was flattered, and figured the past was past. When I was down to my last song, I felt I should introduce this famous man, my former boss, to the crowd. I gave him a big introduction and pointed to his table. The spotlight swung down to reveal an empty table. Benny had shoveled in his food and shoved off with his daughter. He had not said one word to me. He had not even nodded. Nor had he even waited for the end of the show. He was something else—a cold, inconsiderate character.

Much later, when it had been announced in the trade papers that I had signed to do a nostalgia tour with Sam Donahue and the Tommy Dorsey Orchestra, Benny called.

"Hi, Pops, this is Benny. I'm putting a tour together and I want you on it."

I knew he'd seen the announcement of the other tour. I said, "Benny, I just signed to tour with Frank Sinatra, Jr., the Pied Pipers, and Sam Donahue and the Tommy Dorsey Orchestra."

He said, "I don't care about that, Pops. You were never with Tommy Dorsey. You were with me. I want you with me again. I want you as part of my package, Pops."

He made it sound like a real king had commanded it. Clearly, he didn't give a damn about any contract I'd signed with anyone else. Nor did he feel like he had to mention money. But in two minutes I'd had more words out of Benny than I had before in almost two years. I said, "I'm sorry, Benny, but I can't break my contract."

He said, "Sure you can, Pops, just fly on out."

That's when I launched into my tirade about my name being Helen, not Pops. He said, "Oh, sure, Pops. Now why don't you just fly on out——"

I hung up on him.

But Not for Me

They're writing songs of love,
But not for me.
A lucky star's above,
But not for me.
With love to lead the way
I've found more clouds of gray
Than any Russian play
Could guarantee.

I was a fool to fall
And get that way;
Heigh ho, alas,
And also lack-a-day!
Although I can't dismiss
The mem'ry of his kiss,
I guess he's not
For me.

10.

I WAS SO GLAD to get away from Goodman that I didn't care that I was out of work. I knew I wouldn't be out of work long. Any number of bands might have wanted me. But there was a band I wanted. When I heard Harry James was auditioning girl singers, I asked for an audition. I don't know what instinct drew me to Harry, but I loved the way he played, especially on ballads. He had this Yiddish type of phrasing, very "shmaltzy," as they called it, and I just loved it. Harry even had strings. His solo on "You Made Me Love You" had just made the whole country love him. He played jump tunes, too, but he just loved to play love songs.

One thing that distinguished Harry's band from Artie's or Benny's was that Harry had a boy singer—quite a boy, Dick Haymes. Except for Tony Pastor, who did mainly novelty tunes, I don't think Artie ever had one. Benny had a few—Art Lund, who became an actor, and Dick, who was with him for a little while—but not many.

Others did. Jimmy Dorsey had Bob Eberly. Glenn Miller had Ray Eberle. Harry had Frank Sinatra before Dick. Tommy Dorsey had Jack E. Leonard before he took Sinatra away from Harry. Later, when Sinatra left, Tommy took Haymes away from Harry. Dick always seemed to be filling in for Frank, in his shadow, but when I joined James, Haymes was there.

I auditioned at the Lincoln Hotel in New York one night in November 1941. Harry was honest with me. He said, "I'll be happy to hear you, Helen, but I know how well you can sing. The problem is you're a ballad singer. I already have a ballad singer—Dick. I need a jump singer." I spoke to Dick about this. I said, "I don't want to step on your toes." He said, "No chance. Don't be afraid of anything. Don't worry about me. There's room for both of us. Just sing like you can."

Well, Dick was a great guy and a real charmer. He went to Harry and he said, "We can both sing ballads. The band needs a girl singer. Let her sing." So Harry said to me, "Okay, Helen, we'll let the band decide. You sing tonight and later we'll take a vote. If the band wants you, you're in." I sang the beautiful Gershwin song "But Not for Me" and they didn't have to take a vote. The band gave me a standing ovation after my first song. I'll never forget it. Harry grinned and said, "You're in." And Dick seemed happy to share the spotlight with me as long as we were together.

Harry was born in Georgia but raised in Texas. His parents were with a small circus that toured the South and Southwest. His mother was a trapeze artist, his father the bandmaster and drummer. Harry learned to play the drums before his father gave him a trumpet and then he learned to play that. As a kid, he won a state contest. Soon he was playing with touring bands around Texas. Lawrence Welk heard him and talked to him, but because Harry could play only one instrument well and Welk had a small group of guys who doubled on different instruments, Welk passed him by. What a combination they'd have made!

Ben Pollack, who had discovered Goodman, Glenn Miller, Jack Teagarden, and many more, heard Harry and hired him in 1935. Goodman heard about him and hired him in 1937 with a telegram, "C'mon, boy." Benny never doubted for a second that a hot kid would come with him at first call. Harry did and he gave Goodman a terrific lead trumpet and super soloist. He became a star among stars. By the end of 1938 he wanted his own band. Benny, who didn't give away a dime, gave Harry about five thousand dollars for a starter. It was good business. He got twenty-five thousand back.

Harry formed his band early in 1939. He didn't catch on at first. The band bounced around on one-nighters, playing the small spots for small money. He hired a couple of promising singers, Frank Sinatra whom he had heard in a roadhouse in New Jersey, and Connie Haines, but they didn't catch on at first. For about eighteen months Harry battled going broke. Even Sinatra's "All or Nothing At All" didn't catch on at first. I heard a lot of horror stories about the band's struggles before I joined up.

Harry was paying Haymes fifty dollars a week. Dick said that the weeks Harry would pay him, Harry would ask to borrow the fifty right back. Harry was paying his musicians about seventy-five dollars a week, but some weeks he couldn't pay anyone. The guys would borrow a few bucks from Hoyt Bohannon or Claude Lakey, who must have come from rich families because they always seemed to have some money.

The guys would sit in the back of the bus and play poker for the few bucks they had, just to kill the trips. Vido Musso, a great tenor sax man, was also a great poker player, and he used to win a lot. He'd ask the driver to stop at the nearest telegraph office, saying he had to send a wire. What he'd do was wire his winnings home, then return to the game with no more than a small stake so the others couldn't win back their money from him.

Harry was almost as close with a buck as Benny. Harry had a lot of young guys with him who were trying to make it with him and were willing to go along with him. If they'd ask for more money, he'd say, "If you don't like what you're getting, get out." None of them was so good they couldn't easily be replaced. But it was hard for Harry to fire guys. He was soft-hearted in this way.

He had a pianist, Big Jack Gardner, who was a headache to him. Big Jack was really big—maybe four hundred pounds. One time he passed out, stoned, in the pits and the guys had a helluva time lifting him up and out and toting him backstage. Harry hired Al Lerner to replace him, but couldn't bring himself to fire Jack. For a while Harry placed pianos at each end of the stage and used both until Gardner got the message and left.

One of the few times I remember Harry firing anyone was when he got mad at one of his violinists. The violinist was a classical musician, very accomplished, who was traveling with a big band just for kicks. Harry used to really shriek on his trumpet at times and the violinist couldn't stand it so he'd cover his ears with his hands. Harry caught him doing it one time and dismissed him on the spot.

But whenever he let anyone go he gave him money, as much as it took for the fellow to get home from wherever we were.

The band was everywhere, thirty, forty one-nighters in a row sometimes before it could settle down for a week at a theater. The guys would get pretty playful just to relieve the monotony and raise their sagging spirits.

There was a trombonist named Truett Jones who just played melody and never got to solo. He dreamed of the day Harry would ask him to solo. He used to talk about it all the time. One time Harry felt sorry for him and told him he could solo at the start of the next set. Truett was so excited he ran around telling everyone he was going to solo on "Stardust" to start the next set.

While he wasn't looking, Al Lerner stuffed paper in Truett's trombone bell. When he got up to solo, nothing came out but a weird sound. Everyone in the band broke up, but Truett was brokenhearted, close to tears. Harry tried to tell him the guys were laughing with him, not at him, but he wouldn't hear it. Al and the guys felt bad and tried to console him, but they didn't feel so bad they didn't laugh about it for a long time.

Sometimes a comic would be on a theater bill with the band and would do his stuff in the middle of the set. By the fourth or fifth show of the day, when some fans had sat through two or three shows to hear the band, the kids in the audience would call out the punch lines of his jokes before he could tell them, killing his act. Sometimes the guys in the band would do it.

The band was bored stiff listening to the same stuff five or six times a day, no matter how funny the guy was the first time around. One day Al Lerner and Dick Haymes and a few others came to the bandstand with loaded water pistols in their pockets. During the comic's routine, they started to spray the rest of the guys with water, dousing the sheet music and all. Between sets, the other guys went out and got water pistols and loaded them with ink. The war that followed almost finished all of them. Harry was furious. Remember, the boys wore uniform suits at that time, and they did cost money.

They used to have raised stages in the theaters at that time. The stages came up out of the basement on hydraulic lifts, rising dramatically as the curtain parted and the band played the theme. Mickey Scrima, the drummer, leaned back one day and dropped twelve feet, drums and all, to the floor. He wasn't hurt, but it stopped the show.

Scrima was a little on the nutty side anyway. He and Sam Kaplan, a big violinist, were buddy-buddy, like Mutt and Jeff. Scrima used to start fights in saloons, then back off and let Sam finish them. Sam used to beg Mickey to lay off. He was worried about his hands. But Mickey was feisty; he just didn't like to fight.

The guys smoked pot and drank a lot. Harry Rogers, a

trombonist, was one of the heavy drinkers. Everybody called him "Buck" because of the cartoon character. Before we got into World War II, the government started drafting men into the army. Al Lerner tells a story about when he went down for an exam with Buck:

Buck was sweating heavily and the doctor asked him if he drank. Buck said he drank a little. The doc asked him what a little was. Buck said about a quart a day. The doc said he wouldn't be able to get it in the army. Buck said he'd always been able to get it wherever he was. The doc asked him if he had a drink before breakfast. Buck told him a drink was his breakfast. The doc sent him back to the band.

I heard that Buck and his wife are living in Florida now. Mickey Scrima is a maitre d' at an Italian restaurant in Dallas, Johnny Guarnieri is playing piano at a restaurant in the valley in L.A. You run into old friends once in a while. They come out to hear you. When we get together we talk about the good old days. The old days weren't always good, but we remember them fondly. We went through a lot together. We have formed a fraternity. Within the fraternity those old days will never die.

The Depression had ended, but the wartime boom hadn't begun. There wasn't a lot of work available or much money to be made. Some guys did drop off at the side of the road, go "legit," and get a job outside the music business. But most stuck with the music. The band became family and the bus became home.

Sometimes Harry couldn't make the installment payments on the bus and had to scramble to avoid having it repossessed, which would have finished him. He had a bus driver, Lenny Hessinger, who was very loyal to him and to the band. Half the time he hadn't been paid, and he never made much, but he was always available to take a trip.

Lenny would hide the bus in a parking lot somewhere and sleep while the band played a date, then come back to get the guys, and drive down back alleys and side streets to avoid the "re-po" guys, get out of town and make a getaway.

Wheeling those old buses wasn't easy, but he'd often drive seven, eight hundred miles at a clip. Sometimes he'd be so tired he couldn't do it. It was against the rules, but one of the guys would take the wheel for a while, while Lenny slept in the side seat. He'd drive through rain and sleet and snow. It seemed especially dangerous when the roads were wet from rain, and it always seemed to be raining, but he got that bus through without any major accidents.

One time Lenny was driving into Old Orchard Beach, Maine, when the brakes when out as the bus went down a hill leading to the beach. The bus careened down the hill, bumped and jumped over the sandy beach, and came to a stop with the front wheels in the water. Some of the guys yanked off their outer clothes and went into the ocean for a swim.

Those bus rides were wild because those guys were wild. Al Lerner and Dick used to pick up pets and bring them aboard. For a while there were a couple of dogs. At one time there were even some monkeys. They'd run wild. And do their thing, smelling up the bus beyond belief.

The road manager, Don Reed, used to carry a .45 with him. He'd shoot out the lights on the bus, the street lights as we drove along, and sometimes he'd shoot to just miss and scare people walking by. When he was in a hotel room and it was time to turn out the lights, he'd shoot them out.

We'd get to a stop and there wouldn't be enough money for everyone to get rooms, so Harry would take one of those suites salesmen used to rent to display their goods to buyers. These suites had three or four bathrooms and the guys would come in and clean up before we went on, and then we were on our way again, sleeping on the bus. One gal with eighteen or twenty guys really had to fend for herself in those situations.

A lot of the places the band played were real joints, run by mob guys. Dese, dose, and dem guys. But they paid and you played. And they were very protective of me. If I went into the bar for a Coke or a cup of coffee and some customer got out of line with me, one of the owners would show up and chase the fellow away.

Of course the pianos were out of tune and the microphones were out of whack, but you just made the best of things. The customers in these dives didn't know any better. They never got the hot bands.

It took Harry about eighteen months to catch on, and I was on board for several months before we made it to the big time. Harry had recorded "You Made Me Love You" as virtually a trumpet solo in May 1941, but it took many months before it caught on. When it did, it became the biggest hit in the country, the biggest he ever had.

The band became the biggest of the big bands at the Paramount Theater in New York that year just as "You Made Me Love You" became the biggest of hits. The band drew 200,000 people in two weeks. The people were lined up around the block waiting to get in and the kids inside would jitterbug in the aisles during the show, just as they did with Benny three years earlier.

Time, Life, and all the big magazines ran stories on him and soon Harry James and his Music Makers were the hottest band in the business and Harry was the hottest soloist in the business, sweeping all the polls and in demand everywhere.

Martin Block's *Make Believe Ballroom* in New York was the leading daytime musical radio show in the country and when Harry's band beat out Glenn Miller's as the best in the country at year's end Harry was suddenly at the top. He also won the *Metronome* and *Down Beat* polls, the *Esquire* magazine poll, etc.

The band broke the house record wherever it went. At Manhattan's Astor Roof, people paid 8,500 cover charges in one week, topping Tommy Dorsey's record by 500 or 600. At San Francisco's Golden Gate Theater the band grossed more than $40,000 in seven days, breaking Sammy Kaye's record by $5,000 or $6,000.

At the Hollywood Palladium the band drew 8,000 people on opening night, averaged 20,000 a week for eight weeks, and totaled 160,000 for the stay, topping Tommy Dorsey's record for a similar stay by about 20,000.

It was incredible what one hit record could do for a band, but Harry's was one of the biggest of hits. And he loved it. Unlike Artie, Harry loved being a star, a celebrity. He loved hearing the cheers and having the fans reach for him and swoon over him. Soon he was making $10,000 to $15,000 a week and grabbing for the money as fast as it was held out to him.

At one point we were playing the Paramount, six or seven shows a day from nine in the morning to one at night, two shows with radio remotes at the Astor or Lincoln between shows at the Paramount at night, and on radio with *The Fitch Bandwagon* Sunday nights and *Coca Cola's Spotlight Bands* Monday nights. When Glenn Miller went into the army we took over his *Chesterfield Show* three evenings a week. And we cut records in the studios as fast as we could.

The pace was staggering. And some of the guys like Harry and Dick, who kept a fast pace with the ladies every night, might have gotten enough sack time, but seldom enough sleep.

One morning while we were playing the Paramount, Dick was awakened from a sound sleep at the hotel next door. He picked up the phone and heard the music introducing his first number. Harry thought that would be an interesting way to get the word to him that he was late. He got the message. He threw on some clothes, ran out of the hotel, ran into the theater, ran on stage, and started to sing. The guys broke up on the bandstand. He hadn't shaved or combed his hair and he had his clothes only half on. He was a mess, but he made it. He never forgot it and it always was good for a laugh later.

I never missed a show but once in my life that I remember.

I might have been sick a few times and had to cancel out early, but if I didn't cancel out early, I went on. I don't remember being late or anything like that all these years. I always got to a show as early as I could. I'm always an hour early for a trip. I'm just afraid to be late. That's me. And, of course, I didn't dissipate the way some of those characters did. I didn't get drunk or stoned at night and oversleep the next morning. I didn't have to fight hangovers. I didn't have to dump partners out of bed.

I'd break my neck to make a show. One time when we had a few days off, the army asked me to sing at some bases in the South. Al went with me and we went from camp to camp. On a Sunday we had to get back to New York to open at the Roxy Theater. A general offered us a ride in his C-45. As we approached the airport in New York, we ran into thick fog. We were on automatic pilot, but it wasn't working. We just missed some big buildings in downtown Manhattan. It was scary. The following week a plane flew right into the Empire State Building in a fog. Thinking about that was scary too.

We didn't do many one-nighters after we landed the *Chesterfield Show*. We had to be on one coast or the other to do it and sometimes when we were on one coast and moving to the other coast we really had to hustle. One time we were taking a train to L.A. when a French horn player got stoned and pulled the emergency cord. The train ground to a halt with everything flying through the cars. It was hours and hours before everything got straightened out. I think some equipment was damaged. Anyway, we didn't arrive on time.

Harry had flown ahead. Al Lerner caught a train from Chicago. When it came time to do the first show, they were the only ones in. They couldn't hire guys to fill in because they didn't even have the music. Dick Haymes had left the band by then and was living in L.A. with his wife, Joanne Dru. Harry showed up at Dick's doorstep early that morning to ask him to do a one-night reunion. They hired a drummer. With Al on piano and Harry on trumpet they had a trio to play and back Dick. Harry opened the show by saying, "We have a little something different for you tonight."

When we spent some time in California, I decided it was time I learned to drive a car so I wouldn't have to depend on others to get me to work. It wasn't necessary when we worked in New York or Chicago because we usually could take a cab or walk to our shows, but L.A. was spread out and our jobs sometimes were far apart.

This was in 1942. I bought an old Model A Ford, which didn't cost too much and which the salesman said was "a honey." I asked my friend Sid Beller, Harry's road manager, to teach me to drive. One morning we started out in my car. Sid pulled to the curb on a quiet street and told me to get in the driver's seat.

Those cars did not have automatic transmissions. This one had a standing stick extending up vertically from the floor between the driver's seat and the passenger's seat. Sid had showed me how to depress the clutch pedal while I shifted gears with the stick.

I shifted into first gear and started the car moving down the block. When we'd picked up a little speed, Sid told me to depress the clutch and shift into second. When I tried to do it, the stick resisted. I applied pressure and it pulled right out of the floor.

Suddenly, I was waving this eighteen-inch rod in the air and asking Sid, "What do I do now?" He was laughing so hard it took a few seconds for him to react. He grabbed the wheel, guided it to the curb, and told me to brake to a stop.

Once he had resecured the gearshift rod into the floor, we took off again with "never-say-die" Helen at the wheel. Unfortunately, when we came to a curve in the road and I turned the steering wheel to the right, it lifted right off the column.

I had the steering wheel in my hands, but I had no control of the car. Fortunately, Sid suggested that I stop the car before we were killed, and I braked it to a safe stop.

I sold the "honey." I kept Sid as my instructor. And eventually I got another car and did learn to drive and was able to get around Hollywood and the other towns whenever I needed to do so. Poor Sid was a very patient man who is lucky to be alive.

We did the Jack Benny radio show, which was number one on radio at the time, whenever we were in New York or Los Angeles together. During that period we recorded for Columbia Records in both their New York and Hollywood studios. Before any song was recorded, we would rehearse late at night after our normal day was finished, whether it was a radio broadcast or hotel engagement. I would type the lyrics of the new songs on two-by-four-inch cards and palm them each time I got up to sing, when we would try them out on an audience wherever we happened to be. Harry would learn a new arrangement after one run-through and would tease me after a week's time by saying, "Haven't you learned that song yet?"

One reason Harry learned arrangements so quickly was that he would tell the arranger what sound he wanted from each section of the band. After maybe two weeks of including the new songs in our engagements, we were ready to enter the recording studio. The sessions were usually scheduled for either early afternoon before the job or early morning after the job. Most of the band, including myself, preferred the late shift when we were warmed up. Each session would normally include four songs. The band would be set up as if they were on a stage. I would be behind a three-sided screen with a small window cutout to enable me to see Harry. This was most frustrating for me because being isolated I could not get the feel of the band and Harry's trumpet. This physical setup was required in order to prevent the band's sound from seeping into my microphone.

At that time we could not record on tape as is the practice today, but recorded directly on discs. The sound engineer in his isolation booth had to balance sound from three separate microphones—mine, Harry's, and the band's. At that time there was no way to remix the parts together later. But Harry's band and I were known for doing only one take on each song, anyway. We'd rehearse hard, then we'd get it right the first time. In today's recording world, it is unheard of for the first take to be perfect.

One of the reasons Harry could do this was that he didn't mind if there was a "clinker" on a record. He hit one bad note on his big record of "You Made Me Love You" and no one noticed, and it was so successful he felt a clinker here or there along the way was lucky. I never felt that way myself, but I did feel that if I did a record right the first time I'd never get as spontaneous a sound if I tried to do it better. The only thing I disliked about making movies is we had to do one take after another of my songs while they tried to get everything right.

In 1942 we began to make movies. We did a short at Universal, *Trumpet Serenade*, in which I sang "He's 1-A in the Army and He's A-1 in My Heart." Early in the year we did a feature at Universal, *Private Buckaroo*, with Dick Foran and the Andrews Sisters. My one solo in the film was "You Made Me Love You." Harry did his famous trumpet solo, too. But Harry's hit record was strictly instrumental.

I also sang "Nobody Knows the Trouble I've Seen" as a duet with Dick Foran, and a number with the Andrews Sisters, which was cut from the film.

Later the same year we did *Springtime in the Rockies* at 20th Century-Fox. It starred John Payne and cough, cough, Betty Grable. Actually, Harry already had met Betty. Dick Haymes knew her. Dick knew every beautiful woman in the world, I think. Dick had introduced Harry to Betty a couple of years earlier when we were in New York and Betty was on Broadway doing *DuBarry Was a Lady*. And it wasn't until some time after the film was finished that Harry and Betty began their romance.

Although Betty was the star, I had the big song in the picture. I always could sing rings around her. Ha! The fact is I didn't know it was going to be a big song at the time. You seldom do.

Although the setting was supposed to be a resort in Canada, all filming was done on a sound stage in Culver City, and, as usual, we prerecorded all the songs. Instead of the normal sixteen-piece or seventeen-piece band, we had an orchestra of sixty musicians, including woodwinds, French horns, harp, and strings. I was awed by them, but they provided the lush sound the studios wanted for their musical numbers and I loved it.

Later, I had to lip-synch to the tape while I appeared on camera. It was a long time before they got around to it. Every morning we reported at six for makeup, followed by costuming. Then we would wait . . . and wait . . . and wait. Days would go by, sometimes a week, between our calls to camera. Fortunately, I didn't have to wait in costume for my song because they didn't want it to wrinkle. Unfortunately, they chose an American Indian costume for me for my song. I haven't the faintest idea why.

If you catch the movie on a late show some night, you will see Harry and the band play a chorus of the song while couples surround the bandstand and I am nowhere in sight. For reasons I never understood, my voice appears before I am seen. The crowd parts (much as the Red Sea parted) and I come through, walking toward the camera in my squaw getup on heels so high it was impossible to look graceful. I am lucky I didn't trip and break my neck. It took many takes to match my movements to my sound and to get the camera angles and lighting right . . . as usual.

The arrangement of "I Had the Craziest Dream" I did for that film included the verse and ran longer than the revised band arrangement we recorded for Columbia a month later. The record turned out to be one of my biggest hits. I have sung the song countless times in personal appearances and the more I sang it the more I liked it. I have never tired of it and it is the favorite of all my songs, and so I chose it as the title of this book. It doesn't matter to me that the song came from a movie starring Betty. If Harry and Betty were meant to be, they were meant to be. The life I led back then seems like a crazy dream to me now, anyway.

In January 1943 Harry and the band and I went back to Hollywood to do *Best Foot Forward* at Metro-Goldwyn-Mayer. The star was Lucille Ball and the film introduced June Allyson, Gloria DeHaven, and Nancy Walker. Harry had several numbers with the band and accompanied the cast in several production numbers, but the one solo I prerecorded and filmed, "I Cried for You," was cut from the final print. I'm seen sitting on the bandstand, period.

However, someone must have liked my song because I did it again later in *Bathing Beauty* at MGM and got it in this time. I also did a production number with Harry and the cast, which included Esther Williams and Red Skelton. I had a nice reunion with Red. We reminisced about the old dance-athon days in Atlantic City.

I really got the glamour treatment in this movie. I was given a beautiful Edith Head-designed gown and a chance to come on screen from offstage, appearing from behind a pillar instead of rising from my seat on the bandstand.

In between these two films we worked in MGM's *Two Girls and a Sailor*, which starred June Allyson, Gloria DeHaven, and Van Johnson. I sang "In a Moment of Madness," which I later recorded commercially.

I have to say I loved making movies. Being with Harry's band gave me the chance. I have to say that more than anyone else Harry made me a star. I loved him for that. I loved him for other reasons, too, but that's another chapter.

REVIEWS

A secret to the success of the Harry James band is Helen Forrest, throb-voiced torcheuse. She has become the best of the big band singers.

—Time

Helen Forrest is superb. She is in a class with Bing Crosby and Mildred Bailey for persistent class. She never misses.

—Down Beat

Helen Forrest is now number one. She can sing with anyone and has a wider audience than Billie Holiday.

—Metronome

Helen Forrest, not Dinah Shore, is now the Bing Crosby of femme singers. She has helped make Harry James the hottest ticket in town.

—New York Daily News

Singing with Harry James, Helen Forrest has made big-band singing an art as it never was before. She is blazing a trail for others to follow.

—New York Times

Helen Forrest has a bigger, better voice, a wider range of voice and emotion, a more emotional way with a song than any other singer around.

—Los Angeles Times

Helen is simply sensational. She makes every song she sings her own song. She has her own way with a song.

—George Simon

Helen Forrest sings a grand song and sends me. She has

become a real beauty. *I wanted to rush toward her and tear a bit of her dress, as the slick chicks do to Sinatra. But Helen informed me that this wasn't according to the rules. That while it was permissible for the gals to disrobe a male singer, it isn't okay for the guys to disrobe a female singer. Us male hep cats want equal rights.*

—Sidney Skolsky

11.

You made me love you,
I didn't wanna' do it. . . .

I SUPPOSE IF THEY COULD have gotten her, Judy Garland would have been the biggest big band singer ever. Harry and Artie really loved her way with a song. Harry simply copied with his trumpet the way she did "You Made Me Love You" with her voice, and it made him the biggest thing in the music business.

A funny thing about it is that this was the B side of the record. The A side—the one the disc jockeys were expected to play—was a Dick Haymes vocal, "A Sinner Kissed an Angel." This eventually became a big hit for Dick. But at the time "You Made Me Love You" caught on.

Another funny thing about it is that I am associated with it, but I never recorded it, though I did it in the movie. Harry's hit was strictly instrumental. Years later, he did re-record it with Kitty Kallen doing the vocal. But for forty years, when fans ask me to sing my hits, there always are some who ask me

I Had the Craziest Dream

to sing "You Made Me Love You." They don't believe me when I tell them that was Kitty's song. Actually, it was Harry's. They don't believe me when I tell them it never was my song.

I had my songs with Harry, that's for sure. I had five gold records—records that sold one million or more copies—"But Not for Me" and "I Don't Want to Walk Without You," both recorded in 1941; "I Cried for You" and "I've Heard That Song Before," recorded early in 1942 and "I Had the Craziest Dream," recorded later in 1942.

Jimmy Petrillo took the American Federation of Musicians out on strike against the record companies on the first of August 1942, or I might have had many more big hits. The fact is, I was having one big hit after another at that time. The musicians stayed out of the studios for fifteen months, during which time I was at the peak of my career and couldn't cut a single record.

Despite the strike, there were a number of songs that became associated with me that I never got to record. Notable among these was "You'll Never Know." Others were "My Heart Tells Me" and "Somebody Loves Me." I sang them on our radio shows and in public appearances and people started to ask for them. Some still ask for "You'll Never Know." I'm sure it would have been a hit if I could have recorded it with Harry, and some old fans believe I must have recorded it.

That strike started the end of the Big Band Era and the beginning of the era of singers. Singers who were out on their own cut records with vocal choirs behind them and became the biggest things in the business. Sinatra, Haymes, Como went that way and shot to the top. Singers with the bands were stuck with the bands unless they went out on their own, which is why many of them did.

Eventually I did too, but I was hanging on to Harry at the time and didn't go until driven to it by his marriage to Betty. I owed him a lot of loyalty. He had given me the chance to do

129

songs the way I wanted to sing them, which no other bandleader had given singers up to then, and which all others did
after that. But I was the first, absolutely the first, thanks to
Harry.

After I auditioned to a standing ovation by the boys in the
band and Harry offered me the job, I said I'd take it on one
condition. I wanted arrangements built around me, the way
he had arrangements built around him. When we did a vocal,
I wanted to do the entire song. I wanted to start the song and
end the song. I even wanted to do the verse that led into a.
song, if the song had a good verse.

I had been listening to solo singers and band singers for
some time by then, I had been thinking about it a long time,
and I had decided the only way I was going to make the most
of myself was to sing like a singer backed by a band, not a
band singer who sings with a band. I didn't want to adjust to
them, instead of having them adjust to me.

Harry looked at me and simply said, "Okay, babe. It's
yours." I don't know if he had been thinking along the same
lines, but he was ready to go along with me without a second's hesitation. And he followed through, too. He had
arrangements prepared for me in which I did choruses and
entire songs and the band and even his own horn served simply to support me. And the kind of music Harry made with
his horn and his band provided outstanding support.

The guys in the band when I came on board were, if I
remember right, Nick Buono, Claude Bowen, and Al Stearns
on trumpet; Hoyt Bohannon, Harry Rogers, and Dalton Riz-
zotti on trombones; Corky Corcoran, Claude Lakey, and
Clint Davis on saxes; Al Lerner on piano, Ben Heller on guitar, Thurman Teague on bass, Mickey Scrima on drums, and
four or five on strings. Later, Harry added more and more
strings and the band became the biggest in the business,
twenty-seven or twenty-eight pieces.

There wasn't anywhere near the talent here that had been
in Artie's band or Benny's band when I was with them, but

the guys had ability. Harry's was a more versatile band and some critics called it the ideal dance band because it could really belt out a jazz number, play well at dance tempos, and pour out romantic stuff like melted butter.

Vido Musso, a tremendous tenor man, left before I came aboard. He was replaced by Corky Corcoran, a very talented tenor man, but a kid. Corky was only sixteen when he joined James. In fact, Harry had to become his legal guardian to take him on tour. Except for Harry, Corky became the star soloist and the only musician to receive billing out front. And he stayed with Harry forever, or close to it. But he never really realized his potential.

I think a lot of us who were with Harry at one time or another agree that the problem was that Harry had to be the star of any band he ever had. The guys used to say he liked to ride to the rescue of a dull number by hitting high G at the end. The guys used to say that when they played baseball Harry always put himself in to bat with the bases loaded in the last of the ninth.

In fact, one of Harry's problems was he hired guys as much for their ability to play baseball as to play music. We'd pass an open field or land in an open parking lot and he'd get up a game. He'd challenge other bands to games. He'd play anyone anytime. He got up games on studio lots when we were making movies.

Harry was a big Brooklyn Dodgers fan. The Dodgers were from Flatbush. One of our dogs was named Flanagan. Harry wrote an instrumental for the band, "Flatbush Flanagan." He also wrote "Dodger Fan Dance." When the Dodgers left Brooklyn, Harry switched to the St. Louis Cardinals. He hired Corky Corcoran because he was a great infielder as well as a promising sax man.

But Harry didn't feature many soloists. His arrangements featured a lot of strong ensemble stuff with him as the featured soloist. And he could play as well as any trumpeter who ever played. Maybe he won't go down in history as the greatest of jazz trumpeters because he didn't play enough jazz, but when he played jazz, he played it tremendously well, and I think he played more different types of music well than anyone who ever played the trumpet.

Technically, he was certainly the best. He loved to do classical things that required incredibly fast fingering, real showpiece numbers like "Ciribiribin," "Carnival of Venice," "Flight of the Bumblebee," "Sentimental Rhapsody," and "Trumpet Rhapsody." The last two were among his favorites and the first became his theme. He loved to show off on these showpiece numbers and did them beautifully.

If you don't think he could swing, listen to his solo on Benny's big hit from the Carnegie Hall Concert, "Sing, Sing, Sing," or his solos with his own band on "One O'Clock Jump" and "Two O'Clock Jump," "The Mole," "Memphis Blues," or many more. He had trouble with sound. His band played too loud at times. It held to one level—loud. But it swung. It did swing.

And when Harry got into something schmaltzy like "You Made Me Love You" he reduced you to tears. He followed that with "My Melancholy Baby," "Cherry," "Stardust," "My Ideal," "Sleepy Lagoon," and many more beautiful ballads made more beautiful by his syrupy trumpet.

He, his band, and his strings provided the perfect backing for a ballad singer like me. Dick Haymes left before Harry hit his stride, and so Dick had his hits elsewhere, but I got to Harry just in time and had my biggest hits right there. For a while we could do no wrong.

I recorded only eighteen sides with Harry for Columbia before the strike struck us down at our peak. Most of them were hits of one sort or another.

The first side was a novelty tune—"He's 1-A in the Army and He's A-1 in my Heart." People still ask for that one. The other side was "The Devil Sat Down and Cried," another novelty, with Dick Haymes and an ensemble. Both became hits and made the lists.

"He's My Guy" did not sell a million, but did break into the top ten at one time. So did "Mr. Five by Five." "But Not for Me" was in the top ten for a few weeks. "I Heard You Cried Last Night" was in the top ten for eighteen weeks and reached as high as number four at one point. "I Cried for You" did very well, too.

"I Don't Want to Walk Without You," recently revived by Barry Manilow, was in the top ten for thirteen weeks and as high as number one at one point. It was, in fact, voted the record of the year for 1942 on the Coca-Cola *Spotlight Bands* show.

"I Had the Craziest Dream" is my favorite. It lasted eighteen weeks and was number one in the nation for quite a long time.

"I've Heard That Song Before" was my most successful record. It lasted twenty weeks in the top ten and was number one for a very long time. When it passed one and a quarter million in sales, Columbia announced it was its biggest seller of all time and that it had run into a shortage of shellac (with which they made records in those days of wartime shortages) because of the sales of that record.

At one time at the start of 1943 I had the two best-selling records in the country. "Mr. Five by Five" was number two and "I Had the Craziest Dream" was number one.

At another time, in the spring of 1943, "I Had the Craziest Dream" was number one and "I've Heard That Song Before" was number three.

A little later "I've Heard That Song Before" was number one and "I Had the Craziest Dream" was number three.

Hey, it was a great honor. There were some outstanding singers around at the time.

Other hits during this period included "Moonlight Becomes You" by both Bing Crosby and Glenn Miller, "There Are Such Things" by Frank Sinatra and Tommy Dorsey, "Why Don't You Fall in Love" by both Dinah Shore and Dick Jurgens, and "Heartaches" by Perry Como.

Also, "Brazil" by both Xavier Cugat and Jimmy Dorsey, "Why Don't You Do Right" by Peggy Lee and Benny, "When the Lights Go on Again All Over the World" by Vaughn Monroe, "You'd Be So Nice to Come Home To" by Dinah Shore, "Don't Get Around Much Anymore" by the Ink Spots, and "Paper Doll" by the Mills Brothers.

Mack Gordon and Harry Warren wrote "I Had the Craziest Dream" and Sammy Cahn and Julie Styne wrote "I've Heard That Song Before." I will be forever grateful to them. Both records have been voted into the top ten records for the entire 1940s. They are the songs most associated with me and most requested of me. But of course they belonged as much to Harry and the band as to me.

Others that hit high were "I Cried for You," "I Remember You," and "Skylark."

Years later, in 1955 in fact, I had a top ten hit with Harry when he and I reunited for a Capitol album, *Harry James in Hi-Fi*, and we hit with "I'm Beginning to See the Light," the great Duke Ellington composition.

However, this actually was another of Kitty Kallen's hits originally with Harry and I don't consider it one of "my songs." When I am asked to sing it, and I am asked to sing it a lot, I try to explain this to the good people, but they won't believe me. Just as it is when I am asked to sing "You Made Me Love You," which was Harry's hit first and Kitty's second. And Helen's never. Of course, I am confused with Helen O'Connell a lot and asked to sing "Green Eyes" and "Tangerine," which were hits of hers. I'll bet Helen O'Connell is asked to sing "I Had the Craziest Dream" and "I've Heard That Song Before."

When I walked into the recording studio to do "I'm Beginning to See the Light" with Harry, he said, "Let's run through it once for sound." I looked at it and he had Kitty's arrangement ready.

I said, "Hey, hold it, Harry, this isn't my arrangement." He said, "Sure it is." I said, "It is not. I never recorded this with you." He said, "Of course you did."

Even Harry could get confused. After all, those bandleaders recorded a lot of records with a lot of different singers.

I said, "Kitty did this with you." He looked at it and looked at me with a sheepish grin on his face. "Bitch, bitch, bitch, nag, nag, nag," he said. Kitty's key was lower than mine and Harry had to have the key raised for me.

By itself the James band certainly did not make me any better than any of the other band singers, but with Harry I did develop the greatest range of my career.

When Peggy Lee followed me into Benny's band he tried to save a buck by using my arrangements with her. He couldn't because Peggy couldn't sing as high as I could. Peggy sings in that groovy lower register, of course, and she does excel at it.

On that 1955 album with Harry I also did "It's Been a Long, Long Time," as well as "I've Heard That Song Before" and "I Cried for You."

In 1942 and 1943 I won both the Down Beat and Metronome polls as the number one female singer in the country, ahead of Helen O'Connell, Anita O'Day, Peggy Lee, Jo Stafford, Dinah Shore, Billie Holiday, Marion Hutton, Mildred Bailey, Lena Horne, and Ella Fitzgerald.

Looking back, I can't believe how far in front of the field I was in the voting. In 1942, for example, I got two and a half times as many votes as the number two singer. It's sort of sad that so few besides my enduring fans still remember this. But if everyone should have his moments, I'm happy to have had mine.

That year Frank Sinatra beat out Bing Crosby and Bob Eberly as the most popular male vocalist. And Harry beat out Benny as the most popular instrumental soloist. Bandleaders were not eligible in the all-star voting.

The all-star band included Roy Eldridge on trumpet, J.C.

Higginbotham on trombone, Tex Beneke on tenor, Johnny Hodges on alto, Pee Wee Russell on clarinet, Jess Stacy on piano, Eddie Condon on guitar, Bobby Haggart on bass, and my Buddy Rich on drums.

Duke Ellington, Benny Goodman, and Harry had the top swing bands. Tommy Dorsey, Glenn Miller, Charlie Spivak, and Harry had the top sweet bands. Artie Shaw had the top service band. The next year Miller went into service. World War II was, sadly, going strong.

I was singing with Harry and the band at the Hotel Lincoln in New York on December 7, 1941, when Pearl Harbor was attacked and we were drawn into the war. I sang "I'll Be with You in Apple Blossom Time" on a radio remote that night.

Many of the songs we sang in those years were sentimental songs aimed at wives and lovers separated by the war from their men in the service. A lot of the songs had to do with women waiting for their men to come home—"I Don't Want to Walk Without You."

The years I spent with Harry are sentimental ones for me too, of course. They were the years when Harry and I were lovers. They were the years of my greatest song hits and my greatest success. I don't cry for anyone anymore. I'm tough. Toughened by the years. But if I cried for anyone or anything, I'd cry for those years with Harry.

Harry and I were a terrific team. He played and I sang with a single heart. We had the same feeling for a song. Harry had a feeling for what would work that was unsurpassed by anyone I ever worked with.

When Julie Styne brought "I Don't Want to Walk Without You" to Harry and demonstrated it for him, Harry said the tempo was too fast and insisted on doing it slower. When Julie did a demo of "I've Heard That Song Before" for Harry, Harry said the tempo was too slow and insisted on doing it faster. In both cases, Julie argued about it, but Harry had the right to do it his way, and Harry was right. Harry sure was right for me.

Harry took care of me. I got up to $250 in weekly salary with him. And while he, like all the bandleaders, got all the money and royalties from the records, I got up to $450 a week with him in weeks we did records and radio shows. That was a lot of money in those days.

None of the boy singers ever got as much, but then they never had many big hits. After Dick left, there was Jimmy Saunders, then Johnny McAfee, finally Buddy Moreno. All were good. Buddy was very good. Dick was great.

I was close to Dick and got closer later. I was friendly with Buddy. I was friendly with Al Lerner, the pianist; Sam Kaplan, the violinist; and Sid Beller, the road manager. And, of course, I was more than friends with Harry.

After I left the band, he did me the honor of retiring not only the arrangements of my songs but the songs themselves. As far as I know he seldom if ever let anyone else sing them after that, even though they were among his biggest hits.

I still sing them, of course. But then I still carry a torch for Harry.

12.

I don't want to walk without you, baby
Walk without my arms about you, baby. . . .

I THINK YOU HAD to be attractive to be a successful singer with
the big bands. I don't care how good a singer you were, your
appearance was a part of the package. I was successful, so I
suppose I was attractive. I was told I was, but I was always
self-conscious about my looks. I had a pretty good figure in
those days, but I was no raving beauty.

I wanted to be beautiful for Harry. Not that he was so
handsome. He was tall but skinny. Sinatra was supposed to be
skinny, but when Frank sang with Harry, Harry made Frank
look fat. But Harry had wonderful eyes and a lot of charm and
always dressed well. He made an impressive appearance. And
you didn't have to be a beauty for Harry to want you. But I
wanted to be one for him.

I didn't like my nose. Or my chin. And I had dark circles
under my eyes. I went to plastic surgeons to see what could be
done for me. It wasn't nearly as common in those days as it is

today and it took guts to go, but I was determined. However, they didn't do such surgery as fast as they do today. I went to several doctors who wouldn't do anything for me. One in New York, said, "Look, you're Helen Forrest, you're successful and you're famous, the whole world loves you, why change?" And I said, "Because I don't want to look like Helen Forrest. I don't like the way Helen Forrest looks."

Another, a Jewish doctor in Chicago, said, "Helen, you're a nice Jewish girl, you look like a nice Jewish girl, you shouldn't change the way you look." And I thought, Oh, my God, have I gone to the wrong doctor? And I said to him, "I don't mind being Jewish. I'm happy to be Jewish. I tell everyone I'm Jewish. I'll wear a Jewish star. But I don't want to be a nice Jewish girl. I don't want to look like a nice Jewish girl. I don't want my nice Jewish nose."

I lost it to a New York doctor. I have never talked about this before, but I want to be honest in my book. It's no secret, anyway. In his *New York Daily Mirror* syndicated column, Walter Winchell wrote late in December 1942: "Helen Forrest, vocalist for Harry James, is now a 'looker' since her prettifying job on the coast."

In January 1943 *Down Beat* ran a story: "Helen Forrest's New Nose Clicks." The story, out of Los Angeles, read, "Helen Forrest, America's No. 1 lark, emerged as a glamour girl here as she made her first public appearance [at the Palladium] since a plastic surgeon chiseled the Forrest physiognomy into a more becoming outline. Most of the work was performed on Helen's nose, hitherto valuable essentially for breathing and blowing purposes, but now perching piquantly on Helen's attractively pert puss."

Well, that's the way they wrote in those magazines in those days.

The following month the magazine ran a big new photo of me on its front page. Over the picture was the line THIS ONE MAY PUZZLE YOU! Under the picture was this caption: "Ordinarily, we don't play guessing games with our readers, and we share the general dislike for characters who call you on the telephone and chortle, 'Guess who?' But the temptation is too great in this instance. This pretty miss is one of the best known and best liked band vocalists in the country! Can you identify her? If not, turn to page three, column four, and get hep."

On page three, column four, there was a box "Solving the Page 1 Puzzle." It read: "That bundle of glamour on page one, chum, is Miss Helen Forrest, the nation's No. 1 feminine band vocalist, according to our recent poll. We don't have to tell you that she sings with Harry James, but we can tip you off that this is the first photo of Helen to be released since her recent nose operation."

So my secret was shared with no more than a few hundred thousand fans.

Later I had my eyes done and my chin done. For a while I was one of the best customers the plastic surgeons had. They call them cosmetic surgeons now, and it no longer is considered embarrassing to go to them. I was happier with the way I looked later, but I was never really happy with the way I looked. I think it's important to be happy with yourself and the way you look. I don't think that it's any crime to want to look the best you can.

Maybe that's why I kept changing my hair style and my hair coloring. Originally my hair was dark brown, almost black. My scalp showed through white. I photographed as if I had a wig on. Photographers had to soften the lighting. I went red-haired with Harry. Later, I tried to be a blond. All shades of blond. I bleached my hair so much it started to fall out in front. I started a new style for a while, wearing sequined skull caps to match my gowns, but really to cover up the bald spot. I don't dye my hair much anymore. I'm happy to still have hair.

I look different in every photo ever taken of me. Many have noticed it and commented on it. I can't help it. I suppose it has a lot to do with the cosmetic surgery and hair dyeing, but it also has a lot to do with the basic structure of my face. I don't like to be photographed while I'm singing. If I have to be photographed, I prefer it to be in a studio where the lighting can be controlled to my advantage.

I know this is vanity. But I'm in a profession where looks count a lot. Very few homely ladies have made it, so I suspect I'm not too homely. But looks count in a singer, an entertainer, especially a lady. How many homely ones have been successful? Barbra Streisand has refused to have her Jewish nose redone, but I certainly don't think of her as homely. And if I had been as brave as she has been, maybe I'd have been better off.

I've always dressed as well as I can. I've had some marvelous gowns made for me over the years. And a singer has to have a lot of different gowns for different performances. Right now I don't have too many I can wear because I'm in a fat period, and I have to wear my fat gowns. What it's come down to is I've had different gowns made for me over the years; I have a thin wardrobe and a fat wardrobe, and I'm into my fat wardrobe right now. But I'm working hard at it and getting close to being back into my thin wardrobe again. When I started out I wore very conservative gowns. As I developed, people were after me to get some sexy gowns that showed a lot of cleavage. So, I did. Like most ladies, I like to be as sexy as I can be, but I've always known I'm no sexpot. I'm basically shy and not anxious to show off what I've got, which never was what a Betty Grable had. I fell for Harry before he fell for Betty and I wanted to be as much of a good-looking lady for him as I could be.

I knew what Harry was—a womanizer of the worst kind. I had no illusions about that. The guys in the band told me he had to get laid every night or he was in a bad mood the next day. I saw this for myself. You could tell when he'd struck out the night before by his mood. If we had a rehearsal and he was surly and sarcastic, you knew he'd struck out. But he had a helluva batting average. Probably because a lot of ladies were available to him and he wasn't too choosy. Also because he was a romantic figure when he played those love tunes on his trumpet and because he was a charming guy. Usually, he was easygoing and happy-go-lucky. He didn't drive the guys as hard as he might have.

I think our romance started with the Chesterfield radio show. And the other radio remotes from the hotels. The people behind the shows wanted to publicize them, so they shot a lot of photos of us together. At first they'd ask us to have dinner or go here or go there so they could get pictures of us together. After a while they didn't have to ask, we were always together. Somewhere along the way, we went to bed. Soon it was a nightly affair. And the affair was on.

We started to be paired in the gossip columns. I remember Walter Winchell had an item about us—"Hottest twosome in town, Harry James and his chirp Helen Forrest are making real-life love songs."

I have a clip from Down Beat in June 1943 that shows a picture of me standing beside Harry while he plays his trumpet and is headlined "It May Be Love." The caption, out of Hollywood, reads: "This couple may be closer than this in the near future. There is the matter of a divorce formality in each of their cases, Harry from Louise Tobin, and Helen from Al Spieldock."

Well, it was an affair. There's no getting around that. It was not nearly as acceptable in those days as it is today, and I was embarrassed by it and did not seek any publicity about it. But neither Harry nor I had been living with our mates for a long time, and we both wanted divorces so we could marry. Harry was serious, I am sure, because he did get one. I was serious, for sure, but I could not get one. I asked Al and he said no. It was not as easy in those days. You had to have cause. Al had cause, I didn't. He hoped I'd get tired of traveling and come home. He hoped he could make our marriage work. I had no hope for it. For me, it was no marriage.

I wanted to marry Harry. It was not at all unusual for the girl singer with a band to marry the bandleader in those days. Harriet Hilliard married Ozzie Nelson, Dorothy Collins married Raymond Scott, Georgia Carroll married Kay Kyser, Irene Daye married Charlie Spivak, Ann Richards married Stan Kenton, Ginnie Powell married Boyd Raeburn. As far as that goes, Harry had married his former singer, Louise Tobin.

And many girl singers married musicians in their bands. Peggy Lee married Benny Goodman's guitarist Dave Barbour, Doris Day married Les Brown's sax man George Weidner, Mary Ann McCall married Woody Herman's sax man Al Cohn, Frances Wayne married Woody's trumpet player Neal Hefti, Kitty Kallen married Jack Teagarden's clarinet player Clint Garvin, June Christy married Stan Kenton's sax man Bob Cooper, and Jo Stafford married Tommy Dorsey's arranger Paul Weston.

Harry and I were together all the time, on the road, working nights, far from anything you could call home. I had no home at all at that time, nothing I could call home. Like all the others, I found that my home was the bus, my family the band. And my man was Harry whether we were married or not. We were engaged to be married. Since his marriage to Louise no other woman had lasted more than three days with him until I came along. He was notorious for it. Three nights and out. Most usually were one-night stands. I was a one-year stand.

I was domesticated as could be. Harry even had me shopping for presents for his two sons by Louise Tobin whenever one of the boys had a birthday or it was Christmas time. I got good practice for years later when I had my own son. I'd have cooked for Harry if I'd known how to cook and if we'd had a kitchen to cook in. I bought him ties and socks and stuff. He bought his own suits. He had dozens at $125, $150 apiece, which was good money for clothes in those days. Harry loved clothes almost as much as he loved ladies. Clothes hung well on that tall, skinny, well-hung frame of his. He was always well dressed, a delight to be seen with.

He was, as I have said, a great lover, very considerate, gentle, tireless. He was a romantic. He really loved to make love. In a way, he even made love on his trumpet. He loved to play love songs. But he was more than merely a good man in bed. Whatever anyone else thought of him, he was a good man. The guys in the band thought he was tough, but I'd known a lot tougher. All good bandleaders were tough or they wouldn't have had good bands. If you weren't tough with the guys, they'd run wild. He was never tough with me. He called me "Trees." You know, because of my name, Forrest. And he was very tender with me.

He was by nature a bit of a loner. Oh, he had to have his women, but they were just ships who passed in his nights. And wherever he was, whether it was a hotel room or an apartment or a house, he had the guys in the band over. They always had parties together. He was closer to them than Artie or Benny were with their guys. Willie Smith stayed with him twenty years. Corky Corcoran stayed with him thirty years. Nick Buono has stayed with him forty years.

Well, hell, I got a couple of years. I guess I can't complain. I knew what he was when I went with him. He was incorrigible. Still, we had a lot of laughs.

Harry was always trying to break me up. One time I was singing "But Not for Me" on stage. He was standing near me and he pulled a big, juicy delicatessen sandwich from his pocket. While I was trying to sing this serious song, he'd take a big bite and hold out the sandwich to me and offer me a bite. I stood it as long as I could, but finally I just screamed and ran from the stage with the audience screaming.

One night I will never forget. We were in a tiny hotel across from the Paramount, the Picadilly. We were in bed, making love. The room was pitch black. The window was open. Suddenly from the window came a red flash of light. It

144

startled us. Maybe if we had gotten right up we'd have found out what it was. But Harry didn't want to be interrupted.

When he got up he looked outside the window where there was a fire escape but he saw no one. The way we figured it out later someone had come up the fire escape, or more likely down from the roof, and snapped a picture of us in bed. The flash was just like that of a flashbulb on a camera, a sort of pop of light. It was red, not white, but maybe infrared, which they used then to take pictures in the dark.

The funny thing is no picture ever turned up. No one ever tried to blackmail us or anything like that. Maybe it became an underground classic. Remember, we were big stars at the time. And unmarried. I just don't know. I do know we find it funny to think of it and never have forgotten it.

I don't see Harry often these years, but whenever I see him he mentions that red flash and we laugh about it. It sort of symbolizes our love affair. He'll lean over and whisper in my ear, "Remember the red flash?" Or, "Remember the red flash!" with an exclamation mark instead of a question mark! Ha! I asked him if I could use the story in my book. He asked, "Why not?" And why not indeed!

He was straight for about a year, as far as I know. When he went back to his crooked ways, I knew. We fought like cat and dog. I fought for him. Hell, I hated to let go of him. I let him have his one-night stands without letting go of him. If it hadn't been for Betty, who knows? I know. We'd have been married . . . and divorced long ago. And who needed one more divorce? I sure as hell didn't. I wound up with three as it was.

Springtime in the Rockies. I remember driving away from the set at the end of a day's filming and Harry saying about Betty, "That stuck-up broad, who the hell does she think she is?" And a year later she was hanging around the Astor Roof every night, ringside, making moon eyes at him from her table.

Do you remember that picture of Betty in her white bathing suit, looking back over her shoulder at the boys who were looking at her legs? The pinup picture to end all pinup pictures in those war years. And if the boys overseas stuck it up over their bunks and patted her rear end for luck as they went out to fight, Harry had all the luck in the world because he had her. One day they eloped to Las Vegas and that was that.

So I took my midnight walk on a window ledge and maybe if I hadn't been pulled in, I'd have jumped. Who knows? I don't. But I'm glad I didn't. I've had a pretty good life and a lot of laughs since then.

I gave Harry my notice. The last show I did with him was the *Chesterfield Show* from Hollywood, on NBC radio, Friday, the third of December 1943. I still have the script of that show. This is how it starts:

Announcer: *Well, friends . . . tonight we're regretfully saying good-bye to lovely Helen Forrest, who leaves us to become a star in her own right. And so, Helen, from Harry, all the Music Makers, and myself, good luck and lots of success. We'll always remember how sweet you are.*

Helen: *Thanks, Bill. (Music intro in background.) I'm really gonna miss the whole gang and I'd like to sing my song for Harry and all the boys. . . .*
(Harry and the Music Makers play "How Sweet You Are" with vocal by Helen.)

"How Sweet You Are" was the last complete song I sang with Harry's band. It was not the last song. At Harry's insistence on the air I sang our first million-seller, "I Don't Want to Walk Without You," but I didn't finish it.

It was a very emotional moment for me, the last time I would sing with Harry and the boys. It was not a very private farewell. There were all those technicians in the studio, plus a live audience of about two hundred, and a listening audience of many hundreds of thousands.

If you listen closely to the recording, you can hear me crying throughout the broadcast. Harry is tough, but even he had a tear or two in his eyes. We'd had something together. We'd meant something to each other. I got through my first song all right, but the last song was too much. It had too much emotional meaning for me.

I had sung it a hundred times before, but never before with tears in my eyes and a catch in my throat. The tears came running down my face and I started to choke up.

When I reached the part of the lyric that goes "ah baby, please come back or you'll break my heart for me" I came apart and could not go on. With the band still playing behind me, I ran from the stage, through the backstage area, out the stage door, and out of Harry's life.

And out of the big band business. That was it. The end of the road. The end of that road, anyway. And the beginning of another.

I was divorced not long afterward. I had nothing to do with it. I was playing the Million Dollar Theater in Los Angeles when someone showed me a clipping from the local newspaper that said famous singer Helen Forrest had been divorced by her husband of five years, Al Spieldock, on grounds of desertion. He got that right, poor guy. I guess he didn't have to get my story. It's all right. It wouldn't have been any different than his.

I saw Harry a few months later and, as I have said, he sort of propositioned me. Harry was Harry, Betty or no Betty.

Many years later, when I was working in Lake Tahoe, Harry and his band were working across the street. When the timing was right, we'd cross the street to see each other's shows.

One night after our shows were over, we had a few drinks together. Harry knew I had my son, Michael, with me and said he'd like to see him. So we went back to my hotel room so Harry could meet Michael, who was only three at the time.

Harry played with Michael for about an hour, even getting down on all fours to let Michael ride on his back in a game of "horsey." After a while Harry turned to me and said, "You know, he could have been mine."

It touched me deeply.

Years later, he came to play in Phoenix, where I was living at the time. I called him up, and he didn't even recognize my voice. I said, "Harry, it's Trees!" And then he remembered. He insisted I come out to see the show. I did. I stood in the doorway of the ballroom and listened. That sound! Marvelous. It sent tingles down my spine.

When he saw me, he put down his horn, came off the stage with his arms out, took me in his arms, and hugged me. More tingles. Someone yelled, "Break it up!" and we laughed. Harry said, "C'mon up." I said, "No. No tricks, Harry. I'm not going to sing." He laughed and went up on the bandstand and took the microphone and said, "We have a special guest tonight. One of the greatest of singers. The best I ever had." And smiled. And said, "Helen Forrest is going to sing for you." And I hollered, "NO!"

But the crowd cheered and he kept beckoning to me, so I went up. And I sang. I sang "But Not for Me." He had a new arrangement I didn't know, but he played, the band played, and I sang, and we hit every note. It was hypnotic. For a few minutes we were taken back many years. When it was over, the people there just cheered and cheered. Even the guys in his band stood up and applauded. It brought tears to my eyes. Harry hit me on the fanny and said, "You did it, bitch." And that was that.

I have not sung with him since. That was long after I did that nostalgia album with him and that was the last time. Now he will not play with me. We did a Merv Griffin television show and his band played behind me, but Harry didn't. Before my last song, Merv said, "C'mon, Harry, for old time's sake, play that trumpet behind Helen." But he just smiled and shook his head and walked off and I sang all alone with the band.

We have gone our separate ways. Harry has gone on with big bands. The era ended, but Harry went on. Glenn Miller went down during the war. The Dorseys died. Artie lives, but he has been out of the business a long time. Benny lives, but he hasn't had a band for many years. He plays classical clarinet as much as anything, and doesn't play much.

Harry stayed on the road until they put up detour signs. Then he played the lounges in Las Vegas for many years, until most of those closed. He's on the road again, playing concerts and dances. He doesn't play as much as he used to but he still plays.

He and Betty developed a passion for horse racing and became regulars at Santa Anita and Hollywood Park. Harry still hangs out at the tracks.

He had two sons by Louise Tobin, two daughters by Betty, and a son by Joan Boyd, a Las Vegas showgirl he was married to for a few years. That was after he divorced Betty after more than twenty years in 1965. He named his last son Michael, after I had named my son Michael. I asked him once if there was anything to this, but he just smiled.

I remember talking to Betty only once before I left Harry's band, and that was brief. Our paths crossed in the hall backstage at the Astor between sets. We each said hello. She said she enjoyed my singing, and I thanked her. Then, to my surprise, she said, "I would trade my looks to sing like you" and hurried off.

I met her only once after that and that was many years later at La Scala, the Beverly Hills restaurant. There was still some embarrassment there. We were seated only a few tables apart, but we looked at each other without looking, if you know what I mean. Then, I guess we both decided we were being foolish. We both got up at the same time and met halfway between our two tables and stuck out our hands and shook hands and smiled and said, "Hi! It's nice to see you." That's all. But it really was nice.

We smiled and she had a twinkle in her eyes and I suppose I had one in mine. We went back to our tables, but there had been more than just a casual meeting. We had secrets between us. We'd both loved the same man and knew him well.

When she died in 1973, I was sorry to hear it. I'm sure she loved him, but he must have been a hard man to live with. She had only one other marriage—to former child actor Jackie Coogan—and that was before Harry. I've heard she had romances with Artie and with the actor George Raft, but those were before Harry, too. I also heard of one romance she had while she was with Harry, but then I've heard Harry had affairs while he was with Betty, too. Fair is fair, I guess.

It's a funny story because Betty's romance was with my old friend Dick Haymes. This was in the summer of 1946. I was doing a radio show with Dick at the time, but we were on summer hiatus and Dick went to Hollywood to make his second musical, *The Shocking Miss Pilgrim*, costarring Betty at 20th Century-Fox. While Harry and his band were on a summer tour of the Midwest and the East, Dick and Betty kept company at the close of each day's shooting.

Harry returned to Hollywood one night toward the end of August and somehow found out that Betty and Dick were having a rendezvous at a quiet Hollywood restaurant. In a rage, Harry stormed into the restaurant with a pistol in his hand. He threatened Dick while waving the pistol in his face. Fortunately, he did not use it.

I guess what was all right for Harry wasn't all right for Betty. But the story was hushed up and I didn't hear about it until recent years when Dick himself told me about it. He said Harry was cool to him for years, but that some years later they wound up in the same dressing room and laughed it off. I'm sure the story is true. Whatever Dick would do, he wouldn't lie.

It Had to Be You

It had to be you,
It had to be you,
I wandered around
And finally found
The somebody who
Could make me be true,
Could make me be blue,
And even be glad
Just to be sad
Thinking of you.
Some others I've seen
Might never be mean,
Might never be cross,
Or try to be boss,
But they wouldn't do;
For nobody else
Gave me a thrill,
With all your faults
I love you still.
It had to be you,
Wonderful you,
It had to be you.

13.

A LONG TIME AGO I came to the conclusion that charm means the most in a man. Artie was handsome. Harry was good-looking in his way. Both had a lot of charm. Dick Haymes was good-looking, but what he had more than anything else was charm. He could melt your knees with a smile, cause your heart to flutter with a touch.

God, I loved that man! I was never in love with him, I loved him, if you know the difference. We were friends. Never more. I had my affair with Harry, and Dick accepted that. Even after the affair was over, Dick knew my feelings. Oh, once in a while, he'd smile and say, "C'mon, Helen, what the hell, we like each other, let's hit the sack." And I'd say, "I don't want to spoil things between us." And he'd say, "Okay," and grin.

I once was asked what was the secret of his appeal to women. I said, "He's good in bed." I was kidding. I didn't really know, but he had to be. It sometimes seemed like he could get any girl in the world in bed. It sometimes seemed that every lady who met Dick fell in love with Dick. And they never fell out of love with him. Even his ex-wives went right on loving him. When he was dying, Fran Jeffries went to spend weekends with him.

He had six or seven wives. His first wife was Edith Harper. She was singing in the floor show at the College Inn in Chicago while Dick was singing with Harry's band there. They were both young and broke and I guess the marriage never had a chance. After that he marrried Joanne Dru, Nora Eddington Flynn, Rita Hayworth and Fran Jeffries, among others. He had affairs that I know of with Betty Hutton, Betty Grable, Maureen O'Sullivan, Lana Turner, and many that I didn't know of. I used to say, "Who is it this time?" And he'd grin and say, "You really don't want to know, do you?" and I'd grin and say, "No, I don't." And I didn't.

He was selective. Most of his women were great beauties and great gals. Joanne, the sister of television's Peter Marshall, later married actor John Ireland. She was a good actress and made a lot of movies. Dick and Joanne were married eight or nine years in the 1940s and had a son and two daughters. Nora Eddington Flynn was Errol Flynn's ex and she had his two daughters with her during the two or three years she and Dick were married.

Rita Hayworth was, of course, the great beauty of films. She was married five or six times, to Orson Welles and Prince Aly Khan among others. She had a daughter by Welles and a daughter by Aly with her during the four or five years she was married to Dick.

Fran Jeffries was an outstanding singer and though she and Dick were married only about a year, they too remained close. I know Richard Quine, the actor and director, was hung up on her and went around saying he was going to get Dick because Dick had taken her from him, but nothing ever came of it.

Wendy Smith, his last wife, was an English lady and he met her when he was living in England. Their marriage lasted about fourteen years and they had two children. I'm not sure if they were divorced before his death, but they were separated at the end. I am glad Dick finally made a marriage that lasted a long time. From my experience, it's not easy.

Dick had his faults, for sure. He managed his own affairs and he managed them badly. He never took good advice. He always had to do things his way and it usually turned out the wrong way. He was stubborn. He made big money in the middle of his career, if not at either end, but he was always broke.

He turned down the lead in *Pal Joey* early in his career to stay with the bands. It turned out to be a big hit on Broadway, of course. It originally was a singing role, and Sinatra did it in the movies as a singing role. But Gene Kelly did it on Broadway as a dancing role and it made him a star.

Dick always wanted to be a star, and he was a star. Perhaps not as big a star as he might have been. It's said that he was always in Sinatra's shadow, following him into the James and Dorsey bands as he did, following him into the solo ranks after Sinatra became the biggest thing in the business. And Sinatra endured better.

But people forget Frank had his lean years before his acting part in *From Here to Eternity* brought him back. There were years his records weren't selling. They were years Dick's records were selling better than anyone's and he was the biggest name in the business.

He had some memorable number one records—"A Sinner Kissed an Angel," "I'll Get By," "You've Changed," "Little White Lies," "You'll Never Know," "The More I See You," "It Might As Well Be Spring," and others. He had nine or ten gold records.

He made a movie, *State Fair*, and suddenly he was a movie star, making twenty-five thousand dollars a week. He made thirty-five movies in all, including *Diamond Horseshoe*, *Up in Central Park*, and *One Touch of Venus*, opposite some of the great beauties of the day, and he romanced many of them off the screen.

His career really hit the skids when Harry Cohn, the Columbia mogul, attempted to end Dick's romance with Rita by trying to get him deported to Argentina. Dick had been born in Buenos Aires, and educated in France, Switzerland, and England before coming to this country at twenty in 1936. He registered as a resident alien during the war, so could not get United States citizenship. Egged on by Cohn, the government did get a deportation order on Dick, but it was revoked. However, the bad publicity turned his career sour.

He was so hooked on Hayworth that wherever she was, he'd take any date he could get so he could be there with her. And when she left he'd leave with her even if his engagement wasn't over. He was utterly unreliable and missed so many shows it became difficult for him to get jobs. After a while he became a hypochondriac and all it took was a tickle in his throat for him to cancel a show no matter how much in need of a paycheck he was. He used to say, "You guys don't believe I'm sick." He declared bankruptcy twice and drank heavily for many years.

He once said, "I made too much too quickly. I thought nothing could go wrong. When everything went wrong, I couldn't deal with it." He said, "I figured I'd worn out my welcome," when he explained why he left this country to live in Spain, then in England. His last wife, Wendy, straightened him out. He went off the booze and went on a physical conditioning kick. He hadn't been singing well for some time, but he got his vocal cords back in shape and for a while was singing as well as ever when he returned to the United States in 1972.

He didn't get a lot of work. He rented a house in Malibu overlooking the ocean, and spent a lot of time there reminiscing about the good old days with old friends. Dick had a lot of friends, as many as anyone I've ever known in this business.

I'm proud to have been his friend. Our friendship started in our days with Harry's band and strengthened during our radio show. Our paths crossed from time to time after that and it always was a joy to have a reunion.

In November 1977 Merv Griffin reunited Harry, Dick and me on his television program. It was an informal show. Merv asked us about the big band days and we reminisced with a good deal of pleasure.

The following spring we taped a three-hour "Big Band Bash" for public television stations across the country. Dick and I each taped a segment at the Café Rouge in New York's Hotel Pennsylvania. We'd worked there thirty-five years earlier as boy and girl singers. I said to Dick, "It's spooky." He agreed it was.

We did our old duet on "It Had to Be You." We also did this nightly during a "Fabulous Forties" tour during the summer of 1978.

In September 1979, Harry, Dick, and I were reunited for what was to be our last appearance together on the opening part of the tour of "The Big Broadcast of 1944," another nostalgia show.

The idea was to re-create one of those old "live" radio broadcasts on stage, complete with audience warm-ups and the old commercials. Each of the performers did a fifteen-minute "show within the show," so we did not actually appear on stage together until the finale when the performers gathered on stage to join the audience in a rousing chorus of "God Bless America."

Each night I stood between Harry and Dick. I had my arms around their waists, while they had their arms around my shoulders. It was lovely except that they took great delight in silently squeezing my upper arms until I wanted to scream with pain and wound up with black-and-blue welts as souvenirs of their affection.

We played a week at the Valley Forge Music Fair in Devon, Pennsylvania, and drew good crowds. Then we played a week at the Westbury Music Fair on Long Island, New York, and sold out eight straight performances in a two-thousand-seat theater. It was the Jewish New Year, too, when audiences usually are small.

Because I was committed to appear elsewhere before I signed with this show, my last night there was my last night on that tour. The night before, Dick had a backstage party celebrating his sixty-third birthday. A long-time friend from Brooklyn catered it with homemade Italian dishes. Then on the last night we relaxed in our hotel's lounge and reminisced.

Dick looked a little pale, a little thin, but he didn't look bad; his energy level was high and his spirits high. I had no idea he was sick. I don't know that he did. He spoke with affection of his teenage son and how much he was enjoying getting to know him as they shared the apartment which he had rented at Marina Del Rey, after he and Wendy had separated. He spoke about his plans for the future.

I left the show and he went on with it to Detroit. He came down with what he thought was the flu. He developed what he thought was a sore throat. He had to leave the show to return to California for treatment.

It was thought that his condition would be eased if he had his teeth pulled. He went through the agony of having his teeth pulled and replaced with false teeth. These had to be fitted properly and he had to learn to talk and sing with them. It was an embarrassment to him and a difficult experience for him. All to no purpose.

They discovered he had lung cancer and wanted to operate. He was going with a lady who was a psychologist and wanted to treat him with some sort of faith healing, I think. I don't really know. Doctors later said Dick waited a few weeks before returning for more chemotherapy treatments, and by then it was too late.

I spoke to him by phone often while he was at home and when he was in the hospital. I did not visit him in the hospital during his last days. Dick understood because he had been with me on our tours of the hospitals to be with the wounded veterans and he knew I couldn't stand to see suffering. I just couldn't stand to see my dear friend suffer.

Al Lerner, our old pianist with Harry's band, was holding Dick's hand when he died. Dick's friends were faithful to him. We all were angered by his printed obituaries, which dismissed him as a boy singer with the bands of the 1940s and dwelled on his many marriages, his problems with alcohol, and his bankruptcy.

I don't deny he had these things, but there was more to them than appear on the surface and there was more to him than others see. It still hurts me to talk about him, but I think a loving friend should tell it as it really was.

He would do anything for anyone, so others would do anything for him. You know that song: "with all your faults, I love you still. . . ." Well, that was the way we felt about Dick. We forgave him his faults. We all have faults. He was a good man. Few of us are as good as he was. His old friends still talk about him as if he were still alive. The night he died, I got drunk. I can't believe he's dead. I miss him so much it hurts to think of him.

Artie and Harry made romantic music marvelously well with their instruments. So did Dick with his instrument, his voice. He had that deep, deep voice. He sang "Old Man River" as well as the operatic singers it was intended for. He sang it better than Sinatra, who also sang it. He caressed the lyrics of a love song as well as anyone. In my mind, no one ever sang a love song better than Dick, not Sinatra, not anyone. He influenced all the singers that came after him, and at the end, you only had to look at the faces of the ladies in the audience to know he still had the old magic.

He had a chemistry that pulled people to him. He was sensitive, intelligent, articulate, almost a match for Artie, but with much more feeling for people. He won others over without trying, just being himself, just being warm and thoughtful and caring. He was a womanizer, but he didn't use women any more than they used him; less, I think. He had a weakness for women, but they had a weakness for him, too. I've come to the conclusion that these characters can't help themselves. Staying straight may be mostly a matter of temptation. The more temptation a man has, the less straight he's going to be. And my God, did Dick have temptations!

I was with Dick for about six months with Harry, then for three years when we did a radio show together in Hollywood. I never saw women go wild over a man the way they did over Dick. Oh, maybe more swooned over Sinatra, but I doubt they melted when they met any man the way they melted when they met Dick and he gave them that grin of his. Most women who met him would do anything for him.

I lied for Dick. I don't know many men I'd have lied for, but I lied for him. When he was married to Joanne Dru, he made me his alibi. I went along with him even though I really liked her. We used to rehearse songs for the show at their place and I felt terrible about betraying her, but I couldn't help doing what Dick wanted me to do.

He'd tell her we were on business for the show and I'd cover for him if she'd call. We'd go to the Brown Derby or some place for lunch or dinner and sit down and I would stay put and he would go out the back door. At first he was romancing Maureen O'Sullivan, Mia Farrow's mother and the movie Jane to Johnny Weissmuller's Tarzan. Then it was Rita. "I'm going to the Brown Derby," he'd say, and that would be my cue. I covered for him for three years.

Joanne knew we were just friends so she trusted Dick when he was with me, but she should never have trusted him or me. We ran into one another and talked about it during the last year of Dick's life. She understood. She knew how he was. She'd divorced John Ireland by then and married another man and was living in Santa Barbara. But she still loved Dick. We met at the memorial service for him and fell into each other's arms and wept and hugged one another. We had Dick in common.

Dick and I had the same manager, Billy Burton. Less than a

year after I left Harry, Billy put us together on the Autolite radio show, fifteen minutes nationally every Saturday evening. Fifteen-minute shows—musical shows, comedy shows—were common in those days, and many were very popular. Ours was the most popular radio show of all for a while, number one in the ratings. We did the show from September 1944 through June 1947 and we really made it big.

It was terrific fun. Dick was terrific and made work fun. I love to laugh and Dick always was a lot of laughs. In fact, it was on this show with Dick that my laugh got to be famous. Dick would deliberately try to throw me off, throwing me an unexpected line on the air, and I'd start to laugh and smother my laugh. Billy asked me what I was doing and when I told him he told me to let it go. He said, "You've got a great laugh. It'll liven up the show." I said, "A lady doesn't laugh like that." He said, "You do."

So I let it go and I became known for it. I still laugh from my toes when I feel it whenever I'm performing anywhere, and I'm still known for it. Beverly Sills is supposed to have the same sort of laugh. She's heard about mine. And we're supposed to look a little alike. We're both Jewish, anyway. Joe Harnell, a pianist and musical director who's worked with both of us, says we even bitch about the same things. He wants to put us together sometime. I'd like that.

Back then, I can remember being here or there in public and letting go a laugh and people who didn't know my face knew my laugh and would come to me and say, "You must be Helen Forrest." And I'd plead guilty. I still have the same war whoop, but I don't think I let it go as often as I did back in those days with Dick, when he'd tease me and I'd tease him. The ladies would write him letters and call him up. The telephone was always ringing. And when he left the studio, the ladies would be waiting and jump all over him.

It was a great show, and good fun with Dick.

Gordon Jenkins was the musical director. We'd each do a

number, then a third number together, then some sort of specialty number Gordon would write, often with Tom Adair and Matt Dennis. Each week's shows had a theme. They might be based on a city or a season of the year. And the specialty pieces often became major production numbers. Dick and I would be joined by the 4 Hits and a Miss and Gordon's choir. With all those voices we got a marvelous sound.

Sometimes, we had guests like Judy Garland and other stars of the time. The show was promoted and publicized heavily. Dick and I did tours to promote the show. And we did records together that were big hits. Our styles suited each other and our duets worked wonderfully well.

We had six or seven top ten records. "I'm Always Chasing Rainbows" made it for a while. "Oh, What It Seemed to Be" was on the list ten weeks or so and got as high as number four. "It Had to Be You" was on the list a long time and got as high as four. "Together" was on ten weeks and got to be number three. "I'll Buy That Dream" and "Long Ago and Far Away" were on ten or eleven weeks each and each got to be number two. Both were number one on some lists.

"It Had to Be You," "Together," and "I'll Buy That Dream" all sold more than a million copies. Each sold more than half a million pieces of sheet music too.

It doesn't show in the record books, but I believe "Side by Side" was also a big hit. It is well remembered by our fans, I know. Perhaps partly because of our three and one half years together, Dick and I always have had a lot of the same fans, who always followed us and turned up wherever we were. Now that he is gone, they come to me to hear me and see me and talk about Dick.

We were reunited a couple of times in the last years of his life in nostalgia shows, some of which were put together by my current manager, Joe Graydon. We did "The Big Band Festival of the Fabulous Forties" and "The Big Broadcast of

1944" with bands and performers from that era. We did a week here, a week there, mostly one-nighters, as many as forty in a row over eight-week spans.

It was wonderful to be with him again and he was much the same as he'd been before. But like all of us he no longer was young. He'd lost some of his spirit, some of his confidence. Such tours were tough for him. He wasn't well. But he wanted to perform. Sometimes he sang well, sometimes he didn't. He always was nervous singing, he'd lose his strength, and he'd become inconsistent. But at his best he was still the best.

He was on the wagon. He said, "The heavy drinking started when I started to feel sorry for myself. But I have no reason to feel sorry for myself. I had more good days than most. And I accept absolute responsibility for anything that ever happened to me, good or bad." Few were loved as much as he was.

Dick had not recorded much in recent years. His two Capitol albums from 1956 and 1957, *Rain or Shine* and *Moondreams*, are treasured by collectors for he was at his vocal peak then. Yet when Dick recorded his last album, which was released on the Ballad label in 1979, he was still in fine form. This album, entitled *As Time Goes By*, was produced and paid for by members of the Dick Haymes Society and is a lasting tribute to the man and his music.

I think it hurt him a little not to have endured better, not to have remained a star, not to have been a bigger star longer. I think it hurt him a little to be touring with a nostalgia show, playing a lot of small towns. Well, that's the way it is. I'm still touring with these shows and I'm not ashamed of it. The big band days are long gone, but when I left the bands and went on my own I went a long way and had a lot of fun. There have been good days and bad days, but I'm still going and I'm far from finished.

I Had the Craziest Dream

STORIES

Earl Wilson, New York Post syndicated columnist:

I thought it was mighty funny that Miss Helen Forrest let me sit down in her dressing room at the Roxy but kept standing up herself. Miss Forrest, the latest band vocalist to go out on her own as a chantootsie, made me nervous standing up stiff as a post, that I finally said, "Miss Forrest, why don't you sit down?"

"I can't sit down," she replied.

"Why can't you sit down?" I asked.

She looked to me like a girl who could sit down.

After all, I ruminated, what's the use of a girl going into big money if she couldn't sit down?

"I can't sit down in this dress," Miss Forrest said.

I noticed it was long, white, and stiff, and had a skirt about five feet in diameter.

"Unless I throw it up in the back and sit down on my . . . here," she said, coughing modestly.

"I'll turn my head while you throw it up behind and sit down," I volunteered.

"I'll stand," she said firmly. "This dress has about six skirts. They've got horsehair in them. And when I sit down, it sticks me. I mean the horsehair sticks me when I sit down. Do you understand?"

"I understand," I said.

Here, I thought, is a chantootsie problem the frivolous general public has never given a thought to.

I stood in the wings when she went on to sing. Under her wonderful dress her legs were bare, and so, generally speaking, was Miss Forrest.

The audience couldn't tell, but when the lights fell on her dress from in front, I, in back, could.

She is getting $3,000 a week at the Roxy. This is very decent pay now in New York.

For that, Miss Forrest can get a nice meal at 21, including bread, butter, coffee, and one side dish.

Bill Burton said, "She will make more money with me in the next year than she would have made in six years with the bands. She is big box office."

He is her manager and I talked to him while she sang. He said, "I am taking care of everything for her, even her hair.

"Nature gave her a great voice, but didn't take care of her hair. It was just a dull dark brown. So in Hollywood, I took her to the best. We tried on dozens of wigs for color. We cut off a piece of one and went for a dye job."

So now titian-haired Helen is killing 'em at the Roxy.

She came off after stirring up a storm on stage and received a great ovation.

She headed for her dressing room. I noticed her grabbing at her dress.

"Soon I can sit down," she said as she swept by.

Daily Variety reviews:

Los Angeles—Her intimate style and appearance mark Miss Forrest as a draw for top stage, nightclub, and radio bookings. Girl has a way of understanding her songs, selling them without need of physical emphasis or vocal gymnastics. When caught she was garbed in a breath-taking form-fitting gown that took ample care of the visual quality of her turn. Her stage presence indicates her experience at pleasing the public. In fact, entire setup of initial date indicates charisma and showmanship that was expanded to make it a most promising debut. Bridging the gap from band singer to solo vocalist was as easy as should be getting from Hollywood and Vine to Ninth and Broadway, downtown Los Angeles at the Orpheum, her debut as a single, to her second single date, downtown New York at the Roxy.

New York—After warming up her new single in L.A., former big band singer Helen Forrest is a smash hit at the Roxy and should do well on the circuit. This gal looks great and sings great and gives her show a lot of showmanship.

Newark—Helen Forrest presents plenty in the way of eye and ear appeal at the Adams this week. No doubt about it, Miss Forrest has plenty of class and audience shows respect as well as admiration.

Walter Winchell, New York Daily Mirror syndicated columnist:

Helen Forrest is the first of the new Red-Hot Mammas.

Ed Sullivan, New York Daily News syndicated columnist:

Helen Forrest is the Sinatra of femme singers.

I cried for you,
Now it's your turn to cry over me. . . .

LATE IN MY STAY with Harry, we were playing the Paramount Theater in New York when Billy Burton came backstage to see me. I didn't know him, but I knew of him. He was managing Jimmy Dorsey as well as Bob Eberly and Helen O'Connell—in fact he had put them together. He was managing Dick Haymes. Eventually he put Dick and me together again.

He gave me a costly cocktail ring. He said, "This is in appreciation of a great talent. And I'd like you to remember me when and if you go out on your own because I'd like to manage you." I said, "I can't take this. It's very nice, but I don't know when I might go on my own."

He said, "No, you keep it. I'm not asking you to leave Harry. Maybe you never will. Maybe if you do you'll get another manager. All I ask is that you call me. But I want you to have the ring because you've given me so much pleasure."

166

Well, he was the first man who had mentioned managing me as a single. He seemed a very nice man and I knew he was a successful manager. I knew I was leaving Harry. When I did, Billy was the first and only person I called.

Up until then, bandleaders and band managers had told me where to go and when to go, where to be and when to be there. I had no idea how to get bookings or if I could get bookings. Other singers were working successfully as singles. Many told me I would be successful. But I was scared stiff. I was twenty-six years old and about to start a new life.

I asked Billy if I could get bookings, if I would be successful on my own. He said, "Helen, I'll get you more bookings than you can handle. You'll be more successful than you can imagine. The big bands won't last much longer. We're coming into the era of the singers. And you, honey, are one of the great singers."

It was a few years yet before the bands began to die, but during those years the singers—Sinatra, Haymes, Como, Crosby, Eddie Fisher, Frankie Laine, Johnny Ray, Johnny Mathis, Rosemary Clooney, Jo Stafford, Peggy Lee, Patti Page, Kay Starr, Ella, Billie, Sara Vaughan—came into their own.

Billy Burton was a fabulous promoter. I put together an act of my hit songs and he launched my solo career at the Orpheum Theater in downtown L.A. He had a dozen movie stars out to see me on opening night. I remember that after my last song Martha Raye crawled out on stage on all fours pushing a horseshoe of flowers ahead of her. The stage was filled with flowers at the end. The audience was standing and cheering and I did one encore after another. It was a great thrill.

But the big opening was to be in New York, at the Roxy Theater. For one solid month before I opened Billy had a full-page ad in *Variety*, the show business newspaper, with a calendar and the date of my opening circled in red, but no mention of who or what was to happen on that date. Billy had a big mustache and at the bottom of the ad was simply a picture of a big mustache and the signature—"Billy Burton, The Little Manager of Big Stars."

No one knew who was to come out on stage until about a week before opening night. I don't know if I was a disappointment, but that big house was sold out. When my call came, I wanted to take a taxi somewhere. I didn't want to walk out there alone on that block-long stage. I had to force myself to move, my legs were weak and shaking. I was very nervous. But once I started to sing, it was all right. In the end, another standing ovation, more flowers, more encores, another thrill.

I always had been backed by a big band, a band I was used to working with, that was used to working with me. The bandleader was the star, never me. Suddenly I had to learn to rehearse for a day or two, sometimes an hour or two, with different bands—good bands, bad bands. Sometimes I had to sing with small groups for the first time in my life. And I was the headliner and had to carry the show. For a singer this is a terrific adjustment. I made it, but it wasn't easy and didn't come fast.

I went in the month of December 1943 from $250 a week with Harry to $2,500 a week at the Orpheum Theater and $3,000 a week at the Roxy. Billy would not book me for bargain rates. A lot of people figured since I was starting out as a solo they could get me cheap, but Billy would not go along with that. I can remember being in his office with him screaming into the telephone, "What kind of money is that? Whattaya mean, she's a band vocalist? She's a singer, the best in the business! She'll pack your place! She'll make you a lot of money! She has to get top dollar! See her! Hear her, for God's sake!"

I remember he pulled one telephone right off the wall backstage at a theater I was playing, he was so mad at the way the deal was going that he was discussing. He was excitable, which I suppose is why he died of a heart attack about fifteen years later. But he pushed his performers, got lots of bookings for them, got top dollar for them. He did for me.

Although I never thought of myself as a bathing beauty, I didn't have a bad bod at the time and I remember in Hollywood he had me posing for publicity stills in a bathing suit, coming in and out of a swimming pool, coming in and out of my bathing suit. He tried to glamorize me and succeeded to some extent. As far as appearances go, I was at my peak at that time. And I was singing well, with arrangements that featured me even more than those I had with Harry.

I sang in the movies. I sang the title song in the 1945 movie *You Came Along*. I had a fantastic three years of the *Autolite Show* on national radio with Dick from 1944 through 1946. I toured with Dick. I toured on my own. For a few years I worked fifty-two weeks a year.

I had those hit records with Dick—"It Had to Be You," "Together," "Side by Side," "I'll Buy That Dream," "Oh, What It Seemed to Be," "I'm Always Chasing Rainbows," "Long Ago and Far Away." I had hit records on my own— "Out of Nowhere," "Time Waits for No One," "I Guess I'll Hang My Tears Out to Dry," "All of Me," "Don't Take Your Love from Me," "I Love You Much Too Much," "It Was So Nice While It Lasted," "My Reverie," "Deep Purple."

All in all, I recorded seventy-four sides as a single—twenty-two for Decca from 1944 through 1946, forty for MGM from 1946 through 1950, twelve for Bell from 1953 through 1955. The first solo record I cut, in 1943, had "In a Moment of Madness" on one side and "Time Waits for No One" on the other side. The last side I cut was, ironically, "Don't Play That Song Again," in 1955.

"Time Waits for No One" became my biggest hit as a single. It sold close to a million records, was in the top ten for ten or eleven weeks, and got as high as number two on the *Billboard* list. It may have been number one on some lists.

I recorded with such outstanding orchestra leaders as Victor Young, Hugo Winterhalter, Harold Mooney, Earle Hagen, Russ Case, Larry Clinton.

In 1955 I recorded again with Harry, recreating some of our greatests on a Capitol album—*Harry James in Hi-Fi*— as the day of the 33 rpm LPs had dawned.

The next year, I recorded with Billy May and Dave Cavanaugh, recreating many of my hits on another Capitol album—*Miss Helen Forrest, The Voice of the Big Bands.*

By then many of my hit 78s with Artie, Benny, and Harry had been reissued on their 33s. Many of the V-discs I had done with them and Dick were reissued on LPs. These were records we cut strictly for the servicemen and sent overseas to them. And many "air check" recordings cut straight from radio remotes began to appear in the stores as LPs.

For a while there were a lot of records of yours truly selling around. And I made some good money from some of them. No longer did the bandleader get all the money. The singer got it. For a few years I made more than one hundred thousand dollars a year from my personal appearances, radio performances, and records. But I didn't enjoy my money much. Much of it went into arrangements, costumes, musicians, travel.

I had dreamed for years of owning a full-length mink coat. With my increased income I now could afford one. I purchased my coat just before an engagement in San Francisco. I was sharing the bill with Mickey Rooney in the main room of the Fairmont Hotel. I can remember sweeping proudly in my mink into the hotel lobby to register. I was so proud of it I wore it everywhere. Except to my first night's two shows. I hung it in the closet of my room and went to work.

After the second show, Billy, my manager, had arranged an interview with a local disc jockey. After the interview, Billy escorted me back to my room. It was about three in the morning. I couldn't fit my key into the door. We called the hotel manager, who found wax in the tumbler. The house detective came and the police was summoned. They forced the door open.

There were no immediate signs of thieves, but I rushed to the closet. I found an empty hanger where my beautiful coat had been hung six hours earlier. I had not had time to get insurance. All I got was my picture on the front pages of the newspapers the next day. All I have left of that coat is the memory of it and a yellowed newspaper photo showing me sitting on the front steps of the hotel, crying on Mickey Rooney's shoulder.

I felt fate had not intended for me to have a mink, so I never replaced the coat. I worked my fanny off for my money and sometimes didn't get a lot out of it.

I've always done a fair number of benefits for free, or at least for no more than travel money. But I don't do as many as I'd like to because I can't take performing for the seriously injured or sick. I'm too soft-hearted, not tough enough.

Before the war ended, Dick and I visited service hospitals all across the country. They were filled with the mentally and physically crippled victims of battle, many of them "basket cases," as they were called in those days. Attendants would push a piano on wheels from ward to ward and we'd sing for the fellows and talk to them.

But you're supposed to put up a strong front for them, and I'd start to cry when I'd walk in and see them. I didn't know what to say to them. My throat would close up and it was hard to sing. I couldn't entertain them. I couldn't help them.

Bless Dick, he finally said, "Just don't do it, Helen. You can't do it, so stop trying. You tried. It's not your fault. It tears you apart."

It does. I've performed at hospitals for the young and the old, for sick children and the elderly, and it tears me apart, and I don't do well for them, so I've stopped trying. It's an emotional weakness and I feel bad about it, but there's nothing I can do. I still do benefit shows, telethons, and things like that. I do what I can.

One time I agreed to go to Okinawa to entertain the troops for the army. I arrived at Travis Air Force Base about two hours before the plane was to take off. When I got there, they said I was too late. The plane hadn't taken off yet, I said, so how could I be late? They said I was supposed to be there three hours ahead of time. I said no one had told me that. I said I was always early for appointments. I said I was two hours early and the plane hadn't left so what was the problem. They said they'd given my seat to an army wife.

I said, well, I wasn't going to argue against an army wife, but they better get me another seat because I was supposed to be in Okinawa to entertain the troops the next day. They said they didn't have any other flights. I said, well, then, they didn't have an entertainer. I said, goodbye, buddy, and I left and went home. I have a temper and if I feel like I'm being pushed around I'll fight back. I got some bad publicity out of it. There were stories saying I'd missed my flight to entertain the troops overseas, been kicked off the flight because I was late, as if I didn't care. I'm still angry about it.

A lot of times you do things for people and they don't appreciate it. Entertainers are expected to do anything anyone asks of them in the name of charity. I do what I can. I've traveled all across the country for good causes. Sometimes it's tough.

In the late 1960s I ran into my friend Martha Raye, the great comedienne, at a party in Hollywood. She had just returned from one of many visits she had been making to entertain our troops at military bases in Vietnam and other Far East hot spots. I told her I wanted to do that. She grabbed me by the shoulders and said, "Helen, you have to promise me that you won't. You don't know how sick you can get. Everyone who goes gets dysentery, malaria, or some other thing. The heat is unbearable and conditions terrible." I said,

"Martha, you've been there a dozen times or more and you're all right." She said, "I've been lucky. I'm a glutton for punishment. But if you go, I'll come after you and haunt you. You have to promise me you won't go."

I promised and didn't go. I wish I had, but I was scared off. Martha kept right on going. She is an unselfish lady who gives more than she wants her friends to give and the American people owe her a debt of gratitude.

I have made trips all across this country to entertain our servicemen. One time during a summer break from our radio show, Dick and I took a tour of military bases. We flew with about twenty servicemen from one camp to another. Like a lot of the flights I've taken, one of these was scary. We flew propeller planes in those days and couldn't go high enough to get above the storm clouds. The air this time was so rough, the flight so bumpy, everyone on board was sick except me, the only woman on board, and Dick. I travel pretty well actually, and Dick took everything in stride.

At one point, Dick was holding a paper cup of coffee. Every time the plane took a sudden drop, the coffee rose right out of the cup, but each time Dick calmly moved his cup so it caught the coffee without spilling a drop. I started to laugh the first time I saw him do this trick and laughed harder each time after that. The others around us were too sick to laugh, but they watched Dick with fascination and amazement. He started to take real pride in his performance.

When we landed an hour later, we had so much luggage to gather we let everyone else get off first. They were happy to get off that plane, anyway. But when Dick and I got to the top of the portable steps leading off the plane, we were surprised to find the troops lined up, saluting us for our ease under fire.

Dick was great to travel with. He was a man of continuous good humor. One time our plane was in trouble. I was terrified. Dick didn't blink an eye. He started to shake his coffee cup as though in terror. He started to kid around: "Remember the records, Helen. They'll be here long after you're gone. You'll be remembered. But the headlines will go to me. I'm the movie star. They'll say, 'Dick Haymes Killed in Plane Crash.' Beneath the headlines, in small type, it'll say, 'Helen Forrest Also Lost.' " Before long he had me laughing with him. We landed safely, laughing about it.

Some of my trips weren't so funny. I flew to London to record there for Reader's Digest Records with Alan Copeland, in the early 1970s. As we landed, the motor on my side suddenly burst into flames. A stewardess yelled, "Fire, fire, fire." She started to panic and caused others to panic. I tried to calm her, but she was hysterical.

The fire trucks pulled up and tried to put out the fire, but couldn't at first. There was the danger of an explosion that would have blown us all to bits. They popped an emergency door and draped out a chute, down which we were supposed to slide to safety. There was a terrific rush to the door and it jammed up. I was one who stayed seated and waited.

They were telling everyone to leave everything behind— purses, passports, money—and go out the door. They were telling people to take off their shoes, leave their coats behind, and go. It was about 18 degrees outside, bitter cold, and raining and the rainy cold was blowing in the door. It was late at night and dark.

The door was cut into the side of the plane and the chute didn't reach the bottom of the door so there was a sort of metal lip between you and the chute. And a stewardess was grabbing people as they got to the door and slamming them down on this metal lip and onto the chute. There were a couple of maintenance men at the bottom of the chute to catch the people as they came down, but they weren't catching them in time and the people were sliding down fast and going off the chute and hitting the ground hard and yelling in pain as they came out into the dark, into the cold rain.

One young lady holding a baby was in hysterics. I offered to take her baby for her, but she screamed no, she didn't want

174

to let go of her baby. She and the baby went down the chute and she went one way and the baby went another. Fortunately, they were uninjured. Finally, a man and I were the last still sitting and he said, "You think we better go?" And I said, "I guess so." And we went.

The stewardess made a grab for me and I said, "Put one hand on me and I'll put my fist in your mouth." I settled myself onto the chute. I had a long leather cape on. I didn't realize it would make me slide faster. I slid down at terrific speed, flew off the chute, and landed hard on the wet, cold concrete runway. I wound up with my head on the chute, my body on the ground. The ground had little spikes in it to stop the plane and they cut me up. I hit so hard that I think if my head had hit I'd have been killed.

People did suffer fractured skulls and broken shoulders and broken arms and broken legs. No one caught me. One of the maintenance men reached for me to pull me up. I was so mad I asked, "Why didn't you catch me, you idiot?" He pulled back. He said, "Sorry, madam. Sorry for the exposure." I looked down and my dress had slid above my hips. I pulled it down. What the hell, there were worse things happening to me at the moment.

It was bitter cold and raining hard and people were staggering to their feet and bending over and throwing up. Some idiot called to us to run to the grass. What grass? It was ice! The runway had been cleared, but the grass was covered with wet ice. People ran to the grass and slid every which way and fell down all over the wet ice. The ice was red with blood. Hurt and sore and limping, many of us, soaked and in soaked socks or bare feet, worked our way to the terminal with little help.

We waited there two and a half hours while they put out the fire before they sent buses for us. I have no idea why. They did take some who were hurt to hospitals in ambulances. The rest of us sat and nursed our bruised, damp, chilled bodies and drank coffee before they let us sort through and get our luggage and coats and shoes and purses and things we'd left on the plane.

A young boy on the plane was wearing only a shirt and a pair of jeans that must have been washed a thousand times. He didn't have a jacket or anything. I guess as he came down the chute he split his pants. He didn't have on any underwear. As he moved around in the terminal, I could see his bare fanny sticking through his jeans. I thought that was very funny. Every time he moved I laughed. No one knew what I was laughing at. After a while the public address announced, "There's an American lady in a red suit who's hysterical." I was wearing a red dress, so I guess that was me.

Another lady had broken off the heel of one shoe, and when she walked by me she was out of balance, up and down, walking like someone with a short leg. This struck me as funny too, and I let out another of those war whoops of laughter of mine. She turned to see me laughing. She knew I was laughing at her. It made her laugh at herself. She started to laugh too. And then on came the public address announcement again, "There's a lady in a red dress who's hysterical." I don't know why they announced it. No one came to calm me.

The record company had sent a limousine to bring me into town, but the driver had left, thinking I had been taken to a hospital. So no one met me. I took a taxi into town, but didn't know what hotel had been booked for me. I directed the driver to one I thought might be right, but when I got inside they had no reservation for me and no room to give me. I told them who I was and told them the name of the man in charge of the recording and they said he often stayed there, but was not there then, and there was nothing they could do for me.

I told them they could find him, find me another room at another hotel, or get me a reservation on the next flight back to the good old USA and get me back to the airport because I wasn't waiting long. I stormed away from the desk and plunked down into a lobby chair, soaked, chilled, and unhappy.

I Had the Craziest Dream

The concierge was a nice man. He found the man in charge. In any event, they found me another room in a nearby hotel and sent me there in a taxi. I was exhausted. I took off my clothes, fell into bed, and slept twelve straight hours. I heard later that the phone rang for hours before I answered it. I didn't even hear it for a while, I guess.

Finally, it awakened me. It was someone from the recording session saying they regretted the mixup, they didn't know where I was, and they had been trying to locate me. I took a hot bath, changed into clean clothes, got something to eat, and started to feel human again.

The record people came to get me and we went over our arrangements that day. I started to record the next day. After a few days, we were finished and I flew home. No incidents on the flight home. But that was by far the wildest trip I ever took and I hope never to take another trip like it.

I have flown and appeared all over the world, from Australia to Hawaii.

I opened a new club, The Clouds, in Honolulu. Three gals owned the club and one was a friend of mine. We did unbelievable business. It was a tiny club which seated only about eighty people, but we were squeezing in a hundred or more every show, two shows a night, standing room only and the hell with the fire laws. A lot of people came who couldn't get in. I offered to do a third show Friday and Saturday nights for the same money and the owners took me up on it. I was a hit.

At the time there was a major league baseball all-star team in town on a tour. The players came night after night. Some of "the boys" came with them. I hope you know what I mean when I say "the boys." Mafia or plain old mobsters. You can tell 'em every time. They liked the action I was getting. You couldn't get from one table to another in that place, it was so crowded.

A couple of them came to me and asked me if I wanted my own club. They said they'd find a place for me and name it

"Helen Forrest's Club" or "The Forrest" or "The Enchanted Forrest" or something like that. They'd fix it up for me and run it for me, and I'd perform in it. They'd be my silent partners, but I'd have a big piece of the action and almost any salary I wanted.

I told them I'd think about it. I didn't know if I wanted to settle in Hawaii. They gave me an address and a phone number and said all I had to have was a nickel for a phone call and I was in business. I knew they were serious, but I never wrote or called. Maybe I missed my chance, but I was afraid of getting mixed up with them.

I used to play the Colony Club in Omaha, Nebraska. The owner was a nice man. He had terrific food in the restaurant and great booze in the bar. I was drinking by then, Scotch on the rocks, J&B with a splash of water. They were supposed to stop serving drinks after one in the morning. As we approached one, the owner would send me on stage a huge glass of Scotch on the rocks to tide me over.

We had a good drinking crowd. The same people night after night. Familiar faces. Calling out the same song requests. Packed night after night. After a while, on weekends, the owner would close the doors at one and lock up. But the crowd remained. And they'd drink and call out requests and I'd sing for hours and hours. They just didn't do that in those days, but we had a helluva good time. The cops couldn't get in. The customers couldn't get out. But no one wanted to get out.

The place burned down, but he built it again. And renamed it "Tête Rouge." It wasn't a French place, but he liked the sound of it. It meant "The Redhead" in French. I was a redhead by then. The man renamed his place in my honor, and I was honored. He never offered me a piece of the place, but I played there for many years. I think eventually he sold the club and they changed the name.

I remember when I played the dinner room at the Drake Hotel in Chicago, the manager liked me so much he wouldn't allow the waiters or waitresses to serve while my show was on. It cost him money, but he wanted the people to pay attention to me. Well, I wanted them to pay attention to me, too, but I didn't want them to be uncomfortable. I know when you're out drinking and you want a drink, you want a drink. And the food was fantastic there. So I'd open by telling the people to keep eating any food they had in front of them and I wouldn't mind. Maybe it was my Jewish upbringing, but I did mind when good food was wasted. I'd tell them to order a drink before I began. And I'd wait while they got served.

"All ready? All right, let's go!" I'd say. And go into my act. And they'd applaud.

That's the way they do it in Vegas and Reno and Tahoe. If it's a dinner show, you eat first, though there aren't as many dinner shows as there used to be. And you get two or three drinks at a time before the show starts so you can drink during the show without the waiters or waitresses bustling around. I don't mind people drinking during my shows. I don't like smoking because it messes up the atmosphere and hurts my throat, but I accept it. I want people to be comfortable. I want them to have a good time. I hope I'm the biggest part of it, but I don't want anything to get in the way of it.

I didn't have to talk when I was with the bands. The bandleader did all the talking. Once in a while on radio I'd read something from a script: "Hi, this is Helen Forrest. Harry asked me to introduce myself to you." And so on. Nonsense. On my own, on the road, I had to learn to talk to an audience, to make them feel comfortable with me, to bridge the gaps between songs. At first Billy had some lines written for me, but I didn't like them. They came out as if I were reading a speech. And I'm not a comedian. So I found my own way.

If I say something funny, it comes from the moment and from me. I'm not afraid to let loose with that laugh of mine. The audience always loves it. But it's all very informal. I talk to the people as if they were my friends, which most of them are or they wouldn't be there. I may talk about something that happened to me that day or the previous night. I may tell an anecdote about a song. But I never let talking get in the way of singing.

If fans want to talk to me after a show, fine, I love it. They're there to hear me and they're my people. I'm one of the people. I don't feel like a star, set apart from them. I'm a singer. It's just what I do. Other people do other things.

STORIES

Seymour Rothman, Toledo (Ohio) Blade feature writer:

Helen Forrest, redheaded, blue-eyed, perty and petite, bounced happily into the rehearsal hall adjoining the Victorian Room of the Hillcrest Hotel.

She pushed an armload of dog-eared, ragged, tired arrangement sheets at Pretz Russell, the bandleader.

"Treat us gently," she laughed as he turned to distribute them to the musicians. "We've been together a long time."

The band studied the sheets.

"If you play the music as it is written, we may cut this ten-day engagement down to about three days," Helen warned them gaily.

"It's been cut up, marked, and changed quite a bit. We'll have to run through it and fix it up."

She sang her first song softly to herself as the band played the music. She said, "That was good." And everyone smiled and started to relax. The rehearsal started to be fun.

Then came the special material that Helen does—a cute little number about her days with the big bands.

"It gets a little complicated and you'll have to watch the changes in tempo carefully," she warned. "Let's just try the changes."

They tried and Helen was right. They were complicated.

The bandleader suggested, "Maybe you'd like to sort of turn around and direct the band, yourself."

"I'll be too busy emoting," she laughed. "But just keep your eyes on my fanny." She slapped her hips. "You can pick up the cues from these."

"A pleasure," the bandleader smiled.

She turned away as the band picked up the eight bars before the change. All eyes were on Helen's fanny. And the band got through the music without a hitch.

By now, Miss Forrest was "Helen" and she had all the musicians pegged by their first names. There were mixups, but Helen was unperturbed and waited patiently until they were straightened out.

Soon the tricky business was over and Helen was doing all the great sentimental pop classics. By now the band had picked up her style, and there were few interruptions.

Waitresses who were setting up tables in the next room peeked through the door and stopped to listen. Helen wiggled her finger at them and they giggled and picked up the rhythm of the song. She had the whole joint going for her.

Too soon it was time for the opening show and Helen had to dress.

Pretz Russell came up as she left. "I might have to change the name of this band to the 'Helen Forrest Fan Club' " he told me. "They're crazy about her."

Sidney Skolsky, New York Post syndicated columnist:

When Helen Forrest sings a love song, all in the audience fall in love with her. This lady is a singer!

15.

IN THE LAST FORTY YEARS I must have worked with four thousand bands, big and small, big bands and small groups, forty-piece bands or a trio or even just a pianist. If they are good, it is great, and I am easy to work with. If they are bad, it is terrible, and I am hard to work with.

I worked with three of the best big bands of all time. I was spoiled. On tours with bands that have been rehearsed, I have had some good musicians behind me. I had to learn to sing with small groups or just a piano, but I learned. My voice is supposed to carry the song anyway, not the band behind me.

I have worked with many bad bands and bad musicians. Some couldn't even read music. I can't, but I don't have to. They have to. If they don't play my music in the correct key and tempo for me, I can't sing my songs the way I want to sing them.

Recently I worked the Biltmore Hotel in L.A. with the worst band I have ever had to work with. The musicians would start and take off and leave me far behind. I didn't know where they were going. I'd stop them again and again and again and tell them to slow down to my tempo, and they would start up and take off and I'd be wondering where the hell they'd gone.

The bandleader was no help to me. I took over keeping time with one arm while I sang. That helped a little, but by the time we were finished rehearsing my arm was sore.

Usually, a bandleader who's been around has a few key men he calls on every time he plays a date and surrounds them with the best available guys out of the union and on call. I don't know who contracted these characters, but he wound up with the worst. Usually, Joe Graydon, my manager, makes sure the contracter has provided good players, but this time he didn't.

I worked a private party with a pianist in a band who was using one of those little stands on top of the piano to hold his music and who kept turning the music. I was working at floor level with the pianist and from behind the stand he couldn't see me. When he couldn't see me, he couldn't follow me. I was losing him and he was getting lost.

I told him, "You'll have to put the stand down." He asked, "Where will I put the music?" I said, "You can stick it up your rear end for all I care, but I want you to play with me, not against me."

I have worked with drummers who lagged behind the beat. The drummer gives a band its beat and so may be the most important part of a band. If they get behind me or ahead of me, I get on them. I'm sure they go home bitching about this broad who doesn't know anything, but if they know their business there's no problem.

I'll bitch and I can be a bitch. I may not think of myself as a star, but I'm also no angel. I'm good to those who are good to me and bad to those who are bad. I've made a lot of friends among musicians, but when I'm working I'm not trying to please the musicians, I'm trying to please my friends in the audience.

I have found that I personalize each song if I sing to one person or one group of people or one table. I am sensitive to the vibes of an audience, and I can pick out one or two or three or four people up front who are really tuned in to me and I will work to them, and through them to the whole audience.

Many singers don't want to see their audience, but I do. Many are inhibited by seeing the faces and facial expressions of an audience, but I am turned on by it. Most singers sing with the spotlight in their faces, blinded by it to the audience sitting in the dark, but the spotlight makes me dizzy.

When a spotlight is hitting me in the face, I can't see the audience and I can't see the edges of the stage. I have a ver- tigo problem—a fear of falling—and I'm always afraid I'm going to walk right off the stage or fall off in some way, and a few times I almost have. I don't want to work to a blank wall of blackness, anyway.

I always tell the stage manager to turn the spotlight off and light the whole room, audience and all. He always says he can't create a mood without darkness and spotlights. I tell him I'll create the mood with my singing.

I've sung from a lot of stages, but I prefer to sing on the same level with the audience and be able to take a mike with a long cord and walk among the audience and sing right to them. I feel like I'm at home among old friends.

I'm not new. I don't have any new records out. Often the people who come to hear me are old fans. They ask for all the old songs. I'd like to sing some new songs, but I don't mind doing the old songs. Some of them I've done thousands of times, but I don't mind.

When I was appearing at the Drake Hotel in Chicago in the early seventies, I was about to take my bow after the first medley, which included "I Don't Want to Walk Without You," "I Had the Craziest Dream," and "I Cried for You." I received a standing ovation and one man sitting ringside stood up just before I walked off stage and said, "Please sing,

'I Don't Want to Walk Without You.' I looked at him and said, "Sir, where were you? I just finished that song. Did you go potty?" He replied, "I didn't leave the room. I just want to hear the song again."

I stepped off the stage and walked over to his table with microphone in hand. "Sir, would you mind telling us why you want to hear this song again?" The gentleman then told of a time in 1943 when he was in the navy and shipped out on a destroyer for the war in the Pacific. He said that of all the records they had on board the ship, my recording with Harry of "I Don't Want to Walk Without You" was by far his favorite and the favorite of all the men in his outfit.

On the return voyage the song was again the most popular with the men. But that ship did not make it back to our shores. It was torpedoed somewhere in the Pacific. The man lost most of his buddies at sea. He had the record in his hands when he ran on deck and jumped into the ocean and he was still holding it when he was plucked from the water. The audience was deeply moved by this story. So was I. There were tears running down the man's face. I was crying. The band was crying. There wasn't a dry eye in the house.

As I wiped the tears from my eyes, I thanked the man for sharing this touching story. I returned to the stage and signaled to the band to play one more chorus of the song . . . very slowly I sang the song with deep emotion. As I finished the song I looked down at the man and he was beaming. I will never forget. Music often touches us. A song can have significance in a person's lifetime.

Every time I sing one of my old songs I pretend it's the first time. I know it's not the first time, but it's always the first time for some members of the audience. I try to make it new every time. Maybe because these songs have been so good to me, I feel good about them. And, somehow, I always change something—the way I bend a phrase, something. I'm always able to sing these great old songs as if they were new.

It's funny, but I forget the words sometimes. I may have

sung a song four thousand times and draw a blank on a line. This happens to all singers. You don't like it, but you learn to live with it. Usually you hum something. Or make up some words. The audience doesn't even notice. Or if you sing something like "I forgot the words," the audience seems to enjoy it all the more.

I have a strong voice and while I have had my illnesses, I have missed very few performances, even in the big band days when we were doing six or seven theater shows, a radio show, a couple of hotel shows a day. Of course, I didn't sing but a couple of songs at each show, but it still added up, it still stretched over fifteen or sixteen hours a day, it still knocked you out. Now I might sing ten or twelve songs at a show, sometimes two shows in a row, and it's tough. I have not suffered much from what they call "Vegas throat," in which you sing so much your throat simply gives out. But three or four lounge shows a night have taken a lot out of me at times.

Before my throat and my vocal chords developed strength, I did suffer some. I remember once with Artie we were playing a theater in Boston. I woke up with laryngitis. No sound at all. He made an appointment for me with a specialist in New York who treated the top singers in the business—Sinatra, Dean Martin, everyone. I flew down there during the day with orders to return to Boston for that night's shows only if the doc could work a miracle. He was an osteopath, I think. I walked into the office and I couldn't even whisper. He treated me with massage and heat—infrared and diathermy. Ninety minutes later I walked out and I could talk. I flew back to Boston and did the shows that night.

With performers it is like pushing a button. No matter how you feel, you walk out on a stage into the spotlight in front of the audience and you perform at pretty close to your peak. Any performers who have endured can do this or they wouldn't have stayed in the business. I have often seen performers who were bent over, dragging, miserable, straighten

up, prance out to the spotlight, perform as if life were a bowl
of cherries, go off, and drop right back into the blues.

I have been like that. I do not sing during the day unless I
am working during the day. Morning performances are murder. It is tough to get out of bed and go out and sing. But my
vocal equipment needs very little warming up. Usually I can
go out at night without warming up and just start to sing.

We make it look easy. It is not really as easy as it looks, but
a lot of people look at us and wonder why they can't sing, too.
They look at a great clarinetist or a great violinist or a great
pianist and wish they could do what the great ones do, but
they know it has taken years of study and practice and they
know, whatever their talent may be or may have been, they
couldn't do it. But they look at a great singer and they figure
it's easy and they should be able to do it, especially if they
have a decent voice and an ability to carry a tune.

Johnny Carson, the great comedian, is always saying to his
singing guests that he wishes he could be a great singer. A
great singer casts a unique spell on an audience. But it takes a
lot of work, a lot of experience, a lot of practice to get to the
point where you can cast a spell over an audience.

I'd have to say my voice is natural. I never really studied
voice. When I was with the big bands I once went to a voice
teacher because I wanted to raise my range and hadn't been
able to do it. She heard me and told me I didn't need her. She
said, "The range is there, you just have to learn how to use it.
Does everything sound low to you now? Yes, I thought so.
You're straining to reach higher notes. Well, just raise your
key. Have your orchestra leader raise your key. You'll probably feel more comfortable in higher keys as you go along.
You'll still be able to hit the low notes. And you'll find you're
hitting higher and higher notes as you go along."

It worked wonderfully well for me. She was a wise woman.
Someone else might have fouled me up. She simply showed
me how I could start to stretch out on my own.

I started out as a singer copying Mildred Bailey and Ella

Fitzgerald. I suppose all singers start out copying someone they admire, and they were the best singers of my early days. But I did not copy them for long. I found out that when I was at the microphone I wanted to sing my own way. Gradually, working at my new profession, I found my way.

The style that I developed over the years just felt right to me and it is so much my own that I cannot be imitated accurately. Imitators have told me they have tried and failed. Frankly, I like being different from everyone else. It is nice that whatever I am, I am one of a kind.

I admire Barbra Streisand more than any other female singer around today. I think she is marvelous. I also have admired Eydie Gormé's singing for a long time. But I do not try to sing like either of them.

Among the men, I think Frank Sinatra has been tops at communicating the subtle meaning in a lyric and does equally well with slow ballads and up-tempo tunes. But I think Dick Haymes was the balladeer supreme. His voice could caress a lyric like no other I ever heard.

When it comes to vocal dynamics, there is no one more exciting to listen to than my friend Mel Torme. He is exciting to hear and he was exciting to sing with, though that previously unpublished pairing escaped the notice of the general public.

This was in 1944 when I had just started to do the radio show with Dick and was living in Hollywood. I was dating John Carroll, the actor and singer. He was famous for holding open houses for his friends every Saturday night. This Saturday night one of the guests was Donald O'Connor's sidekick, Sid Miller. He was playing a beautiful tune on the piano. I sat down beside him on the bench and asked what he was playing. He said that he was writing a love song for a leading man to sing to his leading lady in a movie, but was having a terrible time fitting lyrics to his melody. In his frustration he had come up with obscene lyrics. He sang the song for me and I found it funny.

Having an impish sense of humor, he had requested an audience with the producer that day to demonstrate his song. Tenderly, he played and sang his dirty ditty. The producer did not share Sid's sense of humor and walked out on him. Sid was mourning the moment that night. Mel Torme and the Mel-tones, his vocal group, were at the party. To cheer Sid up, yours truly, Mel, and the Mel-tones sang Sid's song—less than lovely lyrics to a really lovely melody—to the delight of all on hand.

The song was entitled "Don't Give Me That." I don't know what ever happened to it. I know Sid never found his ballad for that film. I also know it was fun to sing even one song with Mel, as it was to sing all those songs with Dick. But I never wanted to copy them and I always sang my way.

After I left the bands, and got my own arrangements, I really started to stretch. Band singers were limited by the arrangements for the band and the range of the soloist leader, but I think I had the highest range of any of the band singers. With Harry I went from G at the bottom to E-flat at the top. Today I can go to a comfortable C or D at the top. There are few singers around who have a wider range.

But, of course, range is only part of your equipment. It is what you do with the notes, with the words and music, that matters. And you have to hit the notes cleanly and clearly and consistently.

People are always saying to me how great I was on this night or that night. We all like to hear compliments. But I know when I'm at my best and I know when I'm not. People compliment me on my consistency, but no one is consistently at his or her best. I know I'm never exactly the same. Never. No matter how many times people tell me I'm always the same I know when my throat is strong and my voice is clear, when I'm feeling good or bad, when I'm high or low, and it always affects my singing.

I am extremely critical of myself. I hate my old records, which my fans love. I do think I have improved a good deal over the years. I think I hold a high level because singing is the most important thing in my life to me and I work very hard at it, at overcoming any problems I may have. It is not the most important thing to many singers after a while, and it shows. And many good ones get overconfident and throw it away. I am never overconfident and I always give it everything I've got.

It is not for me to say how good a singer I am. That is for others. For critics and fans. For some years now I have not made records or made appearances in many of the most prominent places. I am not reviewed that much. But when I am reviewed, I usually am reviewed favorably. Reviewers say it is a shame more people don't get to hear Helen now. I am not a star now. But I am still singing. And I think I am singing as well as ever.

1950

As the Korean conflict continued, relations between the United States and Russia continued to deteriorate. Almost one third of President Harry Truman's national budget was aimed at a military buildup. Senator Joseph McCarthy intensified his efforts to identify Communists and Communist supporters and drive them out of positions of public influence. Alger Hiss was found guilty of perjury in his spy trial and sentenced to ten years in jail. Secretary of State Dean Acheson announced the United States would support France, Vietnam, Laos, and Cambodia in their fight against Communist-inspired rebels in Indochina.

Entertainer Al Jolson died after returning from a trip to entertain our troops in Korea . . . Ezzard Charles became heavyweight boxing champion after defeating former champion Joe Louis . . . Dick Sisler's tenth-inning home run in the final game of the season gave the Phillies the National League pennant over the Dodgers, but Casey Stengel's Yankees swept the World Series.

All About Eve beat out Sunset Boulevard as the Academy Award movie, while Jose Ferrer won an Oscar for Cyrano de Bergerac and Judy Holliday one for Born Yesterday. . . . Television was in its infancy, but Milton Berle's Texaco Star Theater was the top show and attracted a large viewing audience. . . . Arthur Godfrey was moving up fast as a radio and television star. . . . The big band sound was fading out and rock 'n' roll was coming in.

16.

For a while I was a star, I suppose. In my last two years with the big bands I was voted the number one girl singer in the country. When I went on my own I had a hit radio show and hit records and I was still at or near the top of the polls. My kind of music still was the most popular in the country.

In the early 1950s it started to change. Rock 'n' roll music came in and took over the music scene. A little later, by the time Elvis Presley became the musical sensation of the nation, most of the big bands had disappeared and those that remained had few places to play. Like life, music constantly changes. But it was sad for those of us who loved the sounds of the dance bands.

There was one opportunity to be a big star that got away from me in the late 1940s or early 1950s. That was when they were casting *Guys and Dolls* for Broadway.

I knew the writer, Frank Loesser, who had written songs for me. I called him up and asked if I could audition. To my surprise, he said, "No."

I was shocked. "Why?" I asked. "Because I use a mike and you don't think I can project? Because I'm not an actress?"

He said, "No. You can project. Or be taught to very fast. You can act. I can tell that by the way you sing songs. The problem is, you're too good a singer. You have too strong a style. The part you'd do would be Adelaide. And you wouldn't sing the songs the way Adelaide would, you'd sing them the way Helen would. People would come out of the show saying 'Wasn't Helen Forrest great!' I want them to come out saying, 'Wasn't that a great show and wasn't that gal who played Adelaide great.' "

I didn't believe him at the time, but I soon came to see he was right. Vivian Blaine got the part and she was perfect for it. She played it for many years. In fact, she always played it, no matter what part she was playing.

Still, I lost out on something that might have turned my career upward.

Television was just becoming the dominant medium of entertainment. I appeared on a lot of the early shows. One I remember especially well was *The Jackie Gleason Show* in 1953 because it began a long friendship. I had met Jackie eleven years earlier when we appeared together in the movie *Springtime in the Rockies.* He had a lifetime in show business behind him but was not yet a major star. Television made the comedian a major star. When I appeared on his show, I found out he was much more than just a comedian.

Jackie always had a lot of guests at his home in Westchester County on the water and I spent part of that week as his guest there. We talked a lot about music because Jackie was writing music at the time and conducting lush mood music albums for Capitol. He wrote the theme music, "Melancholy Serenade," for his own show.

He never seemed to sleep. He'd prowl around his house and grounds and the beach at all hours with tunes running through his head. He carried a toy piano around and tapped tunes out on this. When one seemed right to him, he'd rush inside to his grand piano to work it out. Then he'd march through the house, even it if was three or four in the morning, and summon everyone into the living room to listen to it. He couldn't put the music on paper, so he'd call up his arranger at any hour to play it for him so it could be copied.

He knew every facet of putting on a television show and it was especially difficult at that time. This was live television and once the red lights came on those cameras, you were on. If something went wrong, there was no redoing it. Everything seemed to go right for Jackie. He was doing his *Honeymooners* skit as part of the show and that was maybe the best part. But he had guest stars, too. That Saturday night, April Fool's Night, I remember, I sang "I'm Through with Love" and the spirited "Hallelujah," which I still do.

I've never been presented to better advantage musically and I remember it fondly. For some reason, I never got to do as much television as I would have liked. Only a few of the singers from the big bands did. Crosby and Sinatra, of course. And Perry Como. Television made him a major star. TV made Dinah Shore a major star.

Most of the female singers from the bands disappeared almost entirely. For a few years there was still a major market for me. For a few years my fans from the big band days were still going to shows and were faithful to me. But a popular music audience usually is a young one. Young people buy more than half the records that are sold every year. And as my fans grew older, my audience grew smaller. And year by year Billy Burton found it harder and harder to get bookings for me.

Then he died. I think he strained his heart until it just stopped. It was a big blow to me. He was my friend and I really loved that little guy. When I was in L.A. I'd live in his house with him, his wife, and his sister. We were a family. He had other clients, but he seemed to care for me especially.

As a personal manager, he hustled hard, but played fair. He asked good money for his clients' services, but he always insisted we show up on time and work hard and give the clients their money's worth. He would get very upset when a performer like Haymes missed shows. Eventually he dropped Dick. A manager, a good manager, is critical to a performer. You can't book yourself and negotiate for yourself. You can't take care of your travel arrangements and your finances yourself. You have to have help. A good manager can make a good performer a success. A bad manager can kill even a great performer's career. It is a very rough, cutthroat racket and a lot of great talents have not made it to the top because they didn't get the help they needed.

When I went on my own, I went with Billy. When Billy died, I was really on my own. It frightened me. I needed another good manager, but managers weren't beating down my door to get to me. I was supposed to be passé, I guess. A few wanted me, but they weren't the ones I wanted. In the 1950s and early 1960s I drifted. I'd get calls and I'd get jobs, but I didn't work regularly. I made enough money to get by on, but I didn't get enough to be happy.

I had a couple of unhappy marriages, which I will get into shortly. But even if I'd had happy marriages, I don't think I'd have been happy staying home and keeping house. Maybe that's one reason why the marriages weren't happy. That wasn't Helen and still isn't. Singing makes me happy. Working, no matter how hard it is, keeps me content. I'm happy to have something to bitch about. Sitting home, waiting for the phone to ring, makes me miserable, makes me even more bitchy. Up there on the stage, that's Helen. Even as I passed from my thirties into my forties I wanted to work as much as ever. Until I got Joe Graydon as my manager my career really was on the rocks.

At one point I figured I was too closely identified with the big bands. It had been a long time since I was the girl singer with a band. It had been a long time since I was a girl. I was tired of doing the old songs. I was a singer and I could sing any songs. I wanted to do new songs. I wanted a new image.

I talked about it and an agent put me in touch with a man named Carlyle. He used only the one name. He produced magnificent shows at the Hotel Nacional in Havana. He was a fantastic choreographer and musical director. He was in New York and I went to him and told him I wanted a new act, a new image, a new everything. He told me he'd do it for me. For a pretty fat fee, I might add.

He'd heard me and knew my work. He listened to me and watched me work. Then he went to the great Fletcher Henderson and got him to write special material for me. I learned the material and met with Carlyle in Miami, where I was due to open in about two weeks. We went to work in a rehearsal hall that had a stage.

The first thing he did was ask me to walk for him. I thought I knew how to walk. I said so. He said I didn't. He insisted I walk for him. Have you ever had to walk for anyone? If so, you know it makes you so self-conscious you feel like you have two left feet. Heck, you can't even breathe right if you think about it.

He showed me how to walk gracefully and easily, as a performer before the public should. He showed me how to use my hands while singing a song. He taught me how to hold a microphone and work with a long cord. It's not as easy as it looks. You can get tangled up in it, easily. I don't like portable mikes—mikes without a cord. The sound isn't right.

I thought I knew how to do all these things, but I had been doing them all wrong. I got by on my singing, but my movements distracted from my singing. He taught me how to move so it enhanced my singing. In time I became comfortable with the movements. They became natural. And I think they made me a much more attractive performer.

At one point in the performance, he had me turn and walk

196

to the piano. That terrified me. You're not supposed to turn your back on an audience. But today I'm not afraid to show my backside to the people. He had me lean against the piano. He wanted me to sit on top of the piano, but I was too short to get up. "I'm not doing a comedy number," I screamed. "I'm a ballad singer."

He said, "We're going to change that."

I was so nervous I was shaking. I got tangled up in the mike cord. So he told me to leave the mike on its stand and he had another set up for me by the piano. Eventually, he got me to where I could walk to the piano without tripping over my own feet. And lean against the piano, and sing.

He wanted me to vary my moods and work from various places on stage. He created mood by lowering the lights. Because of my vertigo I don't like spotlights. I stumble in the dark. I'm always afraid of falling off the stage. With the big bands, the stage was always well lit. On my own, I found a lot of clubs liked low lighting. I had to argue to get them to turn up the lights. I screamed at Carlyle, "You're risking my life!"

He said, "In life you have to take risks."

It took fifteen days to get it ready. He even got me fancy new gowns. On opening night, I was ready. I walked up a ramp to a new stage while the band played "I Had the Craziest Dream." While I sang, he danced behind me with a beautiful lady. I all but danced. I moved around. I did a medley of my hits, but mostly I did new numbers. I did ballads, but I also did jump tunes. And Vegas sort of stuff. I did the special material. And it was just beautiful. Even though I was in it, I have to say it was one of the most beautiful musical acts I've seen.

I was very happy with it until my fans started to come to me and ask what I was doing. It was beautiful, they agreed, but it wasn't me. They came to see me sing, not dance. They came to hear me sing my songs, not other things. They all tried to be very nice to me and to praise the act, but it was clear they were unhappy with me and my new act. I very fast became uncomfortable with it.

After five nights, I threw it out. It cost me twenty thousand dollars and I threw it out. Twenty thousand out the window. Ha! But it wasn't me. I told Carlyle it wasn't me. I said I was sorry, it was a beautiful act, but it wasn't the act for me. I said he'd done so much for me, he'd earned his money. I meant it and I convinced him.

I still feel it. It was money well spent. The band singer who used to get up from her chair and walk to the mike and sing a song and walk back to the chair and sit back down with her legs close together was gone now. I had really learned for the first time how to move around a stage and work with a mike and sell a song with my hands and my body as well as my voice.

He accepted it. Some years later he dropped in on me unexpectedly and I jumped on him and hugged him and kissed him. I know he knows how much I feel he did for me. I haven't heard from him or seen him for years, but I hope he realizes how fondly I remember him. But his act just wasn't for me.

Maybe I made a mistake. I don't know. I'm still singing the old songs. I'm still not tired of them. There aren't many new songs like the old ones. But there are some. And I could sing them. But my fans don't want me to sing new songs. They come to hear me sing the good old songs. I could make new fans. I could have back then. Others did, I could have. Others changed, I could have. But I didn't want to lose my fans. So I went along with what they wanted. And what I did was date myself.

For a while I did not work as much as I like to work. This bothered me, but I was not deeply depressed because I was still working. Maybe I was not always playing the big dates in the big cities, but I was playing good dates in good cities. There is a lot to the world of entertainment beyond Broadway. Maybe some thought I had retired because I was not on television very often and I was not making records, but I was singing for my old fans and making new fans and getting enough money to get by on and I was not unhappy. I always wanted to perform more than I wanted to be a star. And then, after some years, I began to get real busy again.

Packagers started to put together shows of performers from the Big Band Era of the thirties and forties. Nostalgia shows of the old performers from the good old days for their good old fans. Nostalgia shows. There's always an audience for nostalgia. There always are people who grew up in the sixties who want to hear the music and see the performers from the sixties, and those who want the fifties, and the forties.

They started to put together packages featuring Harry James and his band or Freddy Martin and his band or someone with the Glenn Miller band or someone with the Tommy Dorsey band or someone with the Jimmy Dorsey band and they wanted Bob Eberly or Ray Eberle, Johnny Desmond or Andy Russell, Rosemary Clooney or Connie Haines, Helen O'Connell or Helen Forrest to sing with them.

I was back in business.

REVIEWS

As the strains of the Tommy Dorsey band began issuing forth Saturday night at the Music Hall Theater the near-capacity audience settled back for what looked to be a kind of trip into nostalgia. But the program proved to be a great deal more than that.

Under the direction of Sam Donahue, this "Tommy Dorsey Orchestra," a 15-man group of young musicians, swung their way through the familiar arrangements, but also added a great many more contemporary numbers. . . .

Supposedly the selling point of the concert was the appearance of Frank Sinatra, Jr., but in terms of musical interest the real surprise was vocalist Helen Forrest. Anyone who ever collected records in the 40s is more than familiar with her work. In fact, it was her vocalizing that was one of the best reasons for listening to the Harry James band.

Looking more stunning than ever, Miss Forrest proved Saturday night that she is better than ever as a vocalist. One wished in fact that so much time had not been given to Jeannie Thomas, a new singer, who is all style and no substance, and it had been, instead, turned over to Miss Forrest.

The evening in many ways seems dated. The Pied Piers, for instance, seemed dated. Listening to and watching young Sinatra gave one the feeling they were watching his father. All singers seem somewhat imitative of him. And when you get a singer who sounds like him . . . well, let's say that Sinatra Senior is a tough act to follow.

It was only Miss Forrest who not only seemed as good as one remembered her, but, in terms of singing new material, even better. . . .

—John Voorhees, Seattle Post-Intelligencer.

Ziggy Elman wasn't there, or Buddy Rich, or any of the others who helped over the years to make the name of the late Tommy Dorsey famous, but the Dorsey fans of yesteryear had come to hear those sounds again and they weren't disappointed last night at the Jubilee Auditorium. Unfortunately, the evening was not as enjoyable as a musical performance as it was as a happy recollection.

None of the vocalists except Helen Forrest reached any new heights, and few of the instrumental soloists achieved any brilliance. She never sang with Dorsey, but she sang with the best and is the best. Oh yes, Frank Sinatra, Jr., also sang. . . .

Fraser Perry, Calgary (Canada) Herald.

The cup of nostalgia is bubbling over these fall evenings in New York as the bandstand at the Hotel Americana's Royal Box

Supper Club takes on the looks of a reincarnation. . . . It was Sam Donahue putting the latest version of the Tommy Dorsey band through its paces in a one-hour production.

The engagement produced the New York café debut of 19-year-old Frank Sinatra, Jr., a lad who sings like, sounds like, and gestures like his father, almost to the point where it's unfortunate. He should build his own act and his own image. . . .

Helen Forrest, often called the voice of the name bands, was the hit of the show in the wind-up spot, and showed herself a wow of a performer. Miss Forrest looks fine, almost 20 years after her heyday, and, if anything, sings better than ever.

—Ben Grevatt, Billboard.

Blinstrub's had its largest crowd of the new season at the opening of the Tommy Dorsey Show. Sinatra may have been the name that pulled the customers in but he is really low man on the totem polls, a beginner, but fast mastering stage technique under the guidance of his father.

The red-haired Miss Forrest is the top solo star of the show, coming on last and, as Sinatra, Jr., predicted, she had the crowd begging for more. Junior said, "I've never seen her yet that she hasn't captured the audience and we've played 27 states."

—Alan Frazer, Boston Herald.

17.

I was working with Frank Sinatra, Jr., when he was kidnapped at Tahoe in December 1963.

We were part of a "Tommy Dorsey" package with Sam Donahue leading a band through the old Dorsey charts. I had not sung with Dorsey, but Frank's father had. And the Pied Pipers had. I shared the singing with Frank, Jr., and a new group of Pied Pipers.

It was a great tour and it lasted on and off for three years. We went first class, mostly by plane. We stayed weeks at a time at places like the Americana Hotel in New York and the Flamingo in Las Vegas. It was still exhausting, but we did well with it.

It was young Sinatra's first tour. He was new to performing in public. It was tough for him. But he had talent and got better as we went along. He was supposed to be the star so it hurt him that I got the better reviews, but he never complained about it and always was nice to me.

I never realized how tough it was to be a big star's child. He was compared to his father and that was completely unfair.

Who had a better right? Who can compare to his father? Unfortunately, he did look a little like his father, had many of his mannerisms, and sounded a lot like him. He tried for his own style, but he was called a copy.

He was a great pianist. He wrote beautiful music. He was an electronic genius. He could do a lot of things. He's had a fair career, but I believe he'd have been better off going in any one of several different directions instead of singing. He was a natural as an actor. I saw him do some things that were thrilling. But he wanted to be a great singer like his father.

I have never known anyone who adored another person the way Frank Junior adored Frank Senior. Frank Junior was totally devoted to his father. His eyes lit up when he talked about his father. He carried an unbelievable amount of hi-fi equipment with him on the road and all he ever did was play his father's music at top volume all the time. He drove us nutty with it.

Frank Senior also adored his son. Early in our tour he was always showing up to watch him and hear him and give him advice. He turned up everywhere and he was wonderful to his son. He really cared and it was very touching. The reviews were difficult to deal with, but Frank Senior disliked critics and tried to get Frank Junior to ignore reviews.

One of our first engagements was at the Flamingo Hotel lounge in Las Vegas. Frank Senior would visit Frank Junior backstage frequently. At one point when I was in the room, Senior nodded to me and told Junior, "If you want to learn how to sing, listen to this lady. You have a lot to learn about this craft, so keep listening. She's the best!" Such a compliment coming from the master of song styling flattered me enormously. I've never forgotten it.

Every few months of our tour, we'd return to the Flamingo. One time, Frank Senior was headlining at the Sands, down the strip, when he invited a number of us from our show to his late-night Saturday show. Junior guided me to a ringside table next to him.

At one point in his show, Frank Senior introduced other entertainers or special guests who were in the room. When he had introduced everyone else but Junior and me, he announced, "And now, ladies and gentlemen, I want to introduce the singing star of the Dorsey show playing down the street." He paused and smiled and said, "I realize you're expecting me to introduce my son, but I want you to know that the singing star of the show is truly . . . Miss Helen Forrest."

I was more flattered than ever. The audience applauded and I rose and beamed at Frank and bowed to him in gratitude. When I turned to Junior he had a smile on his face from ear to ear. It was a lovely moment.

At that same engagement at the Flamingo, my dressing room adjoined Ella Fitzgerald's. She was playing the main showroom.

I first met Ella back in the late 1930s, when I was with Artie's band and she was with Chick Webb's, but we never really got to know each other and never had much more than a nodding acquaintance.

Each night of our engagements at the Flamingo, Ella would come to my dressing room to say hello and chat while I got ready to go on. She didn't have to go on until later. I found her to be as sweet a lady as I had heard she was.

On my closing night, she came to me and said, "There's something I want you to know before you go." I couldn't imagine what that might be. She said, "I think you're the greatest singer in the world."

I couldn't believe it. I thought she was. I said, "But, Ella, everyone says you're the greatest singer in the world. Coming from you, that kind of praise is overwhelming, but——"

She cut in, clasping my hands in hers, and said, "Well, let's leave it this way—in this room right now we have two of the greatest singers in the world."

On the heels of the praise from Frank Sinatra Senior, this incredible compliment from "The First Lady of Song" would have made that tour memorable all by itself, but, unfortunately, there was something else.

There was the kidnapping of Frank Junior near the end of our first year on the road, when we were playing Harrah's at the Lake Tahoe resort in Nevada. It took place just before we were to go on stage for our first show that night and it created chaos.

Two men with pistols entered Frank's room at the club's private lodge. They bound and gagged Frank and John Foss, a young trumpet player in the band, who was in the room with Frank. They left John behind when they took Frank. John worked himself free after a while and alerted others to what had happened to Frank.

State police, sheriff's officers, and even the FBI almost immediately were swarming all over the area, questioning all of us. But there was a blizzard and heavy snows stopped them from following the getaway car.

Frank Senior got there as soon as he could get through, offering rewards. Nancy, his ex-wife and Frank Junior's mother, stayed in touch by telephone from L.A.

It turned out later that a new Chevy, with Frank Junior hidden under a blanket in the trunk, had slipped through roadblocks.

This was on a Sunday night. The next afternoon Frank Senior received a telephone call from the kidnappers telling him they had his son. He said he'd do anything they wanted.

The next day he got a couple of calls telling him he should get together $240,000 in small bills and wait at his wife's house in the Bel Air area of L.A. He chartered a plane and flew to L.A.

Late that night Frank Senior had the money together and waited. He got a telephone call telling him where to deliver it and warning him to be alone if he wanted his son released alive.

About two Wednesday morning he left alone. A half hour later he returned alone. But less than an hour later, Frank

Junior turned up in a police car, having been picked up on the highway. He said he talked his way to freedom. But the ransom had been paid.

The next night the Sinatras had a party. Meanwhile FBI agents swarmed into various parts of the L.A. area. Reportedly, they knew the identity of the kidnappers.

The next day they arrested a John Irwin at Imperial Beach with almost fifty thousand dollars of the ransom bills. They arrested Joseph Amsler in Culver City with most of the rest of the money. And they arrested Barry Keenan in Canada.

For a while there was a lot of talk that the kidnapping had been conducted by underworld enemies of Frank Senior or was a hoax in which Frank Junior participated to raise some money. The defense suggested this was the case. But after a two- or three-week trial a couple of months after the kidnapping, all three were found guilty of having taken part in a crime and were sentenced to long terms in prison. I think they're still there.

I remember one of the jurors saying they all were convinced it was no hoax, no farce, but the real thing. When Frank rejoined the tour, he said it was the real thing, serious stuff, and scary. I believed him. I always have believed in him. He was a nice, bright, talented young man.

We all were worried about him while he was gone. We all were thrilled when we heard he was safe. When he returned to us, I thought, "My God, he's really alive, he's really all right." I hugged and kissed him.

We went to Europe to tour after Tahoe and Frank Junior had to fly back to the USA to testify at the trial. It disturbed him and disrupted the tour. But eventually the trial ended and life returned to normal.

What was normal in Europe was a string of one-nighters. Back to the buses. We went everywhere—England, France, Germany, and other countries. We were well received everywhere. But it was tough on the nerves.

When we returned to America, we went on another tour

here. When we finished one tour, we started another. I don't know if we had three weeks off a year in three years. But it was steady work for good money.

When I left the bands, I said I'd never take a bus trip again. One thing I learned was you should never say never again.

I have a little arthritis and riding in a bus or a plane or any confined vehicle kills me. Fortunately, we flew a lot. But it still was very tough going. I did it because I like to work.

I had a son by then. I hated to be away from him. I had divorced his father so there was no father at home to be with him. I had custody. I also had a job that took me on the road, often thousands of miles away. It was lonely for him, I'm sure. It's often been a lonely life for me. But it's been my life. I sure haven't had much luck in my love life.

18.

WHEN I LEFT THE BIG BANDS I was leaving Harry as much as anything. After he married Betty, I stayed four or five months until I just couldn't stand it. When I went on my own, I started to go to parties, I started to date for the first time in my life, really. I was in my mid-twenties and ready to roll.

Booze never meant that much to me. I never became a drunk, but there were a few nights I got drunk. I remember I was dating a doctor in L.A. and on my birthday in 1944 we decided to go out and I asked him if it would be all right if I got drunk and he said I should be his guest. I was.

We went to Ye Little Club in Hollywood. After a while I went upstairs to the john and when I came down I slipped on a step and landed on my fanny and let out that war whoop of mine which let everyone know Helen was there and soon everyone in the place was laughing with me.

We had separate cars and I was supposed to follow him home. Except I was so loaded I couldn't follow the front of my car. Sunset Boulevard had a divider in the middle. I figured if I scrape along the curb, I'd be safe. I scraped every bit of rubber off the sides of my tires. The doc, Eddie, dropped behind me to make sure I made it. He knew all the cops and every time a patrol car passed by he waved to 'em trying to get one of 'em to drive me home, but they just waved and went on by. I didn't know what he was doing. I thought he was trying to get me arrested. I'd lean out the window and scream back, "Hey, Eddie, what're you trying to do to me?"

It's funny, but for some reason I can't forget that drive home that night. That was just one night, but maybe it was typical of too many like it for a while. For a year or two I partied too many nights, dated too many guys. None of them and none of it meant too much to me, but I was trying to learn how to live and get along, reaching out for some kind of normal life.

I met Paul Hogan at a party. His real name was Houlihan, but he changed it to Hogan when he started acting. An Irishman. He was the handsomest man I've ever known. A big, good-looking guy. And the funniest man I've ever known. Very quick with a quip. The life of the party.

He was from Youngstown, Ohio, but he'd been a policeman on the vice squad for ten years in Hawaii. He was in Honolulu when Pearl Harbor was hit. He met some movie people from Hollywood, made friends, and followed them to L.A. after the war ended.

They encouraged him to get into the movies and he was going to acting school and playing bits in films when I met him near the end of 1945. He had the same sense of humor I did and we broke each other up all the time and got along great.

We went together for a while, then started to live together. In those days it wasn't the thing to do to live together. All our friends kept saying, "You two should get married." So in December 1947 we did.

He loved parties and we would have open house around our swimming pool every weekend. Regular guests included

Gloria DeHaven and John Payne, who were married at the time; Rhonda Fleming and Rory Calhoun, who were married; Denver Pyle and Milton Frome, all good friends of Paul's. Among my friends who came whenever they were in town was Buddy Rich.

One time that stands out in my mind was a day that Buddy arrived when a group of us already were in the pool. We called to him to join us in the pool. Dressed in a suit, which was unusual for him, Buddy walked out over the patio and without pause, smile or anything, went right into the pool.

Responding to our hysterics, he deadpanned, "Well, you asked me to join you."

Life was a party for a while and Paul was the life of the party. He wasn't working very much. He played a few small parts in westerns, but most of the time he just did bits. His Hollywood buddies just liked to have him around.

I'd get a call and someone would say they wanted Paul in a picture with them. I'd ask if he had an acting part. The fellows would say, "No, but we want him with us."

"Oh, come on . . ." I'd say. It was so frustrating. I don't know why, but he just never got anywhere with his career. I was the breadwinner and I believe it's bad any time the woman is bringing in the money. It hurts the man's pride. We argued about money all the time.

Also we were apart a lot and he was insanely jealous of me. There's a switch for you. He had beautiful blue eyes, much like Harry's—but he really was a green-eyed monster.

I wasn't running around on him. But he thought I was. He'd be in Durango or somewhere on a western and I'd be in Detroit or somewhere on a tour, and suddenly he'd be standing at the bar, watching me, trying to catch me with a man.

After three or four times, that was it. He just went too far with it. He'd say he was sorry, he just loved me too much. I loved him. I suppose there are many reasons why a marriage doesn't work. For one reason or another, ours just didn't work.

We were separated for a few years. I decided to divorce him in 1956. I recall sitting with him in the attorney's office when the attorney asked, "Why are you getting divorced?"

In California at that time you had to show evidence of cruelty on the part of one partner to get a divorce. The attorney asked, "Has Paul beaten you?"

I said, "No."

He asked, "Has Paul cheated on you?"

I said, "No."

"Does he drink a lot?"

"No."

"Does he embarrass you in front of others?"

"No."

"Then why are you asking for a divorce?" he wondered.

I looked at Paul and admitted, "I don't know."

The attorney said, "You don't have any grounds for a divorce. Why don't you try getting back together again? You don't really want a divorce, do you?"

I looked at Paul and said, "No. Not really. But we just can't live together. We've tried, but it just doesn't work."

We went to court and a divorce was granted on the grounds of mental cruelty. Paul drove me to the courthouse for the final rendering and afterwards took me to dinner. We talked about it and laughed it off. We'd tried and failed at marriage, but we remain good friends to this day.

We were together for ten years or so, married a little less than nine years.

Two strikes on the girl singer.

A couple of years later, in the late 1950s, I fell for a fellow named Charlie Feinman. Again, I met him at a party. He was a businessman. Maybe I was looking for someone outside the entertainment business.

Charlie was outside. His firm manufactured falsies. The

mere mention of it was always good for a laugh. People used to ask him why I didn't wear his product. He'd say he didn't make any big enough. Very funny.

But he was a nice man. He really loved me and was proud of my work. He loved to listen to me sing and would go to my performances as much as possible. When we were at parties he'd ask me to sing.

We were married in 1959 and I was soon pregnant for the first time in my life. I felt I was ready to settle down, raise my baby, keep house for my husband. But he wanted me to go on working as long as possible. It wasn't as though we needed the money.

Our son, Michael, was born in November 1960. As soon as I was able, Charlie wanted me to go back to work. I didn't want to leave my son home. He said we could get someone to take care of the boy. We argued about it a lot.

Soon I saw he wasn't married to Helen, he was married to Helen Forrest, the singer. He always introduced me at parties as Helen Forrest, the singer, not Mrs. Feinman, his wife. He always wanted me to sing at parties. He was proud of me all right, but he was married to the lady at the mike, not the one at the kitchen sink.

He wanted to go out every night to show me off. I've traveled so much that when I'm home I want to stay home. I just got tired of going to parties. I got tired of him. I didn't have a home with him. So I divorced him in 1961, after two years of marriage, when Michael was only one year old.

Three strikes and you're out, old girl. At the least I'm in the last of the ninth with time running out on me. There aren't that many pitches being made to me these days, though I'm still willing to take a good swing at one.

Maybe it's my fault. Maybe I want too much out of marriage. Maybe I'm hard to live with. Maybe I have to have things too much my way. Well, I've had them my way for twenty years now because I've lived alone.

At one point I fell in love with a married man. I didn't want

A Miami, Florida, theater marquee hails the appearance of Helen on stage with a movie, 1949.

Guesting the Ed Sullivan Show on CBS-TV in the early 1960s, Hel-
en has put on a pound or two.

A young Helen Forrest, pre-nose-
bob.

Helen's mother.

Helen's first husband, Al Spieldock.

Helen with her second husband, Paul Hogan, at Slapsy Maxie's in Hollywood.

Artie Shaw played the clarinet while Lana Turner danced on the set of *Dancing Co-Ed*. They met here and married. That's Buddy Rich on drums, Tony Pastor on sax (partly behind Lana) and Georgie Auld on sax (far left). *Duncan Shiedt collection)*

A rare photo—Harry with Betty, Helen with Bud Moreno in 1943.

Helen liked Benny Goodman's playing if not his personality. (Duncan Schiedt collection)

A young Joe Graydon when he was still singing, about the time he started to manage stars.

Frank Sinatra, Jr., at a press conference following release from kidnapping, 1963.

Helen Forrest in late 1960s.

to break up his marriage and he didn't want to break up his marriage so we broke up. It just wasn't meant to be. He died a few years ago.

So I sing all these love songs, but love has passed me by. I'm perhaps most poignant on songs of lost love—"I Had the Craziest Dream," "But Not for Me," and the others.

I wound up leaving my son alone a lot, with a housekeeper or in a boarding school. I took Michael on tour with me when I could, especally in the early years when he was young. On the Tommy Dorsey tour he had fifteen uncles who spoiled him crazy.

In the early years when he was young we were as close as we could be. But I had to earn a living and as the years passed and he got older he started to resent me for being away so much and I can't blame him. You give up a lot to lead the life I've led.

I've lived in the Los Angeles area most of the time I've been on my own, though I lived in New York for a while. But Michael developed a sinus condition, which called for a dry climate, so we moved to Phoenix and lived in Arizona for ten years. I could leave on tours from there as well as anywhere.

It was all right, but it was awfully hot, and I felt awfully far from the mainstream of show business and dreadfully confined. When he went away to school and I was left alone in Arizona I nearly went crazy. Eventually I decided to return to southern California and settled into a town house in Calabasas, a quiet community north of the San Fernando Valley and an easy drive to L.A. I live alone, but I am close to my manager and my friends.

I made new friends in my new neighborhood before I even knew it. Michael, my friend Dominic Scutti, and I caravaned from Phoenix in a rented truck-trailer, towing my car, with Michael leading the way in his car. We expected to arrive in twelve hours. Because of mechanical and other troubles, it took eighteen hours. After we turned off the freeway, we got

213

lost. Fortunately, our new neighbor, who had been waiting for us all evening, sent someone out to try to find us. He found us at about midnight. When we drove up the hill to our new townhouse, our neighbors were still up, worried about us. They greeted us with a warmth I will not forget. I felt I was finally home.

Michael is very bright. He went to Pierce Community College and has been going to Arizona State University. He turns twenty-two this year, but I don't think he knows what he wants to do with his life. He has thought he might want to be a psychologist. He likes people and people like him. They tell him their troubles and he's a good listener.

He's very independent and I haven't been in a position to push my ways on him. I'll be listening to music from my era and he likes it, I know he likes it, but he'll switch on the music of today, turn it up full blast just to bother me, and tell me that's music. Maybe I'm an old fogy, but I can't get with much of today's music.

I think he's proud of me. He calls himself Michael Forrest. His father's name is on his birth certificate but he uses my name.

I guess he was very unhappy for a while. He put on a lot of weight. Went to 250 or 260 and he's only five feet nine or so. But he's come to grips with life and taken off a lot of weight and is down to 180 or 190. He's had a lonely life, but now he has a chance to make a life for himself. I've been as much of a mother to him as I could be. He is my son and I love him dearly.

I did not bring him into this world without pain. It turned out I was seriously sick with physical problems, but I've fought my way past those problems all my life.

19.

I HAVE SPOKEN of my problem with vertigo. Whenever a blinding spotlight strikes my eyes, I feel intensely dizzy. It was some time before I found out the condition stems from a problem in my inner ear.

I first became aware that I had a hearing problem when I was singing duets with Dick Haymes. After our radio shows we'd play back the recording so we could hear how we sounded. I noticed that I was a little behind Dick and the beat. It wasn't so noticeable when I sang alone, but it was when I sang with Dick.

When I mentioned it to him, he heard it. We tried different things, such as changing positions at the microphone. He was willing to try anything to help. Finally, I realized that one ear was bad. When my bad ear was turned to him or to the music, I wasn't picking up the sound fast enough. I realized I wasn't hearing him. I knew the music and I was reading his lips.

I went to five different doctors. Each of them agreed I had a bad ear. None of them could find out what was causing the problem. Several said they might be able to find out with exploratory surgery, which would have some risk. That wasn't for me.

One man I will never forget . . . or forgive. He was one of the most famous men in his field. He has his own hospital on hearing problems today. He told me, "You have nothing to worry about. You'll be deaf within two or three years."

I couldn't believe it. I didn't scream in those days the way I scream today, but I have always had a temper. I said, "You have the nerve to tell a patient not to worry because she's bound to go deaf? And you can't do anything about it?"

Finally, a doctor figured it out. He was a fellow Billy Burton played poker with, Dr. Julius Lemmert. He had studied in Europe and he was ahead of others in the field. He was a dynamic character. He detected that I had otosclerosis, which causes progressive deafness. There was a new operation to correct the condition and he was one of only two or three men in the country doing it.

He said that the operation did not have a high rate of success, but that it also did not have a high risk. He said there was an 85 percent chance my hearing would stay the same, 10 percent it would get worse, and 5 percent it would get better. I told him to give it his best shot because I didn't want to go on the way I was.

The operation was a fenestration. He went through the inner ear canal and raised a large flap to expose the stirrup bone, off which the sound bounces and which had become a spongy mass. Sometimes over a period of years the bone builds up and starts to seal off the stirrup bone again. And now they build an entire new sound board, I believe. But back then, I was happy just to have my good hearing restored. It took a long time, but my hearing was restored.

The recovery was not easy. It was shortly after I met my second husband, Paul, that I decided to have the operation. Fortunately, Paul was supportive and comforting. After the operation, my equilibrium was such that I could not walk a straight line from one side of the room to the other. Paul would stand on one side of the room with his arms outstretched to catch me if necessary. I would weave across the room to him. It took six months before I really recovered and I will forever be grateful to him for his help.

I was extremely lucky that the operation was successful and I was able to continue my career. I felt tremendous relief. However, my problems with vertigo were not eliminated.

After completing the European portion of the tour with the Dorsey package, we were booked into the Paramount Theater in New York. I'd had problems with the lighting at the Paramount before and I felt if I couldn't overcome my vertigo, which was at its most intense, I didn't dare set foot on that stage again.

I wondered if my problem was psychological. Johnny Mercer, the great songwriter, recommended a doctor in L.A. to me. He was a psychologist and hypnotist. I went to him and he explained to me that under hypnosis I might bring forth feelings I was repressing, which might reveal the cause of my problem. Strong-willed subjects are not easy to hypnotize and I turned out to be a difficult subject. It took six visits to his office before I went under.

Asked to describe attacks of vertigo, I was later told I recounted an episode in a Chicago club in the mid-forties when I was working with cornetist Muggsy Spanier. You had to climb about eight steps to get up on the portable stage. I would get dizzy and crawl on all fours to get up. Getting down was even harder.

One afternoon during that engagement I had been shopping in one of the large department stores on State Street. Starting up the street, I suddenly felt tremendously dizzy. Everything was spinning, I lunged for the nearest light pole and clung to it, desperately. I'm sure passersby thought I was drunk.

The doctor brought me out of the trance, explaining I was shaking so hard during my description that I was rocking the huge stuffed leather chair in which I was sitting. As I went back into trances other times, I had similar emotional experiences. However, the doctor decided eventually that the problem was physical, the reaction to it inevitably emotional.

He assured me I had no mental blocks, nothing wrong psychologically. He said I had a very real problem I would have to learn to live with. Before I left for New York he taught me self-hypnosis in the hope I could convince myself I could deal with my dizzy spells.

I had severe problems with my vertigo in New York, but my Paramount appearance was a great success. The self-hypnosis may have helped. The vertigo problems have lessened. But they remain to this day.

Lately, the ear has been going bad again. And the other ear is going bad now, too. I may have to have more surgery. The operation is improved now, I am told, but I may have to get lucky again.

I have been asked how I carried on then and how I carry on now. Most of the time I have heard the music well enough. I have developed a feeling for it. I feel the vibrations. And I do hear it. But I think it is an instinct that keeps my intonation correct. I hear the notes. I hear the sharps and flats. I know when I am flat. I know when I am behind the beat.

I have been told there is a new type of hearing aid that would help, but I do not want to wear it. It is not vanity. I am very sensitive to the dynamics of sound. I am never happy with the sound on a record because it is never right. I am never happy with a battery microphone because the sound it produces is artificial and wrong. I would prefer not to use any microphone at all, but that would be too hard on my throat. But if I used a hearing aid I would hear a different sound than I have been hearing all these years, an artificial sound, and I know I could not be comfortable with it.

I am sixty-four and my voice is as good as ever, but my hearing is not. Hopefully, the condition will not get worse or I will get help to make it better. For now, I am doing all right. I am still able to work well and I want to go on working.

The only other physical problem that has affected my ability to perform is arthritis. Most of the time it is not as bad as it might be, but it often has made traveling for long hours in cramped spaces exceedingly uncomfortable.

It has not struck me on stage too often, but a few years ago when I was touring with a nostalgia show and playing Long Island I was near the end of my first song, "Taking a Chance on Love," when I felt as though someone suddenly had stuck a knife in the back of one leg.

I froze. I could hear the orchestra playing behind me. I opened my mouth, but the words didn't come out. The pain was simply too much. It was frightening. I'm sure that if I hadn't been on stage, I'd have gone to my knees. Somehow I stood there and the pain subsided and I started to sing again.

I was told that I missed only a few words, but those seconds seemed like minutes. It is frightening to know such pain might strike at any time, but that was one of the few times I felt anything from my arthritis on stage. It seldom has affected my ability to perform.

I have had other problems offstage, however.

I was forty-three when I had my one baby. That is old to have a baby. It is more common to have a baby at that age today than it was yesterday. Then the doctor was extremely concerned about both me and the baby.

Actually, he first diagnosed it as a tumor, rather than a baby. He took some tests and told me if it was a baby he'd give his shingle to me. The next day he called and said I could come in for the shingle at any time.

I did have tumors. I had twelve. Little Michael was lying in the middle of them. I went to specialists and several said there was no way I could have this baby. They said the baby would abort naturally or be still-born.

Abortions weren't as common then as they are now. My husband took me to Tijuana, the Mexican town across the southern California border, to have one. A doctor walked into a small room with a bloody apron on and I walked out the door and we drove back across the border.

I was scared. I'd probably have bled to death before I got home. But more than being scared, I really wanted to have my baby. I decided I was willing to risk my life to have it. I guess this is the way of a woman.

Back in L.A., I found a doctor who said I'd have to have my baby by cesarean section, but I could have it. He said he could take care of the tumors after the baby was born. He gave me hope.

I had my baby. He came out howling and healthy. He didn't even have to be slapped. He was five pounds plus and had been lying among tumors, some of which, I was told, were as big as grapefruits.

They put me under and scraped them out. Fortunately, they were benign, not malignant. And they have not, apparently, returned. No one knows what caused them to form in the first place. But once they were out, I felt better than I had in years.

The doctor did feel the need to perform a hysterectomy, so, sadly, I was not to have the opportunity to have another child.

Unfortunately, it was not the last time I would need surgery. Just three years later, I developed a gall-bladder problem.

I was living with young Michael in a house in Hollywood. I had experienced quite a bit of pain for a few days and went to my doctor to find out what the trouble was. After tests, the doctor diagnosed it as gallstones. It was a Monday and the doctor scheduled me for surgery the following Monday.

However, I had an engagement in Bakersfield Wednesday evening, some one hundred miles away. I left Michael with the housekeeper and drove to Bakersfield by myself. The doctor had given me some pills to ease the pain. I took a pill and did the show.

That night in my motel room I had another attack. I was apprehensive about the drive back to Los Angeles the next morning but had no choice. All the way home I prayed that there would be no problem. Fortunately the trip was uneventful.

Friday I drove my son and housekeeper to a nearby department store for some shopping. While in the store I suffered another attack. I didn't know if I'd be able to drive us home, and my housekeeper didn't drive. The pain finally subsided enough for me to drive.

That night, while the rest of the house was asleep, the pain grew so intense I had to call and wake the doctor. He made arrangements for an ambulance to take me to the hospital. He would meet me there and schedule the operation for the next morning.

It was 6:00 A.M. when the ambulance pulled up. I asked my housekeeper to keep Michael out of sight, so that he wouldn't be frightened by the sight of his mother being carried out of the house. The attendants placed me on a stretcher and rather clumsily made their way through the front door and out to the ambulance. I was in terrible pain.

I still had a sense of humor. I thought about asking the driver to hurry or I'd have the baby on the way to the hospital. The pain of gallstones is not unlike that of childbirth. I did ask the attendant why there was no siren. He replied, "I didn't think you're in that much of a hurry to get there." I wanted to hit him.

Finally we reached the emergency entrance and I was wheeled into the waiting area. Then I lay there while the nurse in charge of admissions filled out all sorts of forms. The ambulance driver told me he couldn't leave until he'd been paid. No one seemed to realize I was a very sick lady. Not until I wrote a check for the ambulance and signed the admission forms could I be transferred to a hospital room.

The doctor arrived, took one look at me, and thrust a thermometer in my mouth. Apparently I was jaundiced and had a fever of 105 degrees. He told me he couldn't operate with my fever so high. But he couldn't wait too long because gangrene was beginning to set in. The last thing I remember before I blacked out was asking the doctor to save some gallstones for me as a souvenir.

When I came to in the recovery room I asked the doctor about the stones. He replied, "We couldn't save them. There must have been 150 tiny stones . . . a bag full of poison."

Today I carry a souvenir of that operation, not the stones but a one-quarter-inch-wide scar which the surgeon's knife left due to the speed with which he had to make the incision.

But I wasn't finished yet. During the summer of 1973 I left my home in Phoenix to play one of my favorite clubs in Reno—Harold's Club. I was doing three shows a night. During that engagement I developed an embarrassing problem— a bladder problem. Each time I would hit a high note, I would dribble a little urine. This would happen throughout my forty minutes on stage. By the end of each show, there would be a small puddle where I had been standing.

The problem became increasingly annoying, and by the end of my engagement at Harold's I was wearing disposable diapers during the three shows each night.

I returned home to Phoenix and two months passed before I finally went to my doctor to confess my problem. After a thorough examination he advised me that surgery would be necessary. I entered the hospital the following week. The surgery involved rolling up the bladder membranes very tightly and stitching them.

Following the surgery, the doctor blithely told me that as a result of the required stitching I was once again a virgin. A virgin! My face must have paled at the thought because he quickly went on to explain that after the normal healing process, he would simply de-virgin me with the use of a dilator, a hard rubber tool about three inches long.

A month or so later, the doctor inserted the dilator to permit me to return to normal male-female relations without any discomfort.

Unfortunately it didn't work. As I was to find out, normal penetration was not possible. In fact, no penetration was possible. Each attempt left me in extreme pain and my gentleman friend in an extremely frustrated state.

I returned to the doctor and told him I did not want to spend the rest of my life as a permanent virgin. I explained the frustration I'd been experiencing. He explained that the dilator was a rigid instrument and that only a flexible instrument would do the trick . . . in other words, a man . . . with the right equipment.

I replied, "Doctor, are you trying to tell me that I should walk down the street and tap a gentleman passerby on the shoulder and ask if he would be willing to go to bed with me . . . strictly for medicinal purposes?"

To my chagrin, he said, "That's about it."

I composed an epitaph about my situation:

Here rests Helen,
Who through the years some woo did pitch,
But, alas, alack,
Her doc so tightly stitched,
That no man could pass the test,
So poor Helen got too much rest.

Fortunately, the right man was found. And he was no stranger.

After that, I felt fine physically until 1980. I did a one-nighter with Johnny Desmond, the Modernaires, and Tex Beneke and the Glenn Miller Orchestra at Concord, a colorful little town outside San Francisco. This was on a Friday night, the nineteenth of September.

I remember the show only vaguely. I remember very little of the next couple of days. I remember landing at the Burbank airport, but I don't remember driving home to Calabassas on Saturday. I don't remember anything about Saturday or Sunday.

My manager, Joe Graydon, called me on Monday morning. I don't remember it, but he does. He says he started to say he'd call me back because I sounded like I was sleeping and he'd awakened me, but then he heard me saying over and over again, "Jesus Christ, oh my God!" He realized I didn't recognize his voice and wasn't rational. He lives in Studio City, a half-hour away, so he called to his wife and told her to call the paramedics on another phone.

He says he kept me on the phone until the paramedics got to me, but I don't remember anything about it, except I remember being put on a stretcher and being carried down the stairs and how hard it was for them to get me around the corners. I remember trying to say, Wait a minute, fellas, I'll walk to the door, but I wasn't able to speak, much less walk.

This was the twenty-second of September. They took me to Westlake Community Hospital and a Dr. Sherman Hershfield took my case and Joe and his wife Marion came to see me, but I don't remember any of this. I'm told I was so out of it they couldn't tell if I'd suffered any paralysis or not. They did figure I had suffered a stroke. Joe says he tried to get through to me to find out how to get hold of my son, but he finally had to figure it out for himself.

I was in intensive care for four days and my senses gradually returned to me. I had a terrible time talking at first. I'd try to tell a nurse I had to go to the bathroom and all I could get out was "go . . . to . . . the. . . ." Do you know how hard it can be to say the word "bathroom"? Or how frustrating and frightening it can be not to be able to make yourself understood for the first time in your adult life, not to know what had happened and what was happening to you? I was terrified. I tried to write what I wanted and couldn't control my hands. I was sick with fear.

When you suffer a stroke, an artery (or arteries) leading to the brain has become blocked or broken and the brain is not receiving the proper supply of blood. Sometimes the blood finds other arteries, a new route to the brain, and sometimes it does not. How much damage is suffered depends on how much and how long the brain is starved.

Joe says that for a few days they considered doing an angiogram in which a fluid would be pumped through my veins so they could see on an X-ray machine what had happened and decide if surgery to correct the condition was required. This is a risky process, however, and they hesitate to do it while the patient is in trouble. They decided not to do it with me at that point.

Suddenly I started talking again. And when I started, I talked a blue streak. Joe says I didn't make much sense. I thought I was making sense, but he says I sounded drunk. He'd ask me something and my answer would not make sense. He was trying to get my finances in order so my bills would be paid and he'd ask me what I had in a certain bank and I'd insist I had twelve dollars in the bank, but he found out I had twelve thousand. He'd ask me if I remembered the concert and I'd say, oh, that was last month.

Also I was using profanity all the time. I'll let loose with a cuss word once in a while when I'm intense about something, but I'm not given to stringing four-letter words together. I got flowers and I'd say, "Fix those fucking flowers," and things like that. I kept saying, "Oh, shit."

And I had hallucinations. I have a dog, Buffy, and I'd start to see him in bed with me, a little bundle of fluff, and I'd ask what "my fucking dog" was doing there. I saw smiling faces coming at me.

One time I saw a man in bed with me. He was a very handsome man, fully dressed but with a marvelous body, and I was mad because I was so sick and helpless I couldn't get to him to have intercourse with him.

When I told Dr. Hershfield, he thought that was very funny and he kept asking me later if my lover had returned. He said it was not uncommon for those having suffered strokes to hallucinate and curse abnormally, though they didn't know why.

Joe had a friend who had suffered a stroke and cursed constantly. I heard of an aging nun who suffered one and kept saying "son of a bitch, son of a bitch" over and over again. I suppose some repressions are released, but no one knows.

Freud claimed sexual thoughts, even repressed, motivate us, whether we know it or not. This suggests that, though I don't know.

But I was out of intensive care by the fifth day and started to talk better and more sensibly and with less cursing and fewer hallucinations every day.

Day by day I improved until I was back to normal. They had me doing mathematics tables and so forth and after a while I was doing them better than ever. Day by day I felt better and better and a lot of the fear left me. Joe was there every day and he encouraged me and helped me a good deal.

Dr. Hershfield was marvelous to me. He really cared and I am really grateful. He not only gave me more than the average doctor would, but since I was released he has kept in touch with me and made himself available to me and spent time with me and made sure I made it all the way back.

I never was a pill-popper, but when I felt sick I took different pills that had been prescribed for this or that over the years and it may have hurt me. Dr. Hershfield has me on specific, limited medication, a specific, limited diet, and a little exercise. He says I have made a full recovery and run no greater risk of a recurrence than anyone else does after suffering a stroke.

However, once you have suffered one, it stays in your mind and scares you. I was out of the hospital in about ten or twelve days—the fourth of October—and rested and did not work for about six weeks. I was worried that I would not be able to work again, but the doctor assured me I'd be able to work as well as ever and Joe set about getting bookings for me to build up my confidence.

We did keep it secret for a while because we wanted people to see how well I could work again before they found

out I had suffered a stroke. They could easily become afraid
to book me and I would be out of business. I talk about it now
because it is an important part of my life and because I want
others who suffer strokes to know that you can come out of it
without damage. Just as I speak about my tumors because I
want those who have them to know they can be benign, they
can be taken out, and you can be healthy again.

You have to be lucky, I suppose. I have had my problems,
but I have been lucky. There are strokes and there are
strokes. Some are fatal. Some do a lot of damage, leaving their
victims unable to speak or walk. Some do a little damage. And
some do not seem to leave any residual damage. I suffered no
impairment of my motion or speech.

I went back to work on November 11, about six weeks after
I was stricken. I went to Las Vegas to tape the "Second
Annual Juke Box Awards," which would air on NBC television on the eighteenth. The producers were not told I had
been sick because if they knew they might not take a chance
with me and this was a wonderful way to get national exposure and prove I was fine.

It was a difficult show to do because I not only had to sing a
song, "I've Heard That Song Before," but sing some special
material off cue cards I never had seen before and punch but-
tons on a jukebox to bring on Cab Calloway, Chuck Berry,
Fabian, and others singing their old hits. I had to sing that old
song of mine with different endings, which was difficult.

I was scared half to death I wouldn't sing well, but I am told
I sang better than ever. If I'd made any sort of mistake, even
the kind I might normally make, I'd have blamed it on having
suffered a stroke, but I did not make any mistakes and the
show went off without a hitch.

Joe talks to a lot of agents all the time and none knew I had
had a problem, but all said I looked good and sang great. I
guess I sang well enough. And I have been singing better ever
since, maybe better than ever.

I have gone on tough tours since. It is tough, but after all I am sixty-four. I do not feel sixty-four. Maybe fifty-four. Or forty-four. Let's face it, the old girl is no kid now. But the old girl can still go. Many my age would not admit their age, but I think every time I step on a stage I am young again. I think my performances prove I can still sing with anyone, even those many years younger.

What scares me is being alone—in my house at home, in a room on the road. If Joe had not called me and I had not picked up the phone and he had not realized I was not making sense I have no doubt I would be dead today. But that is the chance a lot of us have to take, especially late in life when we are left alone. Joe goes on the road with me when he can and calls me every day wherever I am. He is more than my manager, he is my friend. He rescued my career and kept it alive and he kept me alive.

JOE GRAYDON

The first time I saw Helen Forrest, I was lying on the beach in Atlantic City, New Jersey. I was a teenager who had made my annual pilgrimage to that resort for the express purpose of spending each night on the Steel Pier listening to the music of the big bands, which I dearly loved. Helen, Dick Haymes, and Harry James were walking on the beach and they came within a few feet of me as I was working on my summer tan. To me, they were superstars. I longed to be a singer. I longed to sing with a band. I saw them at night, singing with Harry James and, a couple of years later, I saw Helen singing on the Million Dollar Pier. She was always the greatest to me.

I sang with bands in high school and in college, enough so that I was able to pay my tuition and buy the books I needed to get me through law school. I attended college in Washington, D.C., where I was born. World War II was just beginning when

I graduated and the FBI was looking for people with law degrees. I believe there were one hundred people in my graduating class and it seemed as though about ninety of us ended up working for J. Edgar Hoover. I had just turned twenty-two and the age limit was twenty-five. To this day, I believe that I am the youngest person ever to be accepted as an FBI agent.

I spent six years in the Bureau and it was a great education but all I really wanted to do was sing. I had made up my mind to pursue a singing career as soon as the war ended. To that end I requested a transfer to the New York City field office. At least I would be in the Big Apple and maybe I could, somehow, land a singing job. Some of my friends from the bands I had sung with had located in Manhattan and through the recommendation of one of them, I had a chance to cut a V-disc with a rather well-known singer, Marie Green. We did two duets, "Easy to Remember" and "It Had to Be You." They were a huge success overseas and I was asked to do more of them, which I did. An agent, in trying to sell Marie Green, had sent copies of these V-discs to all of the major advertising agencies in New York. Foote, Cone & Belding, one of the biggest ad agencies, heard my voice and told the agent they were interested in me. He didn't even know my name and it took him three days to find me. Small wonder, I was still in the Bureau and actively engaged in "tailing" Russian espionage agents.

When I met with the ad agency they asked me to come to a rehearsal of the Lucky Strike Hit Parade show and they would record my voice with Mark Warnow's Orchestra. I did. They liked it and the next week I was singing on the Hit Parade along with Johnny Mercer and Joan Edwards. Not a bad way to start in show business. I resigned from the Bureau immediately.

Since I was a total unknown they decided on a gimmick. I was given three solos each week, as were Johnny Mercer and Joan Edwards. However when they introduced me they would say, Number 2, "It Might As Well Be Spring . . . Sing it, Joe." Quite naturally with an audience of that magnitude, thousands of letters were received asking the identity of "Sing it,

Joe," but few ever found out. I was on the show until Johnny Mercer left it, which was almost six months. I was still "Sing it, Joe" and they never fully introduced me. The week after I left the show I sang on another very big radio show, We the People, and they divulged my true identity.

Singing was good to me. I moved to California where I first was given a contract by Warner Brothers' Studio. Then someone decided I was too much like Bing Crosby. I ended up making a settlement with them so that I could be released to do my own television show. I was on the air two hours a day, five days a week, and one half-hour nighttime show weekly. This lasted for about five years and it was great because I had excellent musicians behind me. Only five, but they were super.

During this time I had an opportunity to record with Gordon Jenkins and the first side we did together was "Again." It went to the top, became number one, and stayed there for an uncommonly long period of time. I made a number of other records for Decca and Coral Records but "Again" was the only one that really made it. I am one of the few guys who can honestly say, "I would like to sing you a medley of my hit."

When rock 'n' roll music came upon the scene, I decided to "turn in my uniform." I knew that I couldn't sing that kind of music and I had always harbored a secret desire to get on the other side of the business. I honestly felt that with a law degree and six years of experience in the FBI, I could do much more than just sing a song. I also wanted to be able to grow old gracefully and not worry about my later years. I decided to become a personal manager. My personal manager, while I was singing, was Tom Sheils, and I had learned a great deal from him. We are still very close friends and work on some mutual deals from time to time.

The last venture I had, before I quit singing, was to become part owner of a nightclub in Long Beach, California. I had a good following from all of my television exposure and some businessmen offered to put up the bulk of the money if I would front the club for them and hire the entertainment. Can you

guess who my first star was when we opened that club? Helen
Forrest! Helen packed the club every night and I think she
stayed with us for four weeks.

Helen and I became very close friends at that time, and from
time to time I would drop in on her when she was singing in the
Los Angeles area. Always, she would sing "Happiness Is Just a
Thing Called Joe" and dedicate it to me. We were pals.

It's no surprise, then, that when she was looking for someone
to represent her, she came to me. I had known Billy Burton and
liked him. I also knew that he was a fine manager and had
acquired great respect in the industry. I don't mind telling you
that I was flattered when, after his death, one by one, his best
clients gravitated to me. The Mary Kaye Trio, Dick Haymes,
Helen Forrest, and a fine comic impressionist, Dick Kerr.

It was very tough getting Helen's career launched again for
several reasons. Rock 'n' roll was still very much in existence
and nostalgia was not in at all. She was at an "in-between" stage
in her career. Not young enough to be current. Not old enough
to be nostalgia.

I remember the first engagement I secured for her was
through an agent in Chicago. He offered me $700 a week for her
to sing at a club called Mangam's Chateau. It was small money
but we had to get her back in circulation again. It was also seven
nights a week, but Helen did it and she killed them. If memory
serves me correctly, she was there for four months.

I was determined to get Helen into Las Vegas as I felt being
seen there could profit her enormously. For one thing, she had
gained a lot of weight while singing with the Frank Sinatra, Jr.,
package and had subsequently lost it all. I drove her to Las
Vegas with me and told her that we were going to have everyone see how great she looked and that we were going to get her
a booking in that town.

Day and night we went from hotel to hotel seeking out the
entertainment directors, all of whom I knew. I made certain that
they all saw her and we "scored" when I introduced her to
Maynard Sloate, the entertainment director at the Tropicana

Hotel. After much negotiating, via the mails and telephone calls, it was decided to put Helen into their Blue Room lounge with comedian Louis Nye. The engagement was a huge success and we began to pick up momentum. Next it was Harold's Club, in Reno, where she became an annual four-week attraction and the most successful in the history of that club.

By this time, nostalgia was beginning to happen and it has been getting stronger and stronger ever since. All of the hard work with Helen is over for me. Whereas I used to spend hours each day trying to sell her to the booking agents who actually get the dates, I now do little more than answer the phone and take orders. Oh, of course I fight like hell to keep getting her more money but I no longer have to fight to get her jobs.

Helen has been with me longer than any other client. Seventeen years. I can remember when our first contract, between us, was about to run out. We were at CBS and she was doing someone's TV show. We went to the coffee shop for a snack, before makeup, and she reminded me that our contract was about to run out. With tears in her eyes she asked me if I was going to sign another contract with her. I said, "Of course, how long do you want to make it for." She said, "As long as the law allows." I said, "Seven years." She said, "Seven years it is." Then we both had tears in our eyes.

Years later we went through that same scene when that contract was about to expire. I don't know where we stand, contractually, at this date, and I don't think she's worried about it. I believe she feels as I do, that this one's for life.

Our relationship has become much more than manager and client. Helen will be the first to tell you that she doesn't trust many people. In fact, she has told me on many occasions that I am the only person whom she really trusts. It tickled me when she moved back to California and bought her current home. The real estate agent had taken her through the house and she fell in love with it. The agent said, "Well, then why don't we make the deal?" "Not until my manager sees it and gives it the okay," said Helen. Are you beginning to understand the rela-

232

tionship? Let me go a step farther. I am also the executor of her estate. Hell, if I were Jewish, I think I'd be her rabbi.

If any of us could have seen what went on in Helen's bedroom, while she was battling for her life against a stroke, it might have been too much for television. I went to her home immediately after leaving her, the first day she was taken to the Intensive Care Unit of the Westlake Community Hospital. The sight of her bedroom made me stop in my tracks. If you can't stand the sight of blood that room was not the place for you. There were large smears of blood on the wall entering the bath approximately four feet from the left side of her bed. There was more blood in the bathroom. It was on the sink and on the cabinet walls to the right of and under the sink. It was in streaks as though she had grasped the wall with a bloody hand and fallen against the bathroom cabinet. She apparently had been staggering around the room.

She recalls very little of this, only that she began knocking things over in an attempt to get to the phone when I called her. Her suitcase, from the engagement from which she had returned, in San Francisco, was partially unpacked and things were generally strewn all over the room. To use an old cliché it literally looked as if a cyclone had hit it. Every object that could have been standing, lamps, clocks, photographs, every one of them was on the floor.

What a terrible ordeal she must have been going through at the time I called. The only words which she could utter, weakly, over and over again, for almost an hour, were "Jesus Christ, oh my God."

"Helen, do you know who I am?" I would ask in a strong voice.

"Jesus Christ, oh my God."

"Don't stop talking, Helen. And keep listening to me."

"Jesus Christ, oh my God."

In the background, over her mutterings, I heard the paramedics enter the house and begin yelling "Helen, Helen?" My wife had given them her name. They took the phone and told me that they would call me as soon as they had run some experimental tests on her. Within minutes they called back with the diagnosis—a stroke. Marion and I were soon speeding toward the hospital in Westlake, some thirty miles away.

There were times during her recovery when I feared for her future, but she has made a remarkable recovery. She now is her old self again.

Helen Forrest is someone very special to me. She has often told me how proud she is to have me represent her. Can you imagine how proud I am to represent her? For the style she sings, she is, in my mind, the greatest of all, and I feel that Helen is singing better than she ever has, and that, as Variety put it, qualifies her as being "a phenomenon." And I was a singer. And I have very well tuned ears. I know whereof I speak.

20.

When I was young with braces on my dentures,
Upon the threshold of life's great adventures,
While other girls around me
Sat sewing all the day . . .
And waited for their prince to come
And carry them away
The only thing I dreamed about
Was how to sell a song.

. . .

When all is said and done,
It's been oodles of fun,
And I'm sure that you'll all understand,
When I remember it,
I'm not sorry a bit,
That I had to sing with a band.

SOME TIME AGO I had six weeks of one-nighters with Joe Graydon's "Fabulous Forties" package with me, Andy Russell, the Pied Pipers, and Bill Green and his band with the music of

Tommy Dorsey and Gene Krupa. We went by bus and we did close to forty shows with few nights off. We went all through the South, the East, the Midwest, small towns, big towns, and it was tough, I want to tell you. I don't know how many more of these tours I can take. I think this one was the last one. But I've said that before.

Before that I did eight straight weeks on the road by bus—forty-eight shows, California to New York—in another "Fabulous Forties" tour with the Dorsey-Krupa band and the Pied Pipers, but this last one was with Andy Russell. And before that I did many months with "The Big broadcast of 1944" with Harry and his band, Hildegarde, Dick before he died, the Ink Spots, Don Wilson announcing. We covered the country. And before that I toured with the big band package with the Bob Crosby band and the Freddie Martin band.

I get three thousand to four thousand dollars for a one-nighter. It's just that there aren't that many of them, so when I get three thousand to four thousand dollars a week for a tour that's going to last six to eight weeks it's hard to turn down that sort of money; that can be a nest egg for the day the old girl gives up.

I got nice money for two private parties for some very wealthy people and the husband gave me a gift of a quarter-inch gold chain. The house was so big they had two Christmas trees. They had a sit-down dinner for eighteen people. Afterwards, I was the entertainment, backed by a trio. Then the wife wanted me to come back for a surprise birthday present for her husband. There was another big sit-down dinner, and above my pay, I was given a bonus check.

I mention the money only because I want you to have an accurate idea of what show business can be for a performer. There are not many wealthy people who throw private parties with real entertainment. I'm not saying I would work for these people for free, but I want to say that these are really nice people or I would not work for them.

Joe Graydon rescued my career. I was down in the dumps,

236

working for seven hundred a night, and lucky to get one night's work in two weeks when he came along. He took me on when times were tough. When he couldn't get me much work, he'd call me to console me. He'd tell me no one like me was working and it was true.

He created a demand. He put me and many like me back to work. Now I can get seven thousand dollars for two nights' work, and I can get two nights a week, two weeks a month, six months a year. I can work today and put money aside for tomorrow. I am far from rich, but I am not far from being safe from the future.

The past is slipping away, but the future looks all right. Joe saved my life, as well as my career. And my career remains my life.

There are a few one-nighters when I can make good money without traveling out of the area. I worked some once with Tex Beneke and the Glenn Miller band at Pasadena and a couple with the Beneke bunch in L.A. and Ontario. I've played Disneyland a few times too. The big bands play there.

There may be a couple of tours a year. I can make good money with them. But there are not many of them. I can't play the same towns every year.

Looking at it realistically, I have to say that I am no longer a prominent performer. I suppose it's because I sing the old songs. I'm not on television enough and I seldom play the big places in the big cities. But I get a warm response wherever I play and I still seem to be able to entertain the public.

I have old fans and a wonderful fan club that show up wherever I am putting on a show. I seem to make new fans wherever I sing. Kids come to me after shows to tell me their parents had to drag them down to see me, but they're coming back to see me on their own the next time I'm in town.

I haven't been making records so only those radio stations that play music from the Big Band Era play my old records. I understand that there are now 900 stations, from coast to coast, that are playing the music of the big bands and that I am being prominently featured on these stations. I'd like to record again, new songs or old.

I can't explain why, but I feel like I am singing better than ever. At my age most singers have lost something, but my voice is stronger and clearer than ever and my range is wider than ever. I still love what I'm doing and I'd love for more people to hear me.

According to my discography, I recorded 207 sides over eighteen years with the bands between 1938 and 1942 and on my own from 1944 through 1955. I have not recorded very much in the last twenty-five years. In 1955 I recorded four big band songs with Harry for Capitol and the following year Capitol issued my *Voice of the Name Bands* album, on which I reprised my hits with Artie, Benny, and Harry as well as a couple of songs from the late forties.

In 1964 RCA Victor recorded the Tommy Dorsey band under the direction of Sam Donahue "live" at the Americana Hotel and I was featured on four numbers. I was reunited with Harry again in 1969, and 1970 when *Reader's Digest* asked us to record four of the band's hits for the first time in stereo sound, as well as four recent popular songs.

A couple of years later I took that flight to London to record four more selections for *Reader's Digest* with magnificent arrangements by Alan Copeland. About the same time Time-Life Records were putting together new packages of the big band hits using the old arrangements. Under the guidance of Billy May many of the original artists were invited to re-create their successful songs. I did two from my association with Harry's band, and one each from Artie's and Benny's catalogs.

Many of my earlier recordings have been reissued in countless LP packages by the original record companies. And also by pirates, who bootleg the records, using cheap material and packaging. Even recorded airchecks from my radio remotes have been turned into LPs, mostly without my permission. There are a lot of thieves out there and I don't get a dime from most of them. It makes me mad, but what can I do?

In 1978 I did a three-hour "Big Band Bash" with Harry and Dick and the bands for public television and the show is reshown from time to time. In recent years I've been on the Johnny Carson show, the Mike Douglas show, and the Merv Griffin show on commercial TV.

Mike and Merv are former big band singers, too. I do Merv's show whenever he takes a nostalgic look back at the big bands, which he does once in a while. The last time I did one, I was on with Harry, but we worked separately. I mentioned my book to Merv. When he asked what I had to say about Harry I said I described him as not only the world's greatest trumpeter, but the world's greatest lover. Merv loved it. So did Harry.

Hopefully, I'll get to do these shows again when this book comes out, to promote it and to promote me.

You can consider it corny if you want, but when I say singing is my life, I mean it, and it's true.

I wouldn't be satisfied to sing in the shower. I can understand how a talent like Artie can put down his clarinet and not pick it up again for twenty years. He doesn't want to perform in public so he doesn't bother to play. But I have to perform in public or I'd be incomplete. I won't sing without an audience—I love an audience.

There are moments I've had out there that no one ever can take away from me.

There was one night I remember when I was working with a big band package at Madison Square Garden. They packed the place with seventeen thousand people. They were enormously enthusiastic. It was as good as the good old days.

They had a revolving stage. Old Helen, she was afraid it would revolve her right into the upper seats. I had them slow it to a crawl and still was hanging on for dear life. I was afraid to work alone at center stage, so I leaned on the piano for my life. There were spotlights hitting me from everywhere. I didn't know where I was. That old devil vertigo.

When the stage started to turn, I started to panic. I leaned against the piano and hung on to the microphone. When the music came up, I started to sing. I sang, "I Had the Craziest Dream," "I've Heard That Song Before," "I Cried for You," all the old songs. I also did "I Wish I Could Shimmy Like My Sister Kate," and a few things like that which I throw in for good measure these days.

I had no idea how well I'd done. When I finished there was silence, so I figured I'd done badly. I wanted to get off in the worst way. I almost did. I had to wait for the stage to reach the point where the steps were, but the spotlight was blinding me and I couldn't see the steps. The producer understood my problem and climbed to the top of the steps, waited for the right moment, and yelled for me to make my move. I let go of the piano and lunged at him and he almost missed me, which would have sent me crashing down the stairs, but he hung on somehow and helped me down.

I was shaking with humiliation, hurried to my dressing room, closed the door behind me, and hid my face in my hands. I was so disappointed in myself, so discouraged. Suddenly William B. Williams, the New York disc jockey, was pounding on the door, demanding I open it. I did and he came in, followed by Steve Lawrence and Eydie Gormé. Eydie said, "What are you doing? Get back out there!

I said, "No way. I'm not going back on that stage again. Anyway, I flopped."

"Flopped?" Eydie screamed. "Flopped? You're the hit of the night. They're going crazy out there. They want you to take a bow."

"But, the silence . . ." I started.

"They were stunned. As you left, they burst into an ovation. Didn't you hear it? They're still cheering."

I hadn't heard anything. I couldn't believe it.

"Go on," Steve said.

"Go on," Bill said.

I went.

I couldn't go back up on that stage, but I came out of the entranceway and the spotlights found me. People were standing and applauding me and yelling for me. Seventeen thousand people were going crazy over me. I couldn't believe it and I will never forget it.

I stood there bowing and crying. They wanted me to do an encore, but I couldn't. I was shaken. It was the thrill of my life and I will never forget it. The cheers just went on and on.

I have not had any other moment like that, but I've had a few that came close. I think most people never have any like that in their lives. I think I've been very lucky. Singing has been my life and I have enjoyed my life.

It has cost me a lot, but it has brought me a lot. It is hard to believe the best part was forty years or so ago, a fast five years or so at the start, but I have had more good years than bad years since, more good times than bad times. I live for today. I look ahead to tomorrow, but it is nice sometimes to look back to yesterday.

We did not know we were living through an era—the Big Band Era—that would last only ten years or so and be remembered and revered forever. We were just getting by, day by day, trying to make the most of every day, trying to get through the days and the nights somehow, do good work and earn a living. Before we knew it, it was over.

We talk about the good old days, but many of them were not that good. Not with those bus rides in soiled, sweaty clothes, sleeping in our seats or in some shabby hotel room, eating greasy hamburgers and drinking cold coffee out of paper cups, the guys getting drunk on bad booze or stoned on marijuana in an effort to save their sanity, moving wearily from one show to another, from one cramped, hot dressing room to another, too many shows, too little sleep. And, for the traveling performer, it hasn't changed that much.

But we did have good old days. And still have good days. We did the shows and we do them and there were and are nights when the music is magic and we and the audience were and are a family with real love for one another. There is always the music, and as long as I can make it, it is marvelous. And there are nights never to be forgotten.

Like when a red light flashes in a hotel room when you are in the arms of your lover.

I've Heard That Song Before

Music helps me to remember,
It helps to remind me
Of things behind me.
Tho' I'm better off forgetting,
I try in vain
Each time I hear that strain.

It seems to me
I've heard that song before,
It's from an old familiar score
I know it well, that melody.
It's funny how a theme
Recalls a favorite dream,
A dream that brought you so close to me.
I know each word
Because I've heard that song before.
The lyric said "Forever more,"
Forever more's a memory.
Please have them play it again
And I'll remember just when
I've heard that lovely song before.

Discography
Compiled and Edited by
Robert A. Sixsmith

SECTION A

COMMERCIAL RECORDINGS

PART 1
Vocalist with Artie Shaw's Band—Studio Material

	Matrix	Recorded	Bluebird	LP Reissue
		New York		
1. "You're a Sweet Little Head-ache"	027233-1	9/27/38	B-7889	RCA 908 AXM2-5517 J6002
2. "I Have Eyes"	027234-1	9/27/38	B-7889	AXM2-5517 RD 25-K J6002
3. "Between a Kiss and a Sigh"	028973-1	11/17/38	B-10055	SOS 123 AXM2-5517 J6002
4. "Thanks for Everything"	028974-1	11/17/38	B-10055	SOS 118 AXM2-5517 J6002
5. "Deep in a Dream"	028975-1	11/17/38	B-10046	RCA 6702 RCA 6039 SOS 123 AXM2-5517 J6002

	Matrix	Recorded	Bluebird	LP Reissue
6. "Day after Day"	028976-1	11/17/38	B-10046	SOS 123 AXM2-5517 J6002
7. "A Room with a View"	030731-1	12/19/38	B-10075	RCA 465 SOS 123 AXM2-5517 J6002
8. "Say It with a Kiss"	030732-1	12/19/38	B-10079	SOS 123 AXM2-5517 J6002
9. "They Say"	030733-1	12/19/38	B-10075	RCA 6702 SOS 123 AXM-2-5517 J6002
10. "It Took a Million Years"	030734-1	12/19/38	B-10079	RCA 6702 SOS 123 AXM2-5517 J6002
11. "Supper Time"	031494-1	1/17/39	B-10127	RCA 515 AXM2-5517 J6002
12. "Bill"	031825-1	1/23/39	B-10124	RCA 515 Tulip 106 AXM2-5517 J6002
13. "I Want My Share of Love"	031866-1	1/31/39	B-10134	SOS 101 AXM2-5533 J6008
14. "It's All Yours"	031867-1	1/31/39	B-10141	RCA 515 AXM2-5533 J6008
15. "This Is It"	031868-1	1/31/39	B-10141	RCA 515 AXM2-5533 J6008
16. "Any Old Time"	032961-2	3/12/39	Victor 20-1575	SOS 116 Tulip 106 AXM2-5533 J6008
17. "I'm in Love with the Honorable Mr. So and So"	032962-1	3/12/39	Bluebird B-10188	RCA 584 SOS 123 AXM2-5533 J6008
18. "Deep Purple"	032964-1	3/12/39	B-10178	RCA 1648 RCA 6701

	Matrix	Recorded	Bluebird	LP Reissue
				RCA 6039
				RCA 2151
				AXM2-5533
				J6008
19. "You Grow Sweeter As the Years Go By"	032999-1	3/17/39	B-10195	SOS 123
				AXM2-5533
				J6008
20. "You're So Indifferent"	035300-1	3/17/39	B-10215	SOS 101
				AXM2-5533
				J6008
21. "If Ever You Change Your Mind"	035302-1	3/17/39	B-10195	SOS 123
				AXM2-5533
				J6008
		Hollywood		
22. "I Poured My Heart into a Song"	036238-4	6/5/39	B-10307	RCA 584
				SOS 123
				AXM2-5533
				J6008
23. "All I Remember Is You"	036240-1	6/5/39	B-10319	RCA 1570
				SOS 123
				AXM2-5533
				J6008
24. "Comes Love"	036265-17	6/12/39	B-10324	RCA 1570
				AXM2-5533
				J6008
25. "A Man and His Dream"	036267-2	6/12/39	B-10347	RCA 1648
				RCA 6701
				AXM2-5533
26. "Easy to Say"	036291-9	6/22/39	B-10345	SOS 116
				AXM2-5533
27. "I'll Remember"	036292-7	6/22/39	B-10345	SOS 116
				AXM2-5533
28. "Moon ray"	036293-3	6/22/39	B-10334	AXM2-5533
29. "Melancholy Mood"	036294-5	6/22/39	B-10334	SOS 101
				AXM2-5533
		New York		
30. "Day In, Day Out"	042606-1	8/27/39	B-10406	RCA 584
				SOS 123
				AXM2-5556
				RDA-49
31. "Two Blind Loves"	042607-1	8/27/39	B-10412	SOS 123
				AXM2-5556
32. "The Last Two Weeks in July"	042608-1	8/27/39	B-10412	SOS 123
				AXM2-5556

	Matrix	Recorded	Bluebird	LP Reissue
33. "Many Dreams Ago"	042755-1	9/28/39	B-10446	SOS 117 AXM2-5556
34. "A Table in the Corner"	042756-1	9/28/39	B-10468	AXM2-5556
35. "Without a Dream to My Name"	042758-1	9/28/39	B-10468	SOS 101 AXM2-5556
36. "Love Is Here"	043316-1	10/26/39	B-10482	SOS 118 AXM2-5556
37. "All in Fun"	043317-1	10/26/39	B-10492	RCA 515 AXM2-5556
38. "All the Things You Are"	043318-1	10/26/39	B-10492	RCA 1244 RCA 6701 RCA 3675 RCA 6039 RCA 1089 AXM2-5556
39. "I Didn't Know What Time It Was"	043368-1	11/9/39	B-10502	RCA 515 RCA 6062 AXM2-5556
40. "Do I Love You?"	043369-1	11/9/39	B-10509	RCA 515 RD-25-K AXM2-5556
41. "When Love Beckoned"	043370-1	11/9/39	B-10509	SOS 123 AXM2-5556

Long-Play Reissues of Artie Shaw's Band—Studio Material

SONGS SUNG BY HELEN FORREST	ALBUM
RCA Victor LPM–1244 (mono) (1956) "All the Things You Are"	Moonglow
RCA Victor LPM–1570 (mono) (1958) "All I Remember Is You" "Comes Love"	Any Old Time
RCA Victor LPM–1648 (mono) (1958) (also subsequently reissued under same number in mono and electronically reprocessed stereo [stereo (e)] under title *Reissued by Request* with different cover) "A Man and His Dream" "Deep Purple"	A Man and His Dream

I Had the Craziest Dream

SONGS SUNG BY HELEN FORREST	ALBUM

RCA Victor LPM-6701 (mono) (1959)
(a 5-record boxed set)
  "All the Things You Are"
  "A Man and His Dream"
  "Deep Purple"
	The Swingin' Mr. Shaw

RCA Camden CAL/CAS-465 (mono/stereo) (e) (1959) "A Room with a View"	The Great Artie Shaw

RCA Camden CAL-515 (mono) (1959)
  "I Didn't Know What Time It Was"
  "Bill"
  "Supper Time"
  "It's All Yours"
  "Do I Love You?"
  "This Is It"
  "All in Fun"
	Artie Shaw Swings
	  Show Tunes

RCA Victor LPM-6702 (mono) (1962)
  "It Took a Million Years"
  "Deep in a Dream"
  "They Say"
	Ten Great Bands
	  (5-record set)

RCA Camden CAL/CAS-584 (mono/stereo) (e)
  "I Poured My Heart into a Song"
  "I'm in Love with the Honorable Mr. So and
    So"
  "Day In, Day Out"
	One Night Stand
	  (1963)

RCA Camden CAL/CAS-908 (mono/stereo) (e)
  "You're a Sweet Little Headache"
	September Song
	  (1965)

Reader's Digest RD-25-K (mono/stereo) (e)
  (RCA Custom) (10-record set) (1965)
  "I Have Eyes"
  "Do I Love You?"
	The Great Band Era
	  (1936–1945)

RCA Victor LSP-3675 (stereo) (e) (1967) "All the Things You Are"	The Best of Artie Shaw

Reader's Digest Set (RCA Custom)
  RDA-49 (stereo) [e] (1968)
  "Day In, Day Out"
	Hear Them Again
	  (10-record set)

RCA Victor VPM-6039 (mono) (1971)
  "Deep Purple"
  "All the Things You Are"
  "Deep in a Dream"
	This Is Artie Shaw
	  Vol. 1

RCA Victor VPM-6062 (mono) (1972)
  "I Didn't Know What Time It Was"
	This Is Artie Shaw
	  Vol. 2

Sounds of Swing LP-101 (mono) (1973)
  "You're So Indifferent"
  "I Want My Share of Love"
  "Melancholy Mood"
  "Without a Dream to My Name"
	The Big Band Years

249

SONGS SUNG BY HELEN FORREST	ALBUM
Sounds of Swing LP-116 (mono) (1974) "Easy to Say" "I'll Remember" "Any Old Time"	The Ballad Years
Sounds of Swing LP-117 (mono) (1974) "Many Dreams Ago"	The Vocal Years
Sounds of Swing LP-118 (mono) (1974) "Love Is Here" "Thanks for Everything"	The Dancing Years
Sounds of Swing LP-123 (mono) (1974) "Day after Day" "Between a Kiss and a Sigh" "Say It with a Kiss" "The Last Two Weeks in July" "Two Blind Loves" "When Love Beckoned" "You Grow Sweeter As the Years Go By" "If You Ever Change Your Mind" "It Took a Million Years" "Deep in a Dream" "They Say" "I Poured My Heart into a Song" "I'm in Love with the Honorable Mr. So and So" "Day In, Day Out" "All I Remember Is You" "A Room with a View"	The Helen Forrest Years
RCA ANL1-1089 (stereo) (e) (1975) "All the Things You Are"	The Best of Artie Shaw
Tulip TLP-106 (mono) (1975) "Any Old Time" "Bill"	The Best of the Big Band Singers
RCA Bluebird AXM2-5517 (mono) (1976) "You're a Sweet Little Headache" "I Have Eyes" "Between a Kiss and a Sigh" "Thanks for Everything" "Deep in a Dream" "Day after Day" "A Room with a View" "Say It with a Kiss" "They Say" "It Took a Million Years" "Supper Time" "Bill"	The Complete Artie Shaw Vol. 1/1938–39 (2-record set)

I Had the Craziest Dream

SONGS SUNG BY HELEN FORREST	ALBUM
RCA ANL1-2151 (stereo) (e) (1977)	Backbay Shuffle
"Deep Purple"	
RCA Bluebird AXM2-5533 (mono) (1977)	The Complete Artie Shaw
"I Want My Share of Love"	Vol. 2/1939
"It's All Yours"	(2-record set)
"This Is It"	
"Any Old Time"	
"I'm in Love with the Honorable Mr. So and So"	
"Deep Purple"	
"You Grow Sweeter As the Years Go By"	
"You're So Indifferent"	
"If You Ever Change Your Mind"	
"I Poured My Heart into a Song"	
"All I Remember Is You"	
"Comes Love"	
"A Man and His Dream"	
"Easy to Say"	
"I'll Remember"	
"Moonray"	
"Melancholy Mood"	
RCA Bluebird AXM2-5556 (mono) (1978)	The Complete Artie Shaw
"Day In, Day Out"	Vol. 3/1939–40
"Two Blind Loves"	(2-record set)
"The Last Two Weeks in July"	
"Many Dreams Ago"	
"A Table in a Corner"	
"Without a Dream to My Name"	
"Love Is Here"	
"All in Fun"	
"All the Things You Are"	
"I Didn't Know What Time It Was"	
"Do I Love You?"	
"When Love Beckoned"	
Joyce 6002 (mono) (1981)	*The Big Bands' Greatest*
"You're a Sweet Little Headache"	*Vocalists Series*
"I Have Eyes"	*Helen Forrest*
"Between a Kiss and a Sigh"	*Vol. 1*
"Thanks for Everything"	
"Deep in a Dream"	
"Day after Day"	
"A Room with a View"	
"Say It with a Kiss"	
"They Say"	
"It Took a Million Years"	

251

"Supper Time"
"Bill"
Joyce 6008 (mono) (1981)
  "I Want My Share of Love"
  "It's All Yours"
  "This Is It"
  "I Cried for You"
  "Any Old Time"
  "Deep Purple"
  "I'm in Love with the Honorable Mr. So and
    So"
  "You Grow Sweeter As the Years Go By"
  "You're So Indifferent"
  "If You Ever Change Your Mind"
  "I Poured My Heart into a Song"
  "All I Remember Is You"
  "Comes Love"

*The Big Bands' Greatest
Vocalists Series
Helen Forrest
Vol. 2*

PART 2
Vocalist with Benny Goodman's Band— Studio Material

	Matrix	Recorded	Columbia	LP Reissue
		New York		
42. "Busy as a Bee (I'm Buzz Buzz Buzzin')"	26366A	12/27/39	35356	COL 32822
43. "What's the Matter with Me?"	26416A	1/16/40	35374	COL 32822
44. "What'll They Think of Next?"	26417A	1/16/40	35374	JAZUM 50
45. "How High the Moon"	26491A	2/7/40	35391	COL 534 P6-15536
46. "Let's All Sing Together"	26492A	2/7/40	35396	JAZUM 36
47. "The Fable of the Rose"	26493A	2/7/40	35391	COL 32822 CSM 890/891

	Matrix	Recorded	Columbia	LP Reissue
		Chicago		
48. "Shake Down the Stars"	2971A	3/1/40	35426	COL 32822
49. "Be Sure"	2972A	3/1/40	35426	JAZUM 36
50. "Yours Is My Heart Alone"	2973A	3/1/40	35445	COL 32822
51. "The Sky Fell Down"	2974A	3/1/40	35420	JAZUM 36
52. "It Never Entered My Mind"	2975A	3/1/40	35420	JAZUM 41
53. "Once More"	2976A	3/1/40	35543	JAZUM 42
		Los Angeles		
54. "Buds Won't Bud"	26714A	4/10/40	35472	JAZUM 41
55. "Devil May Care"	26715A	4/10/40	35461	JAZUM 41
56. "I'm Nobody's Baby"	26716A	4/10/40	35472	COL 32822 P6-15536
57. "I Can't Love You Anymore"	26739A	4/6/40	prev. unissued	NOST 7610
58. "Ev'ry Sunday Afternoon"	26741A	4/16/40	35461	JAZUM 41
59. "The Moon Won't Talk"	26808A	5/9/40	35487	COL 32822
60. "Mister Meadowlark"	26810A	5/9/40	35497	COL 32822
61. "I Can't Love You Anymore"	26811A	5/9/40	35487	JAZUM 42
62. "I Can't Resist You"	26980A	7/3/40	35574	JAZUM 50
63. "Dreaming Out Loud"	26981A	7/3/40	35574	JAZUM 50 P 14302
64. "Li'l Boy Love"	26982A	7/3/40	35594	JAZUM 50
		New York		
65. "Nobody"	29062-1		35820	COL 32822
	29062-alt	11/13/40	prev. unissued	NOST 7610
66. "The Man I Love"	29063-2	11/13/40	55001	COL 534 JAZUM 50
	29063-alt		prev. unissued	NOST 7610

	Matrix	Recorded	Columbia	LP Reissue
67. "Taking a Chance on Love"	29177-1	11/29/40	35869	COL 32822 V-8065 P6-15536 P6-14954 JC 36580 P6-6465
68. "Cabin in the Sky"	29178-2 29178-alt	11/29/40	35869 prev. unissued	COL 32822 NOST 7610
69. "Hard to Get"	29180-1 29180-alt	11/29/40	35863 prev. unissued	COL 32822 NOST 7612
70. "These Things You Left Me"	29255-1	12/18/40	35910	CSP 13618
71. "Yes, My Darling Daughter" with Benny Goodman, Cootie Williams and Chorus	29262-1 29262-2 29262-alt	12/20/40	prev. unissued 35910 prev. unissued	P6-15536 JAZUM 50 NOST 7612
72. "More Than You Know"	29257-1	12/18/40	55002	COL 523
73. "I'm Always Chasing Rainbows"	29274-1 29274-alt	12/20/40	35916 prev. unissued	JAZUM 42 NOST 7612
74. "I Left My Heart in Your Hand"	29276-1	12/20/40	35937	JAZUM 42
75. "I Hear a Rhapsody"	29503-1 29503-alt	1/14/41	35937 prev. unissued	JAZUM 42 NOST 7612
76. "It's Always You"	29504-1	1/14/41	36002	COL 32822
77. "Corn Silk"	29505-1 29505-alt	1/14/41	35992 prev. unissued	JAZUM 50 NOST 7612
78. "The Mem'ry of a Rose"	29532-1 29532-alt	1/21/41	35992 prev. unissued	JAZUM 51 NOST 7612
79. "Birds of a Feather"	29507-1 29507-alt	1/14/41	35977 prev. unissued	JAZUM 51 NOST 7612
80. "You're Dangerous"	29531-1 29531-alt	1/21/41	35977 prev. unissued	JAZUM 51 NOST 7612
81. "This Is New"	29577-1	1/28/41	35944	JAZUM 42

	Matrix	Recorded	Columbia	LP Reissue
82. "Bewitched"	29579-1	1/28/41	35944	COL 32822
				P6 15536
83. "Jenny"	unnumbered	1/28/41	prev.	T-1006
			unissued	
84. "Afraid to Say Hello"	unnumbered	1/28/41	unissued	—
85. "Perfidia"	29578-3	1/28/41	35962	COL 28994
	29578-1	1/28/41	unissued	M-11
86. "Lazy River"	29774-1	2/19/41	36012	COL 32822
87. "Yours"	29776-1	2/19/41	36067	COL 32822
				P6-15536
88. "You Lucky People You"	29777-1	2/19/41	36002	JAZUM 51
89. "Oh! Look at Me Now"	29862-1	3/4/41	36012	COL 32822
90. "My Sister and I"	29864-1	3/4/41	36022	JAZUM 42
91. "Amapola"	30069-1	3/27/41	36050	COL 32822
				V-8065
				P6-15536
92. "Good Evenin', Good Lookin'!"	30419-1	5/5/41	36136	JAZUM 42
93. "I Found a Million Dollar Baby"	30422-2	5/5/41	36136	JAZUM 42
94. "When the Sun Comes Out"	30598-1	6/4/41	36209	COL 32822
				P6-14538
95. "Smoke Gets in Your Eyes"	30599-1	6/4/41	36284	JAZUM 51
				P6-15536
96. "Soft As Spring"	30649-1	6/11/41	36219	COL 523
97. "Down, Down, Down (What a Song!)" with Ensemble	30650-2	6/11/41	36219	COL 32822
				P6-15536

Long-Play Reissues of Benny Goodman's Band— Studio Material

Columbia CL 523 (mono) (1951)
(also reissued by Columbia Special
Products under JGL 523) (1975)
"More Than You Know"
"Soft As Spring"

*Benny Goodman Presents
Arrangements by
Eddie Sauter*

Columbia CL 534 (mono) (1951)
"How High the Moon"
"The Man I Love"

Benny Goodman and His Orchestra

Columbia XTV 28994 (mono) (1958)
(for Texaco)
"Perfidia"

Swing Into Spring

Columbia Special Products CSM 890/891
(for Nostalgia Records) (mono) (1972)
"The Fable of the Rose"

Collectors' Gems 1929–1945
(2-record set)

Columbia KG 32822 (stereo) (e) (1974)
"Busy As a Bee (I'm Buzz Buzz Buzzin')"
"What's the Matter with Me?"
"The Fable of the Rose"
"Shake Down the Stars"
"Yours Is My Heart Alone"
"I'm Nobody's Baby"
"The Moon Won't Talk"
"Mister Meadowlark"
"Nobody"
"Taking a Chance on Love"
"Cabin in the Sky"
"Hard to Get"
"It's Always You"
"Bewitched"
"Lazy River"
"Yours"
"Oh! Look at Me Now"
"Amapola"
"When the Sun Comes Out"
"Down, Down, Down (What a Song!)"

Benny Goodman and Helen Forrest
The Original Recordings of the 1940's
(2-record set)

Jazum 36 (mono) (1974)
"Let's All Sing Together"
"Be Sure"
"The Sky Fell Down"

Benny Goodman and His Orchestra

Columbia House 6P 6465 (electronic stereo) (1974)
"Taking a Chance on Love"

The Music of Long Ago and Far Away

Jazum 41 (mono) (1976)
"It Never Entered My Mind"
"Devil May Care"
"Every Sunday Afternoon"
"Buds Won't Bud"

Benny Goodman and His Orchestra

Jazum 42 (mono) (1976)
"Once More"
"I Can't Love You Anymore"
"I'm Always Chasing Rainbows"
"I Left My Heart in Your Hand"

Benny Goodman and His Orchestra

I Had the Craziest Dream

"I Hear a Rhapsody"
"This Is New"
"My Sister and I"
"Good Evenin', Good Lookin'!"
"I Found a Million Dollar Baby"
Columbia Special Products P3-13618
  (for Nostalgia Book Club) (mono) (1976)
  "The Things You Left Me"
Jazum 50 (mono) (1977)
  "What'll They Think of Next?"
  "I Can't Resist You"
  "Dreaming Out Loud"
  "Li'l Boy Love"
  "The Man I Love"
  "Yes, My Darling Daughter"
  "Corn Silk"
Jazum 51 (mono) (1977)
  "Birds of a Feather"
  "You're Dangerous"
  "The Mem'ry of a Rose"
  "You Lucky People You"
  "Smoke Gets in Your Eyes"
Realm Records V 8064/8065 (stereo) (e)
  (for Vista Marketing) (TV) (1977)
  through Columbia Special Products
  "Taking a Chance on Love"
  "Amapola"
Columbia Special Products P 14302
  (mono) (1977)
  "Dreaming Out Loud"
Columbia Special Products P6 14538
  (stereo) (e) (1978)
  "Smokes Gets in Your Eyes"
Columbia Special Products P6 14954
  (stereo) (e) (1979)
  "Taking a Chance on Love"
Columbia Special Products P6 15536
  (stereo) (e) (1981)
  "How High the Moon"
  "I'm Nobody's Baby"
  "Taking a Chance on Love"
  "Yes, My Darling Daughter"
  "Bewitched"
  "Yours"
  "Amapola"
  "Smoke Gets in Your Eyes"
  "Down, Down, Down (What a Song!)"

Rare Big Band Gems
  1932–1947
  (3-record set)
Benny Goodman and His
  Orchestra

Benny Goodman and His
  Orchestra

Big Bands Forever!
  Four Kings of Swing
  (4-record set)

A Treasury of Sam Coslow
  Songs

Great Vocalists of
  The Big Band Era
  (6-record set)
Big Band Bash
  (6-record set)

The Legendary Benny
  Goodman
  (6-record set)

Columbia JC 36580 (mono) (1980)
"Taking a Chance on Love"

Let's Dance

Meritt 11 (mono) (1980)
"Perfidia"

The Reed Album
Vol. 2

Blu-Disc T-1006 (mono) (1981)
"Jenny"

The Un-Heard Benny Good-man—Vol. 3

Phontastic Nost 7610 (mono) (1981)
"I Can't Love You Anymore"
"Nobody"
"The Man I Love"
"Cabin in the Sky"

The Alternate Goodman
Vol. 2

Phontastic Nost 7612 (mono) (1981)
"Hard to Get"
"Yes, My Darling Daughter"
"I'm Always Chasing Rainbows"
"I Hear a Rhapsody"
"Corn Silk"
"Birds of a Feather"
"You're Dangerous"
"The Mem'ry of a Rose"

The Alternate Goodman
Vol. 3

PART 3
Guest Vocalist with Lionel Hampton's Band— Studio Material

	Matrix	Recorded	Victor	LP Reissue
		Hollywood		
98. "I'd Be Lost Without You"	049675-1	5/10/40	26751	RCA 6702 741.049 AXM6-5536
99. "(I Don't Stand) A Ghost of a Chance (with You)"	049935-1	7/17/40	26696	RCA 6702 741.049 AXM6-5536

Long-Play Reissues of Lionel Hampton's Band— Studio Material

RCA Victor LPM-6702 (mono) (1962)
"I'd Be Lost Without You"
"(I Don't Stand) A Ghost of a Chance (with You)"

Ten Great Bands
(5 -record set)

French RCA Black & White 741.049 (mono) (1972)
    "I'd Be Lost Without You"
    "(I Don't Stand) A Ghost of A Chance (with You)"

RCA Bluebird AXM6-5536 (mono) (1976)
    "I'd Be Lost Without You"
    "(I Don't Stand) A Ghost of a Chance (with You)"

More Hampton's Stuff Vol. 5)

The Complete Lionel Hampton (1937–1941) (6-record set)

PART 4
Vocalist with Harry James's Band— Studio Material

		Matrix	Recorded	Columbia	LP Reissue
			New York		
100.	"The Devil Sat Down and Cried" with Dick Haymes, Harry James, Dalton Rizzotto and Ensemble	31614-1	10/29/41	36466	6009 2P 6159 618
101.	"He's 1-A in the Army (and He's A-1 in My Heart)"	31615-1	10/29/41	36455	RD-4-139 618
102.	"Make Love to Me"	31618	10/29/41	36446	618
103.	"J. P. Dooley III" with Harry James, Dalton Rizzotto and Ensemble	31952-1	12/11/41	36487	620
104.	"I Don't Want to Walk Without You"	31954	12/11/41	36478	CD-2035 P6-14954 620
105.	"But Not for Me"	32074-1	12/30/41	36599	HL-7159 P-13585 620 XTV 82077

		Matrix	Recorded	Columbia	LP Reissue
106.	"I Remember You"	32345	1/29/42	36518	P6-14538 620
107.	"Skylark"	32347-1	1/29/42	36533	HL-7159 P 13585 CSS-1507 620
108.	"You're Too Good for Good-for-Nothing Me"	32618	3/19/42	36566	622
			Los Angeles		
109.	"You're in Love with Someone Else"	HCO-825-1	6/5/42	36614	622
110.	"He's My Guy"	HCO-827-1	6/5/42	36614	622
111.	"I Cried for You"	HCO-828-1	6/5/42	36623	622
112.	"That Soldier of Mine"	HCO-830-1	6/5/42	36650	622
113.	"I Heard You Cried Last Night"	HCO-853-1	7/18/42	36677	622
114.	"Manhattan Serenade"	HCO-854-1	7/18/42	36644	HL-7159 P 13585 624
115.	"My Beloved Is Rugged"	HCO-860-1	7/22/42	36729	624
116.	"I Had the Craziest Dream"	HCO-867-1	7/23/42	36659	COL 2630 CD-2035 8064 624
117.	"Mister Five by Five"	HCO-911-1	7/31/42	36650	624
118.	"I've Heard That Song Before"	HCO-912-1	7/31/42	36668	COL 2630 8064 A-8042 JC 36742 624

I Had the Craziest Dream

Long-Play Reissues of Harry James's Band— Studio Material

Columbia Harmony HL-7159 (mono) (1959)

Harry James and His Great Vocalists

Columbia Special Products P 13585
(stereo) (e) (1975)
"But Not for Me"
"Skylark"
"Manhattan Serenade"

Columbia Special Products XTV 82077
(mono) (1962)
"But Not for Me"

Famous Torch Songs of the 20's

Columbia CL-2630/CS-9430 (mono/stereo) (e)
(1967)
"I Had the Craziest Dream"
"I've Heard That Song Before"

Harry James' Greatest Hits

Columbia Special Products CSS-1507
(stereo) (e) (1972)
"Skylark"

Great Big Band Vocalists

Columbia House 2P 6159 (mono) (1974)
"The Devil Sat Down and Cried"

It's That Time Again
(2-record set)

Tele House CD-2035 (stereo) (e) (1974)
(Columbia Special Products P2-12621)
"I Had the Craziest Dream"
"I Don't Want to Walk Without You"

The Greatest Hits of The War Years
(2-record set)

Reader's Digest RD-4-139 (stereo) (e)
(1975)
"He's 1-A in the Army
(and He's A-1 in My Heart)"

Jukebox Saturday Night
(8-record set)

Adam VIII A-8042 (stereo) (e) (1977)
"I've Heard That Song Before"

The Best Years of Our Lives
(2-record set)

Realm Records V-8064/8065 (stereo) (e)
(for Vista Marketing (TV) (1977)
through Columbia Special Products
"I Had the Craziest Dream"
"I've Heard That Song Before"

*Big Bands Forever!
Four Kings of Swing*
(4-record set)

Columbia Special Products P6 14538
(stereo) (e) (1978)
"I Remember You"

Great Vocalists of the Big Band Era
(6-record set)

Columbia Special Products P6 14954
(stereo) (e) (1979)
"I Don't Want to Walk Without You"

Big Band Bash
(6-record set)

Columbia JC 36742 (mono) (1980)
"I've Heard That Song Before"

Dance the Night Away

Ajax C-618 (cassette format only) (1980)
  "The Devil Sat Down and Cried"
  "He's 1-A in the Army (and He's
   A-1 in My Heart)"
  "Make Love to Me"

The Complete Harry James
Vol. 9

Ajax C-620 (cassette format only) (1980)
  "J. P. Dooley III"
  "I Don't Want to Walk Without You"
  "But Not for Me"
  "I Remember You"
  "Skylark"

The Complete Harry James
Vol. 10

Ajax C-622 (cassette format only) (1980)
  "You're Too Good for Good-for-Nothin' Me"
  "You're in Love with Someone Else"
  "He's My Guy"
  "I Cried for You"
  "That Soldier of Mine"
  "I Heard You Cried Last Night"

The Complete Harry James
Vol. 11

Ajax C-624 (cassette format only) (1980)
  "Manhattan Serenade"
  "My Beloved Is Rugged"
  "I Had the Craziest Dream"
  "Mister Five by Five"
  "I've Heard That Song Before"

The Complete Harry James
Vol. 12

Joyce 6009 (mono) (1981)
  "The Devil Sat Down and Cried"

*The Big Bands' Greatest
Vocalist Series
Dick Haymes
Vol. 3*

PART 5

Duets with Dick Haymes—Studio Material

	Matrix	Recorded	Decca	LP Reissue
		New York		
119. "Long Ago and Far Away"	71714	1/27/44	23317	6P 6465 1P 6265 RDA-053-A
120. "Look for the Silver Lining" above with orchestra directed by Camarata	71715	1/27/44	23317	—

	Matrix	Recorded	Decca	LP Reissue
		Los Angeles		
121. "It Had to Be You"	L3446	6/28/44	23349	DL-5244 CP 98
122. "Together" above with orchestra directed by Victor Young	L3447	6/28/44	23349	DL-5244 RDA-078-A
123. "I'll Buy That Dream"	L3835	5/1/45	23434	DL-5244 RDA-078-A
124. "Some Sunday Morning" above with orchestra directed by Victor Young	L3836	5/1/45	23434	DL-5244
125. "I'm Always Chasing Rainbows"	L3982	11/1/45	23472	DL-5243
126. "Tomorrow Is Forever" above with orchestra directed by Earle Hagen	L3984	11/1/45	23472	DL-5243
127. "Oh! What It Seemed to Be"	L3985	11/1/45	23481	DL-5244 MCFM 2720
128. "Give Me a Little Kiss, Will You, Huh?" above with orchestra directed by Earle Hagen	L4013	12/3/45	23481	DL-5244
129. "In Love in Vain"	L4088	2/7/46	23528	DL-5243
130. "All Through The Day" above with orchestra directed by Earle Hagen	L4089	2/1/46	23528	DL-5243
131. "You Stole My Heart"	L4012	12/3/45	23548	DL-5243
132. "Come Rain or Come Shine" above with orchestra directed by Earle Hagen	L4148	4/14/46	23548	DL-5243

	Matrix	Recorded	Decca	LP Reissue
133. "Stardust" above with orchestra directed by Earle Hagen	L4149	4/14/46	unissued	—
134. "Till We Meet Again"	L4014	12/3/45	23944	DL-5243
135. "Something to Remember You By"	L4147	4/14/46	23944	DL-5243
136. "Why Does It Get So Late So Early?"	L4219	6/28/46	23611	DL-5244
137. "Something Old, Something New" above with orchestra directed by Earle Hagen	L4220	6/28/46	23611	DL-5244

Decca 78-RPM Album A-683
(4-record set)
    "I'm Always Chasing Rainbows"
    "Tomorrow Is Forever"
    "All Through the Day"
    "In Love in Vain"
    "Come Rain or Come Shine"
    "You Stole My Heart"
    "Something to Remember You By"
    "Till We Meet Again"

Dick Haymes Sings with Helen Forrest Vol. 1

Decca 78-RPM Album A-690
(4-record set)
    "Some Sunday Morning"
    "I'll Buy That Dream"
    "It Had to Be You"
    "Together"
    "Give Me a Little Kiss, Will You, Huh?"
    "Oh! What It Seemed to Be"
    "Something Old, Something New"
    "Why Does It Get So Late So Early?"

Dick Haymes Sings with Helen Forrest Vol. 2

Long-Play Reissues of Duets with Dick Haymes —Studio Material

Decca DL-5243 (10″) (mono) (1950)
"I'm Always Chasing Rainbows"
"Tomorrow Is Forever"
"All Through the Day"
"In Love in Vain"
"Come Rain or Come Shine"
"You Stole My Heart"
"Something to Remember You By"
"Till We Meet Again"

Dick Haymes Sings with Helen Forrest Vol. 1

Decca DL-5244 (10″) (mono) (1950)
"Some Sunday Morning"
"I'll Buy That Dream"
"It Had to Be You"
"Together"
"Give Me a Little Kiss, Will You, Huh?"
"Oh! What It Seemed to Be"
"Something Old, Something New"
"Why Does It Get So Late So Early?"

Dick Haymes Sings with Helen Forrest Vol. 2

English CORAL CP 98 (mono) (1964)
"It Had to Be You"

Hollywood Sings—Vol. 3 The Boys and Girls

Columbia House 6P 6465 (electronic stereo) (1974)

The Music of Long Ago and Far Away (6-record set)

Columbia House 1P 6265 (elec. stereo) (1974) companion to 2P 6264 (total of 3 records)
"Long Ago and Far Away"

English MCA MCFM 2720 (mono) (1975)
"Oh! What It Seemed to Be"

The Best of Dick Haymes

Reader's Digest Set (RCA Custom) RDA-053-A (electronic stereo) (1977)
"Long Ago and Far Away"

Remembering the '40s (8-record set)

Reader's Digest Set (RCA Custom) RDA-078-A (electronic stereo) (1981)
"Together"
"I'll Buy That Dream"

Fabulous Memories of the Fabulous '40s (8-record set)

PART 6
The Decca Period (1944–46)

	Matrix	Recorded	Decca	LP Reissue
		New York		
138. "In a Moment of Madness"	71815	1944	18600	—
139. "Time Waits for No One" above with orchestra directed by Camarata	71816	1944	18600	A-8042 RDA-078-A
		Los Angeles		
140. "Every Day of My Life"	L3519	1944	18624	—
141. "I Learned a Lesson I'll Never Forget" above with orchestra directed by Victor Young	L3522	1944	18624	—
142. "Don't Ever Change"	L3521	1944	18646	—
143. "Guess I'll Hang My Tears Out to Dry" above with orchestra directed by Victor Young	L3711	1944	18646	—
144. "He's Home for a Little While"	L3741	1945	18668	—
145. "Ev'ry Time (Ev'ry Time I Fall in Love)" above with orchestra directed by Victor Young	L3742	1945	18668	—
146. "What's the Use of Wond'rin'"	L3838	1945	18687	—
147. "Anywhere" above with or-	L3739	1945	18687	—

	Matrix	Recorded	Decca	LP Reissue
chestra directed by Victor Young				
148. "Strange As It Seems"	L3520	1944	18694	—
149. "(You Came Along from) Out of Nowhere" above with orchestra directed by Victor Young	L3740	1945	18694	—
150. "I'm Glad I Waited for You"	L3980	1945	18723	—
151. "My Guy's Come Back" above with orchestra directed by Mannie Klein	L3981	1945	18723	NW-222
152. "Baby, What You Do to Me"	L4044	1945	18778	—
153. "Everybody Knew but Me" above with orchestra directed by Les Paul	L4045	1945	18778	—
154. "I Like Mike"	L4212	1946	18886	—
155. "Somewhere in the Night" above with the Chickadees	L4213	1946	18886	—
156. "Linger in My Arms a Little Longer, Baby"	L4185	1946	18908	—
157. "Whatta Ya Gonna Do" above with the Chickadees	L4186	1946	18908	—
158. "Love, Your Magic Spell Is Everywhere"		1946	24516	—
159. "All the Things You Are" above with orchestra directed by Victor Young		1946	24516	—

Long-Play Reissues of the Decca Period

New World NW-222 (mono) (1977)*
"My Guy's Come Back"

Adam VIII A-8042 (electronic stereo) (1977)
"Time Waits for No One

Reader's Digest (RCA Custom) RDA-078-A
(electronic stereo) (1981)
"Time Waits for No One"

*Album intended for institution and library distribution only

Praise the Lord and Pass the Ammunition: Songs of World Wars I & II

The Best Years of Our Lives (2-record set)

Fabulous Memories of the Fabulous '40s (8-record set)

PART 7
The M–G–M Period (1947–50)

	Recorded	M-G-M	LP Reissue
	Hollywood		
160. "The Egg and I"	1947	10009	—
161. "Who Cares What People Say?"	1947	10009	—
above with orchestra			
162. "All of Me"	1947	10029	—
163. "S'posin' "	1947	10029	—
above with orchestra conducted by Harold Mooney			
164. "Don't Tell Me"	1947	10040	—
165. "I Wish I Didn't Love You So"	1947	10040	—
above ·with orchestra conducted by Harold Mooney			
166. "You Do"	1947	10050	—
167. "Baby, Come Home"	1947	10050	—
above with orchestra conducted by Harold Mooney			
168. "I'll Dance at Your Wedding"	1947	10095	—
169. "That's All I Want to Know"	1947	10095	—
above with orchestra conducted by Harold Mooney			
170. "Don't Take Your Love from Me"	1948	10105	—

	Recorded	M-G-M	LP Reissue
171. "Don't You Love Me Anymore?" above with orchestra conducted by Harold Mooney	1948	10105	—
172. "You Were Meant for Me" with the Four Woodsmen	1948	10146	—
173. "The Feathery Feelin'" with The Crew Chiefs above with orchestra conducted by Harold Mooney	1948	10146	—
174. "Cincinnati"	1948	10168	—
175. "Worry, Worry, Worry" above with orchestra conducted by Harold Mooney	1948	10168	—
176. "Just for Now"	1948	10215	—
177. "July and I" above with orchestra conducted by Harold Mooney	1948	10215	—
178. "Ain't Doin' Bad Doin' Nothin'" with the Crew Chiefs	1948	10239	—
179. "Help Yourself to My Heart" above with orchestra conducted by Harold Mooney	1948	10239	—
180. "What Did I Do?"	1948	10262	—
181. "I Love You Much Too Much" above with orchestra conducted by Harold Mooney	1948	10262	—
182. "For Heaven's Sake"	1948	10312	—
183. "Down the Stairs, Out the Door" above with orchestra conducted by Harold Mooney	1948	10312	—
184. "I Don't See Me in Your Eyes Anymore"	1949	10373	—
185. "Why Is It?" above with orchestra conducted by Hugo Winterhalter	1949	10373	—
186. "Is It Too Late?"	1949	10430	—
187. "My Mistake" above with orchestra conducted by Hugo Winterhalter	1949	10430	—

	Recorded	M-G-M	LP Reissue
188. "Lover's Gold"	1949	10450	—
189. "Possibilities"	1949	10450	—
above with orchestra conducted by Earle Hagen			
190. "Homework"	1949	10473	—
191. "You Can Have Him"	1949	10473	—
above with orchestra conducted by Earle Hagen			
192. "Give Me a Song with a Beautiful Melody"	1949	10489	—
193. "Just Got to Have Him Around"	1949	10489	—
above with orchestra conducted by Earle Hagen			
194. "It Was So Good While It Lasted"	1950	10597	—
195. "Sweetheart Semicolon"	1950	10597	—
above with orchestra conducted by Russ Case			
196. "I Wish I Could Shimmy Like My Sister Kate"	1950	10680	—
197. "More Than I Should"	1950	10680	—
above with orchestra conducted by Russ Case			
198. "Swingin' Down the Lane"	1950	11128	—
199. "Snowman"	1950	11128	—
above with orchestra conducted by Earle Hagen			

PART 8

Miscellaneous Singles (1953–55)

	Recorded	Label	Matrix	LP Issue
	Hollywood	BELL		
200. "My Reverie"	1953	1003	—	—
201. "Deep Purple"	1953	1003	—	—
above with orchestra conduct-				

	Recorded	Label	Matrix	LP Issue
ed by Larry Clinton				
202. "Lover, Come Back to Me"	1953	1017	—	—
203. "Changing Partners"	1953	1017	—	—
above with orchestra directed by Sy Oliver				
204. "Secret Love"	1954	1030	5007	—
205. "Answer Me My Love"	1954	1035	5008	—
above with The Magic Strings under the direction of Morty Palitz				
206. "Little Things Mean a Lot"	1954	1046	5042	—
207. "If You Love Me (Really Love Me)"	1954	1046	5043	—
above with unidentified orchestra				
208. "Cara Mia"	1954	1068	5093	—
209. "It Worries Me"	1954	1068	5097	—
above with orchestra directed by Larry Clinton				
210. "False Alarm"	1955	New Disc 10021	5108	—
211. "Don't Play That Song Again"	1955	10021	5138	—
above with orchestra and chorus directed by Arthur Norman				

PART 9

The Capitol Period (1955–56)

Capitol album *Harry James in Hi-Fi* (mono)
Selections as vocalist with Harry James and his Music Makers

	Recorded	LP	"45"
212. "I've Heard That Song Before"	Hollywood 7/21/55	W-654	EAP2-654
213. "I'm Beginning to See the Light"	7/21/55	W-654	EAP1-654
214. "I Cried for You"	7/21/55	W-654	EAP3-654
215. "It's Been a Long, Long Time"	7/21/55	W-654	EAP4-654

Long-Play Reissues of Harry James in Hi-Fi Album

Capitol T-1515 (mono) (1960)   *The Hits of Harry James*
  "I've Heard That Song Before"
  "I'm Beginning to See the Light"
  "I Cried for You"
Capitol TT-1515 (mono)/DTT-1515   *The Hits of Harry James*
  (stereo) (e) (1969)
  "I've Heard That Song Before"
  "I'm Beginning to See the Light"
  "I Cried for You"
Longines Symphonette Society   *Dance Band Spectacular*
  LS217-A (stereo) (e) (1972)   (5-record set)
  "I've Heard That Song Before"
  "I'm Beginning to See the Light"
  "I Cried for You"
  "It's Been a Long, Long Time"
Capitol M-1515 (mono) (1978)   *The Hits of Harry James*
  "I've Heard That Song Before"
  "I'm Beginning to See the Light"
  "I Cried for You"
Dutch Capitol T-654 (mono) (1978)   *Harry James in Hi-Fi*
  "I've Heard That Song Before"
  "I'm Beginning to See the Light"
  "I Cried for You"
  "It's Been a Long, Long Time"

I Had the Craziest Dream

Capitol album *Miss Helen Forrest—Voice of the Name Bands*
with orchestras conducted by Billy May and Dave Cavanaugh
Recorded early 1956 in Hollywood

	LP	"45"
216. "The Man I Love"	T-704	EAP1-704
	LC-6834	
	(English 10-inch issue)	
217. "He's My Guy"	T-704	EAP1-704
	LC-6834	
218. "I'm in Love with the Honorab!e Mr. So and So"	T-704	EAP1-704
219. "Out of This World"	T-704	EAP1-704
	LC-6834	
220. "I Love You Much Too Much"	T-704	EAP2-704
	LC-6834	F 3417
221. "Taking a Chance on Love"	T-704	EAP2-704
	LC-6834	F-3417
222. "I Had the Craziest Dream"	T-704	EAP2-704
223. "Make Love to Me"	T-704	EAP2-704
	LC-6834	
224. "More Than You Know"	T-704	EAP3-704
	LC-6834	
225. "All the Things You Are"	T-704	EAP3 704
	LC-6834	
226. "He's Funny That Way"	T-704	EAP3-704
	LC-6834	
227. "I Don't Want to Walk Without You" (English 10-inch issue)	T-704	EAP3-704
	LC-6834	

Long-Play Reissues of Voice of the Name Bands Album

Capitol T-945 (mono) (1958)
  "I Don't Want to Walk
  Without You"

Just for Variety
Vol. 2

Capitol T-948 (mono) (1958)
  "I Had the Craziest Dream"

Just for Variety
Vol. 5

Capitol T-951 (mono) (1958)
  "He's My Guy"

Just for Variety
Vol. 8

Capitol T-954 (mono) (1958)
  "More Than You Know"

Just for Variety
Vol. 11

Capitol Special Markets SL-6990   *Hits of the Forties*
  (stereo) (e) (1975)
  "I Had the Craziest Dream"
Capitol Special Markets SLB-6952   *The Great Girl Singers*
  (stereo) (e) (1974)   (2-record set)
  "I Had the Craziest Dream"

PART 10
1958–1974

	Recorded	Label	Number
Hollywood			
228. "I Don't Want to Walk With- out You" with orchestra conducted by Wilbur Hatch	1958	Warner Bros	W/WS-1216 W/WS-1426

issued in album   *They Sold Twenty Million*
             W-1216 (mono) / WS-1216 (stereo) (1958)
reissued in album   *Remember the Night, and the Girl,*
             and the Song
             W-1426 (mono) / WS-1426 (stereo) (1961)

RCA Victor album   *The New Tommy Dorsey Orchestra*
             Recorded Live at the Royal Box
             of the Americana, New York (1964)
      Four selections as featured artist

	Recorded	Label	Number
New York			
229. "Just One of Those Things"	1964	RCA Victor	LPM/ LSP-2830 (mono/stereo)
230. "The Lonesome Road"	1964	RCA Victor	LPM/ LSP-2830
231. "I Wish I Could Shimmy Like My Sister Kate"	1964	RCA Victor	LPM/ LSP-2830
232. "My Melancholy Baby" above with orchestra directed by Sam Donahue	1964	RCA Victor	LPM/ LSP-2830

Black Magic—Buddy DeFranco & Helen Forrest* (mono)
Eight selections with unidentified orchestra (LP issued 1977)

274

	Recorded	Label	Number
233. "September Song"	1964	Shamrock	LP-1801
234. "I Had the Craziest Dream"	1964	Shamrock	LP-1801
235. "Them There Eyes"	1964	Shamrock	LP-1801
236. "Taking a Chance on Love"	1964	Shamrock	LP-1801
237. "Falling in Love with Love"	1964	Shamrock	LP-1801
238. "From This Moment On"	1964	Shamrock	LP-1801
239. "You Turned the Tables on Me"	1964	Shamrock	LP-1801
240. "I Don't Want to Walk Without You"	1964	Shamrock	LP-1801

*While recorded for *The Navy Swings* Series (non-commercial), these selections have been listed because they were commercially issued. Mr. DeFranco did not accompany Miss Forrest.

	Recorded	Matrix	Label	LP Number
Hollywood				
Reader's Digest (RCA Custom) Session				
241. "I've Heard That Song Before"	6/2/69	XRIS-9671	Reader's Digest	RDA-84-A RD-4-139 RDA-213-1
242. "I Had the Craziest Dream"	6/2/69	XRIS-9672	Reader's Digest	RDA-84-A RD4A-053-1 RDA-213-1
243. "I Don't Want to Walk Without You"	6/2/69	XRIS-9673	Reader's Digest	RDA-84-A RD4A-053-1 RDA-213-1
244. "I'm Beginning to See the Light" above with Harry James and his orchestra	6/2/69	XRIS-9674	Reader's Digest	RDA-84-A RDA-213-1
Hollywood				
Time-Life (Capitol) Session				
245. "I Cried for You"	5/18/70	69	Time-Life	STL-346
246. "The Man I Love"	5/18/70	70	Time-Life	STL-346

	Recorded	Matrix	Label	LP Number
247. "He's My Guy"	5/18/70	74	Time-Life	STL-347
248. "Day In, Day Out"	5/18/70	75	Time-Life	STL-344
249. "All the Things You Are" above with orchestra directed by Billy May	5/18/70	76	Time-Life	STL-344

Hollywood

Reader's Digest (RCA Custom) Sessions

	Recorded	Matrix	Label	LP Number
250. "Call Me Irresponsible"	11/26/70	XRIS-9501	Reader's Digest	RD-4-112 RD-4-141 RDA-213-1
251. "As Long As He Needs Me"	11/26/70	XRIS-9504	Reader's Digest	RD-4-112 RD-4-141 RDA-213-1
252. "More"	11/26/70	XRIS-9505	Reader's Digest	RD-4-112 RDA-213-1
253. "It Must Be Him" above with Harry James and his orchestra	11/26/70	XRIS-9507	Reader's Digest	RD-4-112 RDA-213-1
254. "I Concentrate on You"	*London* 1972	unknown	Reader's Digest	RD-4-107
255. "My Funny Valentine"	1972	unknown	Reader's Digest	RD-4-107
256. "I'm in the Mood for Love"	1972	unknown	Reader's Digest	RD-4-107
257. "Thanks for the Memory" above with orchestra conducted by Alan Copeland	1972	unknown	Reader's Digest	RD-4-107
258. "Once in a While" above with the Serenaders and orchestra directed by Wally Scott	*London* 1974	unknown	Reader's Digest	RD-028-D4

I Had the Craziest Dream

Reader's Digest Set (RCA Custom)
   RDA-84-A (stereo) (1970)
    "I've Heard That Song Before"
    "I Had the Craziest Dream"
    "I Don't Want to Walk Without You"
    "I'm Beginning to See the Light"

Let's Take a Sentimental Journey (9-record set)

Reader's Digest Set (RCA Custom)
   RD4-112-1 (stereo) (1971*)
    "Call Me Irresponsible"
    "As Long As He Needs Me"
    "More"
    "It Must Be Him"

The Big Bands Are Back (6-record set)

Reader's Digest Set (RCA Custom)
   RD4-107-1 (stereo) (1971)
    "I Concentrate on You"
    "My Funny Valentine"
    "I'm in the Mood for Love"
    "Thanks for the Memory"

Stardust (8-record set)

Reader's Digest Set (RCA Custom)
   RDA-139-A (stereo) (1971)
    "I've Heard That Song Before"

Jukebox Saturday Night (8-record set)

Reader's Digest Set (RCA Custom)
   RD-4-141 (stereo) (1971)
    "Call Me Irresponsible"
    "As Long As He Needs Me"

Mood Music from the Movies (6-record set)

*Set distributed only to artists involved in the production; never commercially issued.

Reader's Digest Set (RCA Custom)
   RD4A-053-1 (stereo) (1977)
    "I Had the Craziest Dream"
    "I Don't Want to Walk Without You"

Remembering the '40's (8-record set)

Reader's Digest Set (RCA Custom)
   RDA-028-D4 (stereo) (1978)
    "Once in a While"

Thanks for the Memory (8-record set)

Reader's Digest Set (RCA Custom)
   RDA-213-1 (stereo) (1981)
    "I Don't Want to Walk Without You"
    "It Must Be Him"
    "More"
    "I'm Beginning to See the Light"
    "I've Heard That Song Before"
    "Call Me Irresponsible"
    "As Long As He Needs Me"
    "I Had the Craziest Dream"

Harry James & His Orchestra for Listening & Dancing (5-record set)

Time-Life Set (Capitol)
  STL-344 (stereo) (1971)
  (recreating Artie Shaw arrangements)
  "Day In, Day Out"
  "All the Things You Are"
Time-Life Set (Capitol)
  STL-346 (stereo) (1971)
  (recreating Benny Goodman and Harry James arrangements)
  "The Man I Love"
  "I Cried for You"
Time-Life Set (Capitol)
  STL-347 (stereo) (1971)
  (recreating Harry James arrangement)
  "He's My Guy"

The Swing Era 1939–40
(3-record set)

The Swing Era 1941–42
(3-record set)

The Swing Era 1942–44
(3-record set)

SECTION B

NONCOMMERCIAL RECORDINGS

PART 1
Vocalist with Artie Shaw's Band
—Radio Broadcast Air Checks

Old Gold's *Melody and Madness* Show
Broadcasts: November 27, 1938–August 22, 1939

	Broadcast Date	LP Issue
	New York	
1. "Who Blew Out the Flame?"	11/27/38	JG-1001
2. "Simple and Sweet"	12/11/38	—
3. "My Reverie"	12/18/38	—
4. "My Own"	1/29/39	JG-1003
		J 6008
5. "I Have Eyes"	2/5/39	JG-1005
6. "Deep Purple"	2/19/39	JG-1005
7. "I Cried for You"	2/26/39	JG-1005
8. "I Want My Share of Love"	3/5/39	JG-1005
9. "I'm in Love with the Honorable Mr. So and So"	4/2/39	JG-1007

	Broadcast Date	LP Issue
10. "You're So Indifferent"	Hollywood 4/23/39	JG-1009
11. "Supper Time"	5/7/39	JG-1009
12. "Don't Worry 'Bout Me"	6/6/39	—
13. "Comes Love"	6/13/39	—
14. "I Never Knew Heaven Could Speak"	6/27/39	—
15. "The Lamp Is Low"	Boston 8/22/39	A-11

NBC Radio Remotes from the Blue Room, Hotel Lincoln and Café Rouge, Hotel Pennsylvania, New York; Summer Terrace, Ritz-Carlton Roof, Boston Broadcasts: November 25, 1938–November 11, 1939

	Broadcast Date	LP Issue
	Blue Room	
16. "They Say"	11/25/38	LP-28-128
17. "My Reverie"	11/25/38	LPT-6000 LPM-6701 LP-28-128
18. "Who Blew Out the Flame?"	11/25/38	LP-28-128 SOS 117 J 6002
19. "Night over Shanghai"	11/29/38	HSR-139
20. "When I Go A-Dreamin'"	12/1/38	HSR-139
21. "They Say"	12/1/38	HSR-139
22. "Simple and Sweet"	12/2/38	HSR-139
23. "Deep in a Dream"	12/2/38	HSR-140
24. "I Won't Tell a Soul"	12/2/38	HSR-140
25. "Thanks for Everything"	12/6/38	HSR-140
26. "Who Blew Out the Flame?"	12/6/38	HSR-140
27. "Between a Kiss and a Sigh"	12/20/38	HSR-140
28. "Let's Stop the Clock"	12/20/38	HSR-140
29. "You're a Sweet Little Headache"	12/30/38	LP-28-128
30. "Thanks for Everything"	12/30/38	LP-28-128
31. "Any Old Time"	1/3/39	—

	Broadcast Date	LP Issue
32. "Any Old Time"	1/18/39	LP-1041
33. "This Can't Be Love"	1/18/39	SOS 117
		LP-1041
		J 6002
	Summer Terrace	
34. "Comes Love"	8/19/39	HSR-148
35. "Don't Worry 'Bout Me"	8/19/39	HSR-148
36. "Moonray"	8/19/39	HSR-148
	Café Rouge	
37. "Many Dreams Ago"	10/19/39	HSR-148
38. "Day In, Day Out"	10/19/39	HSR-148
39. "Moonray"	10/19/39	—
40. "Moonray"	10/20/39	
41. "A Table in the Corner"	10/20/39	HSR-149
42. "Melancholy Lullaby"	10/21/39	HSR-149
43. "Two Blind Loves"	10/21/39	—
44. "The Last Two Weeks in July"	10/21/39	HSR-149
45. "Moonray"	10/21/39	—
46. "Lilacs in the Rain"	10/21/39	HSR-149
47. "I've Got My Eye on You"	10/26/39	LPT-6000
		LPM-6701
48. "Any Old Time"	11/3/39	—
49. "Many Dreams Ago"	11/10/39	—
50. "Day In, Day Out"	11/10/39	—
51. "Moonray"	11/10/39	—
52. "Moonray"	11/11/39	LPT-6000
		LPM-6701

Long-Play Issues of Artie Shaw's Band—Air Checks

RCA Victor LPT-6000 (mono) (1961)
"My Reverie"
"I've Got My Eye on You"
"Moonray"
RCA Victor LPM-6701 (mono) (1961)
"My Reverie"
"I've Got My Eye on You"
"Moonray"

Artie Shaw in the Blue Room
(2-record set)

The Swingin' Mr. Shaw
(5-record boxed set)

	Broadcast Date	LP Issue

Sounds of Swing LP-117 (mono) (1974) — *The Vocal Years*
  "Who Blew Out the Flame?"
  "This Can't Be Love"
Air Check #11 (mono) (1974) — *Artie Shaw "On The Air"*
  "The Lamp Is Low"
Jazz Guild 1001 (mono) (1975) — *Melody and Madness*
  "Who Blew Out the Flame?" — Vol. 1
Jazz Guild 1003 (mono) (1975) — *Melody and Madness*
  "My Own" — Vol. 2
Jazz Guild 1005 (mono) (1975) — *Melody and Madness*
  "I Have Eyes" — Vol. 3
  "Deep Purple"
  "I Cried for You"
  "I Want My Share of Love"
Jazz Guild 1007 (mono) (1976) — *Melody and Madness*
  "I'm in Love with the Honorable — Vol. 4
  Mr. So and So"
Jazz Guild 1009 (mono) (1976) — *Melody and Madness*
  "You're So Indifferent" — Vol. 5
  "Supper Time"
Joyce LP-1041 (mono) (1977) — *One Night Stand*
  "This Can't Be Love"
  "Any Old Time"
Fanfare LP-28-128 (mono) (1979) — *The 1938 Band in*
  "They Say" — *Hi-Fi*
  "My Reverie"
  "Who Blew Out the Flame?"
  "You're a Sweet Little Headache"
  "Thanks for Everything"
Hindsight HSR-139 (mono) (1979) — *Artie Shaw & His*
  "Night over Shanghai" — *Orchestra*
  "When I Go A-Dreamin'" — 1938 Vol. 1
  "They Say"
  "Simple and Sweet
Hindsight HSR-140 (mono) (1979) — *Artie Shaw & His*
  "Deep in a Dream" — *Orchestra*
  "I Won't Tell a Soul" — 1938 Vol. 2
  "Thanks for Everything"
  "Who Blew Out the Flame?"
  "Between a Kiss and a Sigh"
  "Let's Stop the Clock"
Hindsight HSR-148 (mono) (1980) — *Artie Shaw & His*
  "Comes Love" — *Orchestra*
  "Moonray" — 1939 Vol. 3

	Broadcast Date	LP Issue

"Don't Worry 'Bout Me"
"Many Dreams Ago"
"Day In, Day Out"
Hindsight HSR-149 (mono) (1980)
"A Table in the Corner"
"Melancholy Lullaby"
"The Last Two Weeks in July"
"Lilacs in the Rain"
Joyce 6002 (mono) (1980)
"Who Blew Out the Flame?"
"This Can't Be Love"

Joyce 6008 (mono) (1981)
"My Own"

Artie Shaw & His
Orchestra
1939 Vol. 4

The Big Bands' Greatest Vocalist Series
Helen Forrest
Vol. 1
The Big Bands' Greatest Vocalist Series
Helen Forrest
Vol. 2

PART 2
Vocalist with Benny Goodman's Band
—Radio Broadcast Air Checks

CBS Radio Remotes from Waldorf-Astoria Hotel, New York, Cocoanut Grove, Los Angeles

	Broadcast Date	LP Issue
	New York	
53. "Does Your Heart Beat for Me?"	12/21/39	IAJRC 21
54. "Devil May Care"	Dec/39	—
	Los Angeles	
55. "Busy As a Bee (I'm Buzz Buzz Buzzin')"	Mar–Apr/40	—
56. "Shake Down the Stars"	4/6/40	—
57. "Too Romantic"	4/12/40	—
58. "It Never Entered My Mind"	4/27/40	—
59. "Where Do I Go from You?"	5/28/40	A-16
60. "Where Do I Go from You?"	6/4/40	A-16

	Broadcast Date	LP Issue

What's New?—The Old Gold Show
New York

61. "There'll Be Some Changes Made"   2/10/41   —

NBC—Radio The Fitch Bandwagon
New York

62. "Perfidia"   2/16/41   —
63. "These Things You Left Me"   2/16/41   —

What's New?—The Old Gold Show
New York

64. "Everything Happens to Me"   3/3/41   —
65. "Good Evenin', Good Lookin'!"   3/3/41   —
66. "The Wise Old Owl"   3/17/41   —
67. "Walkin' By the River"   3/17/41   —
68. "Yours"   4/21/41   —
69. "Everything Happens to Me"   Apr/41   —
70. "Fancy Meeting You"   5/5/41   —
71. "G'bye, Now"   5/5/41   —

Mutual Radio Sustaining Radio Broadcasts from Monte Proser Dance Carnival, New York; Steel Pier, Atlantic City

New York

72. "Bewitched"   5/30/41   —
73. "Smoke Gets in Your Eyes"   6/6/41   —

Atlantic City

74. "Smoke Gets in Your Eyes"   7/5-6/41   —
75. "When the Sun Comes Out"   7/12/41   —
76. "Daddy"   Jul/41   —

NBC Radio Remotes from Hotel Sherman, Chicago

77. "It's So Peaceful in the Country"   8/8/41   —
78. "Soft As Spring"   8/10/41   LP-19-119
79. "Perfidia"   8/10/41   LP-19-119

Long-Play Issues of Benny Goodman's Band— Air Checks

Air Check #16 (mono) (1976)
"Where Do I Go from You?"   Benny Goodman "On The
"Where Do I Go from You?"   Air"

	Broadcast Date	LP Issue
Fanfare LP-10-119 (mono) (1978) "Soft As Spring" "Perfidia" IAJRC #21 (mono) (1980) "Does Your Heart Beat for Me?"	*Benny Goodman and His Orchestra* Vol. 2 *For the First Time,* Vol. 2: *B.G., Louis, Pops & Tram*	

PART 3
Vocalist with Harry James's Band — Radio Broadcast Air Checks

Radio Remotes from the Hotel Lincoln, New York
Broadcasts: October 25, 1941–December 8, 1941

	Broadcast Date	LP Issue
80. "The Man I Love"	10/25/41	JA-31
81. "He's 1-A in the Army (and He's A-1 in My Heart)"	10/25/41	—
82. "I'm Thrilled"	10/25/41	—
83. "Make Love to Me"	11/8/41	—
84. "I'm Thrilled"	11/8/41	—
85. "He's 1-A in the Army (and He's A-1 in My Heart)"	11/10/41	—
86. "Make Love to Me"	11/16/41	—
87. "Will You Still Be Mine?"	11/16/41	JA-31
88. "I See a Million People"	11/16/41	—
89. "I Got It Bad (and That Ain't Good)"	11/16/41	JA-31
90. "Jim"	12/1/41	—
91. "Will You Still Be Mine?"	12/1/41	—
92. "(I'll Be with You in) Apple Blossom Time"	12/2/41	—
93. "I Got It Bad (and That Ain't Good)"	12/2/41	—
94. "(I'll Be with You in) Apple Blossom Time"	12/8/41	—

	Broadcast Date	LP Issue

Schaeffer Band Review
New York
95. "I Don't Want to Walk Without You" — 3/18/42 — —

Coca-Cola Spotlight Band Show #13
Hollywood
96. "I Don't Want to Walk Without You" — Oct/42 — —
97. "The Devil Sat Down and Cried" (with band) — Oct/42 — —

Radio Remotes from the Astor Roof, New York
Broadcasts: August 19, 1942–June 5, 1943
98. "He's My Guy" — 8/19/42 — —
99. "But Not for Me" — 8/19/42 — —
100. "My Beloved Is Rugged" — 8/19/42 — —
101. "Manhattan Serenade" — 8/21/42 — LP-1024
102. "You're in Love with Someone Else" — 8/28/42 — LP-36-136
103. "But Not for Me" — 8/28/42 — LP-36-136
104. "Mister Five by Five" — 9/2/42 — —
105. "Manhattan Serenade" — 9/2/42 — —
106. "But Not for Me" — 9/2/42 — —
107. "But Not for Me" — 6/5/43 — —
108. "The Canteen Bounce" — 6/5/43 — —

Chesterfield Time
Radio Broadcasts: September 1942–December 1943
109. "Can't Get Out of This Mood" — 12/15/42 — —
110. "I Remember You" — 12/30/42 — LP-36-136
111. "More Than You Know" — 3/4/43 — —
112. "Please Think of Me" — 3/18/43 — —
113. "There Are Such Things" — 3/18/43 — —
114. "Savin' Myself for Bill" — 3/25/43 — —
115. "You'll Never Know" — 5/20/43 — —
116. "Somebody Loves Me" — 6/2/43 — —
117. "More Than You Know" — 6/15/43 — —
118. "Always" (with the Song Makers) — 7/20/43 — —
119. "Good for Nothin' Joe" — 7/20/43 — —
120. "The Right Kind of Love" — 7/28/43 — —
121. "Do Nothin' Till You Hear from Me" — 7/28/43 — —
122. "You'll Never Know" — 7/29/43 — —
123. "Somebody Loves Me" — 8/18/43 — —
124. "Between the Devil and the Deep Blue Sea" (with the Song Makers) — 9/7/43 — —
125. "Somebody Loves Me" — 9/7/43 — —

	Broadcast Date	LP Issue
126. "More Than You Know"	9/14/43	—
127. "Where or When"	9/14/43	—
128. "My Old Flame"	9/16/43	—
129. "Good for Nothin' Joe"	9/16/43	—
130. "No Love, No Nothin'"	9/28/43	—
131. "Ice Cold Katie" (with the Song Makers)	10/5/43	—
132. "How Sweet You Are"	10/6/43	—
133. "It's Been So Long"	10/6/43	—
134. "Ice Cold Katie" (with the Song Makers)	10/19/43	—
135. "Shady Lady Bird"	10/19/43	—
136. "How Sweet You Are"	10/19/43	—
137. "Can't We Talk It Over?" (with the Song Makers)	11/4/43	—
138. "My Heart Tells Me"	11/4/43	—
139. "Good for Nothin' Joe"	11/11/43	—
140. "If That's the Way You Want It, Baby"	11/18/43	—
141. "It's Been So Long"	11/25/43	—
142. "I Couldn't Sleep a Wink Last Night"	11/30/43	—
143. "Don't Cry, Baby"	11/30/43	—
144. "Somebody Loves Me"	12/3/43	—
145. "How Sweet You Are"	12/3/43	—
146. "I Had the Craziest Dream"	unknown	—
147. "As Time Goes By"	unknown	—
148. "Now We Know"	unknown	—

Armed Forces Radio Service (AFRS) Transcriptions of Chesterfield Time Broadcasts Harry James Show

	AFRS Reference Number	LP Issue
149. "I Remember You"	2	—
150. "It's Always You"	6, 26	—
151. "The Canteen Bounce"	7, 22	—
152. "I've Heard That Song Before"	Fill 7	—
153. "More Than You Know"	Fill 13	HSR-141
154. "The Right Kind of Love"	14, 19	—
155. "Close to You"	16, Fill 16	—

	AFRS Reference Number	LP Issue
156. "Please Think of Me"	21	—
157. "Somebody Loves Me"	37	HSR-142
158. "But Not for Me"	38, 59	—
159. "My Heart Tells Me"	45, 52	—
160. "My Beloved Is Rugged"	46	—
161. "Do Nothin' Till You Hear from Me"	47, 79	HSR-141
162. "Now We Know"	48	—
163. "Can't Get Out of This Mood"	51	—
164. "My Old Flame"	58	—
165. "You'll Never Know"	60	—
166. "You Go to My Head"	70	HSR-102
167. "It's Been So Long"	80	HSR-102
168. "Pistol Packin' Mama" (with Buddy Moreno)	80	—
169. "If That's the Way You Want It, Baby"	unknown	HSR-102
170. "I Couldn't Sleep a Wink Last Night"	unknown	HSR-102
171. "Between the Devil and the Deep Blue Sea" (with the Song Makers)	unknown	HSR-102

Long-Play Issues of Harry James's Band—Air Checks

Joyce LP-1024 (mono) (1975)
  "Manhattan Serenade"
One Night Stand
Vol. 2

Jazz Archives JA-31 (mono) (1976)
  "Will You Still Be Mine?"
  "I Got It Bad (and That Ain't Good)"
  "The Man I Love"
The Young
Harry James

Hindsight HSR-102 (mono) (1977)
  "If That's the Way You
  Want It, Baby"
"I Couldn't Sleep a Wink
  Last Night"
"Between the Devil and the
  Deep Blue Sea"
"It's Been So Long"
"You Go to My Head"
Harry James and His
Orchestra
Vol. 1, 1943-46

Hindsight HSR-141 (mono) (1979)
  "Do Nothin' Till You
  Hear from Me"
Harry James and His
Orchestra
Vol. 4, 1943-46

	AFRS Reference Number	LP Issue

"More Than You Know"
Hindsight HSR-142 (mono) (1979)
  "Somebody Loves Me"

Harry James and His Orchestra—Vol. 5, 1943–53

Fanfare LP-36-136 (mono) (1979)
  "You're in Love with Someone Else"
  "But Not for Me"
  "I Remember You"

Harry James and His Music Makers

PART 4
The Big Band V-Discs and Studio Transcriptions

	Commercial Source	Recorded	V-Disc Number	LP Issue
with Benny Goodman				
	Columbia		13-A	
172. "Perfidia"	35962	1/28/41	233-A	—
with Harry James				
173. "The Devil Sat Down and Cried" with Dick Haymes, Harry James, Dalton Rizzoto and Ensemble	Columbia 36466	10/29/41	438-B	—
174. "Make Love to Me"	Columbia 36446	10/29/41	380-A 493-B	—
175. "I Cried for You"	Columbia 36623	6/5/42	380-A	—
176. "I Heard You Cried Last Night"	Columbia 36677	6/5/42	57-A	—

	Treasury Department Transcriptions	Recorded	LP Issue
with Harry James		New York	
Treasury Star Parade	#74		
177. "Save the American Way"		Early 1942	LP-36-136
178. "My Beloved Is Rugged"		Early 1942	LP-36-136
Treasury Star Parade	#75		
179. "I Don't Want to Walk Without You"		Early 1942	—
Treasury Star Parade	#76		
180. "That Soldier of Mine"		Early 1942	HIS-1941
AFRS Basic Music Library			
181. "He's My Guy"	BML P-1	Late 1942	—
182. "I Remember You"	BML P-1	Late 1942	—
183. "I've Heard That Song Before"	BML P-1	Late 1942	—
184. "I Don't Want to Walk Without You"	BML P-5	Late 1942	—
185. "Mister Five by Five"	BML P-5	Late 1942	—
186. "I Cried for You"	BML P-5	Late 1942	—
AFRS Basic Music Library		New York Summer	
187. "The Right Kind of Love"	BML P-65	1943	—
Office of War Information (Music of Jazz Bands No. 13)	#7		
188. "You'll Never Know"		Summer 1943	—

Long-Play Issues of Big Band V-Discs and Studio Transcriptions

History in Sound HIS-1941 (mono) (1972)
"That Soldier of Mine" — *World War Two*
Fanfare LP-36-136 (mono) (1979)
"Save the American Way" — *Harry James and His*
"My Beloved Is Rugged" — *Music Makers*

PART 5
Motion Picture Shorts and Features

	Soundstage Prerecording	Studio Disc	LP Issue
Artie Shaw's Band			
Vitaphone Movie Short	*Hollywood Summer 1938*		
189. "Let's Stop the Clock"		—	BS-7128 LP-3004
CLASS IN SWING short	June 1939		
190. "I Have Eyes"		—	LP-3004
SYMPHONY IN SWING short	June 1939		
191. "Deep Purple"		—	LP-3004
Harry James's Band			
TRUMPET SERENADE	Early 1942		
(Universal Pictures musical short)			
192. "He's 1-A in the Army (and He's A-1 in My Heart)"		—	—
PRIVATE BUCKAROO	Early 1942		
(Universal Pictures feature film starring Dick Foran and the Andrews Sisters)			
193. "You Made Me Love You"		UPC-361	LP-3007
194. "Nobody Knows the Trouble I've Seen"—with Dick Foran		UPC-364	LP-3007
195. "Johnny's Got His Gun" (deleted from film) with the Andrews Sisters and Dick Foran		UPC-370	—
SPRINGTIME IN THE ROCKIES	June 1942		
(20th Century-Fox feature film starring Betty Grable, John Payne and Carmen Miranda)			
196. "I Had the Craziest Dream"		TCF-908	JA-19791 507
BEST FOOT FORWARD	Jan. 1943		
(Metro-Goldwyn-Mayer feature film starring Lucille Ball)			

	Soundstage Prerecording	Studio Disc	LP Issue
197. "I Cried for You" (deleted from film)		unknown	—
TWO GIRLS AND A SAILOR (Metro-Goldwyn-Mayer feature film starring Van Johnson, June Allyson and Gloria DeHaven)	Jan. 1943		
198. "In a Moment of Madness"		unknown	—
BATHING BEAUTY (Metro-Goldwyn-Mayer feature film starring Esther Williams)	July 1943		
199. "I Cried for You"		MGM26847	—
200. "I'll Take the High Note" (production number with cast)		unknown	—

Solo

	Soundstage Prerecording	Studio Disc	LP Issue
YOU CAME ALONG (Paramount Pictures feature film starring Robert Cummings and Lizabeth Scott)	Summer 1944		
201. "(You Came Along from) Out of Nowhere"		unknown	—

Long-Play Issues of Motion Picture Shorts and Features

Bandstand BS-7128 (mono) (1975)
  "Let's Stop the Clock"
  Jazz Highlights of the 1930's–40's

Joyce LP-3004 (mono) (1977)
  "Let's Stop the Clock"
  "I Have Eyes"
  "Deep Purple"
  Film Tracks of Artie Shaw

Joyce LP-3007 (mono) (1979)
  "You Made Me Love You"
  "Nobody Knows the Trouble I've Seen"
  Film Tracks of Harry James

JJA JA-19791 (mono) (1979)
  "I Had the Craziest Dream"
  The Hollywood Years of Harry Warren 1930–57

Titania 507 (mono) (1980)
  "I Had the Craziest Dream"
  Springtime in the Rockies/ Sweet Rosie O'Grady soundtracks

I Had the Craziest Dream

PART 6
Solo Broadcast Air Checks and AFRS Transcriptions
1943–1945

	Source	Date
Mostly with Gordon Jenkins's Orchestra	*Hollywood*	
Philco Hall of Fame Show	Broadcast	12/26/43
202. "I Don't Want to Walk Without You"		
Broadway Matinee	Broadcast	1/5/44
203. "Besame Mucho"		
Mail Call #49	Transcription	1944
204. "You'll Never Know"		
Showtime	Broadcast	1944
205. "Where or When"		
Command Performance U.S.A. No. 134	Transcription	8/18/44
206. "He's Funny That Way"		
Personal Album	Transcription	1944
207. "I Don't Want to Walk Without You"		
208. "Exactly Like You"		
209. "He's Funny That Way"		
210. "Is You Is or Is You Ain't My Baby?"		
211. "The Man I Love"		
212. "Somebody Loves Me"		
Personal Album #687	Transcription	1944
213. "You Go to My Head"		
214. "I Didn't Know About You"		
215. "Time Waits for No One"		
216. "Good for Nothin' Joe"		
Philco Hall of Fame Show	Broadcast	12/31/44
Showboat		
217. "Can't Help Lovin' That Man"		
218. "Bill"		
G. I. Journal #52	Transcription	1945
219. "The Man I Love"		
Command Performance U.S.A. No. 164	Broadcast	1945
220. "You Go to My Head"		
AFRS Basic Music Library BML P-373	Transcription	1945
221. "Don't You Notice Anything New?"		
222. "(You Came Along from) Out of Nowhere"		
223. "You Go to My Head"		
224. "Good for Nothin' Joe"		
Mail Call #181	Transcription	1945

	Source	Date

225. "Sentimental Journey"
226. "Ev'ry Time (Ev'ry Time I Fall in Love)"

Downbeat	Transcription	1945

227. "Sentimental Journey"
228. "I'm Beginning to See the Light"

Command Performance U.S.A. No. 255	Broadcast	1946

229. "South America, Take It Away"
230. "September Song"

Part 7
The Dick Haymes Show Radio Broadcast Air Checks

Broadcasts: September 19, 1944–June 5, 1947

	Broadcast Date	LP Issue

With Gordon Jenkins's Orchestra

	Hollywood	
231. "I Surrender Dear"	9/19/44	—
232. "My Man"	10/3/44	—
233. "Can't Help Lovin' That Man"	11/28/44	—
234. "Mad About the Boy"	1944	—
235. "I'm in a Jam with Baby"	1944	—
236. "I Don't Know Why" (duet with Dick Haymes)	1944	—
237. "Make Love to Me"	1/9/45	—
238. "Wish You Were Waiting for Me"	1/30/45	—
239. "He's Home for a Little While"	2/6/45	—
240. "I'm in Love with the Honorable Mr. So and So"	2/13/45	—
241. "I Didn't Know about You"	2/20/45	—
242. "A Little on the Lonely Side"	3/6/45	—
243. "I'm Beginning to See the Light"	3/20/45	—
244. "The Man I Love"	3/20/45	—
245. "Don't You Notice Anything New?"	3/27/45	—
246. "Ev'ry Time (Ev'ry Time I Fall in Love)"	4/3/45	—
247. "Make Love to Me"	4/17/45	—

	Broadcast Date	LP Issue
248. "I Didn't Know about You"	4/17/45	—
249. "He's Home for a Little While"	4/24/45	—
250. "Wish You Were Waiting for Me"	5/8/45	—
251. "Sentimental Journey"	5/15/45	—
252. "If I Could Be with You"	5/15/45	—
253. "Anywhere"	5/22/45	—
254. "You Go to My Head"	5/29/45	—
255. "Sentimental Journey"	6/5/45	—
256. "The Man I Love"	6/12/45	—
257. "(You Came Along from) Out of Nowhere"	6/19/45	—
258. "I'm Through with Love"	6/26/45	—
259. "Summertime"	7/3/45	—
260. "So in Love with Baby"	7/24/45	—
261. "Sunday, Monday or Always"	7/31/45	—
262. "You Belong to My Heart"	8/7/45	—
263. "You Belong to My Heart"	9/11/45	—
264. "Baia"	9/18/45	—
265. "What's the Use of Won'drin' "	9/25/45	—
266. "He's Funny That Way"	10/2/45	—
267. "Homesick"	10/9/45	—
268. "September Song"	10/13/45	—
269. "I'll Buy That Dream" (duet with Dick Haymes)	10/13/45	—
270. "It's Been a Long, Long Time"	10/20/45	—
271. "People Will Say We're in Love" (duet)	10/20/45	LP-4
272. "The All American Game" (production number)*	10/20/45	—
273. "I Surrender Dear"	10/27/45	—
274. "Gee, It's Good to Hold You" (duet)	10/27/45	—
275. "Navy Day" (production number)	10/27/45	—
276. "That Old Feeling"	11/3/45	—
277. "Singin' in the Rain" (duet)	11/3/45	—
278. "The Story of Hopalong Hank" (production number)	11/3/45	—
279. "Autumn Serenade"	11/10/45	—
280. "I'll Buy That Dream" (duet)	11/10/45	—
281. "My Bonnie Lies over the Ocean" (production number)	11/10/45	—
282. "Gimme a Little Kiss, Will You, Huh?" (duet)	11/17/45	—
283. "Hayride" (production number)	11/17/45	—
284. "It's Been a Long, Long Time"	11/24/45	—
285. "Some Sunday Morning" (duet)	11/24/45	LP-2

	Broadcast Date	LP Issue
286. "When the Circus Comes to New York" (production number)	11/24/45	—
287. "You Took Advantage of Me" (duet)	12/1/45	LP-2
288. "The Forrests and the Haymeses" (production number)	12/1/45	—
289. "Oh, Brother"	12/8/45	—
290. "Gee, It's Good to Hold You" (duet)	12/8/45	LP-2
291. "A Bicycle Built for Two" (production number)	12/8/45	LP-2

*All production numbers feature the 4 Hits & A Miss and/or Chorus.

	Broadcast Date	LP Issue
292. "My Guy's Come Back"	12/15/45	—
293. "Honey" (duet)	12/15/45	—
294. "How Ya Gonna Keep' Em Down on the Farm" (production number)	12/15/45	—
295. "Put That Ring on My Finger"	12/22/45	—
296. "Did You Ever Get That Feelin' in the Moonlight?" (duet)	12/22/45	LP-2
297. "The Night before Christmas" (production number)	12/22/45	—
298. "Waitin' for the Train to Come In"	12/29/45	—
299. "A Kiss Goodnight" (duet)	12/29/45	LP-2
300. "Whatever Happened to Vaudeville?" (production number)	12/29/45	—
301. "Isn't It Kinda Fun?" (duet)	1945	LP-1002
302. "I'm Beginning to See the Light"	1945	—
303. "Can't Help Lovin' That Man"	1945	—
304. "You Go to My Head"	1945	—
305. "I Didn't Know about You"	1945	—
306. "I'm in Love with the Honorable Mr. So and So"	1945	—
307. "Once upon a Moon"	1945	—
308. "Don't You Notice Anything New?"	1945	—
309. "He's Home for a Little While"	1945	—
310. "My Mother Was a Lady" (production number)	1/5/46	—
311. "Happiness Is a Thing Called Joe"	1/12/46	—
312. "Come to Baby, Do" (duet)	1/12/46	LP-2

	Broadcast Date	LP Issue
313. "Fairgrounds Medley" (production number)	1/12/46	—
314. "Bewitched, Bothered and Bewildered"	1/19/46	—
315. "Cuddle up a Little Closer" (duet)	1/19/46	—
316. "Waiting at the Church" (production number)	1/19/46	—
317. "Waitin' for the Train to Come In"	1/26/46	—
318. "Too Tired" (duet)	1/26/46	—
319. "Frankie and Johnny" (production number)	1/26/46	—
320. "Ain't Misbehavin'"	2/2/46	—
321. "We'll Be Together Again"	2/2/46	—
322. "Put That Ring on My Finger"	2/2/46	—
323. "You Belong to My Heart"	2/9/46	—
324. "A Kiss Goodnight" (duet)	2/9/46	
325. "MacNamara's Band" (production number)	2/9/46	—
326. "Surprise Party"	2/16/46	—
327. "Button Up Your Overcoat" (duet)	2/16/46	LP-2
328. "Cuddle Up a Little Closer" (duet)	2/16/46	LP-4
329. "Old MacDonald Had a Farm" (production number)	2/16/46	—
330. "Here I Go Again"	2/23/46	—
331. "Did You Ever Get That Feelin' in the Moonlight?" (duet)	2/23/46	—
332. "Love Me"	3/2/46	—
333. "Come to Baby, Do" (duet)	3/2/46	—
334. "Come Josephine in My Flying Machine" (production number)	3/2/46	—
335. "Atlanta, Ga."	3/9/46	—
336. "Oh, What It Seemed to Be" (duet)	3/9/46	—
337. "Home, Sweet Home" (production number)	3/9/46	—
338. "Surprise Party"	3/16/46	—
339. "Two Sleepy People" (duet)	3/16/46	LP-4
340. "St. Patrick's Day" (production number)	3/16/46	—
341. "Here I Go Again"	3/23/46	—
342. "A Kiss Goodnight" (duet)	3/23/46	—
343. "When the Circus Comes to New York" (production number)	3/23/46	—
344. "Laughing on the Outside"	3/30/46	—
345. "Two Sleepy People" (duet)	3/30/46	—
346. "In Love in Vain"	4/6/46	—
347. "Surprise Party"	4/13/46	—
348. "Stardust" (production number)	4/13/46	—
349. "Too Marvelous for Words" (duet)	4/13/46	—

	Broadcast Date	LP Issue
350. "In Love in Vain"	4/20/46	—
351. "Give Me a Little Kiss, Will You, Huh?" (duet)	4/20/46	—
352. "People Will Say We're in Love" (duet)	4/27/46	—
353. "In Love in Vain"	5/25/46	—
354. "Too Tired"	5/25/46	—
355. "Love Is Here to Stay" (production number)	5/25/46	—
356. "I've Got a Feelin' You're Foolin' " (duet)	6/1/46	—
357. "The Gypsy"	6/1/46	—
358. "Automobile Skit" (production number)	6/1/46	—
359. "Linger in My Arms a Little Longer, Baby"	6/20/46	—
360. "Singin' in the Rain" (duet)	6/20/46	—
361. "Who Told You That Lie?"	6/28/46	—
362. "I Don't Know Why" (duet)	6/28/46	—
363. "In Old New York" (production number)	6/28/46	—
364. "George M. Cohan" (production number)	6/28/46	—
365. "Who Told You That Lie?"	9/5/46	—
366. "Sailing Along" (production number)	9/5/46	—
367. "South America, Take It Away"	9/12/46	—
368. "Waiting for the Robert E. Lee" (production number)	9/12/46	—
369. "I've Never Forgotten"	9/19/46	—
370. "In Old New York" (production number)	9/19/46	—
371. "Linger in My Arms a Little Longer, Baby"	9/26/46	—
372. "Oh, You Beautiful Doll" (production number)	9/26/46	—
373. "Without You"	10/3/46	—
374. "South America, Take It Away"	10/10/46	—
375. "What're Ya Gonna Do?"	10/17/46	—
376. "On the Sunny Side of the Street"	10/24/46	—
377. "I'd Be Lost Without You"	10/31/46	—
378. "Either It's Love or It Isn't"	11/7/46	—
379. "Shine On Harvest Moon" (production number)	11/7/46	—
380. "South America, Take It Away"	11/28/46	—
381. "The Other End of a Kiss"	12/5/46	—
382. "Love Is Here to Stay" (production number)	12/5/46	—
383. "Horse Opera" (production number)	12/12/46	—
384. "Christmas" (production number)	12/19/46	—
385. "The Day after Christmas" (production number)	12/26/46	—
386. "Sposin' "	1946	—
387. "September Song"	1946	—

	Broadcast Date	LP Issue
388. "You Ought to Be in Pictures" (production number)	1946	—
389. "We're Going Riding" (production number)	1946	—
390. "The Good Old Summertime" (production number)	1946	—
391. "South America, Take It Away" (production number)	1946	—
392. "The Atchison, Topeka and the Santa Fe" (production number)	1946	—
393. "The Forrests and the Haymeses" (production number)	1946	—
394. "St. Louis" (production number)	1946	—
395. "Waiting for the Robert E. Lee" (production number)	1946	—
396. "School Days" (production number)	1946	—
397. "Cindy" (production number)	1946	—
398. "Football" (production number)	1946	—
399. "California" (production number)	1946	—
400. "The Other End of a Kiss"	1/2/47	—
401. "You Are Everything to Me"	1/2/47	—
402. "New Year" (production number)	1/2/47	—
403. "Sooner or Later"	1/16/47	—
404. "Sun Valley" (production number)	1/16/47	—
405. "School Days" (production number)	1/23/47	—
406. "Trucking" (production number)	1/30/47	—
407. "A Rainy Night in Rio"	2/6/47	—
408. "New York" (production number)	2/6/47	—
409. "The Other End of a Kiss"	2/20/47	—
410. "A Rainy Night in Rio" (production number)	2/20/47	—
411. "Guilty"	2/27/47	—
412. "This Is the Beginning of the End"	3/6/47	—
413. "MacNamara's Band" (production number)	3/13/47	—
414. "Miami Beach" (production number)	3/20/47	—
415. "A Sunday Kind of Love"	3/27/47	—
416. "San Francisco" (production number)	3/27/47	—
417. "The Anniversary Song"	4/3/47	—
418. "Easter Parade" (production number)	4/3/47	—
419. "The Egg and I"	4/10/47	—
420. "Rip Van Winkle" (production number)	4/10/47	—
421. "This Is the Night"	4/17/47	—
422. "When the Circus Comes to New York" (production number)	4/17/47	—

	Broadcast Date	LP Issue
423. "Brooklyn" (production number)	4/24/47	—
424. "Apple Blossom Time" (production number)	5/1/47	—
425. "Hometown" (production number)	5/8/47	—
426. "Show Business" (production number)	5/15/47	—
427. "It's the Same Old Dream"	5/22/47	—
428. "Handbook of Songs" (production number)	5/22/47	—
429. "I've Been So Wrong"	5/29/47	—
430. "Freedom" (production number)	5/29/47	—
431. "Just for You" (production number)	6/5/47	—
432. "Ain't Misbehavin'"	1947	—
433. "Guilty"	1947	—

Long-Play Issues of The Dick Haymes Show
Air Checks 1944–1947

Ballad LP-2 (mono) (1974)
"Some Sunday Morning"
"You Took Advantage of Me"
"Gee, It's Good to Hold You"
"A Bicycle Built for Two"
"Did You Ever Get That Feelin'
in the Moonlight?"
"A Kiss Goodnight"
"Come to Baby, Do"
"Button Up Your Overcoat"

Ballad LP-4 (mono) (1975)
"Cuddle Up a Little Closer"
"Two Sleepy People"
"People Will Say We're in Love"

Standing Room Only SRO
LP-1002 (mono) (1978)
"Isn't It Kinda Fun?"

The Dick Haymes Show
1943–1953
(4-record boxed set)

Dick Haymes/Personal Album 1944–46

The Special Magic of Dick Haymes

PART 8
The Later V-Discs and AFRS Transcriptions
1945–1946

	Source	Recorded	V-Disc Number	LP Issue
with Victor Young's Orchestra				
434. "Some Sunday Morning" with Dick Haymes	Decca 23434	5/1/45	566-B	—
with Gordon Jenkins's Orchestra				
435. "When the Circus Comes to New York" (production number) *The Dick Haymes Show*	AFRS Broadcast	11/24/45	580-B	LP-1001
436. "September Song" *The Dick Haymes Show*	AFRS Broadcast	10/13/45	613-B	—
437. "Mean to Me" with Dick Haymes *The Dick Haymes Show*	AFRS Broadcast	1945	613-B	LP-1001 VC-5017
438. "Button Up Your Overcoat" with Dick Haymes *The Dick Haymes Show*	AFRS Broadcast	2/16/46	645-B	LP-1001
with Mannie Klein's Orchestra				
439. "I'm Glad I Waited for You"	Decca 18723	1945	797-B	—

Armed Forces Radio Service (AFRS) Transcriptions of The Dick Haymes Show Broadcasts

	AFRS Reference Number	LP Issue
with Gordon Jenkins's Orchestra		
440. "I'm in a Jam with Baby"	8	—
441. "I Don't Know Why" (duet)	8	—
442. "Autumn Serenade	28	—
443. "I'll Buy That Dream" (duet)	28	—
444. "My Bonnie Lies over the Ocean" (production number)	28	—
445. "A Kiss Goodnight" (duet)	35	—
446. "Bewitched, Bothered and Bewildered"	38	—
447. "Cuddle Up a Little Closer" (duet)	38	—
448. "Waitin' for the Train to Come In"	39	—
449. "Too Tired" (duet)	39	—
450. "You Belong to My Heart"	41	—
451. "A Kiss Goodnight" (duet)	41	—
452. "Cuddle Up a Little Closer" (duet)	41	—
453. "Button Up Your Overcoat" (duet)	42	—
454. "Cuddle Up a Little Closer" (duet)	42	—
455. "Old MacDonald Had a Farm" (production number)	42	—
456. "Here I Go Again"	43	—
457. "Did You Ever Get That Feelin' in the Moonlight?" (duet)	43	—
458. "Bewitched, Bothered and Bewildered"	44	—
459. "Come to Baby, Do" (duet)	44	—
460. "Come Josephine in My Flying Machine" (production number)	44	—
461. "Oh, What It Seemed to Be" (duet)	45	—
462. "Home, Sweet Home" (production number)	45	—
463. "Two Sleepy People" (duet)	46	—
464. "September Song"	47	—
465. "Oh, What It Seemed to Be" (duet)	47	—
466. "In Love in Vain"	49	—
467. "People Will Say We're in Love" (duet)	52	—
468. "Give Me a Little Kiss, Will You, Huh?" (duet)	unknown	—

	AFRS Reference Number	LP Issue
469. "Hayride" (production number)	unknown	—
470. "Make Love to Me"	645	—
471. "My Man"	646	—
472. "South America, Take It Away"	Here's to Veterans 19	—
473. "Waiting for the Robert E. Lee" (production number)	19	—

Long-Play Issues of Later V-Discs and AFRS Transcriptions 1945–1946

Standing Room Only SRO LP-1001
  (mono) (1975)
  "When the Circus Comes to New York"
  "Mean to Me"
  "Button Up Your Overcoat"
Dan Records VC-5017 (mono) (1980)
  "Mean to Me"

Dick Haymes–The Fabulous Forties (The V-Disc Years)

The Favorite Pop Songs of the '40's (V-Disc Jazz Session Series)

PART 9
World Program Service: World Transcriptions 1948–1952

	Reference Number	LP Issue
with Carmen Dragon's Orchestra		
474. "Mean to Me"	9869	—
475. "Someone to Watch over Me"	9870	—
476. "I'm in the Mood for Love"	9871	—
477. "What's the Use of Won'drin'"	9872	—
478. "They Say It's Wonderful"	9873	—
479. "My Man"	9949	—
480. "How High the Moon"	9950	—

	Reference Number	LP Issue
481. "Too Marvelous for Words"	9951	—
482. "On the Sunny Side of the Street"	9952	—
483. "East of the Sun (West of the Moon)"	9953	—
484. "Why Do I Love You?" (with Dick Haymes)	9999	—
485. "Would You Like to Take a Walk?"	10000	—
486. "They Can't Take That Away from Me"	10001	—
487. "You're the Top" (with Dick Haymes)	10002	—
488. "It's De-Lovely"	10003	—
489. "Ooh! That Kiss" (with Dick Haymes)	10004	—
490. "Bill"	10239	—
491. "Bewitched"	10240	—
492. "My Ideal"	10241	—
493. "I've Got a Crush on You"	10242	—
494. "Stormy Weather"	10243	—
495. "Come Rain or Come Shine"	10834	—
496. "Ain't Misbehavin'"	10835	—
497. "I May Be Wrong"	10836	—
498. "I Wanna Be Loved"	10837	—
499. "I Can't Get Started"	10838	—
500. "My Heart Belongs to Daddy"	unknown	—
501. "Baby, Won't You Please Come Home?"	unknown	—
502. "Dancing on the Ceiling"	unknown	—
503. "I Only Have Eyes for You"	unknown	—
504. "Paradise"	unknown	—
505. "Little White Lies"	unknown	—
506. "Embraceable You"	unknown	—
507. "I'll Always Be in Love with You"	unknown	—
508. "I Gotta Right to Sing the Blues"	unknown	—
509. "I'll Get By"	unknown	—
510. "The One I Love (Belongs to Somebody Else)"	unknown	—
511. "(I Don't Stand) A Ghost of a Chance"	unknown	—
512. "How Deep Is the Ocean"	unknown	—
513. "Mad about the Boy"	unknown	—
514. "Everything I Have Is Yours"	unknown	—
515. "I Can't Believe That You're in Love with Me"	unknown	—
516. "I Keep Telling My Heart"	unknown	—
517. "Under a Blanket of Blue"	unknown	—
518. "You Go to My Head"	unknown	—
519. "Deep Purple"	unknown	—

	Reference Number	LP Issue
520. "Between the Devil and the Deep Blue Sea"	unknown	—
521. "That's My Desire"	unknown	—
522. "I Hadn't Anyone Till You"	unknown	—
523. "They Say It's Wonderful"	Dick Haymes Show Audition Disc	—
524. "Someone to Watch over Me"	Dick Haymes Show Audition Disc	—

PART 10
Department of Defense Transcriptions
1960–1975

	Reference Number	Date
with Ray Bloch's Orchestra		
Stars for Defense	197	1960
525. "Them There Eyes"		
526. "I'm Through with Love"		
527. "Ain't Misbehavin'"		
Stars for Defense	373	1963
528. "Just One of Those Things"		
529. "September Song"		
530. "Almost Like Being in Love"		
Guest Star	919	1964
531. "Almost Like Being in Love"		
532. "I've Heard That Song Before"		
533. "You Made Me Love You"		
534. "Life Is Just a Bowl of Cherries"		
with Unidentified Orchestra		
The Navy Swings	unknown	1964
535. "Happiness Is a Thing Called Joe"		

	Reference Number	Date

536. "All of Me"
537. "My Melancholy Baby"
538. "I Had the Craziest Dream"
539. "Don't Take Your Love from Me"
540. "My Funny Valentine"
541. "How Deep Is the Ocean"
542. "From This Moment On"

The Navy Swings   1964
543. "Falling in Love with Love"   45
544. "From This Moment On"   45
545. "You Turned the Tables on Me"   46
546. "I Don't Want to Walk Without You"   46
547. "September Song"   47
548. "I Had the Craziest Dream"   47
549. "Them There Eyes"   48
550. "Taking a Chance on Love"   48

with The Airmen of Note

Serenade in Blue   390   1975
551. "All of Me"
552. Medley: "I Don't Want to Walk Without You"
                     "I Had the Craziest Dream"
                     "I Cried for You"

Serenade in Blue   417   1975
553. "Taking a Chance on Love"
554. Medley: "I've Heard That Song Before"
                    "You Made Me Love You"

REFERENCES CONSULTED

Brown, Denis. *Dick Haymes * A Discography*, Vol. 1. Birmingham, Eng.: International Friends of Haymes Society, 1974.

Connor, D. Russell, and Warren W. Hicks. *B G—On the Record: A Bio-Discography*, New Rochelle, NY: Arlington House, 1969.

Garrod, Charles, and Peter Johnson. *Harry James and His Orchestra*, Zephyrhills, FL: Joyce Music Corporation, 1975.

Kinkle, Roger D. *The Complete Encyclopedia of Popular Music and Jazz 1900–1950*, 4 vols. New Rochelle, NY: Arlington House, 1970.

Korst, Bill, and Charles Garrod. *Artie Shaw and His Orchestra*. Zephyrhills, FL: Joyce Music Corporation, 1974.

Rust, Brian. *The American Dance Band Discography*, 2 vols. New Rochelle, NY: Arlington House, 1975.

Rust, Brian, and Allen G. Debus. *The Complete Entertainment Discography*. Arlington, NY, 1973.

The files and recorded collections of the following: Miss Helen Forrest, Jimmy Crawford, Richard Dondiego, Alan Eichler, Rodger Robinson and Dominic Scutti.